A LITTLE WAIF JUSTICE

A LITTLE WAIF JUSTICE

MERLIN'S WAIF™

BOOK ONE

RENÉE JAGGÉR

MICHAEL ANDERLE

DON'T MISS OUR NEW RELEASES

Join the LMBPN email list to be notified of new releases and special promotions (which happen often) by following this link:

http://lmbpn.com/email/

LMBPN® Publishing
2375 E. Tropicana Avenue, Suite 8-305
Las Vegas, Nevada 89119 USA

Version 1.01, February 2025
ebook ISBN: 979-8-89354-469-5
Print ISBN: 979-8-89354-470-1

THE A LITTLE WAIF JUSTICE TEAM

Thanks to the Beta Readers
Rachel Beckford, Sean Kesterson, Kelly O'Donnell

Thanks to the JIT Readers
Sean Kesterson.
Daryl McDaniel
Wendy L Bonell
Dave Hicks
Christopher Gilliard
Diane L. Smith
John Ashmore
Dorothy Lloyd
Paul Westman
Jan Hunnicutt

Editor
The SkyFyre Editing Team

CHAPTER ONE

Manniref had no regrets.

Snowflakes settled on her hands and hair as she stood in the clearing. Pine and spruce trees surrounded her, dusting the cold air with their fresh aroma. A bird flittered between their branches, wings whirring as it strove to escape, and unnatural silence settled over the woods.

Until the chief's son screamed.

He lay at the center of the chaos. Feet from his body, the earth looked like a giant plow had done its work on this untouched corner of Mistwood North. Manniref knew what a plow was; she'd seen one in her previous home. The young elf's blood soaked into the snow, a shocking red stain against the neutral hues of the wintry forest, seeping between his pale fingers as he clutched his right leg. Manniref glimpsed bone protruding through his fur-lined boot.

She'd almost started to hope this would work out.

The morning had begun normally. Manniref left the village at dawn, as she always did. The elves weren't interested in her help with chores, so she went to the only place where she felt welcome: the woods.

Everything there called to her. She moved soundlessly beneath the trees, relishing every sight and sensation: the kiss of snow on her cheeks, the song of a red-breasted robin, and the careful movements of a deer family moving through a thicket without stirring a single twig.

She leaned against a mighty dryad. Though rarer here than in Fernwood Deep, Manniref's last placement—the one where she'd learned what a plow was—the dryads were giants among ordinary trees. They moved too slowly for ordinary paranormals like her to communicate with them, but she felt the throb of age and wisdom in the dryad's sap. It calmed her.

A bird's alarm call tore through the quiet woods. Manniref's head snapped up. The high-pitched chirp faded into the distance as the bird fled, but tension rippled through the quiet woods.

She wrapped her woven cloak tightly around her shoulders and hurried in the direction the cry had come from. Morning sunlight flickered through the tight tangle of branches overhead as she darted across the snow, almost weightless on the crust. A stag raced past her, leaping and tossing his antlers to show off his strength before disappearing into the woods with a flash of white tail.

Something dangerous moved through this forest.

A playful yip caught Manniref's attention. She slowed and approached a thicket where the branches of several trees tangled with those of a fallen log, forming a tight-knit shelter. When she crouched and peered inside, she spotted a squirming, furry mass of little bodies. The wolf pups tumbled over each other in their cozy den, play-growling and snapping with milk teeth. Their rambunctious play was practice for the day when they'd pull down full-grown moose.

Manniref grinned. She reached through the tangled branches and stretched her fingers toward the nearest pup. It paused in playing to sniff her fingers, then splashed them with a bright pink tongue. She giggled, making the pup's tail swing.

A low whistle sounded deeper in the woods: the alarm call of a Mistwood nightjar.

Manniref left the puppies and spotted fresh tracks heading in that direction. The wolf pack was hunting.

She followed the tracks at a cautious jog, her deerskin boots almost silent on the snow. When she caught the musky scent of wolf, she slowed and glanced around to find a safe vantage point. A nearby oak's gnarled branches were bare. Manniref climbed it in seconds, bouncing from branch to branch until she reached the top.

The view made her gut twist.

The wolf pack sought suitable prey. They trotted in a disorganized group between the trees, noses low, tails waving high as they looked for a scent. She picked out the alpha female, a pure white wolf whose nipples hung low from feeding pups. She led the way, her nose twitching half an inch from the ground, too absorbed in looking for something to hunt to realize the woods were alarmed about something more dangerous than she was.

Manniref clutched the trunk, her heart slamming against her ribs.

A Mavka Elf crept behind a briar bush, his well-worn boots almost soundless. He was a few yards away from the wolves. A necklace of fox teeth stirred against his deerskin jerkin, and he wore his white hair in a mass of intricate braids behind his pointed ears. He hadn't yet drawn his supple longbow, but an arrow lay ready on the string, and Manniref had never seen him miss.

No, she thought. *Surely not. He knows the rules. He wouldn't.*

Her mouth went dry when the elf's eyes locked on the only white wolf in the pack...the nursing alpha.

Those cubs would starve if he killed her.

If he'd been any other elf, Manniref might have been able to distract him without getting into much trouble, but this was

Neven, the son of the village chief. Manniref couldn't afford to piss off the chief...or let the white wolf die.

She scrambled from the tree and hurried toward the wolves, staying behind a large spruce and praying to Luna that Neven couldn't see her.

"Hey!" she hissed. "Hey, get out of here!"

The wolves raised their heads but didn't flee. The nearest one cocked his head and pricked his triangular ears. His tail twitched.

"Go!" Manniref waved her arms and threw a pebble in his direction.

The wolf's tail wagged. He turned to her and gave a yip of greeting.

"No!" Manniref hissed.

The other wolves took notice. The first sniffed her hands and butted his nose against her fingers as if asking to be petted.

"Run!" Manniref shooed him, but he dropped into a play bow.

The alpha female turned toward Manniref, tail twitching, and a bow creaked in the briars. Neven had found his shot.

The playful wolf pups flashed through Manniref's mind. *"No!"*

The wolves jumped at her changed tone, and Neven's arrow clipped the alpha female's shoulder and drew a line of blood across her white coat. She whipped around, snarling, and hackles rose as the pack rallied. Neven straightened behind the briars, taking aim with another arrow.

"NO!" Manniref roared.

The earth cracked under her boots. She stumbled back as the oak tree's roots erupted from the ground at her feet, spraying dirt across the snow. The wolves yelped and scattered as the mighty roots surged like tentacles through the clearing, ripping grooves as they sped toward Neven.

"Leave that wolf alone!" Manniref shouted.

Neven squealed and stumbled back, but it was too late. The roots ripped through the briars and gripped Neven's ankles. He shrieked as they yanked him into the air, cloak flying, and flung him across the clearing.

He hit the ground awkwardly, right leg first, and bone cracked. Manniref blinked, the sound startling her. He crumpled, curling around his leg as blood seeped between his fingers. The roots withdrew into the earth as quickly as they'd come.

A few moments passed in breathless silence. Manniref spun and watched the white wolf sprint back to her puppies.

Then Neven screamed, and the reality of what she'd done crashed down on her head.

I blew it. Manniref sighed. *Again.*

Hooves thundered. Manniref didn't move as three elk burst into the clearing, saddled and bridled. Two Mavka Elves leaped from their backs.

"*Neven!*" one cried, running to his side.

The other held the elk and stared at the carnage, open-mouthed.

Manniref didn't run. There was no point. Where would she go?

"Neven, what happened?" The first elf crouched beside him.

Neven raised his head, sweat dripping down his ashen cheeks, and raised a trembling finger to point at Manniref.

"It was *her,*" he hissed.

The other elves stared at her. Their expressions registered surprise before their eyes narrowed.

"I knew she would be trouble," the first elf snarled. He left Neven and marched across the churned earth to Manniref. She didn't resist as he seized her arm and yanked her closer. "You'll answer to Myleksa for this."

Manniref allowed the elf to drag her across the clearing and force her into an elk's saddle. The beast rolled its eyes, sensing her fear.

It wasn't Myleksa who scared her. It was Merlin.

The ride back to Wolf Glen was short, but Neven groaned through every step of it. He sat on the elk in front of Yevgen, dramatically leaning his head on his companion's shoulder. He whimpered every time the ground changed or the elk started at a bird in the bushes. Manniref wanted to think he was milking it, but his blood smeared the elk's coat, stark and undeniable.

It was a far smaller degree of suffering, she thought as he squealed and whined, than he would have inflicted on the alpha wolf and her litter of pups. She couldn't summon any regret for what she'd done, though there would be consequences.

She sat silently on the elk's back, hands loosely resting on her thighs as the large animal moved through the woods. Neven's other goon Petro held the elk's reins and thought that gave him total control. Manniref let him believe it.

"Nearly there, Neven," Yevgen comforted.

Neven moaned as the elk stepped over a fallen log onto a trampled path. They followed its smooth curves through the forest to Wolf Glen.

The woods embraced the village, which lay in a half-moon clearing filled with morning sunshine. Snow sparkled between the elves' log homes, and gray wood smoke rose from the stone chimneys. The houses clustered around the most significant building in Wolf Glen: a squat longhouse adorned with the skull of a mighty elk, its antlers bone-white above the door. Paddocks made of woven branches formed a wall around the village, each containing a few curious elk who called to their companions. The elk Manniref rode called back.

A log bridge spanned the stream that defined one side of the village. The elk's hooves thudded over it as curious children came running, their white hair streaming over their shoulders. Their questions beat against Manniref's eardrums.

"Who's that?"

"Is it Neven?"

"Did he kill the wolf?"

"Where's its pelt?"

"Ooh, there's blood!"

"What happened?"

"*She* did it," Petro snarled, casting a ferocious look at Manniref.

The children gasped and backed away, their eyes wide with fear. They bolted into the camp, shouting, "Neven's hurt! Manniref did it!"

When the elk reached the longhouse, a mute crowd had gathered outside the longhouse's door. They glared up at Manniref, silent but hostile, as Petro and Yevgen halted their elk.

"*A healer!*" Petro shouted. "*We need a healer!*"

The door banged open, and Manniref flinched almost as hard as her elk. Chief Myleksa marched out of the longhouse, her hair a tumult of tangled white braids that reached her heels. She wore a night-black wolf-skin cloak over a tunic bisected by a broad leather belt. Manniref had never seen her without the stone knife at her hip, its jagged blade laced with quartz the same ice-blue as the chief's eyes.

Her frigid gaze swept over the group and landed on Manniref like an icicle plunging into her chest.

"The healer comes," Myleksa calmly announced. "Compose yourself, son."

Neven stopped whining.

"Did you bring the wolf?" Myleksa asked.

Everyone in the crowd leaned closer, a total hush falling on the village.

"*No!*" Neven burst out. "But I would have. I grazed it! I—"

"Then your blood is not wolf blood. It is not chief blood." Myleksa's eyes flashed.

"Give me another chance, Mother," Neven pleaded. "It wasn't my fault. It was *her*!" He jabbed a finger at Manniref.

"A true hunter makes no excuses," Myleksa coldly stated.

Neven's Adam's Apple bobbed as he stared into her eyes. "Mother," he whispered.

Myleksa looked away as a willowy male elf, his hair falling around him like a curtain, rushed to Neven's side. Two assistants carried a litter. The crowd silently watched as Yevgen helped Neven onto it. This time, the chief's son gave no cries of pain but lay quiet and pale on the litter as they bore him away.

"Chief, this isn't fair," Petro spoke up.

"Get down from that elk," Myleksa snapped.

Petro dismounted in a rage. Manniref alighted gently as two boys came to take the elk away. She glimpsed a familiar face in the crowd, and a flush of shame crept up her neck to her cheeks. Yulietta stood among the crowd with her arms folded, a worried pinch at the corners of her eyes.

Manniref grimaced. She felt bad for the woman. She'd had worse foster parents.

"Now." Myleksa folded her arms, her stone knife catching the light. "Tell me what happened, Petro."

"I told you, chief. Neven was about to kill a wolf when she arrived and broke his leg!" Petro yelled. "He said he had the perfect shot at a huge she-wolf. When he drew his arrow back, Manniref shouted and tried to frighten the wolves away, but they weren't afraid of a little slip of a thing like her."

"Then she attacked," Yevgen supplied. "She threw him to the ground and broke his leg!"

Gasps and cries of shock ran through the crowd. They nudged one another and pointed at Manniref, whispering behind their hands.

"Silence!" Myleksa snapped.

The crowd hushed.

"Neither of you saw this happen?" Myleksa asked.

Petro hesitated. "I didn't, but Neven did. He'll tell you!"

"I think Manniref saw it, too." Myleksa calmly turned to face her. "Tell me. Did you hurt my son?"

Manniref paused, then raised her chin. "I did what I had to do."

Several elves skittered back, widening the circle around Manniref.

"You should never have brought her here, chief," someone shouted. *"She's been nothing but trouble."*

"The summer fruit looked weird this year!" someone else chipped in. "It was funny colors."

"Prey animals hear us when we're miles away. Nobody's slain a moose or a bear in months," another elf complained. "It's all because of her."

"There's something wrong with her magic!" the first elf added. *"It's poison to the woods. It's poison to the Mavka Elves!"*

A roar of assent affirmed his cry.

"Silence!" Myleksa barked.

The elves quieted more slowly than before.

"The wolf had pups," Manniref murmured.

Myleksa raised a pale eyebrow. "What?"

"The wolf. The one Neven aimed at. She had pups. I couldn't let them die." Manniref spread her hands. "It's not right. I did what I had to do."

"Pups." Myleksa's eyes darkened. "Is this true?"

Yevgen and Petro exchanged glances.

"Dishonesty would be unwise," Myleksa snarled.

Petro cleared his throat. "We didn't see which wolf Neven aimed at, Chief."

"But there was a suckling mother in the pack," Yevgen reluctantly added.

Myleksa sighed. "Neven knows the hunter's code. Fool." She shook her head. "Fool! Now he will never be chief."

The assembled crowd yelled in outrage.

"Quiet!" Myleksa snapped. "I will deal with Manniref alone." She turned and strode into the longhouse.

Manniref looked back before stepping in and met Yulietta's despairing eyes. "I'm sorry," she mouthed, then followed the chief.

The interior was low and smoky, with steady heat rising from the pit at the center in which coals smoldered. Furs and skins covered the floor, and the thatched roof held the heat in. Myleksa strode to a sturdy wooden chair at the back and dropped into the pile of fox furs that cushioned it.

"Sit down, Manniref," she snapped.

Manniref shuffled after her and nervously perched on a nearby stool.

Myleksa rubbed her face. "Neven was really going to kill a nursing wolf?"

"Yes," Manniref murmured.

"Idiot. If anyone found out, he would fail the test anyway." Myleksa sighed. "He would have made a strong and decent chief, Manniref, if not for you."

Manniref said nothing.

"You know the Wolf Hunt is sacred to the Mavka," Myleksa growled. "It has been our rite of passage since wolves and elves were born. No elf can be considered an adult without killing a wolf, and no child can be chief. We give no second chances, so Neven cannot rule the village. I prepared him for the role all his life, and now he will never be anything but a common hunter."

Manniref raised her chin. "No one who would kill a mother wolf with suckling pups is worthy of being chief of anything."

Myleksa's cool eyes met hers. "Perhaps you're right." She folded her arms. "Why did you do it?"

"He was wrong." Manniref shrugged.

"You knew this would be bad for you, though," Myleksa murmured.

Manniref shrugged again. "Didn't make it less wrong."

"No," Myleksa muttered. "I suppose not." She studied Manniref. "I thought you would fit in more easily than you have. When Merlin brought you here, I thought the Leshbolg stories were absurd. You seemed so small, so harmless."

"I can be harmless," Manniref mumbled.

Myleksa sighed. "I don't think you can. That's the difficulty. The villagers aren't wrong about the fruit and the prey animals. Hunting has been harder since you came here."

"The children say the fruits are sweeter." Manniref swallowed. She knew what was coming next. It had happened before.

"They are. Larger, too, but they look...strange." Myleksa shuddered. "The village is suffering this winter without enough prey to hunt. I've thought of a hundred explanations, but I've been the chief for decades, and this winter is different." She paused. "Because of you."

Manniref stared at the fox pelt at her feet. It would have been far more beautiful on a living fox, darting through the undergrowth in the summer, the rich color of copper.

"I'm sorry, Manniref. I don't think you do these things on purpose, or I would have exiled you long ago." Myleksa folded her arms.

Exiled. There it was. Her fate was sealed.

"I have to prioritize my people," Myleksa added. "I cannot let them suffer for the sake of an outsider."

Manniref nodded.

"You are helpful and kind," Myleksa went on, "and you certainly have power, although none of us understands it, least of all you. But this is the last straw. You ruined one of our most sacred rites."

Manniref stared at the floor. "I'd do it again if I had to."

"I know you would." Myleksa grimaced. "I took you in as a favor to Merlin. Who wouldn't honor the request of the most powerful mage in existence?"

"That's fair." Manniref sighed.

"Now I have to choose between currying his favor and caring for my people." Myleksa spread her hands. "You understand that the decision is obvious."

This had been coming. The Mavka had been nice to her, but she didn't belong here. She'd known that when she walked into Wolf Glen.

"I'm sorry." Myleksa sounded like she meant it. "But it's time for you to find somewhere else, Manniref. Somewhere you might fit better than here."

Manniref sighed. "You're right, Chief."

Myleksa rose and marched to the door. "*Artega! Artega!*"

A slender young elf ran up, her steps almost soundless. "Yes, Chief?"

"Ride to the Eternity Throne's garrison on the other side of the river," Myleksa ordered. "Give them an urgent message for Merlin."

"What is the message, Chief?" the elf asked.

Myleksa gave Manniref a long stare, then turned back to the elf.

"Tell him it's time for him to take his waif back," she commanded.

CHAPTER TWO

Merlin Ambrosius marched through the elegant courtyards in the Eternal Palace, muttering to himself.

The cheerful sunshine that almost always shone on the palace's courtyards annoyed him. It made the fountains glitter and the roses trailing over the walls look brighter and more colorful.

Those annoyed him, too.

He walked through three courtyards with arched gateways and elegant signposts before finding a suitable pebble. By then, Merlin was too pissed to kick it. He pointed a finger at it and vaporized it with a blast of moonfire. "*Stupid elves!*"

"Dylan will have your hide for that," Rosa scolded.

Merlin scowled at her. The human strolled across the courtyard, her dark curls bouncing on her shoulders. She wore a scarlet dress with a daring neckline and a massive floppy hat.

"Where are *you* going?" he demanded.

"To Misvyn to visit Sofia." Rosa beamed. "Isn't it nice that I can go there without a bodyguard these days?"

"Very nice," Merlin spat. "Positively peachy."

"Aren't you in a pleasant mood?" Rosa tilted an eyebrow, then strode to the carport on the other side of the courtyard, where her flower-power VW van waited.

"*Hey!*" Merlin yelled. "*Is Julie in?*"

"*You have big juju. Figure it out.*"

Merlin rolled his eyes, but Rosa wasn't wrong. He knew Julie was in her tower. He marched to the double doors, which no one guarded, considering the Eternity Queen was among the most dangerous beings in existence. His silver beard streamed over his chest and tickled the dragonfly wings on his back, making his mood worse.

"Julie!" Merlin banged on the door.

A head popped through an upper-story window. "Come on up. I have my hands full."

Merlin barged into the opulent sitting room at the tower's base and followed an elegant staircase up to the kitchen. Though Julie had an army of brownies at her disposal to serve her any meal she desired, her kitchen was a war zone. Charred bits of bread lay all over the floor and crunched under Merlin's curly-toed shoes. Cheese littered the countertop: string cheese, processed cheese, cream cheese, Swiss cheese, and a neon-orange wheel of Thor goat cheese.

A wisp of smoke rose from the expensive toaster, and the kettle boiled madly on the stovetop. An irate toddler perched in the midst of it all. She sat in her high chair with folded arms, face smeared with cheese. Her frown lessened at the sight of Merlin.

"Yes, of course, Councilor." Eternity Queen Julia Pendragon, a magnificent Lunar Fae with butterfly wings that shed moonlight, was on her hands and knees under the kitchen table. "We can discuss that at the next meeting." She had her phone to her ear as she rescued a toy dragon from under the table.

"*Dragon!*" the toddler screamed.

"Shhhh, Lilli," Merlin hissed. "Mommy's on the phone."

"*Dragon!*" Princess Lillirelda bellowed.

Julie straightened and clocked her head on the table's edge. Merlin grimaced as she rubbed it, not changing her tone. "I fully understand your concerns." Julie straightened and handed the dragon to Lilli. "I will address this inequality as soon as possible. Could you hold for one moment, Councilor? Thank you." She lowered the phone.

"Sorry. This can't wait," Merlin told her.

"Five minutes." Julie pushed a plastic plate across the burned debris on the table. "Feed her, would you?"

Merlin eyed the plate, which contained eight tiny toast squares, each topped with different cheese. "Why doesn't the baby feed herself?" he wondered. "You're a big girl, Lilli. You can do this."

Julie flapped a hand at him and wandered to the other side of the kitchen. "My apologies for the interruption, Councilor. Please tell me more about that corporation's anti-harpy policy."

Lilli giggled and extended a hand toward the plate.

"Seems simple enough." Merlin picked up a square and handed it to her.

Lilli squealed. Silver fire flashed over her fingers, and Merlin cowered, using the plate as a shield. The flames boiled around the toddler, consuming her. A blue ward trapped the flames against Lilli, but they scorched the table and her high chair.

The flames dissipated. Lilli hurled the remnants of the toast at Merlin. He jumped aside, and the former square hit the wall, leaving a sooty mark.

"Ah," he muttered. "Not simple."

Lilli burst out laughing.

"You have terrible manners," Merlin scolded. "No Lunar Fae should behave that way."

Lilli's laughter switched off. "Uncle Merly," she whimpered. "Cheese!" She extended her hands toward the plate.

"Cheese is for eating, Lilli," Merlin severely told her. "Not for burning."

Lilli scowled.

"No more cheese for you!" Merlin added.

Lilli giggled.

"It's not funny, you little toadstool!" Merlin growled.

Julie lowered the phone, cupping a hand over it to muffle her words. "Gentle parenting, Hat!"

Merlin rolled his eyes when she turned her back. "Gentle parenting, my wings," he grumbled. "Fine. Lilli, you may have another piece, but if you set it on fire, that's the last one. Okay?"

Lilli nodded.

"Here." Merlin held out the plate.

Lilli delicately grasped a toast square and ate it.

"Aha!" Merlin punched the air. "Victory! Here, you may have the rest." He gave her the plate.

Lilli chortled and set the whole thing on fire. Melted plastic dripped everywhere, and dark smoke flooded Lilli's ward, hiding her from sight. Merlin yelped and extended both hands over her head. Raindrops poured from his palms, drenching Lilli and extinguishing the flames.

"Of course, Councilor. I look forward to your email." Julie hung up. "Ugh. Councilor Nectarina has her panties in a wad again."

"Does she ever not?" Merlin asked.

"This time, I think it's valid." Julie blinked at the chaos before her. "Whoa, what happened to my child?"

A mass of melted plastic lay on Lilli's tray. Char marks stained her high chair, and the toddler wore a black mask of soot.

"She has no respect for her Uncle Merly," Merlin grumbled.

"Like mother, like daughter," Julie teased. She produced a colossal pack of Wet Wipes and cleaned the toddler, then gave her a fist-sized block of cheddar, which Lillie smeared everywhere with great enjoyment.

Merlin pulled out a chair opposite Lilli and made faces at her while Julie brewed two cups of strong black coffee. She added cream and sugar to hers but pushed Merlin's mug across the table, unadulterated.

"How can I help?" Julie sat beside Lilli, who gnawed the cheese with obvious delight.

Merlin sighed. "It's Manniref again."

Julie grimaced and sipped her coffee. "Aw, man. The Mavka Elves didn't work out?"

"She made it for almost a year. Longest placement yet, but I received a message from the Mistwood North garrison last night. Chief Myleksa wants me to take her back," Merlin explained.

"I'm sorry, Hat." Julie sighed. "I know you hoped the Mavka would work out for her."

Merlin stared into his cup. "It's my fault that she's the last one, Julie."

Julie tilted her head. "Hey, we talked it through. I'm not mad about that anymore."

"I know you're not. Luckily. The Eternal Palace only has so many ceilings," Merlin muttered.

Julie snorted. "In my defense, you were telling me an entire species had died in the Third Pendragon War, and no one had given me a chance to save them."

"The Battle of Fort Elzaphine was more important. You saved thousands of paras that day," Merlin shot back.

"Yeah, and not one of them was a Leshbolg," Julie retorted. She stopped and inhaled. "We're not fighting about this again. You didn't tell me the Leshbolgs were under attack, and I didn't save them. We've come to terms with that."

"You're right." Merlin ran a hand over his hair. "But it left Manniref completely alone."

"I still don't understand how that was possible." Julie frowned. "Have you gone back to the battlefield?"

"We searched every inch in a ten-mile radius. I abandoned the search a few months after the war ended. It was a waste of resources." Merlin shook his head. "I don't have anything new to tell you, Julie, except that Mordred's cult attacked the Leshbolg city, Lichenvale, and Manniref was the only survivor. We found hundreds of cultist corpses and hundreds of Leshbolg skeletons."

"But all the dead Leshbolgs were male," Julie murmured.

Merlin nodded. "That's right."

"How could Manniref be the only female? She was just a kid, too." Julie shook her head. "I don't get it. Did she remember anything new?"

"Not since the last time I spoke with her, and I told her to contact me if she did." Merlin grimaced. "I'm not sure why her memories were lost. She can only remember vague snippets of her past, not enough to tell us anything meaningful about her species."

"Not sure?" Julie raised an eyebrow. "You forgot most of the First Golden Age."

"In my defense, I was a hat for several hundred years," Merlin muttered.

"Trauma does that to you. Can you imagine what Manniref lived through?" Julie's tone softened. "Watching her species go extinct?"

Merlin met her gaze. "Yes. It nearly did."

Julie reached over the table and wrapped her hand around his. "That's why you're the best person to help her."

"I'm not sure anymore," Merlin confessed. He disentangled his fingers and fiddled with the tip of his beard. "I already failed the Leshbolgs once, and now I can't find a place for the last one to feel content. The home in Avalon Town has helped dozens of war orphans, but Manniref didn't cope well there. She's had foster families in Fernwood Deep, the Resurrected Woods, the Spine, and now Mistwood North, without any success. I don't know what to do with her, Julie, but it's my duty to help her find her place in the world."

Julie tilted her head. "Have you talked to Val?"

Merlin frowned. "Val Stonehold?"

"Do we know any other famous heroines named Val?" Julie inquired.

"What do you think she could do about it?" Merlin asked.

"Manniref could stay with her." Julie leaned back. "In Little Avalon."

Merlin snorted. "Little Avalon! Manniref is a woodland creature. I don't see her surviving in the heart of Brooklyn."

"Brooklyn has more trees than you think, and you tried the deep woods. That didn't work." Julie spread her hands. "I sent Tetra Dupont to Little Avalon, and look at how well that worked. She went from a condemned criminal to the princess of the faeries."

"Is there a difference?" Merlin muttered.

Julie snorted. "Fair point, but you know what I mean."

"Manniref has never been to Earth, Julie. I don't think she knows it exists." Merlin shook his head. "She'll be totally lost there."

"Not if she has Val and that community rallying around her." Julie smiled. "You've been to Little Avalon, Merlin. You know how deep its magic runs. It has provided a home to more than one misfit who needed a fresh start. I think Manniref would thrive there."

Merlin sighed. "I don't like to think of a creature like her stuck in the big city, far from green things."

"Val has an excellent park in Little Avalon. Besides, I think you've been concentrating too hard on giving Manniref the environment she needs instead of the *community* she needs," Julie pointed out. "You're worried about her lost magic, but I don't think she can recover her magic until she's with a family that feels safe to her." She smiled wanly. "Trust me. I know."

Merlin sighed. "I suppose you do."

"Of course I do. I'm the Eternity Queen. I know everything," Julie teased.

Merlin scoffed. "Modest, too."

"Of course." Julie tossed her pixie-cut hair.

Merlin snorted. "Oh, all right. I'll talk to Val. Maybe she'll be willing to help."

"Let's hope she hasn't heard the stories about Leshbolgs," Julie murmured.

"Let's hope," Merlin agreed. "Thank you, Julie. I'll email her shortly."

"You do that, DUMB LE Dork," Julie ordered.

Merlin groaned. "Stop calling me that."

Manniref's satchel lay on the pile of furs that served as her bed. The worn leather object had been a gift from Merlin. She wondered if he'd expected how often she would pack and unpack it in new places over the past few years.

She rolled up her spare cloak and slid it into the bottom, then added the two books she owned: *A Brief History of the Griffin Species* and *Growing Lavender from Cuttings: A Comprehensive Guide.* Her small bundle of clothes followed.

The wooden chest at the foot of her bed contained only one other thing. Manniref carefully lifted it and weighed it in her palm. The object looked like a knot of wood from a tree trunk, but its weight suggested it was metal. It felt warm against her skin and buzzed as though it contained lightning.

She had no idea what it was, as she had no idea about anything that came from Lichenvale. Not even herself.

Manniref dropped the amulet into the satchel and closed it. She felt the pressure of eyes on her and looked up. A woven curtain separated her room from the rest of the hut. Yulietta stood in the gap between the curtain and the wall.

"Yevgen said you were leaving today." Yulietta folded her arms.

Manniref nodded. "Merlin's message said he'd be here before noon."

Yulietta grunted.

Manniref buckled the satchel, then slid her stockinged feet into deerskin boots.

Yulietta shifted her weight. "You haven't been bad."

Manniref gave Yulietta a reassuring smile. She'd heard that line from her other foster parents. None of them had hated her. It wasn't their fault she didn't fit in.

"I mean…" Yulietta sighed. "We were all worried when Chief Myleksa said a Leshbolg was coming to live with us. You've heard the stories."

Manniref had, and they were bullshit, but she nodded.

"They were wrong. You're not violent and mindless. Funny things happen when you're around, sure, but you seem…fine." The elf shrugged. "I'm sorry this didn't work."

"Yeah," Manniref murmured. "I'm sorry, too."

"It's not that there's anything wrong with you," Yulietta croaked. "You're different, that's all."

The words were true, but they stung like salt water on scratched hands. She rose and swung the satchel onto her shoulder. The cumulative awkwardness of the weeks she'd spent waiting for Merlin to come now weighed on her shoulders. "I'm going to wait for Merlin on the other side of the bridge. He might come by dragon again," Manniref muttered.

Yulietta stepped aside. "Yes. Of course. Sure. You do that."

Manniref pushed past her and strode to the hut's door. She was halfway through it when Yulietta shouted, "*Goodbye, Manniref.*"

Manniref looked back. "Goodbye." She paused. "Thank you." She meant it.

A hush fell on Wolf Glen as Manniref crunched down the

snowy street toward the bridge. Children gaped at her or waved goodbye. Most of the adult elves pointedly ignored her, continuing skinning carcasses or cutting wood, but some glared as she passed. She heard the whispers behind her but didn't try to make out the words. She didn't want to hear what they said.

The elk pressed close to the paddock fences as she reached the gate. She touched their soft, wet noses and scratched their heads for the last time, then tucked her cloak around herself and shuffled to the bridge.

"Manniref!"

She stopped, then gritted her teeth and kept walking.

"*Manniref!*"

Manniref swallowed the lump in her throat and turned. "Hey, Fedir."

Her only friend scampered up to her, his bowed legs flaring out as he ran. Fedir wore huge round spectacles he had been given by the Eternity Throne clinic near the garrison. The older elves disapproved, but Fedir ran into walls without them. A bow wrapped in leather hung on his back.

"This is *b-b-b-b-bullshit!*" he burst out.

Manniref laughed. "Adalette won't be happy with your language."

"I know, b-b-but it *is!*" Fedir clenched his skinny fists. "Don't g-go, Manniref."

Manniref laid a hand on his bony shoulder. "Thanks, Fedir, but I have to. You and I both know I don't belong here."

His shoulder sagged under her arm. "You're g-going, aren't you?"

"I don't have a choice. Chief Myleksa's orders," Manniref reminded him. "It's for the best."

Fedir scowled. "She's not the Eternity Queen! She can't make you g-g-g-go. We can fight this, Manniref. We can appeal!"

"You've been reading again," Manniref observed.

Fedir flushed. "I don't care if it's forb-b-bidden!"

"I know." Manniref grinned. "You're the village rebel."

Fedir shoved his glasses higher on his nose. "It's not right. We have to stop this. I'll talk to her. *I'll tell the queen!*"

"I don't think the queen cares." Manniref shrugged. "Besides, I...I know it's time for me to leave this place."

"You don't like it here?" Fedir asked.

"It's not that." Manniref gazed at the village. "People have been pretty good, and it's beautiful here. And Lichenvale was in Mistwood North too, so it feels familiar. Merlin thought it would help me to remember what happened to my species, but it hasn't. I need to go somewhere that will help me remember." She smiled. "I'll miss you, though."

Fedir sighed. "You were g-g-g-good to me. Not many elves are."

"I'll write," Manniref promised.

"Letters are forb-b-bidden too, remember?" Fedir rolled his eyes.

"I'll send messages, then." Manniref paused. "Thanks, Fedir. I don't remember if I've ever had a friend before, but you are one."

"If I can't make you stay, at least let me wait with you," Fedir offered.

Manniref smiled. "That'd be nice."

They crossed the bridge together, Fedir's steps halting, and perched on a fallen log by the path. Fedir produced a pouch of wild hog cracklings from his pocket. They handed it back and forth, enjoying the salty snack.

"When's he coming?" Fedir asked.

Manniref shrugged. "Before noon, he said."

"Do you think there'll be a dragon again?" Fedir's eyes shone.

"Maybe." Manniref sighed.

Fedir paused. "I made you something." He reached back, drew the bow, and held it to her.

Manniref stared at it, then at him. "Fedir..."

"I want you to have it," Fedir told her fiercely.

Manniref took the wrapped bow and gently unwound the leather strips to reveal the warm gold of polished yew. The delicate grain shone in the sunlight, and it was supple in Manniref's hands. Strength coursed through the once-living material, unnaturally amplified. When she turned the bow over, she read the flowing elven runes carved into the grip.

"That one makes it stronger." Fedir pointed. "This one makes it more accurate, and this one's your name."

"You gave me a rune?" Manniref asked.

"Yeah." Fedir shyly smiled. "It's not truly your rune until a selenite cutter places it on your soul, but it's an option if you like it. If not, think of it as a decoration."

Manniref gazed at the shape he'd etched into the grain. "I like it."

Fedir flushed. "G-g-good. You'll need a string for it, but we are out of horsehair."

"I'll find one," Manniref promised. "Thank you." She wrapped it again and tucked it into the strap of her satchel. "Thank you for being my friend."

"Outcasts have to stick together." Fedir paused. "Do you know where you're going?"

Manniref shook her head. "Another foster home, I suppose."

"I hope it's nicer than this one," Fedir told her.

Manniref nudged his shoulder. "Hey, this one was pretty cool while it lasted."

She felt a stirring of magic in the woods before the dull booms of dragon wings beating resounded across the sky. The elk snorted and bucked in their paddocks, and birds rose in clouds from the trees. Another resounding thump brought elves spilling from the huts, the children leading the way. They pointed and shouted as everyone searched for the wingshadow.

"Where is he?" Fedir shaded his eyes.

Manniref scanned the sky, heart fluttering.

An elf in the village spotted it first. "There!" He pointed. "There is the dragon!"

The elves gasped and clustered together. Manniref had to squint for several more seconds before she saw the distant shape. The next flap of its wings made the treetops buck and sway, showering snow everywhere.

Then the dragon was upon them. Dark veins streaked the pale gold membranes of its wings, and its colorful scales glittered in the sun: blue, gold, and purple. It soared in a wide arc above the village, filling the sky. It could have fit the longhouse inside its belly.

Manniref hoped it wasn't so inclined.

The dragon spread its wings and swooped to the ground. Trees buckled and shattered as its claws dug into the earth and plowed dark grooves between the snow. Wisps of smoke rose from its flared nostrils. Its amber eyes rested on Manniref with a strange gentleness.

The elves clustered together in awed silence.

"Do I *have* to say it?" the dragon whispered, giving Manniref a glimpse of sword-sized teeth.

"Yes!" its rider hissed.

"Oh, all right." The dragon sighed. "All hail Merlin Ambrosius, High Mage of the Eternity Throne, High Advisor to the Eternity Queen, Stone of the Sword, Oldest of the Lunar Fae, Forger of Excalibur, Shaper of Avalon!"

The elves gasped. A magnificent fae fluttered up from behind the dragon's spreading horns. The slender humanoid's dragonfly wings shed moonlight so bright that its silver glow cast shadows despite the bright sunlight. Silken robes covered with silver stars on a blue background swirled over his arms and legs. His beard shone brilliantly, tumbling in white curls over his chest.

"*All hail!*" Fedir cried, eyes shining.

The elves attempted an organized cry in response but succeeded only in mumbling.

"Thank you, thank you." Merlin inclined his head and waved his arms as though he were calming raucous applause. "It is my honor, friends, to be so warmly welcomed in Wolf Glen."

He gently alighted near Alugon's massive claws. With a wave, he caused a carpet of yellow daisies to push through the snow and bloom across the ground to Chief Myleksa's feet. The elves let out spontaneous gasps of awe.

"Mighty chief," Merlin boomed. His wings stirred, bearing him across the daisies so lightly that his steps bent not a single petal. "Greetings."

Myleksa nodded. "Hail, High Mage."

"I thank you for the care you have shown my ward," Merlin intoned. "I thank you for your protection and hospitality."

Myleksa cleared her throat. "Yes, sir."

Merlin spread his arms, fanning out his long, silky sleeves. "May the blessings of Luna rest forever upon this place!" More daisies popped out of the wooden walls and the paddock fences. The children giggled and picked them.

"Uh, thank you, sir," Myleksa managed.

"I must take my leave now, good people." Merlin gracefully inclined his head. *"Come, Manniref!"*

Manniref couldn't decide if the imperious shout meant he was mad at her. Merlin floated to his seat behind the dragon's head. Manniref followed and scrambled onto the dragon's paw.

"Hello, Alugon," she whispered.

The mighty creature's laughter rumbled like thunder in his chest. "Hello, young one."

Manniref found footholds between his smooth scales and scrambled up to join Merlin on his neck. She straddled the dragon and wrapped her arms around one of the spikes that ran the length of his spine.

"Long live the Eternity Queen!" Merlin shouted. Jets of silver fire burst from his hands.

"Long live the queen!" the elves echoed.

Alugon raised his head, and Manniref hugged the spike as he spread his wings, casting the village in shadow. She squeezed her eyes shut. The dragon's muscles tightened beneath her, and he sprang into the sky. With two heavy wingbeats, he shot over the treetops and swooped away from Wolf Glen, the place that was so like Manniref's home.

CHAPTER THREE

Alugon carried them across Mistwood North. The trees seemed puny from this distance, smaller than thimbles. Their green blended with the snow's white to form a blur of gray far below.

Manniref wrapped her cloak more snugly around her shoulders and leaned against the spike. It wasn't her first dragon flight, and Alugon's movement was surprisingly smooth. She no longer needed to hold on. Fedir's bow pressed into her ribs beneath the satchel's strap.

A gust tugged her hood. She looked up as Merlin fluttered around the spike and sat between Manniref and the next one, facing her. He crossed his legs, utterly at ease, and laid his hands on his lap.

"Want to tell me what happened?"

Manniref was relieved that he'd dropped the pompous tone. She tucked her hands inside her fur-lined cloak. "Not really."

"It wasn't a request," Merlin murmured.

Manniref gazed into the distance. The jagged mountains of the Northern Spine filled the horizon, growing closer as Alugon banked toward them. Their icy peaks caught the sun, rising from an ocean of pale mist.

"I don't know, sir." Manniref sighed. "I did what I had to do, and it got me in hot water."

"You'll have to give me more than that. Myleksa told me no details. The guards at the garrison said the messenger mentioned broken bones." Merlin raised an eyebrow. "What did you do?"

"I don't know," Manniref admitted. "I didn't want to hurt him. I just wanted to scare off the wolves he was trying to kill, but they weren't scared of me, and I had to stop him. Then...the trees..." She shook her head. "Roots came out of the ground. I didn't know how to stop them."

Merlin sat back. "You discovered a new power."

"I try not to. They come too easily, and I can't control them." Manniref's gaze dipped to Alugon's colorful scales. "Sir."

Merlin ran a hand over his beard.

"I didn't mean to hurt him," Manniref repeated, "but I couldn't let him kill the alpha female. She had puppies. I couldn't let them starve."

"I know." Merlin sighed. "It's not your fault they rejected you. Perhaps Julie's right. Maybe Mistwood North's magic is too concentrated for you."

Julie? Manniref wasn't sure who that was. She tried to remember the queen's name and couldn't.

"What about your memories?" Merlin asked.

Manniref shook her head. "It didn't work. Mistwood didn't bring any back."

"Nothing?" Merlin asked. "Truly?"

Manniref looked up. "Nothing new. I can only remember those few images from before the Battle of Lichenvale."

Merlin leaned forward. "What about the battle itself?"

Manniref's throat tightened. She tangled her hands in her cloak and said nothing.

"Come on, Manniref." Merlin touched her knee awkwardly. "I know it's difficult, but your entire species is gone. If you remember more about them, we can try to restore their culture."

"I know," Manniref whispered. She blinked hard to keep her tears at bay. "I remember my mother's face and the tears in her eyes as she touched my cheek. Then she closed something over me...a cloth, a door, I'm not sure. I looked through the cracks and saw an army of Leshbolgs charging to meet a dark host."

"Do you remember any new details about the Leshbolgs?" Merlin asked.

Manniref sighed. "I remember that they were huge. Towering. As tall as the trees. They were humanoid like me, but their skin was like bark. I think they carried weapons. I'm not sure." She paused. "They were all male."

"You don't know where your mother went after she hid you?" Merlin leaned forward.

Manniref brushed her shoulder-length hair out of her face. Alugon's next wingbeat blew it into her eyes again. Annoyed, she shortened it. The strands shrank away from her shoulders and changed into tight curls against her scalp. "No."

"*Mother*. That's the part I can't reconcile with what we found in Lichenvale," Merlin murmured. "We found no female remains."

"I'm sorry." Manniref spread her hands. "I don't have any answers for you. I've tried. Believe me."

"I know." Merlin paused. "I wish I had answers for *you*, Manniref."

Manniref pulled her cloak tighter around her shoulders. "You never found my mother's bones?"

"We found only the remains of male Leshbolgs," Merlin told her.

Manniref bit her lip. "Do you think..."

Merlin shook his head. "I doubt anyone survived except you, since you barely did." His tone softened. "If we'd been ten minutes later, you would have died, too."

"Is that why I can't remember anything?" Manniref asked.

"Possibly. Head trauma can compromise memory temporarily or even permanently, even with magical healing." Merlin shrugged. "Of course, psychological trauma can do the same thing. So can exposure to dark magic, and you suffered all three. It's little wonder you can't remember your past."

"You thought the magic in Mistwood North would help me remember," Manniref observed.

"Yes. Sometimes saturation with powerful pure magic eases the effects of dark magic exposure." Merlin sighed. "Not in this case."

"We approach the Northern Spine garrison," Alugon rumbled.

Manniref peered past the spikes on his neck. The small fortress clung to the rocks and ice of the mountaintop, its battlements dark and unnatural against the snow.

Merlin patted Manniref's knee in a stiff, fluttery motion. "You'll remember eventually, Manniref. Don't lose hope."

"I'm trying," Manniref murmured.

Merlin cleared his throat and sat up. "That's enough of that. Down to business. We're taking the portal at this garrison to Avalon Town. You remember *that*, I trust?"

"I've been there between all my placements. I remember it," Manniref mumbled.

"Good. Your short-term memory works," Merlin grouched.

"Hold on back there." Alugon's words vibrated through his massive body. "Landing."

Manniref swiveled to face the spine and wrapped her arms around it as Alugon banked, the wind whistling over his wings. He circled the garrison, giving Manniref a fine view of the archers on the battlements' armor flashing and bows in hand. Banners snapped from the round towers between the mountain's jagged cliffs. A road traced from the garrison's maw to the lowlands at the mountain's feet.

Alugon descended toward the road, snow swirling in his downdraft as he flapped his wings. He landed with an earth-shaking thump. "Are you doing a grand entrance again?"

Merlin spread his wings and rose above Alugon's head, shedding moonlight. *"Behold!"* he thundered. *"I, Merlin, have returned!"*

An orc guarding the portcullis leaned on his spear, bored. "I remember when the Eternity Queen wore you on her head as a hat. You were a fedora most of the time."

"Shut up and let us in, lout," Merlin snapped.

He landed in front of Alugon's nose and marched to the portcullis as it rose. Manniref slithered down the dragon's scales and over his paw to the ground. Her feet met the road's hard unnatural black surface with an unpleasant shudder. It separated her from the rich earth, making her feel disconnected from her body.

Scales rustled behind her. She looked up as Alugon shrank, colors swirling as he transformed. His scales became fabric, his wings vanished, and his limbs shortened until he stood beside Manniref as a seven-foot humanoid. His silk robe was gold, blue, and purple. The same colors formed scaly patterns on his bald head.

Merlin was already inside the fortress, yelling at somebody.

"Shall we?" Alugon elegantly offered Manniref his arm.

She took it. "Thanks for the lift."

"Anytime, young one." Alugon patted her hand as they strolled into the garrison. Several guards saluted or nodded at him, murmuring, "Hail, Augur." Manniref tried not to stare at them. They all wore navy body armor with strange objects strapped to their backs. These had no blades but emanated violence.

That was where the similarities between guards ended. An elf —Sylthana, judging by the silver hair and sand-colored skin— went to join the orc outside the portcullis. Two dwarves patrolled the inner ward with a gigantic wolf wearing armor. A fae, another orc, and a vampire hustled by in business suits. The vampire wore a veil to protect her face from the sun.

"It's not polite to stare," Merlin snapped.

Manniref cleared her throat. "Sorry."

Merlin stormed toward an open double door in the wall.

"Don't worry about him." Alugon patted her hand. "He's grumpy, but he cares about you."

"I feel like a pain in his ass," Manniref confessed.

"You're not a pain in anyone's...posterior." Alugon smiled. "We are delighted to help you."

Manniref smiled. "Thanks, Alugon."

"Are you two coming?" Merlin snapped.

They followed him into a chamber that was easily the size of Wolf Glen, with stout walls and no windows. Sunlight streamed into the space from a magic portal on Manniref's right. The round portal could have admitted three elk abreast. Its edges shimmering with mysterious power and offered a hazy view of a broad green meadow dotted with wildflowers.

Manniref stepped toward it, but Merlin stopped her. "This way!"

They passed half a dozen portals, many showing landscapes like the first. Merlin stopped by the most depressing of the lot. Manniref saw no natural stone, only concrete walls and pillars with numbers painted on them in poison yellow.

"Hold on to my arm, young one," Alugon reminded her.

Manniref's stomach lurched at the memory of portal sickness. She gripped Alugon tightly as Merlin bounded through the portal with an impatient flick of his wings. Alugon followed sedately, and Manniref closed her eyes and gritted her teeth as they stepped through it.

A lukewarm buzzing sensation raced across Manniref's skin, and nausea clawed up her throat, the bile stinging her tonsils. She kept her eyes squeezed shut but still felt the world spinning. The floor seemed to whirl beneath her feet for several seconds before it steadied.

"There you are." Alugon patted her hand. "Much better than last time."

Manniref opened her eyes and spotted the trash can she'd thrown up in last time, but Alugon was right. She didn't need it.

"You're clammy, poor thing." Alugon retrieved a silk handkerchief from his sleeve and gave it to her.

"Thanks." Manniref dabbed her face with it.

"It gets better with practice," Alugon assured her.

"Are you two coming?" Merlin demanded again.

The polished concrete floor under Manniref's boots was unnaturally smooth. She didn't let go of Alugon's arm as he escorted her to where Merlin waited by a pair of sliding steel doors. Manniref had to fish for the word. "Elevator."

The doors opened as they reached it. Merlin bounded inside and smacked a button as Alugon and Manniref joined him. Its lurch made her wobble, but her nausea was getting better.

As the elevator rose, Manniref couldn't shake off a feeling of unfamiliarity, though she'd spent several weeks here after the Battle of Lichenvale. They'd passed in an uncomfortable blur as she lay in the infirmary. She remembered wounded soldiers in the beds next to her, a few crying out in pain, others worryingly pale and still.

"Are there still so many wounded paras here?" she asked.

"No, no. Not since the war ended," Alugon told her. "The infirmary is all but empty these days."

"Her Majesty's army seems as big as ever," Manniref observed.

"Yes." Alugon smiled. "We fought hard to win this peace. We are ready to fight hard to maintain it."

"It's not politically correct to call it 'the queen's army' anymore," Merlin added. "It's the OPMA these days. Official Para-Military Agency." He scoffed. "Ridiculous."

The elevator halted. Merlin led them into a red-carpeted hallway with walls of near-black stone, which channeled them to a huge entrance hall with balconies overlooking the center.

Manniref drew curious glances from uniformed paras bustling in every direction. Many wore OPMA navy, but others wore green or brown. Their clothes fascinated Manniref. They also wore different shoes, many with heels that seemed to make walking difficult. She couldn't imagine why.

A pretty Sylthana Elf strode past, sleek silver hair spilling down her back like a waterfall. Manniref liked it. She grew her hair almost unconsciously until it reached the length of the elf's and mimicked the soft, straight texture.

A nearby orc did a double-take and hurried off. Manniref smoothed her hair and adjusted her ears to match it, then almost tripped when a passing fae dropped a stack of files on the floor, gawping at her.

"Is there something in my teeth?" Manniref asked.

"I don't think that's the difficulty," Alugon told her.

Manniref tried to remember if all paras were like the Mavka Elves, unable to change their appearance. Surely not. The Green Men she'd stayed with in Fernwood Deep had grown beards, hair, or moss on their skin at will.

They left the lobby and entered a courtyard that echoed like the one at the Northern Spine garrison but was five times the size. Here, too, archers patrolled the battlements, and an iron portcullis guarded the entrance, only its spikes visible as it hovered above the gateway.

White stripes marked spaces for paras to park their various modes of transport. Hitching posts adorned each parking spot. Several magic carpets hung on the nearest one. Beside them, six white horses waited patiently, the leaders tethered to the post. Their carriage was orange and pumpkin-shaped. The vehicle next to the carriage was white metal with wheels and nothing to pull it. Manniref had to fish for the word.

"That's a 'car,' right?" she asked.

"You'll see many of them in Avalon Town," Alugon explained. "You'll take your first ride in one soon."

"I will?" Manniref raised her eyebrows. "Am I staying here?"

"No." Merlin marched to a nearby carriage and flicked a gold coin to the driver.

Alugon gave Manniref a hand up. She scooted onto a velvet seat facing Merlin, and Alugon sat beside her. The horses moved off with irritated shakes of their heads as the driver snapped the whip.

"He doesn't have to crack it," Manniref remarked. "They know what to do. He could talk to them nicely."

"What?" Merlin demanded.

"The horses. They're not stupid," Manniref muttered.

Merlin sighed. "You have bigger problems, Manniref."

The carriage rumbled out of the fortress and into the city's streets. Merlin's piercing eyes bored into Manniref. She knew he was waiting for her to ask where her next placement was, but the question stuck in her throat. She gazed through the window as they passed rows of buildings. No two were the same, and the paras hurrying down the streets were equally different.

Every species seemed to be present on the streets of Avalon Town, including several that Manniref didn't recognize. A beautiful girl with the horns of a gazelle stepped from a building and waved at a well-built man with giant wings and bronze feathers. She saw two elves with red hair and ochre skin. A pair of bleating goats recklessly overtook the carriage, drawing a cart containing two satyrs.

The city's hectic energy skittered over Manniref's skin, fresh and exciting, but she knew from experience that it would eventually become overwhelming. For now, she enjoyed it. The long ears irritated her, so she shortened them and turned her hair golden to match the gazelle-horns girl.

"Well?" Merlin prompted.

Manniref looked up. "Yes, sir?"

"Don't you want to know where you're going next?" Merlin demanded.

Manniref bit her lip. "I'm excited for something new."

"Perhaps you feel safe in this moment," Alugon murmured, "and are uncertain about what the next moment might hold."

Manniref looked into his amber eyes. "That sounds right."

"Your last chance," Merlin snapped. "That's what this is."

Last chance? Manniref swallowed.

"Merlin," Alugon chided. "Don't be melodramatic."

"Don't tell me what to do, you old lizard," Merlin grumbled.

"Don't worry." Alugon smiled at Manniref. "If anyone can help you fit in and fulfill your purpose, it's Val."

"Who's Val?" Manniref asked.

Merlin burst out laughing. His beard bounced on his chest as he threw his head back and guffawed.

"*Merlin*," Alugon hissed.

Merlin stopped. "You really don't know?"

Manniref shook her head.

"They don't have internet in Wolf Glen," Alugon mildly pointed out.

"What's internet?" Manniref asked.

"Oh, yes. You wouldn't know." Merlin snorted. "Good thing I arranged a training orb session for you."

"A what?" Manniref blinked.

"You'll find out soon. We're here," Merlin announced.

The carriage slowed, and Manniref gaped through the window. A colossal plaza stretched around her, its cobblestones sparkling like gemstones in the sunlight. Dozens of buildings in every style surrounded it, from stone cottages to towering masses of steel and glass. Banners hung from every window, filling Manniref's vision with color, and the bustling crowd chattered, punctuating the clatters of hooves and the rumbles of wheels.

"Where's Val?" Merlin grumbled.

Manniref scanned the plaza. "Who is this Val?"

"Oh, no one, really," Merlin muttered. "Only the greatest heroine of her time. The Warrior of the Red Bear. The Duchess of Little Avalon. The protector of all, the leading bodyguard to the most important royals. She built a paranormal community in the heart of New York City, reforged Excalibur, developed the bone runes that quelled the Wild Hunt, and faced Kronos in battle and imprisoned his spirit before beheading him!"

"There's no need for sarcasm, Merlin," Alugon protested.

"It's like she's been living under a rock!" Merlin burst out.

"You sent me to that rock," Manniref stated mildly.

Merlin rolled his eyes. "Don't give me lip, young lady. Ah, there she is."

The carriage creaked to a halt, and Merlin disembarked. Manniref followed him out, and though the name "Val Stonehold" still meant nothing to her, she spotted the only para in sight who could have conquered the Wild Hunt and reforged Excalibur.

The tall woman wore hobnailed boots and tight black pants. Her leather jacket covered shoulders bulging with muscle and strained over powerful biceps. Her skin was the tawny color of Mistwood spruce. She wore her bright blue hair chin length, and a massive dagger jutted at her hip. Manniref's skin prickled in her presence the way it would if she stepped between a bear and her cubs. Danger emanated from every pore of Val Stonehold's body.

Val leaned against the first car Manniref had considered beautiful. There was something far more than utilitarian about its sleek lines. All thoughts of Val and the vehicle fled Manniref's mind when a hairy form sprang through the car door.

Manniref gasped. "Dog!"

The dog would tower over any wolf, but his floppy ears and wagging tail invited Manniref to run to him. She dropped to her knees and flung her arms around his neck, burying her face in his thick red fur.

Hello! The dog's greeting telepathically boomed in Manniref's head. *I Shadow!*

"Nice to meet you, Shadow." Manniref sat back. "I'm Manniref."

You Manniref! I like! Shadow licked her face.

"Wait, what?" Val demanded. She had an unfamiliar accent with harsh, guttural consonants. "Is he talking to you?"

Manniref looked up. "Um, he said hello and introduced himself."

Mom, she hear! Shadow bounded to Val's side and gamboled in a circle around her. *I talk, she hear!*

I thought only I could hear you, Val protested.

Nature magic. Speaks dog! Shadow yipped and chased his tail.

Val's lips tightened. "He only talks to me."

Manniref straightened. Merlin had said Val was her last chance.

Had she already blown it?

"Do you talk to all dogs?" Val demanded.

Manniref shuffled her feet. "I talk to all animals. Sometimes they answer, but I don't usually hear their words like I did with him." She cleared her throat. "He's not really a dog, is he?"

I Shadow! Shadow wagged his tail. *Red Bear!*

Val's eyes narrowed. "No."

Merlin cleared his throat and butted in. "Manniref, this is Duchess Eiravel Stonehold. You may address her as 'Duchess Eiravel,' 'Your Grace,' or 'ma'am.'"

"You'll do no such thing," Val growled. "I'm Val." She extended a hand.

Manniref tentatively shook it and felt shocking strength in Val's fingers. "Manniref."

"Yes, Merlin said." Val released her hand. "I'm starving. Lunch at Meggie's while we get to know each other?"

Manniref didn't know who Meggie was, but lunch sounded great. She nodded.

"I'll never say no to Meggie's." Alugon grinned.

"Oh, all right," Merlin muttered. "If you insist."

Meggie give bones! Shadow barked and raced ahead, coat rippling.

Merlin stomped after the dog. Val fell into step beside Manniref and Alugon.

"Hey, sorry I was cranky back there," Val apologized. "It was a surprise, that's all. Shadow and I are close."

"You'd do anything for each other," Manniref observed, "including die."

Val blinked. "Well, yeah."

"Perhaps those powerful truths don't need to be verbalized at this moment, Manniref," Alugon murmured.

"No, it's okay. You speak your mind." Val grinned. "I like that. What did Merlin tell you about Little Avalon?"

Manniref blinked. "What's Little Avalon?"

"Merlin was not forthcoming," Alugon supplied.

Val groaned. "What else is new?"

They entered a building decorated in an explosion of colors and textures. The wooden floor met a counter covered in white tiles. The back wall was stone. The furniture didn't match, but the paras seated at the tables had food or drinks before them. Manniref surmised that this was a communal eating hall like the one in Wolf Glen.

Merlin chose a table in the back corner with bench-like seats striped red and white. He flung himself onto a bench, and Val sat beside him, facing Manniref and Alugon. Manniref liked the squishy seat. Shadow lay at her feet, to her delight.

"What's Little Avalon?" Manniref repeated.

"It's a paranormal community hidden in New York City." Val grinned.

Manniref stared. "What's New York City?"

"Oh." Val cleared her throat. "Never been to Earth?"

Manniref helplessly looked from Alugon to Merlin to Val. "What's Earth?"

Val's jaw dropped.

A weremouse bustled across the eating hall to meet them, clutching a pen and a notepad. "Duchess Eiravel, it's always an honor to serve you!" She bowed, her gray bun bobbing on her head. "High Mage Merlin, sir, what a privilege! Oooh, and Augur Alugon. How wonderful to have you grace my little bistro!"

Alugon gave an indulgent smile. "Good morning, Meggie."

Shadow licked the weremouse's hands.

"My favorite boy! I saved you the meatiest bones in the kingdom." Meggie giggled. "Who's your lovely new friend? I like your hair very much."

Manniref touched her golden curls. "Thank you!"

"Can we just order?" Merlin grouched. "I'm starving."

"We can't have that, sir. What would you like?" Meggie held up the notebook.

"I'll start with a glass of Fernwood wine, if you please." Alugon inclined his head. "Manniref, would you like wine?"

"Yes, please."

"Beer," Val grumbled.

Merlin inspected a small leather book with shiny pages. "I'll have a venti pumpkin spice macchiato with extra cinnamon. Hold the cream. Three pumps of chocolate syrup. Oh, and don't forget the sprinkles."

"I wouldn't dream of it, sir." Meggie withdrew.

"Let me get this straight." Val turned to Manniref. "You don't know Earth is a thing?"

"I know about ground." Manniref cleared her throat. "You know, dirt."

"I mean Earth as in the dimension," Val told her.

Manniref repeated the stare from Val to Merlin to Alugon and back. "There are other dimensions?"

"What did they teach you in Wolf Glen?" Merlin demanded. "Nothing?"

"Hunting," Manniref offered. "Tanning. Making wattle-and-daub houses. No one mentioned other dimensions."

"Remember, the Mavka are a recently contacted people, Merlin." Alugon spread his hands. "It's possible they don't know Earth exists, either."

Merlin sighed. "Better you than me, Val."

Val shot him a sharper look than most paras would dare, then returned her attention to Manniref. "Earth is another world. It's closely related to this one, which is Avalon. Merlin and King Arthur used Earth as a blueprint when they created Avalon. You know about *that*, right?"

Manniref nodded. "Everyone knows Luna created the universe, and Merlin and Arthur created Avalon."

"At least you know *something*," Merlin muttered.

"Earth has many similarities to Avalon, but there's one major difference." Val paused. "Do you know what a human is?"

Manniref rubbed her neck and glimpsed her sandy Sylthana-like skin. She didn't think it went well with her golden hair, so she made it a few shades paler.

Val jumped. "What just happened?"

"She changes her appearance," Merlin muttered. "What did you think?"

"Oh." Val blinked.

Meggie reappeared with a tray containing two wine glasses, a tankard, and a tall glass mug containing hot milk with colorful additives.

"Thanks, Meggie. I'll have my usual." Val took the tankard.

"Sylthana fish and chips it is, Your Grace." Meggie wrote on the notepad.

Merlin demanded chicken cacciatore, whatever that was, and Alugon asked for a double cheeseburger with fries. Manniref panicked and said she'd have what Alugon was having, drawing an encouraging grin from the dragon.

Manniref clutched her wine as the weremouse hurried away.

"Is she old enough for wine?" Val doubtfully asked.

"You've been on Earth too long, Val. There's no minimum drinking age here," Alugon reminded her.

"Humans?" Manniref asked. "I don't know what they are. I know what 'humanoid' means. That's a bipedal para with hands."

"Humans are bipedal creatures with hands, yeah, but they're not paranormals," Val explained. "You might call them 'normals.' They don't have magic."

"Like Weres?" Manniref asked.

"Uh, no. Not like Weres. They don't shift shape." Val sipped her beer, then wiped her mouth on her sleeve. "Imagine a Were who doesn't have an animal form. That's a human."

"Oh." Manniref tasted the wine, which was excellent. "They live on Earth?"

"Billions of them." Val nodded. "Many in New York, one of the most populous cities in the world. I built Little Avalon inside Brooklyn—that's part of New York—so paras had somewhere to gather."

"That's where we're going?" Manniref asked.

Val nodded. "That's where I live. That's where you'll live too, if you like it there."

"A para community inside a city." Manniref kept her face blank as she glanced through the door at Avalon Town. "That sounds...different."

"It *is* different." Val smiled. "Oh, wow! Your, uh...your eyes."

Manniref grinned. "Do you like them? I didn't think the blue worked with the red hair."

"They're nice," Val croaked, shooting Merlin a wide-eyed look. The wizard was too absorbed in his milky drink to notice.

Val quickly recovered. "Tell me more about yourself."

"There's not much to tell." Manniref shrugged. "Mordred's

cult killed my entire species in the war. I don't remember anything before that. Merlin found me and brought me to Avalon Town to get better."

Val's face softened. "Where did you go after that?"

"Boarding schools and homes in Avalon Town and New Camelot. None of them worked for more than a couple of weeks. They were too depressing. I thought I needed the woods, so Merlin placed me with foster parents near the Eyrie, then in Fernwood Deep, then in the Resurrected Woods, then back to Fernwood Deep, and finally in Mistwood North."

Manniref shook her head. "The woods made my powers go crazy, so none of them lasted. I was with the Mavka for nearly a year. They were the longest placement. I liked them."

Val blinked. "That's a lot of moving around. I'm sorry."

"It's how it is." Manniref sipped wine. "No one goes to Lichenvale, the Leshbolgs' native land, anymore. It's uninhabit-able after what the cult did. I have to find somewhere else to belong, but it hasn't been easy so far." She kept her tone calm, but her chest hurt.

Val tilted her head. "Maybe you'll belong in Little Avalon."

Inside a gigantic human city on a different world? Manniref had reservations but couldn't voice them to the kind para sitting opposite her. "It's something new to try. I look forward to it," she added sincerely.

Val chuckled. "Good."

Manniref no like city, Shadow announced under the table.

"I figured as much," Val murmured. "Look, I know it's nothing like your old home, but trust me. Many paras have found happiness there. You wouldn't be the first outcast to make Little Avalon your permanent home."

Manniref smiled, warmth flickering in her chest. "Thanks. I'm excited to see it."

Meggie bustled over, carrying two trays loaded with food. She slid plates in front of everyone, but to Manniref's dismay, this "cheeseburger and fries" that Alugon had ordered contained nothing green or crunchy except a sad strip of lettuce between the meat and the bread.

Fries were nice, but she now remembered the "burger" from her stint in the hospital, and the memory made her stomach flip. She'd hoped she'd heard wrong when Alugon ordered.

CHAPTER FOUR

"Oh, you poor dear." Meggie clucked. "You don't like it."

Manniref raised her head. "No, it's okay!"

Meggie's nose twitched beneath her black button eyes. "I can always tell, dear. You don't like it one bit."

"It's fine," Manniref croaked.

Meggie leaned disconcertingly closer, her sharp eyes trained on Manniref's. "You'd like something different, wouldn't you?"

"I..." Manniref squeaked.

"You would like a bowl of fresh summer fruits, still damp and crunchy from washing," Meggie murmured. "You'd like a handful of nuts sprinkled on the top, giving buttery pops with every bite of juicy sweetness, and a little honey drizzled over it all. You'd like a few chocolate chips sprinkled in for good measure."

Manniref gulped. "How...how did you know?"

Meggie straightened and briskly removed the plate. "Oh, darling, I always know." She paused. "I'll bring the fries back, don't worry."

Manniref stared after her, open-mouthed, as the weremouse hurried away.

"How did she *know*?" she asked, turning to Alugon. "Did she see it on my face?"

"She's Meggie." Alugon gripped his cheeseburger and surveyed it with deep contentment. "Meggie always knows."

Val raised her eyebrows. "Wait, are you a vegetarian?"

Manniref shook her head. "Not strictly. I eat meat. Sometimes."

Val grimaced. "You and Tetra might not get along."

"Who's Tetra?" Manniref asked.

Val groaned. "You'll find out."

Before Manniref could ask more, Meggie returned with a platter straight from Manniref's wildest dreams. Brightly colored fruit was piled high: scarlet strawberries, pale chunks of apple, juicy orange wedges, dark blueberries, banana discs, shining pomegranate seeds, and half a dozen others Manniref didn't recognize. Golden honey and nuts adorned the top. Her mouth watered.

"That's more like it, isn't it?" Meggie beamed and slid a small plate of fries onto the table. "*Bon appétit*, my dear."

"Thank you." Manniref dug in.

The food was so good that several minutes of silence followed, each member of the group immersed in their taste experience. Manniref only came up for air when the platter was almost empty.

"Wow." Val leaned back. "I've never seen anyone eat so much fruit in one sitting."

"It's very good. What kind of eating hall is this?" Manniref asked.

"It's a restaurant." Val arched an eyebrow. "Now I see why you told me to take her to the NYHQ for a training session, Merlin."

Merlin waved his fork. "Easier to download everything into her brain."

"Let's talk business." Val mopped her fingers with a paper napkin. "First, you'll need a human identity."

"I will?" Manniref asked.

"Yes. Most humans don't know about the paranormal world. This is for their safety as well as ours," Val explained. "The Veil is a powerful concealment spell that hides paranormal details from human eyes. It's why human-presenting paras like dwarves, vampires, elves, fae, and Weres can live among humans without revealing themselves."

Manniref nodded.

"There are things the Veil can't hide, though." Val paused. "Not to rain on your parade, but you have to pick an appearance and stick with it."

Merlin waved a hand. "What she said."

"I can't change my appearance?" Manniref asked. "Does that mean I have to stay humanoid all the time?"

Val blinked. "You can shift shape?"

"I can turn into anything I'm familiar with." Manniref grinned. "I'm a good spruce tree. Do you want to see?"

"No!" Val, Alugon, and Merlin chorused.

"It's more complex than that," Val added. "Yeah, you'll need to stay humanoid when you're in sight of humans." She cleared her throat. "Also, your hair, eyes, and skin tone need to stay the same."

"Oh." Manniref paused. "You mean humans look the same for their whole lives?"

"Not *exactly* the same. They change over the years. But mostly." Val ran a hand over her blue hair. "It'll be safest for you to always assume the same appearance."

"Okay." Manniref looked around for a reflective surface and chose the back window. She liked the gold hair but decided that she wanted to be a redhead for her permanent identity, and gave herself freckles to go with it and shortened it to a shoulder-length bob, then added curls. Her nose seemed slightly off, so she tilted it up at the end. She enlarged her eyes and made them jade green. Val's tawny skin appealed to her, but it didn't work with her hair when she tried it. She lightened it several shades and added a pink undertone.

"How do you do that?" Val wondered.

"I don't know. I just do." Manniref sat back. "How do I look?"

"Perfect." Val nodded. "You'll fit in with no problems. We'll get you a change of clothes, but you can get away with that outfit for a while. It *is* New York City."

Manniref wondered if everyone on Earth wore the kind of clothes Val did, but didn't ask.

"There's one more thing." Val rubbed her chin. "Your name."

"What's wrong with my name?" Manniref asked.

"Nothing's *wrong* with it, but it's too paranormal for humans. I think you should change it." Val nodded.

"What?" Merlin's attention snapped away from his chicken. "No! You can't ask Manniref to leave her culture behind, Val. Let her keep her name. It might be the last Leshbolg name in Avalon!"

"She has to fit in with the humans," Val argued. "It doesn't have to be her real name. Paras can still call her Manniref. It can even sound similar. My human name is Valerie."

"She's lost so much already." Merlin shook his head. "Don't ask her to lose that, too."

"No, it's okay." Manniref held up her hands. "Seriously, it's fine."

Merlin and Val stared at her.

"I want to change my name." Manniref paused. "I don't remember my past or my people, and I've been trying so hard for so long that I forgot to think about my future. I want to leave my old name behind and try something new."

Val smiled. "I get that."

"Are you sure about this, Manniref?" Merlin asked.

"I'm not giving up on my species. I'll keep trying to remember them," Manniref promised, "but I need a new start."

"I can understand that," Alugon rumbled.

"Okay, pick a name." Val groaned. "I should have brought Tess. She's good at this."

"Myrtle," Merlin suggested. "Mabel. Meg. Maggie. Molly."

"She's not a starving street urchin in Victorian London, Merlin," Alugon remarked.

Manniref had no idea what he was talking about.

"He's right. We need something more modern." Val tilted her head. "Mackenzie? Maya? Melody?"

"None of them really fit," Alugon observed.

Manniref shook her head. She couldn't imagine referring to herself by any of those names.

"I've got it." Merlin snapped his fingers. "Merritt."

"Merit? What kind of name is that?" Val demanded. "You might as well call her Excellence."

"I like Excellence," Manniref murmured.

"Not Merit, as in the word," Merlin grumbled. "Two Rs, two Ts. Merritt."

"Merritt," Val slowly repeated.

Alugon smiled. "I like that. It suits her."

"What do you think, Manniref?" Val asked.

Manniref considered the name. To her, it connoted goodness, accomplishment, and value. Three things she longed to bring to her new placement.

"Merritt," she murmured. "I love that. I want to be called Merritt, please."

"Done." Val beamed. "Merritt it is. You'll need a last name, too. Everyone in New York has one."

"Take something from her place of origin," Alugon suggested. "Merritt Vale."

"It has a nice ring to it." Val nodded. "I'll have Qenzi whip up a human ID with that name if it works for you."

The para who now thought of herself as Merritt smiled and nodded. "I really love it."

"Fantastic." Val ate her last fry.

Merritt. I like! Shadow wagged his tail.

Merritt rubbed his ears. *Yeah. So do I.*

<hr>

They left the eating hall—the restaurant or "bistro" as she had read on the sign, Merritt corrected herself—with bellies so full that Merlin cradled his like a pregnant woman.

"Ah, Meggie. Contributing to obesity since the bistro's inception." Alugon discreetly belched.

"I suppose this is another parting," Merlin muttered.

Alugon gave Merritt a gentle hug. "Luna be with you, young one."

"Thanks for everything, Alugon." Merritt returned the hug.

"I would like a moment alone with her," Merlin announced.

Alugon inclined his head and wandered off. Val and Shadow headed to the car.

Merlin turned to Manniref. His piercing eyes were unreadable beneath his mop of white curls. "Listen." He cleared his throat. "I said this is your last chance because if this doesn't work out, I can't think of anywhere else to send you."

Merritt bit her lip. "Maybe it will."

"I hope it does, for your sake. Listen to Val. She's as wise as she is badass. She can help you," Merlin ordered.

Merritt nodded.

"Keep trying to remember. Keep working on your powers. Don't forget who you are," Merlin added, "and try not to ruin any important rituals."

"Yes, sir," Merritt mumbled.

Merlin patted her shoulder. "Be good." He cleared his throat. "I'll be in touch."

"Yes, sir."

"Good. Good." Merlin stared at her for a moment, then turned on his heel and strode away.

Merritt watched him go. He hadn't said it, but she'd heard the unspoken words. *"Don't screw this up."*

"Merritt?" Val called. "Ready to go?"

Excitement replaced the pressure in her chest. "Yes!" She strode over as Val opened the door to the beautiful car. "I've never ridden in a car."

"Never?" Val asked.

Merritt shook her head. "In one of those magical vehicles the OPMA uses, once, and on dragons, but never in a car."

"You're in for a treat." Val grinned. "Gennie is much more than a car."

Merritt stared at it. Its aerodynamic shape and flattened angles made her think of speed.

"*She* is." Val patted the roof. "Her name is Genevieve. She's amazing."

Genevieve honked. "She says hello," Val added.

Merritt curtsied. "Hello, Genevieve."

Genevieve's lights flashed.

"She liked the curtsy. She's vain." Genevieve rolled forward and butted her bumper into Val's knee.

"You know it's true. Don't be snippy," Val grumbled. "Okay, hop in. Shadow, you've got the back seat."

Val folded the front seat down to allow the big dog—well, dog-ish—to jump into the back. She returned the seat to an upright position and gestured. "In you get, Merritt."

Merritt awkwardly wriggled into the seat. Val shut the door with an unexpected thump. A belt slipped over Merritt's shoulder and clipped itself into a buckle by her hip.

"Help!" Merritt squealed, struggling. "Help! I'm trapped!"

"It's okay! It's okay." Val slid into the seat beside hers. "You're not trapped. You can unbuckle it by pressing this button, see?" She touched the buckle, and the belt magically retracted.

Merritt gaped. "Why did it do that?"

"Gennie's trying to keep you safe. She has to, given the way she drives," Val told her.

A lever rapped Val on the arm.

"Ow! Hey! You know it's true," Val grumbled. "Put your seat belt on, Merritt. You'll need it. Oh, and grab the handle over the window if things get hairy."

Merritt pulled the strap over her body and buckled it as Val inserted a key into a slot beside the big wheel she guessed was for steering. Val turned the key, and Genevieve snarled. The deep sound came from the car's front end and vibrated in Merritt's bones.

"Oooh." Merritt grinned. "I like that."

"You ain't seen nothing yet." Val chuckled. "Take it easy, Gennie. There are pedestrians here."

Genevieve purred forward. Merritt sensed the car was only using a fraction of her power. She gazed around the interior, which featured leather seats and shining wooden finishes. Dials and gauges decorated the front. The wheel for steering had a steel emblem in the shape of a galloping horse.

"Why a horse?" Merritt asked.

"What? Oh, the emblem." Val smiled. "It stands for the type of car she is."

"A horse car?" Merritt wondered.

"No." Val laughed. "She's a 1971 Ford Mustang Mach 1. The big one." She patted the wheel. "The 429."

Merritt had no idea what any of that meant. "Mustang," she echoed.

"That's right." Val nodded.

Genevieve puttered across the plaza to a round gateway on the other side. The edges shimmered with magic.

"Do you get portal sickness?" Val asked.

Merritt grimaced. "Badly."

"There are puke bags in the glove box." Val sighed. "Genevieve sometimes has that effect on people."

Genevieve growled.

"I'm not lying," Val insisted.

Merritt gripped the handle over the window and screwed her eyes shut. Portal sickness seized her as the Mustang edged forward. Merritt's stomach lurched as the world spun. This time, the spinning lasted longer.

Val's hand on her shoulder steadied her. "You good?"

Merritt opened her eyes, gasping and sweaty. "That was *much* worse."

"That's because it's an interdimensional portal. Makes the sickness more severe." Val paused. "Merritt, welcome to Earth."

Merritt looked up and gasped.

Earth was nothing like Avalon Town. It was nothing like anything Merritt had seen. The towering buildings dwarfed the towers of any castle she'd visited. They featured shimmering glass windows between brick and concrete pillars, and many had breathtaking curves and fixtures that told Merritt she was in another world. The road was hard and black, overlaid with white and yellow paint. Lights of different colors guarded the crossroads as Genevieve purred onto the street. Merritt saw no carriages or magic carpets, but cars of every color and shape were everywhere.

"Wow!" Merritt whispered.

"It's quite something," Val agreed and pointed. "There is your first human!"

Merritt plastered herself against the window, staring. The creature hurrying beside the road wore a long black coat and had short gray hair. He held a rectangular object to his ear and frowned as he strode along, carrying a leather case. The creature was Were-like, but his features were bland. Merritt saw no wolfish grin or slit-pupiled eyes.

"He's so...humanoid," Merritt murmured.

"They're all like that." Val snickered. "Cool, right?"

"*So cool!*" Merrit cried.

"Did you know that the Eternity Queen grew up in this city?" Val asked as Genevieve joined the flow of cars.

Merritt shook her head. "I didn't. I didn't even know this city existed." She pointed. "Look, trees!"

"That's Central Park. The portal to Avalon is at its edge," Val explained. "We're in Manhattan, some of the most crowded real estate on Earth. There are humans *everywhere.*"

"Amazing," Merritt whispered.

"Gennie, roll down the window for her."

The car's window disappeared as magically as the seat belt had. Merritt leaned out and gaped open-mouthed at the city. At first glance, the steel, glass, and concrete surrounding her made it seem dead. The thick walls muffled Merritt's senses and made the people behind them seem less alive. As her senses adjusted, she was bombarded by life forms, and many were not human.

Genevieve passed a truck whose driver's tusks jutted from his lower lip. A vampire hastened by, sticking to the shadows, although the day was gray. Chilly air flooded Genevieve. The trees lining the street had bare branches, and the park beyond them was covered in snow.

Humans were everywhere: in cars as they raced by, thick beside the road, and crowding the buildings. Weeds clung to cracks in the concrete. Splashes of green announced the presence of plants through windows. Merritt sensed hundreds of animals, too—dogs, cats, pigeons, peregrine falcons soaring among the buildings, rats skittering in every alley, and birds congregating in the park.

People, animals, plants, and paranormals popped out at Merritt like explosions from behind the bridges, buildings, and walls. She clapped her hands over her ears, but it did nothing to muffle her magical senses. She'd felt the buzz of life in the rich depths of Fernwood, but this was different. There, everything moved more slowly. A giant vehicle rushed past containing more than a dozen humans. They flitted in and out of Merritt's senses with disorienting speed.

Breathe. Shadow pressed his wet nose to the back of her neck. *Merritt breathe.*

Merritt inhaled, chest aching.

One thing at a time, Shadow added. *Smell Genevieve. Hear voice. One thing at a time.*

Merritt exhaled and ran her hands over the seat, then focused her magical senses on Shadow's potent life force. If her magic was auditory, he would have sounded like a symphony. The depth and complexity of his life force told her he was more than a dog.

"You good?" Val asked. "It can be overwhelming."

Merritt raised her head. "I feel like I'm being bombarded by fireworks while going blind and deaf." She concentrated on Val's words, and her thudding heart slowed.

Val raised her eyebrows. "Sounds intense."

"Yeah, it is." Merritt grinned. "But it's the most exciting thing I've ever experienced."

Val inclined her head. "Nice, as long as I don't get a demonstration of those powers that keep getting you into trouble."

"I don't think so." Merritt frowned. "I feel disconnected from my magic, like I did in Avalon Town or New Camelot. It feels...far away."

"The city does that to you. Your magic is nature-linked, right? Of course all the manmade stuff around here muffles it. I feel the same thing if I'm on a boat, in the air, or high up in a building. I need to be connected to the earth, or my powers don't work." Val touched the bear-shaped amulet hanging from a thick chain around her neck.

Merritt nodded. "Merlin said the same thing."

Val cocked her head. "What are your powers, anyway?"

"I hardly know." Merritt spread her hands. "The only thing that comes easily is shifting shape. Sometimes plants do weird things when I'm emotional. That was what happened to Neven, the Mavka chief's son. He made me mad, so a tree attacked him."

"Whoa." Val grinned. "That's cool."

"It was until it got me banished." Merritt sighed.

"I guess." Val paused. "The stories they tell about Leshbolgs are scarier than you are, to be honest."

"I've heard the stories. Many paras are suspicious of me because of them." Merritt frowned. "Something about Leshbolgs being violent fighters with scary earth and plant powers."

"Yup," Val agreed. "There's a lot of bullshit about you being mindless creatures without language, too. If anyone in Little Avalon gives you trouble about the Leshbolg legends, let me know. I don't tolerate prejudice in my duchy."

Merritt looked up. "You don't?"

"No." Val shook her head. "I dealt with enough of that back home."

Genevieve reached a stretch of open road and accelerated. Merritt relished the powerful pull of the Mustang as her growl's pitch increased.

"Is it because you're so tall for an Iron Dwarf?" Merritt asked.

Val blinked. "You know I'm an Iron Dwarf? I thought you didn't know who I was."

"I didn't, but anyone can sense your species." Merritt frowned. "You have greater magic than most Iron Dwarves."

"I'm a Warrior of the Red Bear." Val grinned. "It's epic."

"I can see that," Merritt agreed.

The road turned to follow a glittering river, and Merritt gasped. The water passed more built-up land. A tall statue crowned an island in the river: a woman in green copper, her hand stretched toward the sky.

"The Statue of Liberty," Val supplied. "Cool, isn't she?"

"Beautiful," Merritt whispered.

They plunged into the city again, then took a long, straight bridge across the river. Genevieve accelerated until she was moving faster than a galloping elk. Perhaps faster than a flying dragon. The bridge's pylons flitted past in blurs. Merritt laughed in exhilaration.

"Easy, Gennie," Val grumbled, but she was grinning.

Genevieve slowed when they left the bridge. The buildings were smaller here, with lawns and gardens surrounding them, and Merritt's raging senses calmed.

"This is Staten Island," Val explained. "It's not as densely populated as Manhattan. We're not far now from the NYHQ. That's the New York headquarters of the OPMA."

"What are we doing there?" Merritt asked.

"Getting you trained." Val raised an eyebrow. "I thought it was overkill when Merlin suggested it since I moved from Avalon to Earth without training, but I knew Earth was a thing. I suppose Leshbolgs have less contact with other species than Iron Dwarves do."

Merritt looked away. "I wouldn't know. I don't remember them."

Silence filled the car like smoke.

"You don't?" Val asked after a few seconds. "Merlin mentioned that you lost your memory."

Merritt shook her head. "I remember a few flashes before the Battle of Lichenvale, and my mother's face. After that, nothing. Maybe the Leshbolgs were isolated. No one knows much about my species, but if I knew about Earth before the battle, I don't now."

Val cleared her throat. "You lost your whole family and everyone you loved in one night. I can't imagine, girl. I'm sorry."

"Thanks." Merritt forced a smile. "I'm sorry, too."

"The training orb will fix your Earth knowledge, at least," Val added.

"'Orb?' What does it do?" Merritt asked.

"Really cool shit. It's hard to explain, but you'll see for yourself," Val told her. Genevieve slowed and turned right. "We're here."

The Mustang pulled up to a solid gate with a small guard-house beside it. A Copper Dwarf relaxed in the guardhouse, looking at one of the little rectangular things everyone in the city seemed to have.

"Hey, Fred," Val called. "Bringing a new resident for a training session."

Fred waved a hand, and magic slowly rolled the gate open. "You don't have to explain anything to me, Val. Genevieve gets automatic admission."

"Genevieve?" Merritt queried. "Not you?"

"Genevieve used to belong to the queen. She's more famous than I am." Val patted the wheel.

Genevieve drove onto spacious grounds, which had beautifully trimmed bright green lawns despite the snowy landscape outside. The manicured trees had verdant green leaves, and the clear sky was blue. A squat five-story brick building stood at the center of the grounds.

"Welcome to the NYHQ," Val announced.

Merritt had never seen anything so unremarkable…except for the paras moving around the grounds. Their diversity reminded her of the Avalon HQ. These also wore uniforms of different colors, but most wore forest green. Several waved at Genevieve. Val didn't wave back.

They drove into a low building filled with cars, carriages, boats with golden wings, magic carpets, broomsticks, and mounts of various species. Genevieve purred into a space next to a large stall that held a gray stallion with eight legs.

Val disembarked and petted the stallion's neck. "What's up, Slippy? Looks like you're about due for shoes. You coming to Little Avalon for them this time?"

The stallion nickered.

"He says yes," Merritt supplied as Genevieve's door opened and the seat belt released her.

"You understand him?" Val's eyebrows shot up.

Merritt shrugged. "I understand many animals."

"Coolest power ever," Val muttered. "C'mon. We'll be late."

Sleipnir watched Merritt go with mysterious dark eyes.

Shadow stayed close to her side as she followed Val across the campus and into the building. The buzz of magic gave Merritt goosebumps, and she kept a hand on Shadow's ruff to ground herself as they headed for steel doors at the other end. Another elevator. Several paras hurried past, but none spared Merritt a second glance, although several nodded at Val.

"Short elevator ride," Val muttered. "Luckily. I hate going up in these things." She mashed a button with her fist, and the doors slid shut. Merrit braced herself on Shadow as the elevator jolted into motion. Her magic felt dull and distant. Thinking about Neven, Merritt decided that wasn't a bad thing.

The elevator disgorged them into a quiet, cream-carpeted hallway. A troll in a white lab coat waited there, ornate rings decorating her tusks. She held a larger flat rectangle but gazed at it with the same intense concentration as the humans showed their little rectangles.

"Hey, Qtana," Val greeted.

The troll looked up. Her layered yellow-blonde hair complemented her olive-green complexion.

"Afternoon, Val." The troll tucked the big rectangle into a case with a strap over her shoulder. "Is this our trainee?"

"This is Merritt Vale." Val gestured.

"Qtana." The troll extended a hand.

Merritt shook it.

"You're taking the Basic Earth package?" Qtana asked.

Merritt nodded.

"Excellent. This won't take long." Qtana marched down the

hall, her hair bobbing over the blue letters on the back of her coat: IT.

"'Won't take long?'" Merritt echoed. "Is this like a class at school? I hated school in New Camelot. I don't remember a single thing."

"This is much simpler." Val inclined her head. "Granted, it has a slightly higher mortality rate."

Merritt blinked. *"Mortality rate?"*

Qtana pushed open a nondescript door on their left. "Welcome to the training orb."

Val gestured for Merritt to enter. The Leshbolg shuffled within, feeling disoriented since Shadow waited outside.

The room was white and featureless except for a pedestal in the center with a bright blue orb resting on it. Merritt felt deep, ancient magic emanating from the orb, making the hairs on her neck rise. Prints in many different shapes covered the orb's surface: paws, claws, and hands with too few or too many fingers.

"It's a simple process." Qtana busily swiped on the big rectangle. "Put your hands in the prints that fit you and try not to throw up."

"Okay," Merritt squeaked.

"We'll be in the observation room," Val added. "Good luck."

They shut the door, leaving Merritt alone with the orb in the silent room. Her heart thumped, but its magic was as irresistible as it was frightening. She edged closer.

"Okay, Merritt." Qtana's words came from nowhere, making her jump. "Place your hands on the orb. It is ready for you."

Merritt reached for the handprints with five fingers and slowly pressed her palms into them. A warm crackle of magic ran across her skin, but nothing else happened.

"Do you think we should've given her a chair?" Qtana muttered. "We used to."

"I never got a chair," Val protested.

Their disembodied voices creeped Merritt out. "Um, guys? Is something supposed to—"

Everything vanished: the orb beneath her fingers, the room, and the floor under her feet. She whirled with a gasp and saw a mighty ship crashing across the ocean, spray cold on her face, sails catching the wind. A human stood at its prow, pointing. *Land ho!* The words echoed through her mind, but the ship disappeared before Merritt could cry out, and she stood amid a gruesome battle. Booms and explosions surrounded her as humans clashed on a bloodstained field. She yelped and covered her ears, turning away from the horrific sight, and looked up at a half-completed building swarming with human workers.

The images came and went too quickly for her to grasp. Faces, objects, events, and devices streamed past her like leaves on the wind. Words flashed through her mind too fast to hear: *America, microwave, scaffolding, skyscraper, money, gun, phone.*

Merritt gasped. Her eyes snapped open, and she stood in the training room, hands on the orb, sweat trickling down the small of her back.

"H-hello?" she quavered.

The door opened. "There!" Qtana grinned. "You're done. You can take your hands off the orb now."

Merritt reeled away from the pedestal. Shadow trotted to her side, and she grabbed his coat for balance.

"Wh-what happened?" Merrit croaked. "I don't think I learned anything. It happened so fast."

Qtana waved the big rectangle. "What's this?"

"A tablet." Merritt blinked. "Whoa. I didn't know that five minutes ago."

"That's how the orb works," Qtana explained. "You won't be able to access everything you learned at once. Definitions will come to you as you need them. It's mildly inconvenient, but it prevents your brain from turning to liquid and running out of your ears."

Merritt stared at her.

"Good luck with your transition to Earth." Qtana patted Merritt's shoulder. "I'd better go. We're working on increasing the connection speed using redcap energy."

She bustled off.

Merritt smart! Shadow wagged his tail.

"Let's get out of here," Val suggested.

They left the building and returned to the parking lot. Information flooded through Merritt's mind as they approached Genevieve. The voice in her head sounded like hers, but it knew things she didn't. As she gazed at different parts of the car, their names flashed through her thoughts. *Fender. Tires. Hood. Windshield. Passenger side. Driver's side.*

"Is it working?" Val asked, unlocking the Mustang.

"Yeah." Merritt grinned. "It's great."

"Cool." Val nodded.

They entered Genevieve, and Val backed out of the parking space.

"This city still feels totally foreign," Merritt admitted.

Val laughed. "The orb doesn't negate your need to learn about Earth and Little Avalon, but it'll protect you from major mistakes like running into the street and getting squished."

Merritt nodded. "That's helpful."

"Indeed." Val chuckled. "Let's get out of here. I can't wait to show you Little Avalon."

CHAPTER FIVE

Genevieve's engine roared as she sped across the bridge, the river glinting on either side. Merritt gripped her seat belt in one hand, grinning at the car's breathtaking speed as she wove through traffic, avoiding other vehicles by inches.

"Easy, Gennie!" Val burst out, gripping the wheel.

Genevieve ignored her. She squealed off the bridge and skidded around a turn but slowed as traffic thickened.

"Phew." Val's hands eased on the wheel. "Your love for that bridge will get us killed someday."

Merritt's skin prickled as the Mustang purred north, overtaking cars with insulting ease.

"There are higher concentrations of magic here," Merritt observed.

Val nodded. "You're sensing Little Avalon. It's in the heart of Brooklyn."

"Brooklyn?" Merritt asked. Her orb training didn't elaborate. "Is that the name of a kingdom?"

"Kingdom!" Val burst out laughing. "It's a part of New York City."

"Doesn't the city have a king?" Merritt asked. "Or a chief?"

"Oh, no. Humans make it *way* more complicated than that." Val waved a hand. "I'm not sure how it works, to be honest. We serve the Eternity Queen."

Merritt sniffed. "The magic's getting stronger."

"It's powerful in Little Avalon, not only because many paras live there but because we created a pocket dimension," Val explained. "Humans see it as a single street, but since we made the new dimension, it's a whole village."

Merritt didn't understand.

"Here we are," Val announced as Genevieve slowed and turned left. "Welcome to Little Avalon."

Magic stirred on Merritt's skin. Young trees lined the street, tiny green buds studding their branches. A pack of young were-wolves played on the paved area beside the street—*sidewalk*, Merritt's training supplied—and waved as Genevieve rolled past. A beautiful building stood on their left, fairy lights sparkling in the windows. A few paras sat at tables outside. The wooden sign over the door read The Second Fist.

More businesses crowded on either side of the street. *Gold, Manns, and Sax* the sign on the sleek, modern-looking one read. *Bank*, Merritt's training told her, though she wasn't sure what that was.

"What's that?" Merritt asked, pointing at the Second Fist.

"That's the local watering hole." Val grinned. "Where we go to drink, although we don't drink water there if you get my drift."

Merritt nodded, and a memory hit her like a hammer between the eyes. She remembered the taste of something sharp but tooth-achingly sweet. An image flashed through her mind: spiky bright green fruits in a stone vat, feet trampling down on them to squeeze out the juice.

The memory disappeared as quickly as it had come. Merritt gasped, touching her hair.

"You good?" Val asked.

Merritt cleared her throat. "I'm fine. I just remembered something from my past."

"That's *all*?" Val's head snapped toward her. "You remembered something?"

"A flash," Merritt admitted. "I remember my people distilling the spirits we drank. I remember tasting them, but nothing more than that."

"It's progress." Val smiled. "Maybe Little Avalon will help you remember more."

Merritt forced a smile. "Maybe, but it's not the first time I've remembered a flash like this. It never leads to anything except frustration, even though Merlin keeps telling me to lean into the memories since I'm the only one left who can continue the legacy of my species."

"Wow." Val blinked. "No pressure, huh?"

"No pressure." Merritt shrugged.

"A few drinks at the Second Fist will solve most problems in the world. I'll take you there soon," Val promised.

Merritt grinned. "Thanks."

They passed several other businesses and a grandiose building with white walls and blue trim. An Aether Elf strolled from the building and waved at Val, who returned the gesture.

"Arion Woodskin, the Aether Elf Councilor," she told Merritt. "He's an unofficial advocate for Little Avalon. You'll like him."

Merritt had no idea what the title meant, but she nodded.

They slowly rolled down the street as para kids in school uniforms ran down the sidewalk. After a few minutes, they reached several nearly identical houses, each two or three stories, with flowers blooming in window boxes and wrought-iron balconies, rails, and light fixtures.

"Welcome to the Stonehold Houses. These are the apartment buildings that started it all." Val grinned. "I've arranged for you to live in Stonehold One, the building next to my house, so I can keep an eye on you and make sure you're comfortable."

"Thanks," Merritt murmured.

Genevieve halted in front of the last Stonehold House on the left. Merritt noted with dismay that it had no yard, with only strips of concrete separating it from the building. Window boxes provided the only pops of life and color. A fresh coat of sand-colored paint gleamed in the veiled sunlight, and an ornate wrought-iron 1 hung over the arched wooden door.

"Welcome home." Val exited the car.

Merritt retrieved the satchel from the space at her feet and followed Val, staring at the building. She doubted she'd ever been inside a home this size. The big buildings in her life so far had all been fortresses or institutions.

"It's enormous," she managed.

"You won't live here alone. Each floor has three bedrooms, including the three floors below ground," Val explained. "The underground ones house two redcap families and the three dwarves who work in my smithy. There's a nice mixed-species family on the ground floor, and a bunch of IT trolls on the second floor. You're on the third floor with two housemates."

Merritt nodded. "Do we each have our own bed?"

Val blinked. "Yeah. You each have your own bed*room*, and bathroom, too. You only share the kitchen."

"Oh." Merritt brightened.

"You're not used to having a bedroom?" Val asked.

"My Mavka foster mother Yulietta curtained off a small part of the cottage where I slept," Merritt told her.

Val smiled. "I thought you might find it crowded to be with housemates, but it sounds like this might be more space than you've had in years."

"In the hospital, I shared a bathroom with three other paras," Merritt admitted.

"This one's all yours." Val beckoned. "Let me show you to your room."

Merritt stayed on Val's heels as the dwarf strolled through the door into a tiny room containing another door and a staircase. Val took the staircase with shocking speed and agility. Merritt was quick, but she had to fight to keep up with Val as they climbed two flights of stairs and emerged on a small landing.

"Here we are." Val pushed the door open. "Your new home."

They entered a spacious room lined with cabinets and shiny appliances Merritt didn't recognize. *Kitchen*, her orb training told her. *Room used for the preparation of food.* Merritt wondered where the fire was, but the space was cozy and welcoming, with richly colored hardwood floors, butter-yellow walls, and cabinets of smooth red mahogany. A colorful mosaic of red, yellow, and blue tiles decorated the space above two items that her training told her were the *kitchen sink* and *stove*.

"Here's the kitchen." Val gestured at another door to her left. "There's a small living room through there. The bedrooms are down the hall." She led Merritt through a door to the right, boots thudding on the hardwood floor. "This first door is the laundry. The other two belong to your roomies. This one is yours."

Val opened the first door on the left. "It's been empty for a few months. My mother stayed here, but that's a long story."

Merritt stepped into a space so big that she thought Val had made a mistake. Surely this couldn't *all* be for one para. The room could have swallowed Yulietta's hut without difficulty. A squishy couch upholstered in bright red faced a dark screen on one wall. Another door and the most enormous bed Merritt had ever seen presided over one corner of the room.

"The bathroom's through there." Val pointed at a door in the back.

"Is this all for me?" Merritt asked.

Val smiled. "It's all yours."

"Wow," Merritt whispered.

"Val?" someone called from the kitchen.

"That's one of your housemates. You'll love her." Val grinned. "Let me introduce you."

When they returned to the kitchen, a ripple of powerful magic surged through the room. The para waiting for them there was a Lunar Fae like Merlin, but much younger. Her wings were diaphanous and butterfly-shaped, shedding only a faint sparkle from their tips. Her skin was the color of moonlight, contrasting sharply with a cascade of scarlet hair. Though her eyes seemed blue at first glance, their color shifted as the sunlight coming through the window struck them.

Val nodded at the fae. "Merritt, this is Tess Mendoza."

"It's great to meet you, Merritt!" Tess beamed and extended a delicate hand. The delicate piercings protruding from her lower lip bobbed when she spoke, causing the gemstones to sparkle.

"Hi." Merritt shook her hand.

"I'm so happy you're here. It's good to have the third bedroom full again." Tess shuddered. "Not with Val's mom, though. No offense, Val."

"None taken." Val chuckled. "Where's Damian?"

Tess glanced at her little rectangle. *Phone*, the orb training whispered. "He'll be up later. Damian's a vampire," she added for Merritt's benefit. "He's nocturnal."

Merritt nodded. She couldn't stop staring at Tess. The fae's lunar magic caressed Merritt's senses like gentle rain on parched earth.

"I'll leave you in Tess' capable hands. She'll help you with anything you need. I'm right next door, too." Val laid a hand on Merritt's shoulder. "There are many friendly people around you, Merritt. Don't hesitate to ask for help."

A knot closed Merritt's throat. Little Avalon might be at the heart of chaos in concrete, but no one had ever welcomed her like this. "Thank you."

Val squeezed her shoulder. "You got it. C'mon, Shadow."

Bye, Merritt! Shadow licked her hand.

Val and Shadow left, and Tess turned to Merritt, beaming.

"What do you need?" the Lunar Fae asked. "Something to eat? Coffee? Water?"

"We had lunch at Meggie's eating hall," Merritt mumbled. "Sorry, I mean 'bistro.'"

"Meggie makes the best food in Avalon. I bet you're stuffed." Tess giggled.

Merritt grinned. "Yeah."

"Well, let me show you around your room. Val didn't tell me much except that you hadn't lived in a place with modern amenities before. She took you for orb training, right?" Tess asked, striding to Merritt's room.

Merritt followed. "She did."

"I went for orb training after Queen Julia found me. I didn't even know the paranormal world existed," Tess chattered.

Merritt blinked. "How? You *are* a paranormal."

"Right. Val mentioned you didn't know about other dimensions." Tess laughed. "At least you know what species you are, which I didn't. I'm a changeling. My parents surrendered me to a human family when I was a baby."

"That's horrible," Merritt cried.

"They had no choice. Mordred's cult murdered all the Lunar Fae children it found. That was the only way they could keep me safe, and it worked. Her Majesty later found me and helped me to shake off the concealment spell and become a Lunar Fae." Tess marched to the closet and paused, blushing. "If this is too invasive, let me know, but I figured you wouldn't have much stuff to bring with you."

Merritt glanced at the satchel. "I have a change of clothes and a bow."

"Bows are good." Tess nodded. "There's a weapons rack in here, and Val will know where to get arrows. But I didn't think you would have clothes for the city."

Merritt thought about the humans and paras she'd seen so far. "No," she admitted. "My other clothes look like these." She gestured at the homespun shirt and pants and her fur-lined cloak.

"I took a liberty." Tess bit her lip. "You don't have to keep any of it if you don't want to. I'm not trying to overstep. I wanted to be welcoming, and, well, I got carried away."

She swung the door open, and Merritt's jaw dropped. Outfits in every color hung inside. Her orb training provided words she'd never heard before: *jeans, blouse, skirt suit, blazer, trench coat, sweater,* and *slacks* were among them.

Tess pulled out a bright pink dress with a figure-hugging skirt and cleared her throat. "This might not be to your liking. It's all para-made. It'll adjust to fit you when you put it on."

"Tess, this is so kind," Merritt told her housemate.

Tess perked up. "You think so?"

"Yes!" Merritt stepped closer and ran a hand over the fabrics, enjoying the textures. "Thank you so much."

Tess beamed. "You're welcome. Do you know how the TV works?"

TV, Merritt's training told her. *Screen used for entertainment.*

"I've never had a TV," Merritt confessed.

Tess led her to the screen and showed her a black oblong— *remote*—that turned it on and changed the channels. Merritt gaped, thinking that Fedir would love having a constant stream of information available at the touch of a button.

"That concludes your tour." Tess placed the remote on the couch's back.

Merritt perched on the couch. "What should I do now?"

"Whatever you like. Settle in. Relax. Watch TV," Tess suggested. "I have a few things to take care of, but I'll be back with dinner. Do you like Chinese food?"

"What's a Chinese?" Merritt asked.

"Girl, you haven't lived. You'll love it," Tess promised. "See you later."

She left the door open behind her as if inviting Merritt to go into the rest of the apartment. She had free access to her new home.

The TV bombarded her with information. Merritt's orb training flashed new words through her mind with every new scene, from *streetlight* and *tie* to *doorknob* and *coffee mug*, and she pressed the red button to switch it off when it gave her a headache.

Merritt wandered into the bathroom and stared at the knobs on the wall. She'd had a shower in the institution at New Camelot, but there, she'd used a lever to run the water.

Faucets, her orb training announced. *Devices for controlling the flow of water.*

Great, Merritt grumbled. *That doesn't tell me how to use them.* She prodded one of the knobs, but nothing happened. Visions of flooding the apartment filled her mind, and she decided to ask Tess about the shower when she returned. Bathing was a once-a-week thing in Wolf Glen, so though she gave the closet full of clothes a longing look, she wandered around the bedroom instead. A dial on the wall looked interesting.

Forced warm air distribution system, her training told her. *Method of heating homes via a central furnace and ducts.*

The dial had numbers on it ranging from seventy to ninety. Merritt assumed those related to the distribution system's efficiency. She twisted the dial until the arrow pointed to ninety.

It was getting dark, so she did a lap around the room, looking for a light switch like the one she'd seen at the institution. The thing on the small table by the bed—*nightstand*—looked like a light. Her training confirmed that it was an *electric lamp*. Merritt found a rope running from its base toward the wall with a switch on it and experimentally poked it. The light turned on.

"Cool," Merritt whispered.

Sweat trickled down her back as she peered at the other end

of the rope, which disappeared into a thing on the wall with holes in it.

Electrical plug, her training supplied.

The holes seemed finger-shaped. Merritt extended a hand toward them.

Supplies electricity to the household. A regular cause of death or injury by electrocution, her training added.

Merritt withdrew her hand and decided to check the kitchen out instead.

New words clamored through her head as she gazed at the shiny appliances. *Toaster. Air fryer. Microwave. Refrigerator.* It was cooler in the kitchen, but she still sweated under her fur cloak, so she removed it and hung it on the back of a chair. A gleaming metal dome captured her attention. Her training told her it was a *rice cooker.*

Merritt tried to remember what rice was. She was too hot to think, but the word sounded familiar. The idea of a device for cooking one thing fascinated her. She poked it, and it gave an interesting beep.

"Wow," Merritt murmured.

She wandered around the kitchen, opening cabinets in search of something to drink.

A strange stench suffused the air. Merritt sniffed; it smelled like something burning but had an unfamiliar acrid edge. A wisp of smoke caught her eye, and she spun to see flames coming from the rice cooker.

"Oh, crap!" Merritt squealed.

The lights abruptly went out, leaving the kitchen in twilight, but the flames grew. Merritt grabbed the nearest door and yanked it open. A bottle of liquid stood in the door of the *refrigerator,* so she grabbed it, twisted the top off, and dumped it out on the rice cooker. Bubbles went everywhere and sizzled, but the fire went out.

Merrit exhaled. "That could've been bad."

She tucked the empty bottle into the garbage can. Thirst clutched her throat; she felt like she was baking inside her clothes. When she went to close the refrigerator door, a welcome gush of cold air came from within.

Refrigerator, her training supplied. *Device for cold storage, usually for food and drinks.*

All Merritt cared about was that the refrigerator was deliciously cool. She leaned into it and pressed her hands against the blissfully cold glass shelves. The door almost swung shut on her as her shape subtly changed, melting into the refrigerator. Her breath steamed, reminding her of crisp mornings in Wolf Glen. She would have to ask Tess about getting a message to Fedir. He'd love all this human-made stuff.

Footsteps plucked Merritt from her reverie. She tensed, squeezing herself tighter into the refrigerator.

"What in Merlin's name?" someone muttered. A switch flicked. The refrigerator gave a rumbling noise that made Merritt flinch.

The footsteps proceeded across the kitchen. A sigh came from the direction of the rice cooker, and the footsteps came nearer.

Merritt tried to remember what Val and Tess had said about her other housemate.

The refrigerator door swung open and Merritt spun. A disheveled vampire in checkered pajamas and fluffy slippers stared at Merritt, his black hair sticking up and his fangs protruding under his upper lip. His red eyes snapped wide, and he leaped back with a high-pitched scream.

Merritt fled the kitchen, heart pounding. She couldn't screw things up with her new housemate on the first day! Panic gripped her, and she sprinted into her bedroom. The only hiding place was under the enormous bed, and Merritt squeezed into the warm, dark space, flattening herself against the floor.

The vampire's fluffy slippers appeared in her vision as he padded to her door.

"Um, hello?" he called.

Merritt squashed herself against the floor.

"Hello? You're the new housemate, right?" the vampire queried. "I'm sorry if I scared you. I didn't expect you to be in the fridge."

Merritt held her breath. She now regretted running to hide. She could have said something awesome like, *Hey, I'm just chilling in here.* She couldn't bring herself to crawl out from under the bed, so she froze, cursing herself for being an idiot.

"Wow, it's hot in here." The vampire sighed. "You'll come out when you're ready. Did you melt the rice cooker? FYI, you're not supposed to turn it on without anything in it. So. Yeah. Okay, bye."

The vampire shut the door behind him. Merritt waited until she couldn't hear his footsteps before squeezing from under the bed.

"Phew," she muttered. "That was bad."

Maybe Tess would introduce her to the vampire. He seemed nice. Merritt made a mental note about the rice cooker thing as she padded to the curtains on one side of the room. She cautiously lifted one and found a large window overlooking the street.

The sight of the outdoors stilled Merritt's thudding heart. She pulled the curtains wide and gazed at the view, which mainly consisted of roofs, their dark shingles all matching. Streetlights illuminated sidewalks bustling with paras who called cheerful greetings to one another. They carried coffee cups and laughed, showing off flashing fangs. Several wolves trotted past in a pack, yipping, tails high.

Merritt pressed her nose against the window, fogging the glass. Val's words from earlier came back to her. *Look, I know it's nothing like your old home, but trust me. Many paras have found happiness there. You wouldn't be the first outcast to make Little Avalon your permanent home.*

The thought of a permanent home made Merritt's heart surge. Her gaze rested on the two trees she could see, delicate saplings rising from planters on the sidewalk. Her sigh made the fog grow.

This place seemed wonderful, but she saw so few trees and so little greenery that she wondered if there was any grass in Little Avalon.

The thought made her chest hurt, so she turned away from the window and wandered to the couch. Its thick cushions embraced her as she sank onto it and picked up the remote. The press of a button made the screen turn on.

A serious-looking human male stared into the camera, his hair neatly combed over his forehead. "Brooklyn Bridge Park has long been a popular haven for lovers of the outdoors and a magnet for tourists from across the globe. But in light of a recent crime spike in the park, New Yorkers and visitors alike have to ask themselves if it is still safe. Jill Wheaton reports."

The image cut to a windblown woman in a wool coat. "A recent spate of muggings has left tourists and locals wondering if Brooklyn Bridge Park remains a safe space."

She kept talking, but Merritt barely heard the words. She leaned forward, holding her breath, her eyes locked not on the woman but behind her. An expanse of pale grass stretched out to meet the shimmering river. Merritt noted the bridge in the background but stared at the trees that stood everywhere: deciduous trees beginning to bud and spruces scattered across the grass and lining the paths to the river.

So many trees!

Merritt's hands curled into trembling fists as she memorized the name: Brooklyn Bridge Park.

There *was* grass in this city.

Val grabbed a cold six-pack from the fridge, put it on the kitchen table, and ripped the plastic wrap off with a practiced movement.

"The best emergency meetings have beer." Tetra Dupont sat on the table, her wasp-like wings twitching in anticipation. A scrap of plastic fell in her direction. She seized it and stuffed it into her mouth.

"Do you *have* to sit on the table, Tetra?" the young human beside her grumbled. He didn't look up from his tablet.

"Do you have to be anal about furniture, Liam?" Tetra retorted.

"Focus," Tess chided, accepting a beer from Val. "We're supposed to be having a serious meeting."

"It's not as bad as Tess makes it sound," Val intervened. "We need to talk, though."

"Nothing good starts like that," Tetra grumbled.

"One second. Sorry." Liam touched his tablet and frowned. "Okay, done. Val, I'm sending you the draft notice about fighting in the streets."

"Thanks. I'll get it to the residents." Val huffed. "Can you believe it? A werewolf and orc physically going at each other in broad moonlight! Half the nocturnal kids in the neighborhood saw them. Scared the crap out of them."

"What was the orc doing out of bed?" Tess asked.

"Fighting a werewolf, apparently." Val opened a can of her favorite craft beer from Anvil Brewery and pulled out a chair.

"Never a dull moment," Liam's fiancée Qenzi observed. The troll helped herself to a beer.

Val snorted. "Got that right. Okay, let's talk about Merritt."

"Who's that?" Tetra asked.

"The new resident. I picked her up in Avalon Town this afternoon." Val sipped beer.

"Oh, yeah. Merlin's waif." Tetra nodded. "What about her? Is she edible?"

"*What?*" Liam demanded.

"Kidding." Tetra smirked, displaying pointed gray teeth between black lips.

Antin cleared his throat. The well-groomed Sylthana Elf, Tetra's improbable boyfriend, muttered, "I don't think you are."

"Don't look at me like that. I don't want to eat her. It's good information either way," Tetra protested.

"I'm worried about Merritt," Val confessed.

"Poor thing. She lost her whole species in one night." Liam shook his head. "I can't imagine that trauma."

"That's not what worries me. She seems pretty level-headed." Val sighed. "The trouble is that she doesn't know *anything* about functioning in the type of society we have here."

"You took her for orb training. Surely that will help," Tess pointed out.

Val raised an eyebrow. "You went for orb training about the paranormal world. Could you navigate it on your own afterward?"

Tess grimaced. "No. I only functioned in the para world after I'd been at Tintagel for a while."

"Exactly. Merritt doesn't have that background." Val straightened her bright blue wig. "The orb training will help, but she seems so lost. I'm not sure Little Avalon is the right place for her."

"Val, don't say that," Tess protested. "She's so nice!"

"She is. Smart, too, and gutsy. I like her, but I want what's best for her. I'm not sure Little Avalon is it," Val admitted.

"Why?" Tetra demanded. "Because she's a bit feral?" She bit into her beer can and slurped.

"*You're* feral," Liam pointed out.

"Precisely." Tetra mopped foam off her chin.

"She's not feral." Val sighed. "She's clueless."

"Yeah? So was I," Tetra reminded her. "I didn't know my ass from my elbow when it came to *anything* in the human world. I wanted to flash Genevieve back to greet her, remember?"

"You what?" Liam asked.

Tess grinned. "We need to hear this story."

Val chortled. "It was hilarious, but another time."

"The point is that I figured it out," Tetra added. "Little Avalon might not seem like the place for a woodland para, but it could be. If I can adjust, anyone can." She bit the top of her beer can off and ate it.

"*You're* so well-adjusted," Liam muttered.

"Tetra's right." Antin folded his arms. "She came from a background almost as troubled as Merritt's, and she's happy here. So am I, despite my history."

Val tilted her head. "You guys aren't wrong."

"Have some faith, Val. Trust Luna, but also in yourself." Tess smiled. "Look at us. An elf who was a lieutenant in a rebel army, a human, a troll, a changeling who only recently learned about the paranormal world, and a faerie."

Tetra munched on the rest of the beer can.

"You brought us together. You can get Merritt together with the right paras, too," Tess told her. "Nothing will stop you."

Val smiled. "Thanks, Tess. I'm just worried about the time I can commit to her. Being a duchess and having Little Avalon grow at this rate keeps me so busy that I don't know if I'm coming or going."

"I get that." Tess nodded. "But *I* can commit time to helping her. Let her be my responsibility, Val. I want to help her. She's awesome."

"I'm here, too," Qenzi added.

Liam protested, "Qenz, you're burned out. There's a reason you're taking three weeks of vacation time."

"I know, but I'm here if needed." Qenzi smiled.

Liam squeezed her hand. "You rock, did you know that?"

"So I'm told." Qenzi grinned.

"I can show her the ropes, too. I'll teach her to survive in modern society." Tetra grinned, aluminum shining between her teeth.

"No!" Val, Liam, and Tess chorused.

"Be that way." Tetra snorted.

"You guys are the best. Thank you." Val paused. "I'm honored to have you on my team."

"We're more than your team, Val." Tetra nudged her. "We're your family. You know that."

Val smiled. "Merritt needs something like this."

"We can be that for her." Tess touched Val's arm. "We've got this."

"You sure do." Tension eased between Val's shoulder blades. "Thanks, Tess."

"The first order of business is to get Merritt settled in and feeling safe in the community." Liam spread his hands. "Why don't we invite her over for dinner tonight? That okay with you, Qenz?"

"Absolutely!" Qenzi smiled. "I'll try that new Bolognese recipe you found online, Lee."

"Perfect. Then she can get to know us, and we'll talk about what to do next." Liam nodded. "I'm betting the Eternity Throne is covering her costs for now, like they did with Tetra and Antin."

"Yeah, but ideally, she should find a job." Val finished her beer.

"There are many opportunities in Little Avalon." Tess grinned. "We'll find something."

Val leaned back in her chair, studying the eager faces at the table.

"You guys are incredible," she murmured. "You know that, right?"

Tetra mock-punched Val's arm. "Not so bad yourself."

CHAPTER SIX

Merritt stood inches from the TV, mouth open as she gazed at the trees behind the woman, who spoke earnestly about crime and violence. Merritt barely heard her. Her attention remained fixed on the branches, the sparrows fluttering from twig to twig, and the alluring sparkle of the river beyond.

"Where is this place?" she whispered, extending her hand toward the screen as though she could touch the rough bark and feel the tight buds on her fingertips.

A knock on the door made Merritt jump. She stepped away from the TV and used the remote to mute it. "Who's there?"

"Hey! It's me," Tess called.

"Come on in." Merritt turned off the TV.

Tess opened the door. "Do you know what happened to the rice cooker?"

"That was me." Merritt felt a swift kick of nervousness. "I turned it on without water in it. I didn't know that was bad for it. I'm really sorry, Tess. If there's something I can do to fix it..."

"Hey, no worries. I accidentally lit a tapestry of Sir Galahad on fire during my first day at Tintagel. I was not popular." Tess chuckled. "We'll get another rice cooker."

"Oh." Merritt's shoulders relaxed. "I also sort of met our housemate."

"Damian? He texted me, but it made no sense." Tess raised her eyebrows. "Were you in the fridge?"

"I was hot," Merritt confessed.

"No wonder." Tess turned the dial on the warm air distribution thing. "Somebody cranked the heat up."

Merritt rubbed her neck. "That was me. I thought the numbers meant something else."

"It's all good." Tess touched her arm. "I know I promised you Chinese food, but our neighbors across the street invited us to dinner. Would you like to go?"

Merritt blinked. "They want me to come, too?"

"Absolutely. That's the point. They'd like to get to know you." Tess grinned. "They're close friends, and you'll love them. It's okay if you'd rather stay in, though."

"I'd love to come!" Merritt gushed.

"Fantastic." Tess hesitated. "Did you want to change?"

"Yeah, but the shower faucets are all weird." Merritt blushed.

Tess laughed. "I know, right? Let me help."

Thirty minutes later, after the most delicious hot shower of Merritt's life, she stood looking at the full-length mirror in the wardrobe door. Tess helped her pick appropriate clothes for the occasion: a pair of stretchy pants ("Jeggings," Tess said) and a green turtleneck sweater that brought out her eyes. The clothes looked strange, but no stranger than her Mavka Elven outfit had initially looked, and they were far more comfortable.

Tess knocked on the doorframe. "Ready?"

Merritt smoothed her sweater and inhaled. *This is it. This is my chance to have a real home.* She grinned. "Ready."

They took the stairs to the front door and stepped into a crisp evening with the promise of frost in the air, though Merritt felt the stirrings of spring in the trees lining the street. Music floated from an upstairs window nearby. Muffled clanging came from the large house next door—the one where Val lived.

"That's Val working in her smithy," Tess explained. "She can't make it tonight, but everyone else is really nice, too."

Merritt nodded. "Val must be busy."

"She always has her hands full," Tess agreed. "I'm glad she sold the Second Fist to Dante. It was one thing too many. Her jewelry business is booming. She's the duchess and always in demand to provide security to royals and celebs. Whoa! What's wrong?"

Merritt stopped short, one hand clenched tightly around Tess' arm. She sniffed the air as blood pounded in her ears. She had to be wrong, but no. The stench was unmistakable. It stung her nose like a cross between spilled acid and crushed capsaicin.

"What is it?" Tess asked.

"Shhh!" Merritt backed away, dragging Tess after her. "Don't you smell that?"

"Don't I smell what?" Tess frowned, confused.

"Stay calm." Merritt lowered her voice. "We need to get back to the apartment before it finds us."

"Merritt, you're not making sense," Tess protested.

Merritt whispered, "There's a faerie here!"

Tess stopped. Then she threw her head back and laughed.

"Tess, no! Shhh! It'll hear you!" Merritt cried. "They're the most dangerous predators in any forest."

"Sorry. I do." Tess tried to stop laughing. "But it's okay. We know her."

Merritt's jaw dropped. "You know a *faerie?*"

"Yeah. She's your neighbor." Tess grinned. "She's having dinner with us."

"A faerie," Merritt croaked.

"It's okay. She won't eat you," Tess promised, her tone serious.

Merritt gulped, not reassured. "She's domesticated?"

Tess rubbed her neck. "Uh, sort of."

Merritt stared at the house across the street, amazed that such a terrifying creature had been this close to her all afternoon.

"She's scary, but it's fine. I promise she won't hurt you." Tess gently detached Merritt's clenched hand. "She's friendly."

"A friendly faerie?" Merritt whispered.

"You don't want the people here to treat *you* with prejudice." Tess smiled. "Maybe extend that same grace to her?"

Merritt flushed. "Sorry."

"It's okay. Honestly, everyone reacts like that." Tess grimaced. "I think Tetra enjoys it. Oh, and don't be alarmed when you see her. She's chosen to be human-sized."

A five-foot faerie? They were terrifying at six inches tall. Merritt swallowed her fear and followed Tess to the two-story house across the street. They climbed several steps to the front door, which was set in an ornate stone facade.

Tess knocked. A handsome young male opened the door, beaming. One glance at his bland features made Merritt realize, with a skip of excitement in her chest, that he was human.

"Hi!" The human grinned. "You must be Merritt Vale. It's great to meet you." He shook her hand, his grip unusually soft and warm. "I'm Liam Miller."

"Hello, Liam Miller," Merritt greeted him. "You're a human!"

"I am indeed. Come on inside." He laughed. "Call me Liam."

He led the way into an enormous kitchen filled with savory smells. Merritt spotted the faerie and stayed half a step behind Tess for protection. The faerie was even more terrifying in human size, with her ragged wasp-like wings twitching and her eyes midnight-black. Faerie dust sparkled beneath the skin on her fingers. Merritt had seen that dust blow holes through full-grown moose.

"What's up?" The faerie met Merritt's eyes and grinned, displaying flesh-rending teeth.

Tess nudged her. "Hello," Merritt managed.

"I'm Tetra."

Merritt gaped. Faeries never shared their names.

"It's not my real name, obviously. It's what people call me." Tetra patted the head of an elf sitting beside her. "This is Antin. He's mine."

The elf, who was a reassuringly normal para who wore his hair in a ponytail, waved. "Hello, Merritt."

"This is my fiancée Qenzi," Liam added, wrapping an arm around the waist of a troll who wore comfortable clothes and slippers.

The troll grinned, showing off her tusks. "Hi. Welcome to our home."

"Hello," Merritt squeaked.

"Glass of wine?" Qenzi offered. "Beer? We have faerie wine, too."

"Isn't it poisonous?" Merritt asked.

"It's normally not lethal." Tetra gave another toothy grin.

"Normal wine it is, then." Qenzi laughed.

Tess pointedly sat next to Tetra. Merritt edged into the seat beside the Lunar Fae, using her as a shield. Tetra wiggled her fingers, and bright pink dust trickled from them, making Merritt cringe.

"I'm so scary," Tetra hissed.

"You are. Stop spooking her. She's new," Antin protested.

"Thanks, babe." Tetra nibbled his ear.

Liam turned his attention to the stove, busily stirring the pots that bubbled on mystifying round plates that glowed red hot. "I hate waiting around for dinner at parties, so it's nearly ready."

Qenzi dispensed glasses of red Fernwood wine. Merritt sipped and raised her eyebrows. "You have good taste!"

"Straight from the hills of Beltane." Qenzi swirled the wine and sniffed. "The human stuff can't match it."

"Hey," Liam protested.

Qenzi swatted his ass. "It's true."

"Are you making pasta?" Tetra asked.

"Yes, Tetra. That's what Spaghetti Bolognese is," Liam grumbled.

"You're doing it wrong," Tetra observed. "You should put iron filings in it."

"Given how it went the last time you and I cooked, Tetra, I don't think we're in a position to comment," Antin murmured.

"Shut up, Antin." Tetra amiably patted his head.

Antin wrapped his arms around the faerie's waist. Merritt gaped. Tetra and Antin were a couple? But he was an elf, and she was a faerie. Merritt had never heard of such a thing. Most elves couldn't go near faeries without having their faces melted.

"How much leave do you still have, Qenzi?" Tess asked.

Qenzi leaned back in her seat, her chestnut hair straggling over her shoulders. "Officially, I still have two weeks. Vacation time piles up if you never take any."

"I'm sure you can get more paid time off if you want it." Liam flashed a proud grin. "You saved the world, after all. The OPMA owes you everything."

"Oh, Lee." Qenzi rolled her eyes, but she was smiling. "You talk like I was the one who turned into a giant and beheaded Kronos."

Merritt gaped.

"That was Val," Tess whispered.

"Anyway, two weeks is more than enough time to relax. I'm excited to get back to work." Qenzi smiled.

"Qenzi's in IT at the NYHQ," Tess explained to Merritt. "She's on Qtana's team."

"I met Qtana today. She's nice," Merritt offered.

"She has high standards, but she's a good para to work for." Qenzi swirled her wine and sipped.

Liam piled the food into several large dishes. Merritt watched in fascination as long, squiggly worms of dough fell onto the plates. *Spaghetti*, her training murmured. *Cylindrical pasta, popular in Italian cooking.*

Liam turned to another pot and ladled a thick sauce over each bowl. Merritt's stomach twisted as he piled reddish blobs of dead animal in another dish, but she kept a smile on her face. She'd eaten meat before. She could do it again.

"There we are! Dinner is served." Liam added a bowl of grated cheese to the table.

"Let me help, honey." Qenzi rose and assisted Liam in placing the dishes on the table.

Liam proudly grinned as he set a bowl of the doughy stuff before Merritt. He had fine hair along the back of his hands and forearms, unlike the elves she'd met, but much finer than the average werewolf's. Merritt couldn't help stroking it. The lack of magic in the human's blood made him feel weird but not unpleasant. It was like squeezing a marshmallow.

"Uh, Merritt?" Qenzi laughed. "Hands off my man, if you please."

"Oh." Merritt snatched her hands back. "Sorry. You're so interesting."

"Thanks, I think." Liam tilted his head. "Never seen a human up close?"

"Never seen a human before today," Merritt admitted.

"Find a different one to pet." Liam winked. "This one's taken. Okay, let's say grace."

This, at least, was a familiar ritual. Merritt joined hands with Tess and Antin as Liam offered a brief prayer of thanksgiving to Luna.

"Dig in!" Liam released Qenzi's hand and kissed her cheek. "I'm excited to see what you think. Don't forget the parmesan."

Tess scooped grated cheese over her Bolognese, then handed the bowl to Merritt. Merritt helped herself to a generous pile of parmesan. It might be the only way she could ingest this gunk.

"When's your next gig, Antin?" Liam asked.

Antin inclined his head. "This Friday. I'm booked every Friday for the next four months."

"Wow, dude!" Tess beamed. "That's fantastic. Well done!"

Antin flushed. "Thank you. It puzzles me that many bookings are from human-owned establishments. Humans apparently like my music. I thought it might be too weird for them."

"Have you met humans? They like weird shit." Tetra grasped her bowl in both hands and raised it to her lips. She noisily slurped.

Merritt wrapped her hands around her bowl.

"No, no." Tess pressed a fork into her hand. "No."

Relieved, Merritt took the fork and scooped up a few strands of spaghetti. When she lifted the fork, they slipped off, splattering Tess and Antin with meat sauce.

Antin dabbed his sleeve with a napkin. "I'm happy. It feels good to have a job and pay my own way."

Pay your own way? Merritt had no idea what he was talking about.

"Have you heard Antin play?" Tetra demanded, turning her disconcertingly dark eyes on Merritt.

Merritt gulped. "N-not yet."

"She's only been here a few hours, Tetra," Tess chided.

Merritt reattempted the spaghetti scooping. This time, one strand made it to her mouth. Despite the queasy richness of the sauce coating it, the pasta tasted great.

"Yeah, well, Antin's music is the best thing in Little Avalon," Tetra retorted. "You *have to* hear him play. Is that clear?" Sauce coated her mouth.

Merritt nodded, wide-eyed.

"Tetra, quit bullying her," Liam ordered.

"I'm not bullying. I'm introducing her to the experience of a lifetime!" Tetra plunged her face into her bowl and ate with horrific smacking noises.

"Thanks, honey." Antin pushed a wad of napkins across the table to her.

Merritt watched Liam. He appeared to have no difficulty eating his spaghetti, and his technique seemed simple. He put the fork into the bowl tines-down and turned it until the pasta wrapped around it. Merritt gave it a shot and came up with a giant roll of spaghetti. She subtly widened her mouth to fit it all inside.

"You okay, Merritt?" Tess asked.

Merritt couldn't answer. Her cheeks puffed out like a chipmunk's.

"Spaghetti might not have been the best choice." Liam grimaced. "Sorry."

Merritt choked the mouthful down. "It's really good," she offered after she swallowed.

Tess handed her a napkin.

"So, Merritt, what's your plan?" Qenzi asked. "Any ideas on what you'd like to do when you join the workforce?"

Merritt wiped her mouth. "Um..." She looked at Tess for help.

"Qenzi's wondering what you'd like to do to earn money." Tess smiled.

Merritt blankly stared. *Money,* her training supplied. *Currency used for buying and selling.* That did not help.

"What are you good at?" Liam added. "That's often the right place to start."

Merritt rubbed her neck. "Well, in the villages, I cut wood, carried water, and gathered food. I'm good at those things."

"That is interesting." Qenzi leaned forward. "You're used to living in a society where everyone does everything, right? Did you trade things with each other?"

Merritt chased spaghetti around the bowl with her fork. "We shared everything. Chores and resources."

"Incredible." Qenzi smiled. "That sounds like a simple life."

"I guess, although it wasn't always a friendly one," Merritt admitted.

"Have you ever used currency?" Tess asked.

"Currency." Merritt slowly stated. "A country's money system."

"That's an orb training answer." Qenzi smirked. "You're going to have a learning curve."

"We don't need to worry about that now." Tess grinned. "I'll explain everything and give you a tour of Little Avalon tomorrow, Merritt. Val asked me to help you. I've got you."

Merritt met the fae's blue eyes and smiled. "Thank you. I've..." She looked around the table and spoke quietly. "I've never felt so welcome in a new place. Little Avalon is different."

"It's the best place in any dimension," Tetra declared.

Antin desperately tried to offer her a napkin. She ignored him and returned her face to her bowl.

"She's not wrong." Liam nodded. "You'll love it here, Merritt."

"We'll see more of it in the morning," Tess added. "I think a good night's sleep is what you need right now."

Merritt rolled up another forkful of spaghetti as the conversation flowed around her. She decided not to tell Tess—or anyone —that she did not sleep. Yulietta had been weirded out when she discovered that.

So far, so good, Merritt thought. She didn't want to blow it.

Despite the dulling effect of Little Avalon's walls, Merritt sensed life around her as she and Tess crossed the street. Lights shone in the windows, and snatches of conversation drifted across the cool air. Two young vampires strolled past arm-in-arm, so absorbed in one another that they almost bumped into Tess and Merritt on the sidewalk.

"Everybody's got somebody," Tess reflected. "Even Tetra." She grinned. "It's good to have a new female friend who's single."

"Does Val have someone?" Merritt asked.

"Boy, does she have someone." Tess laughed. "She's dating a smoking hot weredeer who also happens to be a vet. He's setting up an animal clinic here in Little Avalon."

"Wow." Merritt blinked. "Sounds like the perfect man."

"I know, right?" Tess exclaimed.

They strolled across the street, feet slapping on the hard black surface. *Asphalt.* The trees' bare branches made Merritt long for more.

"Hey, Tess, can I ask you something?" Merritt murmured.

"Of course." Tess touched her shoulder. "Anything. That's what I'm here for."

"Where's Brooklyn Bridge Park?" Merritt asked.

"Northwest of here. It's about fifteen minutes by car." Tess pulled out her phone. "Yep, seven-point-four miles and sixteen minutes, depending on the traffic. Did you see it on TV?"

"Yeah." Merritt hugged herself. "It looks great."

"I bet you miss being in nature." Tess tilted her head. "Little Avalon has a park, too. We can go there tomorrow if you like."

Merritt forced a smile. "Sure." They'd passed the park in Genevieve on their way in. It was little bigger than Val's house and had few trees.

They climbed the stairs to their apartment. Tess had thrown the half-melted rice cooker in the trash. She put the kettle on the stovetop.

"Cup of hot chocolate before bed?" the Lunar Fae asked.

Hot chocolate. Warm, sweet, creamy beverage. A reason to live, Merritt's orb training announced.

"Sounds great!" Merritt grinned.

"It's amazing." Tess spooned powder into mugs and added milk.

"Where's our vampire housemate?" Merritt asked.

"Damian? He works the night shift at the NYHQ. I'm not sure what he does, but it seems to be important," Tess explained.

"I think I scared him," Merritt admitted.

Tess waved a hand. "Damian can handle it. Don't worry about him." She filled the mugs with hot water and handed one to Merritt, stifling a yawn. "I'm turning in. I look forward to that tour tomorrow."

"Me too." Merritt wrapped her hands around the mug.

"Sweet dreams." Tess turned to the hallway.

"Hey, Tess?" Merritt piped up.

Tess turned. "Yeah?"

Merritt squeezed the mug. "Thanks for everything."

Tess beamed, and moonlight spilled from her wings. "You're welcome."

Merritt padded to her bedroom and kicked off her boots. She sagged onto the couch and raised the mug to her lips. The first sip was the most fantastic experience she had ever had. Buttery, creamy flavors flooded her senses, with the rich, earthy aftertaste of dark chocolate, and warmth filled her belly.

"Wow." Merritt lowered the mug and stared at it with respect. "That *is* a reason to live."

She drank slowly, giving the beverage her full attention, and felt a pang of regret when it was gone. Given the adventure of the rice cooker, making more seemed like a bad idea. Instead, Merritt gazed around her room, trying to decide what to do.

She used to roam Mistwood North at night. When she closed her eyes, she could picture moonlight on snow, the smell of damp pine trees, and the distant wail of wolves. After opening them, she longingly gazed through the window, seeing only rooftops and the straggle of sidewalk trees.

Yearning flooded her.

No, Merritt, she ordered herself. *We're not screwing this up.* She grabbed the remote and turned the TV on. A stylized wolf ran across the screen with giant blue eyes and unnatural eyebrows.

Merritt frowned. It looked like a moving drawing, not a real thing.

Animation, her training whispered. *Motion pictures created with art instead of filming live action.*

It was beautiful in its way, Merritt decided, but the fake wolf in its fake woods made her heart long for the real thing.

She turned off the TV and stared through the window. The night called to her, but the air smelled of plastic, smoke, humans, and carbon. She itched to touch grass and earth.

Merritt slipped her boots on and fished her fur-lined cloak out of the laundry hamper. She wrapped it around her shoulders, flipped the hood up, and quietly left the room.

No sound came from Tess' bedroom. Merritt left the apartment unopposed.

A few nocturnal paras moved around Little Avalon when she reached the street. One or two gave her cloak a curious look, but no one said anything.

Northwest of here, Tess had said. Merritt sniffed the air, detecting a whiff of polluted water, and remembered the river in the background of the picture. She had an unerring sense of direction, so she didn't need the stars to guide her, which was a good thing. The streetlights rendered them barely visible. If she could find the river and follow it to the north, she'd reach the park in no time.

Seven-point-four miles. Merritt could reach the OPMA garrison, which was ten miles from Wolf Glen, in a little over an hour if she ran. It wouldn't take her that long to get to the utopia called Brooklyn Bridge Park.

She wrapped her hands in her cloak, protecting them from the chilly air, and set off along the sidewalk. She didn't look at Val's house as she passed. The wrought-iron sign outside dubbed it *Lillie House.* Merritt briefly wondered why, then yanked her thoughts away from Val. The dwarf didn't need to know where Merritt was going.

No one did.

Merritt took the next street to the left, leading toward the river, and felt the ripple of magic as she left the concealment wards surrounding Little Avalon. The stench of pollution grew stronger. Merritt could almost feel particles of filth entering her lungs as she hustled down the sidewalk. A few cars swished by, their headlights messing with Merritt's vision. Her orb training told her to avoid the road or get squashed. She stuck with the sidewalk.

A gaggle of young human males turned toward her. They wore gold and silver chains on their necks and pants, and one had a different style of skull ring on every finger.

One wolf-whistled. "Hey, beautiful," the one with the rings called.

Their attention crawled over her like bugs on her skin. She calmly kept walking.

"Hey, I'm talking to you," the human barked.

Merritt met his eyes. "I heard you."

"Then say something, bitch." The human stopped a few feet from her. "I want to see you smile."

"Why?" Merritt asked.

The human's eyes narrowed. "Why? Because I want to. Come here." He grabbed her arm. "You smell nice."

Merritt placed her free hand on his chest. "Let go of me."

"C'mere." The human pulled her closer, his breath fruity with stale alcohol.

Merritt shoved. His fingers slipped off her arm, and he stumbled back with a yelp of alarm, chains swinging and jingling as he reeled. His friends jumped as he crashed into a row of garbage cans.

"*Hey!*" he yelled.

Merritt ignored him. She wrapped her cloak around her hands and kept walking.

"*Hey!*" the human bellowed, but he didn't come after her. Merritt was almost disappointed.

She followed the street toward the alluring scent of water but halted when another road crossed her path. A few vehicles rumbled across the intersection. Red and green lights hovered over the crossing, apparently governing the cars' movements. A nearby sign depicted a walking figure with a red line through it.

No crossing sign, her orb training whispered. *Illegal to cross the street.*

Where can *I cross the street?* Merritt wondered.

Crosswalk, the training supplied. *Black-and-white striped symbol allowing the passage of pedestrians.*

Merritt looked up and down the street and spotted the bulky white stripes across the next intersection. She strode down the block, dodging a scrawny human with wild eyes. He looked like Yevgen and Petro the day they'd discovered those weird mushrooms in the woods. Maybe those mushrooms grew here, too.

She paused at the crosswalk's edge. Her training told her that a green light in the shape of a walking person would tell her when it was time to cross, and cars swished by with no regard for the white stripes as she waited. They all seemed boring to Merritt, with bulky shapes and scraped paintwork. Nothing like shimmering Genevieve.

At last, the green walking symbol appeared on a post opposite Merritt. She stepped forward, and white metal filled her vision as a blaring sound emanated from the car speeding toward her.

The light was green! Merritt jumped back, but the car kept coming, tires squealing. She glimpsed a human's wild eyes behind the wheel and stuck out both hands to protect herself. Her palms slammed into the car's hood with a thump that reverberated up her arms. The vehicle spun aside, leaving black streaks of rubber on the sidewalk, and its hood met the nearest streetlight with an unpleasant crunch.

Merritt shook out her hands, which stung.

The car door crashed open, and a human in a suit sprang out. *"What do you think you're doing?"*

Merritt raised her eyebrows. "What do you think *you're* doing? The light was green. It was my turn to walk!"

"Didn't anyone ever tell you to stop, look, and listen?" the guy screamed. *"Are you insane?"*

Several cars stopped, and blaring horns filled the night. A few pedestrians pulled out their phones and pointed them at Merritt, who stared at the driver.

"I don't understand why you're angry with me," she snapped. "I'm not the one who nearly killed someone. You could have crushed me."

"But I didn't!" the driver barked. "Instead, you—" He stared at his car's crumpled nose. "You totaled my car! How did you do that?"

"I pushed it," Merritt growled.

"How did you push a speeding car?" the driver demanded.

"She's a superhero!" someone in the crowd yelled. "Look at her cape!"

Merritt rounded on them. "Excuse me, sir. This is a cloak of the finest Mavka make." She gathered her dignity. "Good night."

"Where do you think you're going?" the driver snapped. "Look what you did to my car!"

He stepped toward her, fists clenched, and Merritt made a subtle change to her posture. She lowered her weight on hunkered knees and moved one foot back, balanced enough to dodge or strike. Her eyes calmly met the driver's. She'd fought far scarier beasts than him.

When? she wondered, but no clear memories came to mind. All she knew was that she was ready.

The driver raised his fists but froze when a yipping sound tore across the street. Blue lights reflected in his eyes. Merritt spun as a blue and white car pulled up, brilliant lights flashing from its roof. They stung her eyes, making it difficult to read the words on the car's side: *NYPD* and *POLICE*.

Police, the orb defined. *Law enforcement.*

That didn't sound good. Merritt glanced at the crumpled car.

"Officer, you're finally here!" The driver strode toward the police as he exited his vehicle. "Look what this woman did to my car!"

Oh, crap. Merritt couldn't get in trouble now. She'd only been in Little Avalon for a day.

CHAPTER SEVEN

Merritt bolted toward the river. A gap between two buildings offered her an escape route. She darted into the gap and sprinted down it.

"*Get her!*" the driver yelled.

Merritt's eye caught a stout pipe running down the side of the building.

Drainpipe, her training explained.

I don't care what it is! Merritt ran to it and grabbed it with both hands. It felt nothing like a tree branch, but it was sturdy, and she skittered up it in seconds. Her supple deerskin boots embraced its contours. She scaled the building before the police human reached the gap.

Not even breathless, Merritt pulled herself onto the roof and crouched at its edge. The police human jogged down the alley, shining a *flashlight* around the corners.

"*Hey! Police!*" he yelled. "*Show yourself!*"

"Sorry," Merritt whispered. "Not today."

She moved away from the edge and straightened. Water sparkled, catching her eye, and she realized she'd nearly reached the river.

Merritt silently strode across the roof and gazed at the neighborhood lights. Their reflection rippled on water a block away, and the broad river stretched to another line of city lights on the horizon.

North, Merritt thought. She turned, orienting herself. The rooftops were low here, nothing like the towering buildings she'd seen in Manhattan, and as her eyes adjusted to the darkness, she realized that no one moved up here. The rooftops were abandoned.

Merritt grinned. No humans would bother her up here, and though there were gaps to hurdle between the buildings, the terrain was nothing compared to rushing through the canopies of Fernwood Deep to get away from the local bullies who'd tormented her.

She flung her cloak back to free her arms and broke into a run.

The wind whipped against her hair, nipping her ears with the last of winter's chill. Her boots thumped on the roof as she darted around antennas and chimneys with the agility of one who could run through treetops. Her body reveled in the activity, and tension leaked from her muscles, making her bark a laugh.

A step down took her onto the next one so lightly that she barely felt the impact. Shingles tilted under her boots and she changed course, racing to the top of the pitched roof. She ran along its peak with barely a sound.

A space loomed between this rooftop and the next. Merritt gathered herself and accelerated. Her boot touched the edge, and Merritt launched into the air, flying, the wind lifting her cloak, her body weightless. She adored the floating moment and soundlessly landed on the other side.

Rooftop after rooftop passed beneath her quick feet. The city lights shone around and beneath her. She reached the last house before the river and swung north toward the place of trees. Two more houses, and the street gaped ahead, the mighty jump over two lanes of traffic beckoning. Merritt sprinted toward it. Strength surged through her limbs, and when she reached the roof's edge, she jumped.

This leap took longer. Metal vehicles sped beneath her. A pedestrian looked up, jaw dropping, as she soared over his head. She extended her arms and was shocked by the sheer distance. She landed hands first, her arms crumpling, and rolled to her feet on the opposite rooftop.

A laugh burst like a bubble from her as she allowed her momentum to carry her across the rooftop, her legs pistoning, her feet silent.

This was *much* more fun than the sidewalk.

Seven-point-four miles passed in a flash. Merritt spotted open ground with trees and paths and snow, and her heart soared.

She skidded to a halt at the roof's edge and gazed at the park. Though its borders were artificial, with square-edged piers jutting into the river, the trees and shrubs called her name. The river made it feel roomier by far than anything she'd seen since she left Mistwood North.

"I'm coming, trees," Merritt whispered.

This building made it easy. A metal ladder on the outside—a *fire escape*—allowed her to scramble to street level without breaking a sweat. This time, drivers stopped at the crosswalk when the light turned green, and Merritt skipped across it.

At last, she strolled into the park, and her boots met real earth for the first time in hours.

A shuddering exhalation rippled through Merritt's body as something tight and uncomfortable released in her chest. She ignored the paths and strolled across the cold ground, her boots squelching in melting snow. A few lamps illuminated the paths, and Merritt turned away from them into the soothing, natural darkness beneath the trees.

She walked up to the first tree and threw her arms around it. The rough bark scraped her cheek, and she pressed her body against the trunk, feeling the sap pulsing through its heart.

"Hello, tree," Merritt whispered. "I love you."

The green buds on the branches swelled and burst, and the leaves trembled with new life. Merritt beamed and ran her fingertips over the little leaves. They sang like wind chimes in her senses.

Merritt closed her eyes and spread her arms. The cool breeze rippled over her skin, bearing notes of river water, fresh dirt, and new grass. She laughed and spun, reveling in the abundant life around her. It felt like her first deep breath since that fateful moment with Neven and the wolf.

Arms still wide, Merritt allowed her knees to buckle. She fell full length on the beautiful, natural ground, so rich with roots, dormant seeds, and the tentative germination of spring's first plants. It felt like she was sinking into a warm bed or floating in a hot bath.

She gazed at the stars through a tangle of branches. Though she saw only a few, their brightness made her heart take wing. She could have lain on the fragrant, frigid earth for hours, except for the surge of energy that the cool breeze and starry sky brought her. Before she could stop herself, she flipped to her feet.

Her senses told her this part of the park was empty of humans. This was a place to explore with four strong legs and a twitching nose, not the cumbersome limbs of this humanoid form. She closed her eyes and felt magic crackle through her cells in response to the earth and trees. The shape she took was deeply familiar, and the transformation felt as natural as a shrug. Her front paws hit the dirt as her tail grew. Her snout lengthened, teeth sharpening. Fur prickled as it spread over her body, her clothes fading under the magic.

Merritt opened her eyes and saw the world without red and green. The night suddenly seemed brilliant. A tapestry of smells extended around her, far more intense than sight. Her whiskers twitched at the acrid reek of the city, but an exciting smell consumed her attention: the pulse of blood in the body of a mouse.

Merritt lowered her nose to the earth and trotted across the park, her white-tipped tail low and twitching. Her soundless paws carried her from tree to tree like a shadow. The mouse fled into a hole beneath a tree root, still sluggish from hibernation. Merritt could have dug it up, but she wasn't hunting tonight. All she wanted to do was run.

She turned her sharp nose into the wind, stretched her tail out behind her, and sprinted across the grass. The breeze sang in her fur. Her paws landed lightly on the cold ground. Her world was a swirl of tree trunks and stars as scents brought a constant stream of information to her nostrils. Pheromones, vibrations, and distant sounds were thrilling to her canid senses.

When her lungs burned, Merritt slowed to a trot. She dipped her twitching nose, letting her whiskers caress the earth, and recoiled a step when the dirt changed to asphalt. The footpath gleamed in the moonlight. It felt strange under her paws, but she smelled water on the other side, so she stepped onto it.

A loud noise came from her left, and Merritt dropped to a crouch. A moment later, her fox mind processed the sound as English.

"Look, look!" someone cried. "It's right there!"

"Where?" another human demanded.

Merritt raised her twitching nose and tilted her head in curiosity. A pair of humans were blurred in her canid vision, but she saw light glinting on the shiny badges on their shirts. Their smells told her one was male and one female.

"It's a fox," the male whispered. "It's so close."

"Isn't it gorgeous?" the female murmured. "Don't move too fast. You might scare it."

Merritt's tail twitched. She tilted her head the other way for a better look.

"Get a pic, quick," the male hissed, "before it runs away."

The female pulled her phone out. Merritt's training labeled it a communications device, so she wasn't sure why the female aimed it at her.

"So pretty." The female turned her phone. "All these years of patrolling, and I've only seen them once or twice."

Merritt was still thirsty. She twitched her tail again and trotted off.

Her nose led her to the river's edge, where a concrete barrier separated the park from the water. The unnatural straight line unnerved her, but she watched the edge and found no danger after several moments, so she lay down and dipped her muzzle into the water. It tasted stale and unwholesome, but the welcome cold refreshed her.

The roots of a huge old tree nearby gave her a safe space to resume her human shape. To her relief, her clothes returned after she transformed. She sat cross-legged among the roots, her back pressed against the tree trunk. The sap pulsed through it like impulses through neurons, and she leaned her head back. Her breathing slowed.

New York City isn't so bad. Merritt grinned.

Out of habit, her mind wandered back to Lichenvale. She tasted alcohol sweetness on the back of her throat again. All her memories from childhood were like that: flashes of sensation, as intriguing as they were useless.

Merlin told her that she had to remember since she was the last hope for her species to have a legacy. She leaned against the tree, feeling its magic thrum through her cells, and closed her eyes.

Cool grass under her bare soles.

The shape of butterfly wings against bright sunshine.

The taste of alcohol.

Someone laughing—a voice that rushed like a river.

The touch of her mother's hand. Her fading vision as something passed over her. The yammer and howl of monstrous creatures spilling through the woods, bringing darkness with them as a hopeless line of Leshbolgs turned to fight—

Merritt gasped and sat up as pain pierced her head. She rubbed her temple, grimacing. It faded as she released the memory and let it float back into the flotsam of her fractured mind.

She remembered telling Merlin that she felt crazy. "You're not crazy," he'd assured her. "You have amnesia, that's all." Her mind was fine as long as she didn't stray too close to the edge of her memory and tumble into the abyss of what she'd forgotten.

Merritt shook herself, then rose and marched back toward Little Avalon. Remembering her past had done nothing for her so far, but a new memory flooded her mind as she walked, filling her with warmth. She remembered the taste of spaghetti, Liam rolling his eyes at Tetra, Qenzi cracking jokes with Tess, and Antin's arm around Tetra's waist.

A smile lifted her cheeks as she jogged across the street. This group accepted everybody, even a faerie.

They would accept her, too.

Merritt felt pleasantly out of breath as she trotted up the stairs to her apartment. She'd skipped the streets on the way home, darting from rooftop to rooftop, dodging trouble with the humans.

She barged into the kitchen before she realized that the lights were on. Her vampire housemate whipped around, clutching a bowl. He stood beside the open microwave, next to the charred spot where the rice cooker used to be.

Merritt swallowed. "Um, hi."

"Hey." The vampire arched an eyebrow.

Don't ask me where I've been, Merritt silently begged. *Please don't ask.*

"Nocturnal too, huh?" the vamp inquired.

Merritt nodded. Technically, it was true.

"Cool." The vamp turned to the microwave and shoved the bowl inside.

Merritt took the opportunity to slip past him and darted to the safety of her room.

"You have a good night?" Tess asked at the table the next morning.

Merritt looked up from her cereal. The colorful blobs floating in the milk appeared to contain grain, but they were so heavily processed that Merritt couldn't begin to guess what kind. Sugar sparkled on her tongue as she chewed.

"Oh, sorry. I caught you with your mouth full." Tess splashed the spoon in her bowl.

Merritt swallowed. "I had an excellent night."

"Great! There's nothing like a solid night's sleep to make the future seem brighter." Tess grinned.

Merritt shoved a spoonful of cereal into her mouth. "Mmhmm."

"About our tour." Tess beamed. "We have the entire day to ourselves. We're between contracts right now—"

Contract. Agreement between two parties, Merritt's training supplied.

"So I have a few days before I need to play bodyguard to a celeb or royal again," Tess continued.

Bodyguard. Person employed for the personal protection of another.

"Between contracts?" Merritt queried. "You can't agree on something?"

"What?" Tess blinked.

"I'm misunderstanding my training. What's a contract?" Merritt asked.

Tess chuckled. "I see how the context could screw that up. You know what Stonehold Security Services does?"

Merritt frowned. "You said something about protecting important paras."

"Val would say that *all* paras are important, but yeah, that's what the company does. We go around with humans and paras who are at risk for whatever reason and make sure nothing happens to them," Tess explained.

"I work for Val, but also for the High Magic Division. That's a crack team of Lunar Fae who work to advance the species, educate changelings like me, and preserve our history. Anyway, I'm saying I don't have anything on for the next few days. I'm usually busy, but I'm devoting this time to helping you settle in."

Merritt lowered her spoon. "Thank you, Tess."

"Aw, don't mention it." Tess squeezed her arm. "It's a pleasure. What do you want to see first? The Second Fist? The bank?"

"I wouldn't know where to start," Merritt admitted.

"We'll start with the Fist, then," Tess decided.

After breakfast, the Lunar Fae led Merritt down to the street, which was full of paras. A few cars crawled along, patiently stopping for pedestrians to wander across. An orc tipped his hat to Tess, making her grin. Two elegant centaurs strode past, hooves clopping, with bows and quivers on their backs. Each carried a paper cup of coffee, and one scrolled on her phone. The other grabbed her arm and tugged her away from a streetlight before she could walk into it.

"Ourania and Hector. They work for the OPMA. Val had to make them special amulets to be human-presenting," Tess explained as she led Merritt up the sidewalk. "We don't have many humans in Little Avalon, so we're more free to be paranormal here than in the rest of the city, but there are a few."

Merritt remembered Val saying something about not allowing humans to see paranormals and nodded. She touched her hair to make sure she'd returned it to the same length after leaving her fox form the night before.

"You'll love the Second Fist," Tess told her. "It's a popular drinking hole for humans and paras alike, but it's more than that. Half the businesses in the duchy have their meetings there, or at Kalyna's Kitchen on the other side of the neighborhood. It's like Little Avalon's unofficial town hall."

"A tavern for a town hall?" Merritt grinned. "I like it."

Tess giggled. "It's a very Val idea."

She led Merritt past the apartment buildings and businesses she'd seen the day before from Genevieve's window. They reached the Second Fist and found the chairs stacked on the tables and the doors closed.

"It's too early to open, but Dante will be around." Tess knocked.

Merritt peered through the glass door and gasped when she saw the bar—a huge deadwood trunk from Fernwood Deep split in half. Merritt recognized the Shajara Elven craftsmanship. Bright blue bolts of resin traced through the magnificent wood.

"You like the bar?" Tess asked.

"I used to watch the Shajara Elves make stuff like this when I lived with them." Merritt straightened. "It's beautiful. I never thought I'd see anything like it again."

"You'll see everything in Little Avalon," Tess told her.

Her words proved true a moment later when a para of an unfamiliar species came to the door. His tawny skin didn't match his bald head and the traditional orc tattoos encircling his scalp, but that wasn't why Merritt stared at him. She couldn't drag her eyes away from his mouth.

This guy had tusks *and* fangs.

He opened the door and smiled. "Hey, Tess! This must be the new resident."

Merritt gaped at him.

Tess cleared her throat. "This is Dante Diaz, the owner of the Second Fist."

Merritt dragged her gaze away from his teeth and met his eyes, which didn't help. They were deep brown, flecked with scarlet.

Tess elbowed her.

"M-merritt," she managed. "Merritt Vale."

"Great to meet you, Merritt." Dante extended a hand.

An unfamiliar mix of magic shot through Merritt's arm when she shook it.

"You're in luck. Uncle Enzo is here today, too." Dante turned away. "Hey, Unk! Come say hi to the new resident. Want a beer, Merritt?"

"It's nine in the morning," Tess protested.

"Yes," Merritt croaked.

"Only a taste." Dante flashed his too-toothy grin. "Uncle! Where are you?"

He retreated to the back wall, where wooden kegs stood on thick shelves among glasses and electrical appliances Merritt didn't recognize.

"What *is* he?" Merritt hissed.

Tess raised her eyebrows. "Mixed-species paras aren't a thing in Mistwood North, are they?"

"The Mavka Elves don't live with other species," Merritt thought about Tetra and Antin, then about what Tess had said about Val's boyfriend being a Were. "Is that...common here?"

"Growing increasingly more so, especially now that Princess Lillirelda is in the public eye," Tess explained.

Merritt stared at her.

"Princess Lillirelda? Daughter of Queen Julia and King Taylor?" Tess prompted.

"They're Lunar Fae," Merritt protested.

"Her Majesty is, but King Taylor is an Aether Elf," Tess explained. "The training orb should've taught you about paranormal affairs, too."

"That's really cool," Merritt murmured.

Clearly, things were very different in Little Avalon compared to the strict traditions of Wolf Glen, but the thought intrigued and excited her. If Weres and dwarves or elves and faeries could fall in love, a Leshbolg could find a way to fit in.

Dante slid a glass across the bar. The liquid within was so cold that water condensed on the outside of the glass. A tall layer of white foam bobbed on top of the sparkling amber fluid.

"Anvil Brewery's pilsner," he announced. "A house favorite. Try it."

Merritt raised the glass to her lips, glancing at Dante's broad grin. Tusks and fangs. She guessed he was half-vampire, half-orc.

"What's this, Dante?" someone inquired gruffly. "Serving booze before opening time?"

Merritt lowered the glass. A burly orc stumped across the bar, confirming her guess. His thick accent—one she'd heard only here in New York City—made him sound cranky, but the dark eyes were kind.

Dante explained and introduced her.

"Enzo Lombardi." The orc shook her hand. "Come to the Fist whenever you like. We always have cold drinks. The original bar, the Iron Fist, is in Williamsburg. I'm usually there. Swing by if you're in the area."

Merritt had no idea where Williamsburg was, but she nodded.

"What do you do for work, Merritt?" Dante asked.

Merritt finished her beer. "I don't know yet."

"We're looking for a job for her," Tess explained.

Dante grimaced. "Aw, Merlin's beard. I hired a new waitress

last week. We're full up, but I'll let you know if I need a pair of hands for a shift or two."

"Thank you." Merritt smiled as her training defined *waitress*. Serving drinks didn't sound so bad. Maybe this "job" thing would be easy.

"C'mon. We have lots to see," Tess announced.

She led Merritt out of the bar, and they walked to the corner. Here, several businesses overlooked a large parking area dotted with weird objects with tubes snaking out of them.

Gasoline pumps, her training told her.

"What's gasoline?" Merritt asked. "Why do we pump it?"

"It's fuel for vehicles," Tess explained. "These pumps fill cars with diesel and gasoline. That's an electric charging station for human-made battery-powered vehicles." She pointed at a port beside it, which seemed identical but emanated a soft blue glow. A rune shimmered on the wall above it. "That one's for charging the magic crystals that power para-made vehicles. The Veil keeps humans from noticing it."

Merritt nodded. The thing with the humans seemed complicated.

"You'll love this place." Tess avoided the pumps and led Merritt to the first business. The sign over the doors read *Fern-wood Grocery: Avalon's Finest in the Big Apple's Heart!*

Tess didn't touch the doors. They magically slid aside, though Merritt didn't see any runes powering them. She followed Tess into a store the size of their apartment. Shelves were crammed into it, so close together that Tess had to fold her wings to fit between them. The Lunar Fae marched down the first aisle, giving Merritt little time to stare at the items on the shelves. Jars of colored stuff had labels that said *Lotus Jam, Mandrake Reduction,* and *Shamrock Jelly, Silphium Flavor.* A box of tentacles wriggled as Merritt passed.

"Wow!" Merritt stopped. "You have goldensap!" She picked up a tiny jar.

Tess delicately took it. "Yes, and it costs eighty-five dollars."

"We used to drip it in our tea in Fernwood Deep. I sometimes helped the little kids extract it from the trees," Merritt enthused.

"I knew you'd like this place." Tess beamed. "Let me introduce you to Jackson. He's great."

They approached the counter at the back of the store. As they approached, smells took Merritt back in time, coming from the bundles of dried plants hanging behind the counter. She spotted fern flowers, moly, and aglaophotis, but she didn't recognize the others. Glass jars on the counter contained colorful candy and grain. The air was spicy and dusty. Dryad music played softly. Merritt looked around but didn't see anyone with pipes.

The para behind the counter straightened as they approached. "Hi, Tess! Back for more Southern Spine coffee?"

"Not today." Tess smiled. "I'd like you to meet Merritt Vale. She hails from Mistwood."

"A cousin from the north." The para leaned on the counter. He was a Woodland Fae. Two-inch antlers protruded from his tight brown curls, freckles spotted his cheeks, and the tip of his nose was rubbery and black. "Are you an elf?"

"No." Merritt squared her shoulders. "I'm a Leshbolg."

She waited for fear to flood the Woodland Fae's features, but he just blinked. "Really? If you'll pardon my saying so, I guess the legends aren't true about you guys. You don't seem particularly savage."

"No, sir." Merritt smiled.

"Good to meet you. I'm Jackson." The fae patted a jar beside him. "I have Mistwood marzipan if you like it. Have a piece on the house."

Merritt eagerly accepted a slice of the sticky, nutty sweet and crunched it while Tess poked around the store, choosing golden-fleece cheese, milk from Wingtip Peak, and a pack of elven strawberries so fat and red they seemed ready to burst.

"The marzipan is amazing," Merritt declared. "Exactly like Granny Alta used to make in Wolf Glen."

"Good to know." Jackson grinned.

"A bundle of silphium too, please," Tess requested.

Jackson took it from the ceiling and handed it to Merritt. "Thanks, Jackson. It was nice meeting you."

"Hold on!" Tess laughed. "We have to pay for this first."

The orb training informed Merritt that *paying* involved the exchange of that *money* stuff it had mentioned earlier. She watched as Tess rummaged in her purse for a flat plastic rectangle—*bank card*, the training unhelpfully defined—and tapped it on a thing with buttons.

"Thank you." Jackson gave Tess a piece of paper. "See you around, Merritt."

"See you." Merritt followed Tess to the door, grabbing the bottle of goldensap as she went.

"Nope." Tess took and replaced it. "Not paying eighty-five dollars for that."

"Dollars?" Merritt asked. "Is that money?"

"It is, and eighty-five is a lot of them," Tess informed her. "I'll show you the other stores."

They wandered through stores selling potions, car parts, clothing, and mystifying devices Tess called "thaumatech." Merritt liked them all, even if she wasn't sure what thaumatech was.

"We'll get you a phone," Tess told her as they left the store. "But first, I need to introduce you to my friend Isabella."

They turned right and walked down the opposite side of the block from their apartment building. A new row of identical buildings greeted them, with wrought-iron numbers over the doors, labeling them Stonehold Houses eight through twelve.

"These are my favorite buildings in Little Avalon." Tess' wings buzzed. "They're apartments on top but businesses on the bottom. It's so cool. Everything is close at hand, even my hair-dresser." She touched her stunning red mane.

"Hairdresser." Merritt quoted her training. "A professional who styles your hair."

"Red is my natural color," Tess hastily informed her, "but Isabella takes it to another level. You'll love her."

She strolled to the ground floor of Stonehold Nine, where a revolving glass door admitted them to a place full of wonder and color. The pastel pink wallpaper featured white polka dots, and the floor tiles alternated between white and pink, too. Tables lined the wall on Merritt's left, with three swiveling chairs and enormous mirrors in gilded frames.

An enormous painting presided over white basins with shower heads on the room's far side. Merritt fell in love with the painting, which was an explosion of wild colors, streaked and splattered with reason behind the placement. It depicted nothing, but her heart thrilled when she looked at it.

Several comfortable chairs stood by the door, containing humans and paranormals who read magazines and scrolled on their phones. A Sylthana Elf sat before one of the giant mirrors, smiling at her reflection as a human fussed over her hair.

The human ran a brush over the elf's straight silver locks. "Look at that. I've never seen this natural blonde color in my life."

"It's a family thing," the elf explained.

Most Sylthana Elves had similar hair. The elf's statement was technically true.

"You give me so little to do. Trim the ends so you don't trip over it, and that's all." The human stepped back and looked into the mirror. "How do you like it?"

The elf ran a hand over her hair. "Perfect. Thank you!"

"Doing your hair is daylight robbery." The human shook her head. "Sure you don't want highlights? Or a different cut?"

"Absolutely sure." The elf rose.

"Good. You look amazing." The human patted her shoulder.

The elf left, drawing envious glances from the waiting group.

"Next, please," Isabella called.

A vampire with a straggly bob approached the chair.

"Oh, Anne." Isabella sighed. "What did you do?"

The vampire sheepishly grimaced. "I don't think you'd believe me if I told you. Suffice it to say, my last diplomatic trip to…ah, Europe was more interesting than usual."

Isabella fluffed Anne's hair. "It looks like you took a blowtorch to this."

"Can you fix it?" Anne asked. "I have a council meeting tomorrow. I can't go looking like this!"

Isabella laid a hand on Anne's shoulder. "Of course I can. I'm a wizard!"

Anne's lip twitched. "You are."

Isabella guided the vampire to the basins and washed her hair. She applied tons of something white and sticky to it. "Give that ten minutes to work."

"Ten minutes of doing nothing." Anne sighed. "Bliss."

Isabella left the vampire reclining against a basin and strode to the door. "Tess Mendoza, tell me that you didn't do something stupid to your hair, too. You were here two days ago!"

"I didn't." Tess rose, laughing. "I'm here to introduce you to a new resident."

Isabella raised an eyebrow. "The natural look. It works on you. I like it."

Merritt touched her red curls. "Um, thanks."

"Isabella Sanchez." The human extended a hand.

Merritt shook it and introduced herself for what felt like the hundredth time that day.

"Merritt's a recent immigrant," Tess added. "She's learning the ropes of life in Little Avalon."

"I've lived in Brooklyn all my life, and sometimes *I* feel like an immigrant." Isabella chuckled. "It's a whole new world here. If you ever need an ear or a safe space, come over, Merritt. We newbies have to stick together."

Merritt smiled. "Right."

"You're busy today," Tess observed.

Isabella nodded. "Business is picking up. Soon I'll be able to justify having space for three hairdressers. Hey, I have to get back to work, but we'll meet for drinks sometime. Sound good?"

Merritt's smile widened. "Sounds great."

"Let's grab lunch," Tess suggested. "There's one more place I want to show you."

CHAPTER EIGHT

Fantastic smells emanated from the house on the far end of Little Avalon's main street. Merritt's mouth watered as they approached. The scents of garlic, lemon, seafood, spices, and butter reminded her how hungry she was.

She sniffed again. "Garlic?"

Tess groaned. "That was a complicated one. Chaplin's Kitchen has two owners, a Sylthana Elf and a human. Hank couldn't understand why Kalyna resisted using garlic in their recipes. She eventually convinced him that many of Little Avalon's 'immigrants' are deathly allergic to it."

"I suppose that's true," Merritt murmured.

"Kalyna discreetly managed to establish a garlic-free zone for our vampire customers. It works. The vamps are safe, and the garlic-loving humans are happy." Tess shook her head. "Humans love that stuff."

She led Merritt up the broad steps to a porch with stone pillars with fairy lights twined around them. Humans and paras alike sat at several tables on the porch. Many nodded and waved at Tess.

Inside, more tables stood around a blue and white tile floor.

Lacy curtains hid the street but admitted plenty of sunshine, making the room feel sheltered from the outside world. A massive portrait hung on the opposite wall, depicting a gray-bearded human with his arm around a smiling female. The couples and children surrounding them shared their features.

"I'm told you've been to Meggie's." Tess picked a table and sat. "You're familiar with ordering? Menus?"

"No," Merritt admitted. "I ordered what Alugon ordered. It was a cheeseburger. I hated it."

"No cheeseburgers here," Tess assured her. "I'll talk you through it."

A well-dressed young dwarf came over to welcome them. He placed a jug of water, two glasses, and a basket of rolls on the table. Then he slid a leather-bound little book in front of each of them and drifted away.

"These are menus." Tess lifted her book. "You look at them and order what you want." She explained that the numbers next to each item were the amount of money customers had to exchange for the food.

Merritt felt like she was starting to get the hang of the "buying" thing.

"I'm telling you, we can't do it without a good baker." The strident words cut through the room. "I've never known a cook like you, but you could make a flop of a box cake."

"That's Hank and Kalyna." Tess grinned. "They're the owners."

Merritt craned her neck. A striking Sylthana Elf in a white uniform hurried from table to table, exchanging a few words with each diner. She wore a tall white hat that Merritt really liked. The scruffy human stumping beside her looked like a goblin, but he had kind eyes.

"Thanks, Hank," Kalyna grumbled, tucking a stray silver hair under her hat.

"I'm not trying to insult you. People want baked goods for breakfast," Hank growled.

Kalyna sighed as they approached Tess' and Merritt's table. "I know they do, but how can we be sure that breakfast will take off and justify the expense of hiring a baker?"

"Don't use long words to confuse me, young lady," Hank grumbled. "It won't work. You know breakfast will be popular. Look at this place!" He spread his arms. "Lunchtime on a Wednesday, and it's packed."

"I suppose." Kalyna nodded. "Hey, Tess."

Tess introduced Merritt, but the elf and the human didn't stay long. They bustled back toward the kitchen, still arguing.

When their waiter returned, Tess and Merritt ordered Sylthana wine and seafood dishes.

"You like shrimp?" Tess asked.

"I love seafood. I haven't had much, except when I was in the hospital in Avalon Town next to the sea. It's my favorite. The only meat I really like," Merritt admitted.

Tess raised her eyebrows. "You did avoid the meatballs."

Merritt said nothing.

"Oh, man." Tess laughed. "You poor thing. I'll put the word out that you prefer vegetarian cooking."

"Thanks." Merritt smiled.

Their Sylthana wine, which humans called ouzo, arrived. Merritt found it spicy but delicious.

"Okay, let's talk business." Tess sipped. "We need to find you a job you'll enjoy, preferably in Little Avalon, where you would have plenty of support."

Merritt nodded. "Everyone should contribute to the duchy."

"Precisely. What have you done in the past?" Tess asked. "You're barely of age."

"All paras work in the forest villages where Merlin placed me." Merritt shrugged. "I'm no stranger to hard work."

"You mentioned helping with stuff like chopping wood and fetching water." Tess nodded. "What else?"

Merritt rubbed her neck. "Animals like me."

"Niall recently hired a new nurse for the clinic he's opening, so that's out." Tess swirled her glass. "What about magic? Do you have any?"

Merritt bit her lip. "I have plant powers." She didn't mention shapeshifting.

Tess raised her eyebrows. "Can you make them grow?"

"Easily," Merritt told her.

"Then I know just where to place you." Tess grinned. "Lawrence Davies is the groundskeeper at our park in Little Avalon, and he mentioned needing someone younger to help him with weeding and planting. I think you'd be great at that!"

"Working in the park?" Merritt smiled. "I'd like that."

"It's perfect. You can be out in nature, doing what you love and getting paid for it." Tess beamed.

Merritt frowned. "Getting paid? You mean, getting money for work?"

"Exactly. That's how jobs work," Tess told her. "You do things, and people give you money in exchange."

"What would I do with money?" Merritt asked.

Tess chuckled. "Whatever you want. You could start by buying your own groceries or paying your rent. The Eternity Throne will pay for those things until you don't need them anymore. Then you can be independent."

Merritt slowly nodded. "Then no one would have control over me."

"I wouldn't say the Throne *controls* you," Tess murmured, "but working gives you an element of freedom."

Freedom. Merritt liked the sound of that.

"We'll meet with Lawrence tomorrow morning," Tess decided. "Ooh, here comes our food."

They were soon far too busy eating to think about anything else.

Fat clouds hung low over Little Avalon the next morning, promising rain. A chill breeze nipped Merritt's nose and chin. She tugged her beanie over her ears and tucked her hands under her armpits.

"Another lovely spring day in New York," Tess grumbled. "You'll feel better when we get to the park."

"It's nothing compared to Mistwood," Merritt admitted. "I'm not sure how we'll grow any plants in this weather."

The park looked dead. Frost sparkled between the playground equipment. A single pine tree leaned into the wind, a carpet of needles at its feet.

Tess patted her shoulder. "You'll see."

The elderly Woodland Fae leaning on the park's gate seemed too ordinary to be the source of the powerful magic Merritt sensed as they neared him. Lawrence Davies had wiry hair striped in black, white, and gray. His stumpy hands ended in sharp claws, and whiskers twitched on either side of his long nose.

"Morning, Lawrence!" Tess beamed.

Lawrence looked Merritt up and down. "Is this her?"

"Merritt Vale, sir. At your service." Merritt extended a hand.

Lawrence ignored it. "You're a slip of a thing. Can you garden?"

Merritt hoped so. "Yes, sir."

"Fine. Come on." Lawrence hoisted a bag of gardening tools and turned to the gate. "Let's see what you can do."

He stepped through the gate. Merritt followed, and the magic rippled over her skin like she was sinking into warm water. Her vision blurred, and she stumbled a step. Tess grabbed her arm to steady her as she blinked to clear her hazy eyes. Then she saw Little Avalon Park as it truly was.

Merritt gasped.

A carpet of deep green grass extended hundreds of feet from her, undulating over the uneven ground. Stately oaks reigned over the space, their leaves rustling in the breeze. Merritt's beanie was suddenly too hot. A massive playground occupied the park's center, with monkey bars, a slide, jousting lists, archery butts, and twenty-foot-tall rings. A few young harpies played on the rings, giggling and fluttering from one to the other.

"Merlin's beard!" Merritt whispered.

"Concealment spell fooled you, did it?" Lawrence grunted. "I'm not surprised." He stomped to a small shed and clanged around in it.

"It's amazing!" Though the park was less than half the size of Brooklyn Bridge Park, the magic coursing through the earth made her heart pound.

"It's a gateway to Little Avalon's pocket dimension," Tess explained. "See over there? All those buildings are in the dimension. They're putting up a new shopping mall."

She pointed across the park, where construction equipment and scaffolding jutted against the clear blue sky.

"Is it always summer in this dimension?" Merritt asked.

Tess shook her head. "Weather adjustment thaumatech is *really* expensive. Val could only afford it for the park, but still, that way, Little Avalon's residents always have a piece of summer to visit."

"I love it," Merritt gushed. "I love it *so* much."

"You'll adore working here." Tess beamed.

"If you make the cut." Lawrence stumped past, carrying a shovel. "Come on."

Merritt couldn't resist kicking off her boots. She carried them in one hand as she followed Lawrence across the park, the deep green grass caressing her bare soles, sending ripples of magical energy through her muscles.

Lawrence paused beneath one of the trees. Merritt desperately wanted to hug it, but she put her boots down and attentively listened to Lawrence instead.

"See this flowerbed?" He indicated the soft circle of earth

around the tree's roots. "I want you to grow primroses here." He handed her a package of seeds. "I'd like them to bloom right away."

"'Right away?'" Merritt queried.

Lawrence raised an eyebrow. "Tess, you said she had plant magic."

"I can do it," Merritt hastily told him.

"Then do it." Lawrence nodded at the flowerbed.

Merritt tore the package open and shook the seeds into her palm. They were rich with promise and latent life. She closed her hand over them and inhaled the scents of summer as the seeds trembled in response to her magic.

"Get on with it," Lawrence growled.

"Let her work," Tess chided.

Merritt ignored them. She knelt on the glorious, thick grass and scattered the seeds over the damp earth. Then she ran her palms over the dirt, closing it over the seeds. The earth trickled between her fingers and under her nails, rich with nutrients.

She pressed her fingers deep into the flowerbed, lowered her head, and concentrated. Seeds responded: the primroses and dozens of other seeds in the earth from the wandering plants the wind and birds had dropped there.

Merritt's magic flowed through her hands, and Tess gasped. Merritt guessed her hands were glowing green. Her energy surged through the ground and awakened the seeds. She felt them germinate, sprout, and stretch across the flowerbed until leaves curled around her wrists and fingers.

"Merlin's wings!" Tess whispered.

"What are you doing?" Lawrence demanded.

Merritt opened her eyes and withdrew her hands from the flowerbed, satisfaction blooming in her chest. She grinned at her handiwork. A tumult of plants rose from the once-barren earth, tangling around the oak's trunk, two feet tall in places. The brilliant yellow of primroses tangled with white fleabane and purple violets. Spiky crabgrass and delicate mugwort added texture to the mass of flowers, overlaying the delicate shapes of lambs quarters' leaves.

"Isn't it beautiful?" Merritt smiled.

"Beautiful? It's a disaster!" Lawrence waved his arms. "I asked you to grow primroses!"

"You didn't see them?" Merrit pointed. "There they are! There's plenty."

"Of course I see them, fool!" Lawrence yelled. "Lost in a huge bed of weeds!"

Merritt frowned. "Weeds, sir?"

"Plants that don't belong here. Don't you know what a weed is?" Lawrence pointed at the next oak tree, where a little knot of lonely primroses bloomed around its roots. "That was what I wanted, not this mess!"

Merritt blinked. "Oh." She didn't say that plants were meant to grow together or ask what made violets and fleabane less valuable than primroses. Lawrence didn't seem to be in the mood for questions.

"You told me you'd found me a gardener, Tess," Lawrence snapped.

Tess laughed. "Look at what she's done, Lawrence! Have you ever seen a para grow plants that quickly?" She spread her hands. "I'm a Lunar Fae, so I have creation magic, and I can barely keep my peace lily alive. You're looking at raw talent!"

"'Raw talent?'" Lawrence growled. "More like a disaster. I have to pull up all those weeds or clear the whole bed and start again!"

Merritt slowly rose. "Kill all the flowers? Why?"

"Because they're the wrong ones!" Lawrence threw his hands up. "Never mind. This isn't the job for you. Go away."

"Hey!" Tess protested before Merritt could say anything. "You can't do that to her, Lawrence. Give her a second chance. You asked her to grow primroses, and she did it. Really fast, I might add."

Lawrence scowled. "I don't have time for this."

"You don't?" Tess raised her eyebrows. "Should I remind you, Lawrence, that the Shajara Elf company who used to do the landscaping here only left because I begged Val to give you this job?"

The old badger fae shuffled his feet. "All right. One more chance. But if you screw this up," he told Merritt, "that's the end of it. Understand?"

Merritt nodded. "Yes, sir."

"I'll leave you guys to it." Tess patted Merritt's shoulder. "You've got this, girl!"

She strode away, and Merritt wished she hadn't.

"Clearly, you don't have control over your growing magic," Lawrence growled. He pawed through the bag of tools and pulled out a fork about six inches long. "Take this to that flowerbed on the other side of the park. It's got geraniums in it. Weed it."

"Weed it?" Merritt queried, taking the fork.

"Pull out the weeds. Make sure you get the roots," Lawrence ordered.

Merritt studied the fork. "Which plants are the weeds?"

"Any that aren't geraniums," Lawrence snapped. "Go over there and leave me alone. I have your mess to clean up here."

He pulled out a similar fork and attacked Merritt's flowerbed, ending the conversation.

***

Merritt's hat, coat, and sweater lay in a heap on the grass beside her. Her jeans felt too hot. She longed for a pair of shorts or a leaf dress like she'd worn in Fernwood Deep as she dug the fork into the geranium bed.

She had to admit the geraniums were lovely, their bright red and pink flowers providing a screen at the back of the park. Merritt dug beneath a sprig of clover and gently lifted it from the dirt. She shook the soil from its roots and laid it on a little pile beside her, careful not to crumple any of the leaves.

"I'll plant you somewhere," she murmured to the clover.

In response, a small pink flower blossomed at the tip of one stem.

Merritt smoothed the dirt over the patch she'd disturbed to pull out the clover. The pile of weeds beside her grew, and she moved a few feet to remove a patch of crabgrass from beneath a red geranium bush.

Though dirt smeared her hands, the city surrounded her. Across the street, vehicles rumbled, machines whined, and something clanged insistently. Humans and paras swarmed over machinery and scaffolding on a dusty residential site with half-built walls. A dwarf paced on the sidewalk, wearing a yellow helmet, watching everything.

Merritt hummed as she added the crabgrass to the pile of weeds. She waved her fingers over the heap, and green light seeped from her skin. The wilted plants perked up.

"I'll get you out of the sun," Merritt promised.

She looked at the flowerbed, admiring the clean dirt beneath the geraniums. It looked bare and ordinary to her, but it was tidy. She could see why Lawrence liked it.

Merritt smiled. He would be happy with her work. She was sure of it.

A car door's thud caught her attention. She looked up as the dwarf climbed a series of steps into the enormous blue vehicle—*pickup truck*, her training told her—parked by the construction site. He grabbed a water bottle from inside and stepped out, then drank.

"Hey, Ronnie!" someone yelled. "Need you to look at this."

The dwarf turned away, leaving the truck door open, and hurried toward another dwarf on the site.

Merritt hummed as she dug up more clover. Movement made her look up. A human trotted across the street, slinking like a fox trying to scavenge a piece of a wolf's kill. He wore grubby clothes and low-slung pants that wobbled as he moved, and a black mask covered his face. Merritt hadn't seen other humans wear clothes like that.

She lowered the fork, frowning, as the human ran over to the truck. He glanced around, but the dwarf named Ronnie was squinting at the scaffolding and didn't see the human.

Merritt's belly knotted. The human scrambled into the truck and reached under the steering wheel. He concentrated briefly, and the truck's engine sputtered to life.

Ronnie whipped around. "Hey! My truck!"

The human slammed the door, and the truck headed down the street toward Merritt.

"Hey!" Ronnie sprinted onto the sidewalk. "*Stop!*"

The human ignored him. Merritt knew that he *was* like a fox at a wolf kill—taking something that didn't belong to him.

She plunged through the geraniums and ran onto the sidewalk as the truck lurched toward her.

"Lady, look out!" Ronnie yelled.

Merritt lunged at the speeding vehicle and gripped the side mirror, then pushed off the running board and pulled herself beside the open window.

The thief screamed, "*Get off!*" He swung a wild punch.

Merritt easily avoided the puny blow and grabbed him by the collar. "Stop the truck," she commanded. "Give it back."

"*Get off me!*" the human shrieked, trying to punch her again.

Merritt grabbed his arm to stop him. The human wailed and yanked the steering wheel, making the truck swerve across the street. He yanked again, and the vehicle swerved back.

"Stop the truck now," Merritt ordered.

The thief grabbed her hand and tried to wrench it off his collar, but Merritt was done talking. She hauled him through the window and threw him across the street. His high-pitched shriek ended when he hit the asphalt.

Merritt let go of the truck and jumped off.

"My *truck*!" Ronnie screamed.

She turned toward him, smiling. The dwarf was ashen and horrified as he ran toward her.

"Noooooo!" he moaned.

Merritt turned.

Her training had neglected to inform her that vehicles didn't stop without a driver. The truck careened across the street and bucked onto the sidewalk, heading for the geraniums.

"Oh, shit," Merritt squeaked.

"Stop!" Ronnie squealed.

The truck ignored him. It plowed headlong into the geraniums, flower petals flying as it mowed through the plants, tires digging trenches in the soft dirt. The geraniums barely slowed it down. Horror pooled in Merritt's gut as the truck continued across the sloping lawn, ripping the grass, and trundled toward the oak trees.

"Oh, *shit*," Merritt mumbled.

"No!" Ronnie cried. "It'll hit the tree!"

The truck was going faster than it had been. Merritt concentrated, and the oak's roots responded. They rose, ripping gaps in the lawn, and stood up before the truck's speeding tires. It bumped and bucked over the first few, but creaked to a halt mere feet from the trunk.

"Shit! That was close." Ronnie broke into a run.

Merritt followed him through the destroyed geranium bed. They stopped by the truck's side, and Ronnie anxiously inspected it from front to back.

"Not a scratch on it." The dwarf sighed. "Thank Merlin for that. That was close!"

"Sorry." Merritt grimaced. "I didn't know it'd keep going."

"Hey, you got my truck back in one piece." Ronnie grinned. "You have nothing to apologize for."

"Hey, boss!" a dwarf yelled from the street. "We got him!" Two dwarves held the groaning thief by the arms. The human didn't look to be in any condition to run away.

"I'll call the police to pick him up." Ronnie pulled out his phone.

"*Merritt!*"

The roar came from deeper in the park. Lawrence marched across the grass toward the Leshbolg, his cheeks flushed and his sharp yellow teeth bared as he gaped at the ruined lawn and the smashed geraniums.

"*Get your ass over here!*" Lawrence bellowed.

Merritt looked to Ronnie for help, but he had walked away, phone to his ear.

"*What did you do?*" Lawrence roared when he reached her.

Merritt pointed. "I stopped a human from stealing his truck."

"*You destroyed half the park!*" Lawrence thundered. "*Look at this lawn! Look at my* geraniums! *What were you* thinking?"

Merritt clenched her fists. "I didn't know the truck would keep going. I was trying to help Ronnie, and I did."

"*Help Ronnie? I'm paying you to help me!*" Lawrence roared.

Merritt raised her chin, anger flaring. She wanted to yell that he hadn't paid her yet, but the words stuck in her throat. Merlin's words flashed through her mind. *Last chance.* She couldn't screw this up.

Her hands trembled as Lawrence yelled about his geraniums. The oak's roots shivered in response, and she struggled to stop them from moving. Dandelions grew and blossomed around their feet.

"*Hey!*"

Her head snapped up as Tess strode toward them, wings outspread, fists clenched. Wisps of smoke escaped between her fingers.

Lawrence stopped yelling and pressed his lips together in a bitter line.

"How dare you speak to her that way?" Tess demanded.

"Look at what your little friend did!" Lawrence gestured.

"What happened, Merritt?" Tess asked, folding her arms.

Ronnie rushed over before Merritt could respond. "Tess, there you are!" he cried. "I touched my panic amulet, but everything's okay, thanks to Merritt here." He reached up to lay a hand on Merritt's shoulder. "She stopped the thief who tried to steal my truck."

"I didn't know it wouldn't stop," Merritt mumbled. "It went through the geraniums. I thought it would hurt the tree, so I made the roots stop it."

"Ruining the lawn in the process." Lawrence snorted.

Tess' eyebrows shot up. "You fought the guy, Merritt?"

Merritt shuffled her feet.

"She was great. She threw him out of the truck," Ronnie enthused. He slapped Merritt's back. "I owe you a beer. Thanks."

Tess' gaze wandered to the crushed geraniums and the torn-up lawn. "Whoa."

"You single-handedly caused more trouble in my park than the average pack of werewolf cubs does in a day," Lawrence grumbled. "This won't work. Get out of my park and let me clean up your mess."

"Lawrence!" Tess protested.

"Don't talk to her like that," Ronnie snapped.

"It's okay," Merritt murmured. "I...I'd rather go home, Tess."

Tess surveyed the ruined park and the groundskeeper's irate face.

"Okay." She took Merritt's arm. "Let's go."

Ronnie cheerfully waved as Tess led her away, and Merritt waved back.

———

Merritt sat cross-legged on her bed, staring at the wall. Dirt still covered between her fingers and lay beneath her nails, and she rubbed it over her hands for comfort, seeking the tiny sparks of magic in every grain.

The morning's events replayed in her mind as they'd done a dozen times. The more she thought about it, the less easy it was to remember Ronnie's grin, and the more she saw the disgust on Lawrence's face.

I screwed up badly, and I've only been here for three days. Nice.

Merritt swallowed hard.

A knock on the door made her jump. "Merritt? It's Val. May I come in?"

Let in! Shadow whimpered and scratched the door.

Merritt straightened. "Sure." Panic lanced through her as the door swung open. She could already hear Val saying the words she'd heard before. "*It's not your fault, but this isn't working out. You have to go back to Merlin.*"

Shadow barged through the door and leaped across the room.

"*Shadow, no!*" Val yelled.

Shadow landed on the bed with enough force to slam it against the wall. Merritt squealed as he jumped on her, squashing her against the mattress, and licked her face.

Hello, Merritt! Hello! Hello! Hi! I love you! Shadow yipped.

"Dude, come on." Val grabbed his collar. "You're squishing her."

Sorry. Shadow jumped to the floor.

Merritt sat up, wiping dog drool off her face.

Val chuckled as she rumpled Shadow's ears. "I'd say I'm sorry, but you don't look upset."

"He's the best." Merritt touched his nose.

Val sat on the bed's edge. "Tess told me what happened today. Ronnie, too." She smiled. "Lawrence got pretty detailed on the phone."

Merritt's nervousness returned, knotting her belly. "Okay."

"I'd like to hear it from you," Val added.

Merritt bit her lip. "I crashed Ronnie's truck through Lawrence's flowers and messed up his lawn."

Val tilted her head. "Something tells me there's more to the story. That something is Ronnie, but I want *you* to tell me."

Merritt rubbed her neck. "I saw a human jump into Ronnie's truck and drive it off. Ronnie yelled, so I realized the human was stealing the truck. It wasn't right. That was Ronnie's. So I grabbed the human and threw him on the road. I thought the truck would stop, but it didn't, so I used the tree roots to stop it."

"Hold up." Val raised her eyebrows. "You threw the guy out of a moving truck?"

"The window was open. It wasn't hard." Merritt swallowed.

Val studied her as the seconds passed. Merritt wondered what Merlin would do with her. Send her to the OPMA's containment unit, maybe.

Val nodded. "I believe you."

Merritt cleared her throat. "When, um, when is Merlin coming to get me?"

Val frowned. "What?"

"I messed up." Merritt sighed. "When's he coming?"

"Oh, Merritt." Val laughed. "Did you think one ruined lawn would make me send you out of Little Avalon?"

Merritt stared at her.

"Girl, quit worrying." Val laid a hand on her shoulder. "You belong here. You proved that today."

"What?" Merritt squeaked.

"You protected a resident of Little Avalon." Val's eyes shone. "That tells me everything I need to know about who you are. We don't understand your powers yet, and, okay, Lawrence is spitting mad, but when is he not?" She laughed. "I'm not throwing you out, Merritt. I'm thanking you."

Merritt's jaw dropped.

"We'll find you another job." Val winked. "It'll be okay."

Tears of gratitude prickled Merritt's eyes. She blinked to hold them back. "No one's said that to me in a long time," she croaked. "*Thank you.*"

"It's all good." Val patted her shoulder. "We'll figure this out together."

Merritt exhaled. "Thanks, Val."

"Don't mention it. You're one of us now." Val grinned.

Shadow rested his head on her knee, tail slashing from side to side. Merritt ran her fingers through his thick coat and felt glorious relief spread through her tense body.

CHAPTER NINE

Tess had shown Merritt how to use the most magnificent invention she'd ever seen: tea bags. Instead of fiddling around with leaves, making tea was now breathtakingly simple. She poured hot water into the mug, grinning as the water turned rich reds and browns.

So simple. Merritt replaced the kettle on the stove and stirred the tea. *So elegant.* She squished the tea bag with her spoon, pressing more of the herbal goodness into the water, and sighed in contentment.

The door banged open. *"Hello!"* Tetra screamed.

Merritt squealed and jumped. The spoon and the tea bag sailed across the room and landed on the table with a splat.

"Did I scare you? Sorry." Tetra picked up the spoon, considered it for a second, and ate it.

"That was Tess' teaspoon," Merritt squeaked.

"She has too many. She won't miss it." Tetra perched cross-legged on the table. "Heard you kicked ass today."

Merritt clutched her mug in both hands. "Um, yes." She eyed the hall door, wondering if she could run for it.

"Sounded awesome. I hear that guy has a concussion." Tetra throatily chuckled. "Love it."

Merritt gulped.

"Val says you thought we'd throw you out for it," Tetra observed. She lifted the tea bag between her thumb and forefinger and inspected it.

Merritt cleared her throat. "Other places haven't been so...understanding."

"Val's cool about shit like that. Don't worry. I get it, though. Adjusting to Western civilization wasn't easy on me, either." Tetra ate the tea bag, then gagged. "Wow! That's hateful." She retched it up into her palm and delicately placed it on the table. "Disgusting."

Merritt had lost her appetite for her tea. She set the mug on the counter.

"You got any raw meat?" Tetra asked, sliding off the table. "Any still-beating hearts of your enemies?"

"What?" Merritt yelped.

Tetra opened the refrigerator. "Oooh, what's this?" She pulled out a plastic bag with red fluid. "Human blood? Gross, it's synthetic. I bet it's Damian's." She sniffed it. "Yuck. Smells like plastic. Is this milk going off?" Tetra shook the carton. "Ooh, yes it is. Perfect." She bit off the top and crunched it.

Merritt backed toward the door as the faerie slurped the souring milk. If she moved fast, she could escape.

"I know exactly what you need." Tetra whipped around, a mustache of congealing milk on her upper lip.

"You do?" Merritt managed.

"Yeah. This is a microwave, by the way." Tetra opened and shut the door with a clang. "You press buttons to make stuff hot. Like this." She hit several buttons at random, achieving only sad beeps. "Okay, this one's lame. Where was I? Oh...what you need."

Merritt stared in mute horror. She jumped when her vampire

housemate wandered past in the hallway, rubbing his rumpled hair and yawning.

"Get out of here, Damian," Tetra ordered.

Damian rolled his eyes, turned around, and left.

"What you need," Tetra announced, "is an outing to make you feel better."

"An outing?" Merritt quavered.

"Yeah. A night out. Booze, dancing. Something fun!" Tetra beamed, displaying pointed gray teeth. "Luckily for you, Antin's playing a gig at a human-owned bar nearby. He invited us both to come."

"With you and Antin," Merritt asked.

"Yeah!" Tetra grinned. "Don't worry, I don't bite. Okay, I do bite, but not friends. Well, I don't bite friends *hard*. Don't look at me like that. It's fine. Live a little!"

Merritt looked around for help as Tess wandered up the hall, book in hand. It was an ancient leather-bound tome with moonlight rising from the runes on its pages.

"Tess," Merritt squeaked.

"Hey, Tetra." Tess raised her head from her book. "What's up?"

"I want to take Merritt out for drinks at the bar where Antin's playing tonight. Wanna come?"

"No, thanks. I'm doing research." Tess waved the book. "High Magic Division stuff."

"*So* lame." Tetra rolled her eyes.

"You should go, Merritt." Tess smiled. "You'll enjoy it, and Tetra will keep you safe."

"See?" Tetra grinned.

Merritt stared at the faerie, realizing she had more friends in Little Avalon than she thought.

"Okay." She smiled.

"Yeah?" Tetra grabbed her arm. "Awesome! Let's go!"

A human arrived in a car to take Tetra and Merritt to the bar. Tetra called it an "Uber," though the name on the car's back was "Toyota." Merritt decided not to ask questions.

Tetra explained that Antin was already at the bar, playing his "gig." Merritt wondered if that was a musical instrument, but when they walked into the smoky space, the music resounding through it belonged to a Sylthana lyre. Neon lights gave the bar a twilight appearance. Humans were everywhere: crowded around the small tables, lining the bar on the other side, and paying very little attention to Antin. He sat in a back corner, lyre in hand, crooning into a fluffy thing that the training called a *microphone*.

The Sylthana ballad appeared to fall on deaf ears. No one looked at Antin. The humans seemed occupied with slurping their drinks.

"Tough crowd. Poor guy." Tetra grimaced. "This doesn't seem like his type of place."

"Why would he play here, then?" Merritt asked.

"Merlin only knows. Something about paying the bills. Let's get a drink." Tetra grabbed her arm.

Merritt realized that the population was overwhelmingly male. She and Tetra drew curious glances as they crossed the floor. Two open seats at the bar's far end allowed them to sit side by side. Merritt struggled to scramble onto the high stool and panted as she clutched the sticky bar for support.

A sweaty human leaned closer to Tetra. "Hey there, sweetie. Want a drink?" His words whistled through the gap where a front tooth used to be.

Tetra sweetly smiled. "Your blood in a cup made from your skull would be amazing."

The guy slowly eased away.

A human with many tattoos approached them. "What can I get you ladies?"

"Do you have any Bacchus mead?" Merritt asked.

"Ignore my friend. She's got voices in her head." Tetra smirked. "We'll have two Long Island iced teas."

"Sure." The tattooed human nodded and wandered off.

"Iced tea?" Merritt asked. "I thought this was a place for drinking alcohol."

Tetra patted her head. "There's plenty of alcohol."

Antin's tune changed. A few people looked up from their drinks, but most ignored him.

"Poor guy. This isn't his idea of a good time," Tetra observed.

The tattooed human returned with a pair of innocuous-looking glasses containing a brown fluid, ice, and lemon slices. Merritt politely thanked him and lifted her glass. The contents tasted like soda with a lemony kick, but she barely detected the alcohol.

Tetra downed hers. "Like it?"

"It's refreshing." Merritt tried to be polite. It wasn't her idea of an alcoholic drink, but she supposed she might feel a buzz after a few. It used to take two or even three glasses of spiced wine to make her tipsy in Wolf Glen.

"Give it a second." Tetra smirked. "It's more than that."

The concoction was tasty, and Merritt drank it swiftly. She hadn't drunk her tea at the apartment and was thirsty. When she finished the drink, Tetra ordered another one.

"These are really good!" Merritt announced, grabbing the second.

The tattooed human raised an eyebrow.

"I got her," Tetra assured him.

Merritt slurped the drink. "Everyone here is stupid," she trumpeted. "They should be clapping for Antin. His music's great."

Tetra smirked. "I know, right?"

The bar was still annoyingly applause-free several minutes later when Merritt finished her second drink. She raised her hands above her head, clapping. Her palms frequently missed each other. "Wooo! You're the best, Antin! Keep singing!"

Antin missed a beat as his eyes darted to Tetra. She grinned and gave him a double thumbs-up.

"*Another drink for my friend here, barkeep,*" she yelled.

"*Yeah!*" Merritt yelled. "*Another drink!*"

The bartender arched an eyebrow but brought another of the yummy things to Merritt anyway. She raised it to her lips, missed, and dripped it on the front of the cute sweater she'd chosen.

"Aw, man," she moaned. "My sweater."

"It's all good." Tetra paused. "Maybe you should go easy on those. They're not meant to be downed like that."

"But they're so good!" Merritt sipped. "So frereshing! Rerefshing." She concentrated. "Re-fresh-ing. That's it."

"Yeah, that's it." Tetra grinned.

Merritt belched. "I wanna dance!"

"That is an excellent idea," Tetra told her.

"Yeah!" Merritt planted her empty glass on the bar and slithered off the stool. She almost slithered to the floor, but Tetra grabbed her arm and kept her upright.

"Whoa!" the faerie exclaimed. "Easy there. You okay?"

"*Never been better!*" Merritt yelled and threw her arms in the air. "Woohoo, dancing!"

"That's...not dancing," Tetra observed.

Merritt wiggled her body, hands high, and noisily sang along to Antin's music. Although the song was in Sylthana Elven, which she did not speak, it sounded great to her. Antin gave Tetra a wide-eyed look over the microphone but kept singing.

"*Dancingggggg!*" Merritt sang and tried a flashy jump. She nearly fell on her ass.

Tetra grabbed her arm again. "I think you should sit down."

"But I'm having an *amazing* time!" Merritt grabbed Tetra by the cheeks and tried to focus on her eyes, which was difficult.

They drifted in and out, and there seemed to be four of them. "You are the best friend anyone has ever had. You were exactly right. I needed an outing to beer me chup. Cheer me up. Whatever." She giggled.

"Loving that color on you, but you're making flowers grow from the floor," Tetra pointed out.

Merritt looked down as a handful of snowdrops bloomed from the hardwood at her feet. She giggled. "Look at that! They're so cute!"

"You'll freak out the humans." Tetra glanced around, then trickled faerie dust on them. The flowers evaporated.

"Hey, my flowers!" Merritt complained.

"You can grow flowers when we get back to Little Avalon," Tetra promised. "Which should be soon, I think."

"No," Merritt protested. "I'm having too much fun. Oooh, do you know what we should do?"

Tetra smirked. "What?"

"We should make friends!" Merritt yelled.

She released Tetra and marched toward the bar. The floor tilted annoyingly under her feet, and she swung to the right to keep it from tipping more. She then crashed into the bar, knocking several stools over.

"Whoops." Merritt giggled. She staggered to the sweaty human with the gap in his teeth. "Hey! My name's Merritt. Let's be friends!"

The human glanced at Tetra and cleared his throat. "Leave me alone."

"But look what I have for you." Merritt opened her hand. "A pretty flower." She'd grown it from the bar's wood and plucked it when he wasn't looking.

The human sneered. "Bitch, I'm not in the mood. Leave."

"But we should be friends," Merritt wheedled, waving the flower under his nose. She lost her balance and reeled forward, almost ending up in his lap.

The human grunted, grabbed her shoulder, and pushed her away. "Seriously. You're looking for trouble."

Merritt reeled several steps before coming back, giggling. "No, *you're* looking for trouble."

"Merritt—" Tetra began.

Merritt playfully shoved the human back. He let out a yelp and sailed over the bar, landing in a clatter of broken glass on the other side.

"Oopsies!" Merritt chortled as she leaned over the bar. "You okay?"

The human lurched to his feet, fists clenched. *"Bitch!"* he roared and swung a wild punch at her face.

Merritt grabbed his hand, scowling. "That's not very nice."

"Let go of me, freak!" the human squealed.

"That's even worse." Merritt frowned. "Say you're sorry."

"Let me go!"

"Hey, bitch!" Another human stormed up to her and grabbed her arm.

"Nope. No touching my friend." Tetra kicked him in the balls.

The human bellowed in pain and doubled over. His friend twisted his fist from Merritt's grip and scrambled away, clutching his hand. Two more men charged, one aiming a roundhouse kick at Tetra, the other grabbing for Merritt's sweater. She slapped his hands aside and pushed him away. He stumbled, crashed into a row of bar stools, and tumbled to the floor amid splintering wood.

"Get them out of here!" the tattooed bartender yelped.

Tetra had a burly guy in a headlock. More males surrounded Merritt, yelling ugly words and throwing their fists. Merritt jumped aside since the punches flew with almost comical slowness. One human accidentally hit another in the face. The man wailed in agony and grabbed his attacker by the collar. A third pushed past them and seized Merritt by the arm.

"Don't touch me," Merritt protested.

"I'll take you down!" the guy thundered, aiming a kick at her shins.

Merritt effortlessly twisted her arm from his grasp, then swarmed onto his shoulders and locked her legs around his neck. He staggered, wheezing and clawing at her limbs, but she didn't let go until he crumpled to the floor.

"*Hey!*" a massive human in a black suit shouted, rushing toward Merritt.

Tetra seized her hand. "Time to go. You don't need to spend one of your first nights on Earth in a cell."

"He looks like fun!" Merritt protested, waving at the suit-wearing human. "Hi! Can we be friends?"

Antin appeared beside them, lyre case under his arm. He grabbed Merritt's other hand. "Run!"

They dodged the suit-wearer and hurried through the door. Merritt's feet felt a long way from the ground. She giggled as Tetra and Antin half-dragged and half-carried her to the corner.

"Don't come back!" the suit-wearer yelled, then slammed the door.

"Shit, Antin. Sorry." Tetra grimaced. "I didn't realize that Merritt is a lightweight. Three cocktails and she doesn't know which way is up anymore."

Merritt hiccupped. "I want another one. So yummy!"

"Should we get an Uber?" Antin asked.

A handful of humans burst from the bar. "Where'd they go?"

"Let's take the subway," Tetra suggested.

They swerved to one side and dragged Merritt down a flight of steps into a space full of noise, light, and people. In her blurred vision, it looked like a forest of humans.

"Again, sorry. I didn't mean to screw up your gig," Tetra muttered.

Antin laughed. "You saw that crowd. They were awful, and they already paid me. You did me a favor by getting me out of there."

"Thanks for saying that, dude." Tetra smiled. "You're cool. I like you."

"That's good to know," Antin teased.

"I think I'm gonna throw up," Merritt groaned.

They dragged her over to the nearest trash can, and she did.

Merritt had no idea how they reached her apartment. Now she lay full length on the kitchen table, groaning as the world spun around her. Tetra proudly stood beside her.

"Don't look at me like that," the faerie grumbled. "I didn't even drag her. I carried her."

"Tetra, what did you do?" Tess wailed. She touched Merritt's face. "Merritt, are you okay?"

Merritt sighed. "Want more iced tea."

"No more iced tea for you," Tetra chided.

"She looks half-dead!" Tess complained.

Merritt giggled.

"Oh, relax. I only fed her a few cocktails." Tetra grabbed Merritt's arms. "Let's get you to bed." She hoisted Merritt over her shoulder.

The Leshbolg chortled and burped.

"Why does she have broken glass in her hair?" Tess demanded.

Tetra dumped Merritt on the bed. "We got in a fight."

Merritt punched her arms in the air. "Best night ever!"

"Merlin's ass crack," Tess grumbled.

"Never seen it." Merritt chortled. "Probably saggy and wrinkly."

"Gross." Tess pulled her shoes off. "Okay, sleep it off, you wild creature."

To Merritt's surprise, she did.

The sunlight made Merritt's eyeballs feel like someone was stabbing them. She sat at the kitchen table, holding an ice pack to her head. Every sound drummed through her skull: the refrigerator's hum, music from their downstairs neighbor, and the thump of Tess' footsteps.

Is this what sleep does to you? Merritt wondered. She remembered sleeping when she was in the hospital, badly wounded and drugged to the eyeballs for pain. She didn't remember feeling *this* bad.

"Good morning, sunshine!" Tess trilled.

Merritt groaned. "Don't yell."

"That's the hangover talking." Tess snorted. "I'm guessing that whatever your people drank in Lichenvale didn't have the alcohol percentage of vodka, tequila, rum, and gin."

"I don't think that stuff was iced tea," Merritt whispered.

"It was not, but it sounds like you had a good time last night." Tess put a cup down with a deafening clang at Merritt's elbow. "Drink this. It'll help."

Merritt slowly raised her head, which weighed as much as the average anvil, and eyed the glass. It contained a clear liquid, but last night had taught Merritt not to judge a drink by its color.

"What is it?" she croaked.

"Fernwood dew. It'll help. Trust me," Tess insisted.

Merritt sipped and gasped in relief. Inexpressible freshness rushed through her blood, instantly cleansing the stuffy feeling in her head. She blinked the soreness from her eyes and chugged the rest of the liquid.

"You weren't kidding." Merritt drained the glass. "I feel like a new person!"

"Good." Tess grinned. "Seems you had a good night out."

"Tetra's not so scary." Merritt paused. "Wait. She's terrifying, but she's also genuinely caring. A dozen things could have gone wrong last night, but she didn't let anything happen to me."

"That's Tetra for you. You're never safer than with her around." Tess rose. "Cup of coffee?"

"Sounds great." Merritt nodded. "I can make it, though. You showed me how the plunger works."

Tess inclined her head. "Go ahead. I'll help if you need it."

Merritt rose, placed the kettle on the stove, and turned on the burner. "At least there's one thing I can do in this house." She bit her lip. "What are we doing today? May I look for another job?"

"I'll help you to set up a résumé. That's a document that tells prospective employers about you," Tess offered. "We can do it with pen and paper to start since I know you haven't used tech yet, and I'll type it up."

Merritt flushed. "Thanks, Tess. You do so much for me."

"I love helping kind and deserving paras like you." Tess beamed. "Truly."

"I would like to do more," Merritt added. "If there's anything I can do to help *you*, I will."

Tess tilted her head. "There's lots to do around the house and plenty of skills for you to learn in the process. Do you know how to cook?"

Merritt opened her mouth to say no but hesitated. A fragment of memory fluttered beneath her consciousness, tugging at her attention. She remembered a soft texture between her fingers, stretching, punching, rolling, and a delicious taste on the back of her tongue.

"Merritt?" Tess prompted. "You okay?"

Merritt realized she had a hand pressed to her head as if she could seize the memory and drag it into the light, but it fled at Tess' words.

"Sorry." She cleared her throat. "I...think I remembered something."

Tess straightened. "What?"

"I'm not sure. It was only a fragment." Merritt stared at her hands and flexed her fingers. She mimicked the motion from her memory, and her fingers performed it like they'd done it a thousand times before. "I think I baked before the Battle of Lichenvale."

"That's great!" Tess jumped up. "What did you bake?"

"I'm not sure. My brain doesn't remember, but it feels like my hands do." Merritt let them fall to her sides. "This is stupid. No one in my other placements trusted me to cook or bake."

"It's not stupid. Muscle memory is a thing," Tess told her.

"I haven't cooked or baked anything since I can remember." Merritt shrugged.

"No, but if you try, maybe the memory will come back to you." Tess flung the cabinets open. "Let's give it a shot. I have a bunch of ingredients here. I'm the designated cupcake maker for friends' birthdays."

Merritt made the coffee while Tess piled baking supplies on the table. They made Merritt's heart sink. She didn't recognize any of the boxes, packets, and bottles.

"I don't know, Tess." Merritt placed two coffee mugs on the table. "This feels like a stupid idea. I don't know what any of this is. I might make a huge mess."

"Bullshit. Don't call my idea stupid." Tess winked. "We can do this. If you make a mess, we will clean it up. No big deal."

"It all seems unfamiliar," Merritt hedged.

Tess studied her, then grabbed Merritt's hand. She reached into the nearest bag and trickled a handful of its contents onto Merritt's palm.

Merritt blinked. "Flour." She'd read the label on the bag without knowing what it was, but the texture was familiar. "That's flour."

"Yeah!" Tess beamed.

"I know what to do with this." Merritt grinned.

Tess placed a sizeable plastic bowl on the table. "Go for it."

Merritt measured the flour with her hands, flicking it into the bowl with practiced motions that became more confident as she continued. "There's something else." She paused. "Something that makes it get big and fluffy."

"Maybe yeast? Or baking soda or powder." Tess looked at the stuff on the table. "Are you making bread or a cake or something else?"

Merritt recalled the flavor from her memory. "I think it's bread."

"Then you'll want yeast." Tess retrieved a tiny packet and handed it to Merritt.

Merritt shook it. Dead, dry grains rolled around on the inside.

"I don't know," she murmured. "This doesn't seem right. We used to use something else." She flexed her fingers. "It was squishy and smelled weird."

Tess frowned. "Mmm. Sounds like sourdough starter."

"What's that?" Merritt asked.

"It's made by mixing flour and water and letting it ripen," Tess explained.

Merritt tilted her head. "That sounds familiar. I think that's what I'm looking for. Do you have any?"

"It's not something you buy from the store," Tess admitted, "but I'm sure somebody in Little Avalon has a starter to share." She grabbed her coat. "Let's find out!"

Merritt cleaned herself up, and they strode into a dry, chilly morning with a clear sky and pale sunshine. "Val won't have any," Tess murmured. "She doesn't have the time for that. Liam tried, but his flopped after a day." She turned. "Let's try Stonehold Two. I think Kenna bakes."

She crossed the street to the house beside Liam's and knocked. A Copper Dwarf answered the door, silver streaks in her fox-red hair. Merritt remembered her from the potions store Tess had taken her to the other day.

"Hi, Kenna." Merritt waved.

"Merritt! Good to see you again. Morning, Tess." Kenna beamed.

"We have an odd request." Tess smiled. "Do you have any sourdough starter?"

"Bless your heart, I don't." Kenna shook her head. "The last thing I want to do after a day of brewing potions is baking. Sorry."

"No worries." Tess smiled. "We'll try somebody else."

"Wait a second." Kenna went back into the apartment and returned a few moments later, carrying a crystal bottle with a wax-sealed stopper. "This is for you, Merritt."

"Thank you!" Merritt took it. "What is it?"

"Fernwood dew." Kenna inclined her head. "Judging by how loud you were singing last night, you'll need it."

Merritt blushed to the hairline but thanked Kenna and tucked the bottle into her pocket.

"Merlin's beard," Tess muttered as they walked away. "That's, like, a hundred dollars' worth of Fernwood dew. I think you're Kenna's favorite."

Merritt didn't know how much a hundred dollars was, but she assumed it was a lot.

"Hmm, who shall we try next?" Tess wondered. "Maybe Gertie does. She's a teacher at Little Avalon Academy. She seems like the type."

She crossed the street to Stonehold Four and knocked. A young werewolf with tousled hair and bright eyes opened the door several minutes later, breathless. He wore a thick coat and a scarf pulled up to his chin.

"Oh, hey, Rory." Tess smiled. "Is Gertie home?"

"Hi, Tess. She went out to get pizza." Rory grinned. "Can you believe it? Pizza! I've had it twice this week!"

Tess tilted her head. "I'm glad you're spending your weekends with her instead of being stuck at school."

"Gertie rocks. So do you," Rory informed her.

"Do you know if Gertie has any sourdough starter we can borrow?" Tess asked.

Rory shook his head. "I don't think so, but I heard Mrs. Ricci talking about sourdough starter the other day. She went on and on about it. I bet she has some."

"Cool." Tess bumped Rory's fist. "Thanks."

"You're welcome. Bye, Tess. Bye, Tess' friend." Rory shut the door.

"Nice kid," Tess murmured, leading Merritt to another apartment building. "He's a war orphan who used to hide out in Little Avalon. Val and I got him into school, and he's shaping up well. We both feel bad that he ended up on the streets here and nobody knew."

"On the streets?" Merritt echoed. "He had no home?"

Tess shook her head. "He was alone with his six little siblings."

"Wow." Merritt blinked. "I guess I'm not the only one who lost everything in the war."

"It'll leave scars on our society for generations, but let's not go into the doom and gloom. We're here for sourdough starter!" Tess grinned. "We'll have to go upstairs to Mrs. Ricci's apartment. She's not mobile anymore."

They climbed two flights to a landing identical to theirs. The orc who answered the door wore a housecoat and a string of pearls. She blinked at Merritt over her half-moon glasses and beamed, displaying yellowed tusks.

"Hello, dear," she croaked. "You must be the new girl. Everyone's talking about you."

"They are?" Merritt squeaked.

"All good things, dear. All good things." Mrs. Ricci patted her arm. "Would you girls like a cup of tea?"

"That sounds wonderful," Tess told her.

Mrs. Ricci led them into a living room that brought a spate of new words to Merritt's mind from the training orb: *chintz, doilies, china, knickknacks, lace, crochet,* and *paisley.* She perched on an overstuffed armchair while Mrs. Ricci fussed in the kitchen and prattled about her children, whose baby photos were all over the room, although the old orc said that most were several hundred years old with families of their own.

"Twelve grandbabies," Mrs. Ricci told them, beaming, as she returned with a teapot on a pewter tray. "Twelve of them! All perfect, of course. Most moved to Avalon after the war, but I couldn't leave the city."

Loneliness draped the old woman like a cloak, but Merritt watched it lighten as she and Tess politely listened to her stories about her children, occasionally mixing up their names, and drank the truly excellent tea she brewed.

"Do you like it, dear?" Mrs. Ricci asked, watching as Merritt closed her eyes in pleasure as she sipped.

"It's the best I've ever had," Merritt admitted.

"I'll bring you a packet. My dear Alphonso brings it for me when he visits from the Sylthana Islands. They grow the most wonderful tea there." Mrs. Ricci painfully creaked to her feet.

"Actually, Mrs. Ricci, we wanted to ask you something else," Tess chipped in.

"What's that, dear?" Mrs. Ricci asked.

"It's a big favor," Merritt confessed, "but I'm looking for sourdough starter. Rory mentioned you might have some?"

Mrs. Ricci's wrinkled face produced a radiant smile. "Of course I have some! I love sourdough! I made a rosemary and olive loaf this morning. Come, come. You have to taste it and tell me what you think."

Tess and Merritt dutifully followed the orc into a spotless kitchen cluttered with figurines, tapestries, and pictures of chickens. The dishtowel hanging by the sink featured embroidered chickens, the egg cups were chicken-shaped, and the bread tin from which Mrs. Ricci retrieved the loaf was decorated with a pattern of alternating chicks and eggs.

"You like chickens, Mrs. Ricci?" Merritt asked.

"Dreadful things. They pecked my toenails when I was a girl

on my grandfather's farm." Mrs. Ricci sliced the loaf. "Here, here. Taste it."

Tess and Merritt made encouraging noises, which wasn't easy since Mrs. Ricci's bread was the texture of a brick and tasted like being choked to death with olives.

"Isn't it wonderful?" Mrs. Ricci beamed.

"Amazing," Tess rasped.

"The best I've tasted," Merritt spluttered.

The orc's eyes shone. "You're such darlings. Did you want to make your own sourdough, Merritt, dear?"

"Yes." Merritt paused. "I think so."

"I'll share my best recipes," Mrs. Ricci enthused.

She fetched a glass jar from the top of the fridge, and Merritt recognized the substance within. She had no name for it, but she knew it from her memory. It would be soft and filled with bubbles when she touched it. It was goopy and a creamy light brown, but Merritt sensed the magic within.

"*Oooh, yes!*" she cried, holding out her hands. "That's it. That's what I need!"

Mrs. Ricci gave her the jar. "It's good to see young people sharing a passion for sourdough."

They left ten minutes later with half a loaf of the inedible bread, an armful of handwritten recipes, and the jar of starter proudly clutched in Merritt's hands.

"Everyone here is so nice." She held the jar up to the light, admiring the bubbles within.

"They're the best," Tess agreed as they reached their building. "Let's bake bread!"

CHAPTER TEN

The recipe Tess found on her phone—they'd agreed not to try Mrs. Ricci's recipes after Tetra almost choked on the rosemary and olive bread—led them through steps that seemed easy enough. Merritt's vague memories swirled to life as Tess read the instructions, and she added flour, water, salt, and oil to a few ounces of the starter. She couldn't remember any measurements except for the handfuls of flour, which Tess made her weigh on a scale, but the shaggy ball of dough felt familiar.

They had another cup of coffee while the dough rested.

"This could take a while," Tess admitted, scrolling through the recipe. "The dough has to double after we roll it into a ball. It says that could take as much as twelve hours in winter."

Merritt checked the kitchen clock. "We'll be baking bread at eleven tonight, I guess."

"That's cool. Midnight baking sounds fun." Tess grinned. "That's our thirty minutes. Now you have to make it into a ball. Don't knead it, though. Just shape it."

Merritt uncovered the bowl and smiled at the shaggy mess within. She plunged her fingers around its edges and squished it together, the texture familiar. Her hands knew what to do, though her mind did not. They formed the dough into a ball and tipped it into a clean, oiled bowl on the table.

"Whoa." Tess blinked. "Looks like you've done that before."

"I have," Merritt murmured, staring at the ball.

"Next, we cover it and leave it alone until it doubles. I—" Tess stopped. "What are you doing?"

Merritt didn't know, but it felt right. She wrapped her hands around the bowl and lifted it. The magic in her blood felt different from the energy that grew the flowers in the park. This was a gentle, warm glow, like the first rays of the rising sun instead of coursing lightning.

Tess gasped. "Merritt, something's happening!"

Merritt knew. The starter responded to her magic, pulsing with life. Activity hummed within the bowl, loud in her senses. The yeast multiplied by a factor of a hundred at the touch of her magic energy. Gas flowed into the dough, swelling it, and the tiny organisms within seemed to sing with happiness.

Merritt opened her eyes and replaced the bowl on the table. The dough had almost doubled, now fat and fluffy.

"*Look at that!*" Tess cried. "It's exactly like the video says it should be." She held up her phone.

Merritt didn't look at the screen. She kept her eyes on the dough, knowing in her soul that it was right. "I love it," she murmured. "Now I have to shape it."

"The recipe says to—" Tess began.

Merritt dusted flour on one side of the wooden cutting board Tess had provided but left the other side clean. The dough sagged as she scooped it from the bowl, dropped it on the floured side, then stretched and folded it. Her hands lost themselves in the familiar motion as she worked the dough and felt its wonderful, smooth texture between her fingers. She used no magic energy for this part, but as she folded and kneaded and squeezed the dough, it felt as though her hands were the best magic of all.

She rotated it several times on the non-floured side and ended with a round ball of smooth dough.

"Amazing," Tess whispered.

"It needs to rise again." Merritt didn't know how she knew, but she did. "For about half an hour. Then I...I'll need leaves." She frowned. "Big ones like this." She held her hands several inches apart.

"Big leaves?" Tess inquired. "What for?"

"I have to wrap the dough in them. I don't know why, but I remember it from before the Battle of Lichenvale," Merritt murmured.

Tess' eyes widened. "Are your memories getting stronger?"

"They are," Merritt confirmed.

"We'll do whatever we need to do to keep them coming." Tess scrambled to the fridge and pawed through it. "Here, I have cabbage!" She held them up. "Will it work?"

Merritt sniffed the head that Tess gave her and slowly nodded. "Yes, it'll work."

She gently peeled the leaves from the head and washed them while the dough rose for the second time. Tess turned the oven on, and Merritt sipped a cup of tea while the thirty minutes passed. After that, Merritt laid the cabbage leaves on the table and delicately scooped the dough into them.

"Won't it taste like cabbage?" Tess asked.

"I don't know. I have to do something to the leaves, though." Merritt frowned as she enclosed the dough in the leaves. "I vaguely remember..."

"Just try," Tess encouraged her.

Merritt exhaled. She wrapped her hands around the leaf-wrapped dough and bowed her head. The leaves responded to her magic, cooling and strengthening, their cells tightening as her energy touched them.

"What did you do?" Tess asked, wide-eyed. Pale green streaks now ran through the deep-green cabbage leaves.

"I have no idea," Merritt admitted, "but I want to put it in the oven."

"Won't the leaves burn?" Tess asked.

They eyed the magic-streaked leaves.

"I don't know." Merritt grimaced.

"Let's try." Tess opened the oven.

Merritt slid the loaf onto a sheet pan Tess had lined with parchment paper. Tess showed her where to place it in the oven, and Merritt winced at the heat. "Can we turn it down a little?"

"Whatever your instincts tell you." Tess turned the knob.

"There. I think that's right." Merritt shut the door.

"Now what?" Tess asked.

"Now we wait," Merrit murmured.

She sat cross-legged in front of the glass door and stared intently at the dough. It swelled in its leaf wrappings, but they didn't burn. The edges just curled as they heated.

"How long do you bake it?" Tess asked. "The recipe says an hour, but the recipe didn't include making it rise by magic or cabbage leaves."

"It's not ready yet." Merritt rested her elbows on her knees and gazed at the baking bread.

Tess didn't ask questions. Merritt kept her eyes on the oven, and a delicious scent filled the kitchen.

"I feel like it's going to be cabbage-y," Tess muttered.

"Shhh." Merritt raised her head. "It's ready."

Tess handed Merritt a pair of oven mitts, and the Leshbolg gently drew the pan from the oven. She placed it on the granite countertop, and Tess hovered close by as she grabbed a knife and gently pried the leaves away from the dough.

A ball of fragrant steam rose into the air, filling the room with the heady aroma of freshly baked bread. Merritt smiled at a pale, perfectly cooked loaf, smoothly split where she'd scored it.

"Oh, wow. Look at that." Tess leaned closer. "It's like it steamed in the leaves."

"No crust." Merritt gently tapped the outside. "Perfectly soft all over."

"I know people who love the crust, but that fluffy white inside is the best part, hands down," Tess declared.

"Let's cut it!" Merritt gripped the bread knife.

She tossed the crunchy cabbage leaves in the trash and sliced the bread, creating perfectly white sheets filled with bubbles.

"I've never seen anything like it," Tess whispered. "Do you know what it's called?"

The name came to Merritt like a thunderbolt. "We called it bellyfill. As in, you fill your belly with it. I think it is a traditional Leshbolg bread," she slowly added.

"I've certainly never heard of anyone baking it like you did. Do you know what you did to the cabbage leaves to keep them from burning?" Tess asked.

Merritt shook her head. "I hardly know how I made it, but I can make it again. My hands remember."

"Look at you, Merritt." Tess squeezed her arm. "A few hours ago, no one in the world knew how to make Leshbolg bellyfill. Now we do. Paras will taste your people's food again because you remembered."

A knot tightened in Merritt's throat.

"Do we have butter with it?" Tess asked.

Merritt nodded. "Lots of butter."

Tess spread a generous layer on the first slice, broke it in two, and gave Merritt one soft, squishy half. The flavor made tears well in her eyes when she bit into the bread. Emotions crowded her, too thick to sort out. All she knew was that she had eaten bellyfill many times.

"Merlin's wings, Merritt." Tess groaned with pleasure. "I've never tasted anything like this."

"Is it good?" Merritt asked, blinking her tears away.

"It's incredible!" Tess finished her slice. "We need to show this to everyone. Val texted me a few minutes ago asking if I could join the team at her house for a meeting about next week's security contracts. Why don't we bring this and give everyone a piece?"

Merritt's eyes widened. "Do you think they'll like it?"

"They'll adore it." Tess beamed.

"Okay!" Merritt laughed. "Let's do it."

They arrived at Lillie House a few minutes later, Merritt proudly carrying the bellyfill in a basket. They passed through the garage to the back door. Genevieve honked as Merritt strode by, and Merritt paused to pat the Mustang's roof.

Shadow greeted them at the door with a wagging tail. *Merritt hi! Smell good!*

"Not for you, Shadow." Tess bopped him on the nose with a finger.

Smell good! Shadow snuffled the basket.

"Maybe later." Merritt held the basket out of his reach, no mean feat with her short frame.

"I smell food!" Tetra bounded from the kitchen, flexing her fingers.

"It's not *all* for you, Tetra," Tess scolded.

"Is that fresh bread?" Val called.

Shadow and Tess led Merritt into the kitchen. Liam and Val were sitting at the table with coffee. Liam had his large rectangular thing—*tablet*—propped on the table before him.

"I made Leshbolg bellyfill." Merrit placed the basket on the table. "Tess thought you'd like to taste it. Help yourselves."

"I'll never say no to carbs." Val reached for a buttered slice.

Liam nibbled a corner, then groaned in delight and shoved the whole thing into his mouth. His cheeks puffed out like a chipmunk's. "Wow!"

"Don't talk with your mouth full," Tetra protested, spraying crumbs.

"This is *so* good." Val took a second piece. "Wow, Merritt. What did you call this?"

"Bellyfill." Merritt raised her chin, smiling. "It's Leshbolg bread."

"It's fantastic. Are you taking orders?" Val asked.

Merritt laughed.

"Girl, I'm serious." Val waved the slice, splattering the table with melted butter. "I'll buy this all the time."

"I'll make another loaf for you," Merritt promised. Warmth spread through her chest as everyone nodded and agreed, enjoying what she had made. She had brought something good into Little Avalon, she realized. Something that people liked.

"Awesome." Val sucked butter from her fingers. "Save me a slice, everybody. Merritt, I have something for you."

She rose, Shadow at her heels, and led Merritt through the dining room to a short flight of stairs going down to a basement. The muscular dwarf unlocked the door with a mysterious panel she only had to touch. It swung open, revealing a wonderland of metalworking.

The earth-walled cavern beneath Val's home was far more extensive than her house's ground floor. Its rich magic rippled over Merritt's skin like harmless fire. A workbench stood on her left, with designs on parchment above it, and numerous anvils ranged across the floor. Racks of tools and weapons were everywhere.

The wall opposite the workbench held dozens of pigeonholes, gemstones gleaming in many of them. A mighty forge occupied the far wall. Runes glowed on its chimney and the flames in its heart were blue, orange, and yellow.

"Cool, right?" Val grinned at Merritt's expression.

"It's amazing!" Merritt gushed. "So many runes!"

"Yeah. Rune magic is my thing." Val crossed the floor to the workbench. Shadow followed her and collapsed into a comfortable dog bed under it with a habitual sigh. Merritt had the impression he had spent many hours in that bed. "I made you a little something."

"Tess said you made jewelry." Merritt gaped at the weapons hanging near her. "I didn't realize you were a smith, too."

"I'm a dwarf, remember?" Val chuckled. "I make jewelry for a living, but many of my pieces are weapons or protective devices, too. Like this." She held up her left arm, displaying a sturdy round disc of an unfamiliar metal that appeared to be copper but caught the light in strange ways. When Val shook her arm, scales unfolded from the disc and formed a huge shield.

"Whoa!" Merritt jumped. "I love that!"

Val shook her arm again, making the shield fold up. She lifted a shining object from the workbench. "This is for you."

Merritt held her hands out and gasped at the beautiful thing Val dropped into them. She tilted it to catch the forge's light. The amulet filled the palm of her hand. It gleamed like polished steel, shaped like a delicate leaf, the tip curling as though Val had composed it of plant matter instead of metal. Tiny emeralds encrusted the edges and trapped the light in their deep green hearts. Jets of the same jewel shot through it in fine patterns like veins.

"Wow," Merritt whispered. "It's gorgeous."

"It's more than that." Val pointed. "See those runes?"

There were three down the amulet's length. Merritt didn't recognize their jagged shapes. Runes were younger and more brutal magic than the woodland types she'd encountered so far.

Val named the runes one by one. "*Muffle, amplify,* and *contact.*" She smiled. "I didn't always know I was a Warrior of the Red Bear. When my powers came in, they were hard to control. I once threw a caber through the window of our local fortress. Everyone was pissed."

Merritt thought about the ruined lawn in the park. "I know how that feels."

"I get that." Val paused. "That was why I made this for you. It will help you control your powers and use them to their full potential."

"How does it work?" Merritt asked.

"It's calibrated to your magical signature, so no one else can activate it," Val explained. "To use one of its functions, press on the relevant rune. Try touching the *contact* one." She placed her phone on the workbench.

Merritt poked it. Val's phone lit up and buzzed.

"See?" Val touched the phone, silencing it. "When you touch *contact*, it'll call me. If you talk, I can hear you. That's a clever piece of thaumatech Liam and Qenzi helped me with."

Merritt made a mental note to thank them. "That's fantastic. Thanks."

"These other two runes relate to your power. *Amplify* strengthens any magic it touches," Val continued.

Merritt made another mental note never, ever to touch *amplify*.

"Finally, there's *muffle*. That could come in handy if you struggle to control your powers," Val added. "When you touch it, your powers will lessen. Both only last for a few minutes. Then they wear off, and you can switch between them at will. For example, say you're training your powers, and you touch *amplify*. If your powers feel too intense, touch *muffle*, and they'll calm down."

"This is incredible, Val." Merritt inclined her head. "Thank you."

"No worries." Val smiled. "I'm here to help."

Merritt thought about the amulet that had come with her from Lichenvale. It lay at the bottom of her underwear drawer now, but Val might be able to tell her more about it. The thought made her belly tighten. She decided against asking just now.

Val rose. "We need another cup of coffee and more of that excellent bread."

Merritt paced.

She'd mastered most of her apartment. She'd set the heat to a comfortable level, had a fresh cup of tea on the nightstand, and had taken a luxurious bath with candles that smelled nice. The amulet bumped her chest from the chain around her neck as she crossed the room again, her feet protesting the dead feeling of the floor.

They longed for green grass and rich earth.

I could go to the park, Merritt told herself, but she quailed at the thought of the buildings surrounding the green space. She needed the place of trees. The memory of its vast lawns and the wide river made her limbs cramp with longing.

Merritt flopped onto the couch and turned on the TV. When she saw the reporter standing in the place of trees again, it felt like a sign.

"There has been a recent rise in violent crime at Brooklyn Bridge Park." The reporter earnestly stared from the screen. "Two suspects reportedly approached the victim near the riverfront armed with knives and demanded their valuables. When the victim attempted to resist, they received four stab wounds before the suspects fled. The victim remains in critical condition."

Merritt bared her teeth. Someone had stabbed an innocent person in Brooklyn Bridge Park? She thought about Neven, and her fists clenched.

"Security camera footage identifies one of the suspects as Jimmy Barton, a local gang member," the reporter continued.

An image appeared on the screen depicting a sour-faced human in front of a white wall with numbers on it. The human had black stubble, saggy jowls, and baleful eyes glaring from beneath heavy lids.

"Jimmy Barton," Merritt whispered.

She turned off the TV, her mind made up, and pulled on her cloak. In minutes, she was jogging down the street toward the river. She didn't stay on the sidewalk for long but darted down the first alley and climbed to the first roof.

A gentle drizzle fell as Merritt raced across Brooklyn's roofs, heading for the string of lights on the bridge in the distance. Her cloak rippled over her shoulders, and the cool rain sent fresh strength to her limbs. Laughter trickled from her, unstoppable, as she raced to her destination.

She was not even breathing hard when she trotted down the fire escape and dropped onto the street. The rain had cleansed the world of the last slush and snow. The earth felt warm and wide awake when Merritt ran into the park. The tree she'd previously touched had a thick crop of green leaves. Merritt blew it a kiss, prompting several new leaves to grow and unfurl as she jogged past it. Though she longed to spread herself across the dirt and feel the plants awakening within, she had work to do.

The open space and the presence of the trees strengthened her magic. She stopped beneath a tremendous oak and scanned the footpaths, thinking of Jimmy Barton's jowly face.

She'd have to move fast to find him before dawn, if he was even here tonight. A nasty itch between her shoulder blades told her all was not well in the place of trees. Finding him was a slim chance, but Merritt would take it.

She closed her eyes and summoned her magic. The transformation felt awkward as her body shrank, her bones turning hollow and feathers sprouting from her skin. When Merritt, now a sparrow, opened her eyes and spread her wings, dizzy freedom flooded her senses. She flitted into the air and winged between the tree's branches, chirping in laughter, her widespread tail balancing every swoop and turn.

Merritt's delicate wings carried her higher than the trees. She flitted across the park, tilting her head left and right as she scanned the ground. Sparrows had keen vision. A few humans wandered through the park. She spotted the security people from last time, and several sleeping on the benches or jogging down the paths, wearing earphones like Tess sometimes did.

All seemed well at first, but the uneasy feeling remained. She perched on a streetlight to rest her wings and chirped with pleasure at the sight of a dog trotting along on the end of a long leash. She was a scruffy, wire-haired creature no bigger than a fox, but her tail wagged with pleasure as her twitching nose investigated the ground. Her human strolled behind her, gazing at the river, enjoying himself.

Merritt would have smiled if she'd had lips. It was good to see a responsible dog taking her pet human for a walk to keep him from getting angsty and depressed.

Movement caught Merritt's sharp eye, and she tilted her head. She chirped when she spotted a heavy silhouette creeping through the shadows behind the dog and her human. The man darted behind a tree, looked left and right, and pulled something from his pocket. The light glinted on a sinister blocky object, and the bad human glanced around, his face out of the shadows for a brief moment.

Merritt gasped. It was Jimmy Barton. He'd come back to the park for another victim after all, and though she didn't recognize the thing in his hands, her orb training identified it. *Gun: a deadly weapon.*

With both humans distracted, Merritt fluttered to the ground and transformed. She threw her hood back and yelled, *"Hey! You! Stop!"*

The dog bayed, and her human spun, clinging to her leash. *"Shit!"* the human yelped. "Where did you come from?"

Barton burst from behind the tree, holding out the gun. The dog's human shouted and staggered back, hauling the dog closer.

"Phone and jewelry!" Barton yelled. "Now!"

"I don't have a phone, and if I did, I wouldn't give it to you," Merritt snapped. "You're an asshole."

The dog's human tried to back away but struggled to hold on to the irate dog, who reared on her hind legs and barked.

"I see that pretty thing on your neck, you stupid bitch," Barton growled. "Give it to me!"

"Why would I do that?" Merritt demanded, hands on her hips. "You need to stop hurting people."

"Give it to me or I'll shoot you. Don't you see this?" Barton gestured with the gun.

Merritt stepped closer. "Put the weapon down."

"*Lady, run!*" the dog's human cried. "*It's not worth it. Get out of here!*"

Merritt came a step closer, relishing the terror in Barton's eyes. "Put it down," she growled.

Barton swung the weapon's black muzzle away from her face and pointed it at her arm. White light flashed from the gun, and something slammed into her right arm, spinning her around. She gasped as pain blossomed in the muscle. The force threw her to one knee. She clutched her wounded arm, and the dog's barking became a roar of hysterical fury.

"Cassie!" the human wailed. "No!"

Merritt raised her head, breathing through the pain. Barton wheeled away from her and tried to flee, but the wire-haired dog leaped in front of him, teeth flashing. He pointed the gun at her.

He'd shoot her, as he'd shot Merritt.

She clawed at the amulet, fumbling for the *contact* rune that would summon Val to her aid. Her fingertips slid across its surface and hit one of the runes. Was it the middle one, *amplify*, or *contact* at the bottom?

There was no time to wonder.

"Cassie!" the dog's human sobbed.

Barton's finger tightened on the trigger, and Merritt lurched upright. The sound that tore from her throat was unlike any she'd uttered before. It sounded like a hurricane wind in a thick forest or a rushing waterfall plunging over rocks—inhuman and unstoppable.

Barton's head snapped to Merritt as she strode toward him, hands balled into fists. While he was distracted, Cassie lunged. The dog's jaws snapped shut on Barton's arm, and he shrieked in pain and fury. The gun flashed as he raised it over his head, then smashed it into the dog's shoulder.

Cassie's yelp of agony resounded through Merritt's soul.

"Leave her alone!" Merritt roared. As she spoke, her voice deepened, becoming fuller and more husky.

Before she knew what she was doing, Merritt transformed.

There was no gradual lengthening of her limbs or teeth. The thing Merritt changed into came from inside her. She was not a Leshbolg pretending to be a fox. She was a Leshbolg taking her true form, and it happened in a heartbeat.

One moment, Merritt, a five-foot-two female, stood on the path. The next, Merritt towered over Barton and the dog's human, almost the height of the smaller trees. Bark had replaced her skin and wood her bones, but she had no roots. Merritt moved forward on massive feet and raised fists like gnarled tree burls.

Merritt realized that another profound change had taken place. He was no longer female. In this form, he was undeniably and unequivocally male. *"I said, leave the dog alone!"*

Cassie threw her nose up and howled in approval.

Barton stumbled backward, screamed, and fired again and again. Projectiles slammed into Merritt's arms and torso, but they couldn't penetrate the thick bark. Splinters puffed from his body as he strode toward the would-be mugger, that roar of ancient fury escaping his mouth. Barton scrambled backward in terror.

The dog's human seized Cassie's lead. *"Come on, girl!"* They bolted down the path to safety.

Barton fired another shot into Merritt's shoulder. "Get away from me, freak!"

Merritt raised his fist. A last shot ricocheted from his knuckles before he struck. The blow crashed into Barton's chest with the force of a tornado. His scream ended in a breathless grunt, and the impact threw him through the air like a rag doll. He smashed into a tree so hard that it shuddered, and he hit the ground, limp and motionless.

Merritt roared again. In the distance, Cassie bayed in response.

Merritt raised his head and felt the wind tangle in the thick creepers and lichen that poured like hair from his scalp. A delicious strength rushed through him. He could do anything, he realized. Anything at all.

"It came from over there!" a human shouted.

Merritt hesitated. *Humans!*

The security guards from a few nights ago rounded the turn, breathing hard, their flashlights playing over the scene. They found no juggernaut. Merritt was a sparrow again, flitting away from the fight with her little heart hammering between her fragile ribs.

CHAPTER ELEVEN

Merritt's magic weakened half a block from Little Avalon. She tumbled to the ground in an alley, breathing hard, feathers and leaves sticking to her hair as she resumed her humanoid shape.

Shit, shit, shit! What had happened back there?

Merritt coughed as she stumbled out of the alley and sprinted toward Little Avalon. Her limbs felt like overcooked noodles. Exhaustion clogged her eyes, an intense burning sensation she'd last felt in the hospital in Avalon Town.

Her lungs ached as she jogged up the street to her building. She slapped dirt out of her hair as she ran up the stairs, panting, and shoved the door open.

Merritt froze. The vampire stood by the counter, milk bottle in hand, stirring a mug of coffee.

Damian turned. "Hello, Merritt." He focused on her arm, and his eyes widened. "Merlin's puckered asshole! What happened to you?"

Merritt glanced at her arm. An ugly black and purple bruise extended over her bicep, its yellowish epicenter marking the place where the bullet had struck her.

"What have you been doing?" Damian demanded.

Revealing magic to humans. Merritt didn't know what would happen if anyone realized she'd done that, but it would be bad. Panic gripped her, and she bolted across the kitchen for her room.

"Hey!" Damian yelled. "I'm talking to you!"

Merritt scampered into her room and slammed the door.

"Where are you going?" Damian demanded from the hall. "C'mon, Merritt. Open the door. What happened to you?"

Merritt threw off her cloak, still breathing hard.

Damian knocked. "Merritt, come on. Tell me what's going on!"

"Hey!" Tess barked.

Her tone held an edge Merritt hadn't heard before. She huddled under the blankets, holding her breath to listen to the argument in the hallway.

"What are you doing?" Tess demanded.

"Don't take that tone with me," Damian grumbled. "I'm trying to help."

"You are? It looks like you're scaring the living daylights out of Merritt," Tess snapped.

"She won't tell me where she's been," Damian growled.

"Why should she? She can do what she wants. Back off!" Tess barked.

Damian snorted. "Fine, whatever. I don't want to be part of this drama anyway." His footsteps receded into the kitchen.

Tess gently knocked. "Merritt? You okay in there?"

Merritt just looked at the door, not wanting to answer.

Tess knocked again. "Merritt? You good?"

"I'm fine!" Merritt called. "I'm fine. Come in." She grabbed a sweater and yanked it over her head to hide the bruise on her arm.

Tess popped her head around the door. "Sorry about Damian. He gets a little intense, but he usually means well."

Merritt perched on the couch's edge and ran her hand over her hair. "It's okay."

Tess frowned. "You're covered in mud. Are you okay? Damian said you'd been somewhere, but it's the middle of the night."

Merritt cleared her throat. "I was restless, so I went to the park."

As she had hoped, Tess assumed she meant Little Avalon Park.

"I imagine the park calms you down." Tess gave a sympathetic grimace. "You startled Damian when you came in, that's all. It's the weekend, so he probably slept late."

"Yep."

"Sure you're okay?" Tess asked. "You seem peaky."

"I'm tired," Merritt admitted.

"No wonder. It's the middle of the night." Tess smiled. "Sleep as late as you like tomorrow. We have no reason to rush around."

Merritt nodded. "Thanks."

She didn't think she would sleep, but she was mistaken. After a hot shower that soothed the bruise, Merritt dropped onto the bed and sank into slumber.

Merritt woke up feeling like her mouth had grown hair on the inside. She probed her cheeks with her tongue to ensure that it hadn't. It felt dry and gross.

She groaned and pried her eyes open to see bright sunlight filling her room. What? Last she remembered, it was night.

Stupid sleep. Merritt sat up. *So disorienting.*

She hauled herself to the bathroom and started at the apparition in the mirror. Her hair stood up in red corkscrews. Deep shadows colored the contours below her eyes, and though she tried to warm her skin tone, her cheeks stubbornly remained pale.

"Gross," Merritt whispered.

She felt little better as she stumbled into the kitchen.

"I'm telling you—" Tess stopped. She gripped her mug with white knuckles, leaning against the fridge.

Damian sat at the table, facing her over a bowl of chili. He glowered at Merritt, scarlet eyes like smoldering coals.

The Leshbolg paused in the doorway.

"Good morning, sunshine," Tess greeted her. "Sleep well?"

"Yeah. Weirdly well." Merritt shuffled to the nearest chair and slid into it.

Damian snorted, whipped to his feet, and stalked to his room with the bowl.

"What's up with him?" Merritt asked.

"Who knows?" Tess shook her head. "Are you okay?"

Merritt ran a hand through the hair she'd attempted to tame in the shower. "I am still tired."

"I'm sorry. You're usually so chipper in the mornings." Tess started the kettle. "I'll make you a cup of coffee."

Maybe it's because I transformed into a seven-foot male Leshbolg, Merritt thought, but she couldn't get the words past her lips. How would Tess take the news? Could she admit that she'd been sneaking out to Brooklyn Bridge Park? Her toes curled inside her slippers, and she swallowed a nervous knot in her throat.

No. It was better that nobody heard about the transformation or her nocturnal activities. Tess, Val, and the others were different from the people in her other placements, but she didn't want to push her luck.

"Do you feel sick?" Tess asked.

Merritt shook her head. "Just tired."

"I bet the change and excitement is catching up with you." Tess' lips turned down at the corners. "Poor thing! I have one more day to spend with you, and I'll make it a fun one. That's the pick-me-up you need."

Merritt grinned. "Sounds good."

"We'll start with a good breakfast." Tess extracted a pan from the nearest cabinet. "I know you're not into meat, but how about eggs?"

Merritt brightened. "I *love* eggs. Actually..." She paused. "This is weird, but I'm craving meat this morning."

"You're in luck. Ever had breakfast sausages?" Tess asked.

Merritt shook her head. "Never willingly."

"Then you're in for a treat." Tess grinned.

She wasn't wrong. The meal she placed before Merritt a few minutes later made her feel better simply from looking at it. Scrambled eggs, toast with butter and jelly, crispy hash browns, and a pair of sausages adorned the plate. Merritt barely waited for Tess to say a brief grace to Luna—a typical Lunar Fae thing—before plowing into the food.

"Whoa!" Tess laughed. "You're not lacking an appetite."

"These are amazing," Merritt groaned, chomping into a sausage.

"There's more in the pan," Tess promised.

Merritt finished those on her plate and the extras in the pan before slowing down. Her eyelids felt less leaden when she pushed her clean plate away and sipped orange juice to help the food go down.

"Feel better?" Tess asked.

"A little."

"I know what'll make you feel like yourself again." Tess paused. "I took another liberty."

"So far, I have liked all your liberties," Merritt assured her.

Tess grinned. "I booked an appointment with Isabella for you to have your hair done if you'd like that."

Merritt straightened. "Really?"

"Yeah, but you don't have to go if it isn't your cup of tea."

"I like all tea," Merritt told her.

Tess laughed. "Then let's do it."

Isabella's salon was almost empty when Merritt and Tess arrived. A werewolf relaxed in one of the chairs by the mirrors, scrolling on her phone while product coated her hair. Isabella fussed with the shelves of shampoos and conditioners by the basins.

"Hey, Merritt!" the human chirped. "I knew you wouldn't be able to resist my charms forever. Whoa, you're really pale."

"She needs a pick-me-up," Tess informed her.

Isabella beamed. "You've come to the right place. What can I do for you? Cut, color, blow dry?"

Merritt touched her hair. "I like its length and color, but it's going in all directions today."

"I have products that will fix that for you." Isabella grinned. "Let me work my magic."

Merritt gasped. "You have magic?"

Tess elbowed her.

"Sure I do." Isabella winked.

She grasped Merritt's arm and towed her to a chair before one of the basins. In seconds, Merritt was wrapped in a cape, tucked into the chair, and leaning back with her head against the basin, a surprisingly comfortable position.

"You've got leaves in your hair." Isabella laughed as she directed a stream of warm water onto Merritt's scalp. "What *have* you been doing?"

"Um..." Merritt began.

"You'll never guess who came in the other day," Isabella added.

Tess asked, "Who?"

Isabella worked shampoo through Merritt's hair, her fingertips making figure-eights against her scalp. The sensation was so delightful that Merritt's hair lightened several shades before she could stop it. She gritted her teeth, fighting for control as her hair turned platinum, curled excessively, or transformed into grass. No one had ever touched her scalp like this, or not that she could remember, and she loved it too much.

"Arion!" Isabella announced. "You know, that guy high up in the agency you all work for."

"He's nice. I'm not surprised he came in." Tess perched on a nearby chair. "I recommended you."

"You're the best." Isabella laughed. "I told him I'm not a barber, but I did my best. His cut came out quite nice. I might have more male clients in my future."

"That's good news." Tess smiled. "You've had plenty of practice on Liam."

"Speaking of which, have you seen how quickly Qenzi's hair grew? I love it. Any idea when they're getting married?" Isabella gently rinsed Merritt's hair. "It feels like they're dragging their feet. Do you think anyone's having second thoughts?"

"It's only been a few weeks," Tess pointed out. "I think they're basking in the joy of being engaged."

"Liam sure looks like he's basking. I haven't seen him this happy in my life." Isabella rubbed something sweet-smelling into Merritt's hair. "Hard to believe he was so depressed he could barely leave the house a year ago."

"Why?" Merritt asked.

"That's for Liam to—" Tess began.

"Liam lost his sister in an accident when they were teenagers," Isabella happily informed her. "He blamed himself for a long time."

Merritt blinked. "Wow."

"He's worked through it." Isabella rinsed her hair. "Let's get you to the chair."

She squeezed the water from Merritt's hair and led her to a chair before one of the mirrors. Merritt stared into it as Isabella produced a thing that blew hot air—a *hair dryer*—and directed it at Merritt's hair. Its roar drowned out all conversation for several minutes, and Isabella's face pinched with concentration as she brushed, primped, and poked.

"Wow," Merritt gasped at the end.

Her hair looked better than she could have imagined. The long bob's curls were perfectly defined, forming an attractive shape around her head, and it shone like rubies under the salon's lights. Isabella had parted it at the side so the front slanted over Merritt's forehead.

"Like it?" Isabella asked.

"Love it!" Merritt touched her hair.

"Come back anytime." Isabella grinned. "Tess, did you want anything?"

"I wouldn't complain if you wanted to practice those braids you told me about," Tess told her. "I don't have time for a wash, though. Already washed it this morning."

Isabella frowned. "Did you use the products I told you to?"

Tess shuffled her feet. "Yes."

"Sit." Isabella removed Merritt's cape with a flourish.

Tess and Merritt traded places, and Isabella spritzed Tess' hair with some liquid before brushing it out.

"What did you spray on it?" Merritt asked.

"It's a detangler. Tess' hair knots up like nobody's business. Without this stuff, brushing it is torture for both of us." Isabella chuckled.

"You never pull." Tess smiled.

Isabella parted Tess' hair and secured most of it to one side with a gigantic clip. Her fingers moved with incredible speed as she braided another part.

"How do you do that?" Merritt moved nearer.

"Braid this quickly? I'll show you." Isabella slowed. "Hold the ends like this. Then you don't have to go all the way to the bottom with each braid." She sped up, braiding the strands in what felt like seconds. "Oooh, did you guys hear the latest about Amber and Aurelio?"

"Who?" Merritt asked.

"The worst neighbors in Little Avalon." Tess groaned.

"They own houses next to each other and don't get along."

Isabella grinned. "Last week, Aurelio filed *three* noise complaints about Amber with the cops. *Three.*"

"The hu…I mean, NYPD?" Tess asked.

"Yep. The cops showed up at, like, three in the morning, Jenny from across the road told me. Val had to come out and talk to them to make them go away." Isabella smirked. "Amber retaliated last week."

"What did she do?" Merritt leaned closer to watch as Isabella started a new braid.

"She dumped her rose clippings over the wall onto Aurelio's lawn. Do you know how big Amber's rose garden is? It was a *huge* pile." Isabella chortled. "Aurelio was furious."

"Those two," Tess grumbled. "I can't believe they're at it again."

"It's always entertaining. I can't wait for Jenny to come in for her weekly blow-dry to tell me what they did after that." Isabella added a dab of something to Tess' hair from a pot on the table.

Merritt moved nearer. "What's that?"

Isabella didn't seem to mind her questions, so she asked half a dozen more in the next few minutes as the human transformed Tess' long, straight hair into a complex series of tightly woven braids that flowed over each other like copper chains. Isabella secured the last one with a pin and stepped back. "What do you think?"

Tess touched the thin braids that dipped over her forehead and smiled. "It's perfect. I love it!"

"Not bad for a practice run." Isabella beamed. "Thanks for letting me work on you. A lot of long-haired girls around here are *really* into braids like this for some reason."

As they left the salon, Tess explained to Merritt, "Elves. Elves dig braids."

"Ah." Merritt nodded. "Do you know the real story with Amber and Aurelio?"

"She's a werewolf, and he's an orc. One nocturnal, one diurnal. It normally works out in Little Avalon, but not for them." Tess groaned. "They're awful. Poor Val has enough on her plate without having to wrangle their petty drama."

"There must be a way to make peace between them," Merritt murmured.

Tess sighed. "We haven't found it yet."

The place of trees was calling.

Merritt paced along the bedroom wall with the window. It faced away from Brooklyn Bridge Park, but she'd flung it open despite the cold air, hoping the faint smell of spruce would soothe her desire to sprint across the rooftops.

Her body ached for open spaces. She wanted to dig her fingers into the dirt, press her cheek against a tree's bark, and sit on the pier and watch the river flow inexorably into the sea.

She shook her head. *Focus!* What if she turned into Merritt-the-seven-foot tree-thing again? She might reveal her magic to humans, and if Val found out, she'd be furious.

She didn't want to push her luck in Little Avalon. Val was tolerant and kind, but everyone had limits.

She brushed her fingertips over the edge of her amulet, where emeralds studded its surface. Maybe she could use the *muffle* rune to make sure her powers didn't get out of control. It would help her slip in and out without anyone ever knowing.

A sound from outside froze her in her tracks.

Merritt breathed slowly. *You're wound too tight. Relax.* She listened for a moment but didn't hear the scraping noise again.

Her legs hurt from pacing. She sagged onto the couch and turned on the TV. Two humans argued over something on the screen, and Merritt glanced at the time: 5:37 am. Damian had gotten home almost an hour before. She'd heard him enter his room and shut the door.

She could easily slip away, and she could be back before Tess woke if she was quick.

Something creaked outside, and Merritt tensed. The unfamiliar sound made the hair rise on the back of her neck. Her magic senses prickled. Something strange and sinister hovered in the air. A pungent scent reached her, one she'd smelled in abundance at Chaplin's Kitchen.

Garlic.

Damian was a vampire. Tess never brought garlic home.

Merritt slipped off the couch and opened the hallway door. "Damian?"

The garlic smell intensified, but she heard no response from Damian. His room was soundproof, an advantage for cohabitating nocturnal and diurnal paras, so she knocked on the door. "Damian!"

Nothing.

Merritt's stomach clenched. That uncomfortable feeling crawled on her skin like she'd fallen into a pit of cockroaches. Something was wrong.

She jogged down the hall to Tess' door and knocked. "Tess!"

"Merritt?" she sleepily called. "Come in."

Merritt shoved the door open. Tess sat up in bed, rubbing her eyes. A giant portrait of Queen Julia presided over her room, Excalibur in hand.

"Tess, something's wrong," Merritt hissed. "Do you smell garlic?"

Tess' eyes widened. "Shit. Damian."

She scrambled out of bed and trotted down the hall on bare feet. Merritt stayed close behind her, clutching her amulet, as Tess hastened to Damian's door.

"*Damian!*" she yelled, hammering on it.

Something thudded inside the room. It didn't sound like footsteps.

"Do you sense that?" Tess hissed.

"What is it?" Merrit whispered.

The Lunar Fae's eyes narrowed. "Silver."

She slammed a flat hand against the door, and silver fire enveloped the lock. Tess punched the door, and wind burst from her sleeve, its hurricane force smashing the door to splinters.

The stench of garlic rolled through the room. Damian sprawled on the floor by the open window, eyes closed, as a hooded figure stood over him. The object in the figure's hand gleamed silver, its sharp point poised over Damian's heart.

"Oh, shit!" Merritt squeaked.

Tess punched both hands forward, and twin balls of moonfire exploded from her knuckles. The attacker ducked the first, but the second slammed into his chest, knocking them against the wall. He screamed, and the silver stake clattered to the ground.

"Show me your hands!" Tess thundered. "By order of the Eternity Throne!"

The unidentified para grabbed the windowsill and tumbled over it. Merritt heard the clang as his feet hit the fire escape.

"Crap!" Tess hissed. "Merritt, stay with him!"

The fae's wings whirred as she shot through the window. Merritt ran to Damian. He sprawled on his side, head pillowed on one arm, dark hair falling over his face.

"Damian!" Merritt shook him.

He moaned but didn't stir. Though the vamp was always pale, the sickly green undertone of his skin scared Merritt.

The garlic. Merritt glanced around but saw no bulbs. The smell permeated the air like someone had sprayed it into the room.

"C'mon, Damian." Merritt grabbed the vamp by the arms. "You need to get out of here." She hoisted him over her shoulder and stomped out of the room, slamming the door behind her. It would have been fun to clear the kitchen table dramatically, but there was only a salt shaker in the middle, so Merritt carefully placed it on the counter before lowering

Damian to the surface. She rolled him onto his side to let him breathe.

The kitchen door crashed open. Merritt tensed until Shadow bounded through it, baying.

Where? he thundered. *Where he go?*

"Tess chased him through Damian's window." Merritt pointed.

Mom, outside! Shadow raced onto the stairs.

Val put her head around the door. She wore dwarven armor of polished steel with glowing runes. The warhammer in her hands was as tall as Merritt and glowed red hot.

"You good?" Val barked.

Merritt nodded.

"He good?" Val nodded at Damian.

The vampire rolled over and noisily gagged.

"I think he's fine," Merritt hazarded.

"Stay with him!" Val charged back down the stairs.

Merritt supplied a bucket and held Damian's hair out of his face for lack of anything better to do as he puked his guts out. He lay face-down for several trembling seconds afterward, sweaty forehead pillowed on his arm, spasms running through his body.

"You'll be okay." Merritt patted his shoulder.

"Merlin's testicular torsion," Damian croaked.

"Merritt! Damian! Are you guys okay?" Tess shouted from the stairwell.

"In here!" Merritt called.

Tess jogged into the kitchen, breathless and smelling of smoke. Cinders trickled between her fingers as she slammed the front door and brushed her braids out of her face. Val was on her heels, armor gone. She still had her warhammer on her back.

"Did you get him?" Merritt asked.

"Get who?" Damian croaked.

"The asshole who tried to kill you," Val growled.

Damian raised his head. "What?"

"What do you remember?" Tess asked. "What happened?"

Damian slowly swung his legs over the table's edge and sat. Merritt grabbed his arm to steady him, but he shook her off.

"I was in my room, working late on my laptop," he murmured. "Then I felt sick and got up to get water. Then, nothing."

"You were on the floor when we found you," Tess explained. "Someone stood over you with a…with a silver stake in their hands."

Damian stilled. "A silver stake."

"It would've killed you," Val snarled. "Tess and I chased him, but he lost us. Tetra and Shadow are trying to track him. Are you okay, Damian?"

The vampire shakily mopped sweat from his face. "Better now."

"You should go to the new clinic and get checked out," Val suggested.

Damian shook his head. "I'm fine. Just garlic poisoning."

"It was in the air, like someone had sprayed it into his room," Merritt explained.

Val bared her teeth. "Aerosolized garlic. An illegal but effective sedative for vampires. It wouldn't have killed you, Damian, but it knocked you out in seconds."

"No," Damian growled. "The silver stake was meant to kill me."

"Whoever this guy is, he's a pro. This was a well-planned and well-executed attack. How did you know something was up?" Val asked.

Tess smiled. "Merritt woke me."

"I was up early and smelled the garlic," Merritt mumbled. "I sensed the silver, too. It felt wrong."

"I'll transmute it to iron and get it safely out of the apartment." Val touched Damian's shoulder. "We'll catch that son of a bitch."

Damian ran a hand through his hair. "I was waiting for something to happen, given the nature of my work at the OPMA."

"What do you do there?" Merritt asked.

Damian shot her a glare. "It's classified." He pushed off the table and tried to stand, but his knees buckled.

Val grabbed his arm and steered him to a chair. "Easy. What kind of classified?"

Damian shakily inhaled. "The dangerous kind."

Val and Tess exchanged meaningful looks over his head.

A bark resounded from the stairwell. Shadow trotted into the kitchen, his raised hackles making him the size of a small horse. He bared white fangs and loped into the hall.

"Any luck?" Val asked as Tetra followed him inside.

The faerie shook her head. "None. He used faerie dust to cover his trail. It obliterates organic matter like scent particles and evaporates into nothing. I caught a few whiffs, but we lost him."

"Shit," Val muttered.

"He was a pro. I'm surprised he didn't succeed." Tetra raised her eyebrows. "Damian, you look like crap."

"Thanks," Damian muttered.

"Is he a faerie?" Tess asked. "One who changed his form like you did?"

"I doubt it. A faerie wouldn't have messed around with garlic and shit. We'd simply melt Damian's flesh from his bones." Tetra smiled.

Damian groaned. "Lovely."

"One thing's clear." Val folded her arms. "Whoever's after you, Damian, they sent a professional to kill you. A hired assassin."

Damian remained stone-faced. "In my line of work, it's hardly a surprise."

"Maybe, but he won't touch you again in Little Avalon." Val bared her teeth. "You have my word."

CHAPTER TWELVE

The kitchen seemed painfully empty with Tess at work and Damian asleep the following day. Val had insisted on placing alarm amulets outside Damian's window, and Merritt kept half an eye on the selenite blocks scattered around the house. They would light up if anyone tried to open the window.

"If that happens," Val had told Merritt, "hit your amulet, and someone will be there in seconds." She'd added that Liam would watch the amulets, too.

Merritt regularly sniffed for garlic, too, but as she ate the last slice of Leshbolg bellyfill, it wasn't assassination attempt that worried her.

It was boredom.

She tried to stop thinking about Brooklyn Bridge Park by considering her options for the day. Tess had told her to feel free to wander around Little Avalon, but the thought made her shy. A visit to Little Avalon Park seemed appealing...unless Lawrence saw her. Merritt wasn't in the mood for drama.

The last piece of bellyfill was fluffy and delicious on her tongue. Merritt eyed the book Tess had left on the kitchen table for her.

Baking for Beginners.

She pulled it over and flipped it open. The recipes delighted her. She'd eaten plenty of bread in her lifetime and knew what a cupcake was since paras lucky enough to know their birthdays got one at the New Camelot institution, but she'd never imagined all these baked goods.

The pictures on the pages made her jaw drop: pies with glorious golden crusts, brownies dripping with nuts, cakes with fluffy interiors, and big fat cookies laden with chocolate chips.

"Chocolate brownies," Merritt whispered, gazing at the picture. The confection on the page appeared dark and gooey and amazing. She skimmed the ingredient list and poked around in the cabinets, quickly finding butter, salt, and flour but no cocoa powder or granulated sugar.

"Tess said it was okay to wander around Little Avalon," Merritt whispered. She squared her shoulders and marched outside into a drizzle that nipped her ears and fingers with cold teeth. Elves and fae miserably hurried this way and that on the sidewalks, but a group of young werebears played in the street, growling and shaking their ears as droplets settled in their coats.

No one paid the werebears any attention, so it was not surprising that Merritt attracted only a curious glance or two. She tucked her hands into her armpits and shuffled along. Mrs. Ricci waved from her window. Merritt grinned and waved back, then relaxed, allowing her arms to swing by her sides as she walked.

The Second Fist's doors were closed, raindrops dancing down the glass, but Enzo sat at the bar inside with paperwork spread around him. He waved as Merritt strolled by. She beamed as she returned the gesture. It was easy to make friends in Little Avalon.

Merlin will be proud. The thought drifted through her mind like an unexpected snatch of music.

She held her head high as she reached the grocery store, where a handful of other paras browsed the shelves. A bunch of werewolf pups brawled in one aisle, yelping and pulling one another's ears.

"Stop it!" their mother snapped, squirting them with a spray bottle of water.

The pups yelped and hid behind baskets of Fernwood fruit, almost knocking them into an elf, who scrolled on her phone and didn't notice. Merritt dived to grab a basket before it could bump into the elf's legs.

"Thanks." The elf flashed a quick smile.

"You're welcome." Merritt returned the smile.

She turned down the next aisle and found promising-looking bags and cans. It didn't take long to locate a package labeled Granulated Sugar (Feldgeister Friendly) and an eight-ounce can of Southern Spine Cocoa Powder.

"Perfect." Merritt tucked the items under one arm and glanced at the counter. She remembered Tess saying that one exchanged money for items but hadn't seen Tess give Jackson any real money. She'd simply touched the *card machine* with her bank card. She glimpsed Jackson in the storeroom at the back, counting things, and didn't want to disturb him.

Merritt went up to the counter and looked at the card machine. She reached out with a finger and touched the card machine. "Boop!"

The machine did nothing.

"Okay, bye." Merritt turned and strolled through the front door.

"Hey!" someone yelled. "Hey, that chick's shoplifting! Jackson, come quickly!"

Merritt looked around, expecting to see a giant pick up the whole store, but all seemed fine. She contentedly kept walking.

"Hey, you!" the elf shouted. "Stop!"

A mass of werewolf pups poured from the store and charged Merritt. Several grabbed her pants leg in their sharp little teeth and tugged, making it hard to keep her balance.

"Hey!" Merritt shook her leg, laughing. "You're so playful!"

"We got her, Momma!" one of the pups barked. "We got her!" He ran wild laps around Merritt.

"*Thief!*" the elf shrieked.

Merritt realized with a ripple of shock that the elf was looking at her.

"Wh-what?" she stammered.

Jackson burst into the parking space. An orc washing his car's windshield stood gaping, suds dripping from the squeegee. Several people appeared at the door of the potions store to stare.

"Merritt!" Jackson cried. "What do you think you're doing?" His rubbery nose twitched with disgust.

"I...I'm getting sugar and cocoa," Merritt croaked.

"You have to pay for those!" Jackson burst out.

Merritt blinked. "I did. I touched the card machine."

"With her finger. I saw her!" the elf yelled.

"Hey, what's going on?" someone asked.

Merritt spun. Dante wandered over, his smile hinting at tusks and fangs. The half-orc, half-vampire swept Merritt with that mysterious auburn gaze and turned his attention to Jackson.

"We caught a thief!" one of the wolf pups barked.

"She's shoplifting!" The elf pointed.

"I can't pick up the whole store," Merritt wailed.

"She means you're taking things." Dante raised his eyebrows. "Did you pay for these?"

Merritt swallowed hard. "I thought so, but I-I don't know how it works. I touched the card machine. I thought it made money."

Dante's expression softened. "That's not how it works, Merritt." He laid a hand on her shoulder. "Let's go back inside. Jackson, we'll give her a crash course on capitalism."

Jackson relaxed into a smile. "We can do that."

The elf snorted and marched away, but the pups had already gotten distracted. Their mother hurried over to stop them from chewing on the gas pumps, and Merritt gratefully returned to the store with Dante and Jackson.

When Merritt peeled the foil cover off the can, the cocoa powder smelled heavenly. She dipped her fingertip into the brown substance and gazed at it under the kitchen light.

So, this is how you make chocolate.

Sweet things had been scarce in Wolf Glen. The self-sufficient elven community had no access to sugar. They'd used honey, mostly for brewing mead. Merritt had tasted chocolate in New Camelot and Fernwood Deep, and she'd never forgotten it.

She dabbed the cocoa-coated finger on her tongue, and bitterness seized her by the tonsils. Spluttering, Merritt stumbled to the fridge, splashed milk into a glass, and washed down the shocking flavor with a gulp.

"Wow." Merritt cleared her throat and eyed the recipe. "No wonder we need one and a half cups of sugar."

She cautiously followed the steps, aware of two loaves rising on the windowsill since that morning, one Leshbolg bellyfill, one from the recipe book. Merritt had her doubts about the dried yeast she'd used for the latter, but she'd felt life in it when she mixed it with sugar and warm water as the recipe suggested, and the loaf had doubled in size.

The brownie recipe made a sticky, gooey mess in the mixing bowl. She cautiously tasted it and grinned as chocolate overwhelmed her senses.

I can make chocolate anytime I want, she realized. It was a magnificent thought.

Merritt poured the brownie batter into a cake pan—she hoped it was a cake pan since it matched the picture in the recipe book—and tucked it into the preheated oven. That left her hands free to play with her bread dough for thirty minutes.

She left the second batch of dough, the one she thought of as "human bread," and turned her attention to the fluffy bellyfill dough. When she'd mixed it that morning, the memory of adding spices to the mixture had come back to her. The dough contained swirls of cinnamon and cumin and speckles of rosemary. Merritt grinned in appreciation at the rich texture as she scored it, revealing the rich spices within.

"This is gonna be good," she murmured.

By the time she wrapped it in the cabbage leaves and added Leshbolg magic to them, the oven's timer beeped. Her brownies were ready.

Merritt hummed a song she'd heard in last night's movie as she fetched the brownies from the oven, adjusted the temperature, and tucked both loaves of bread inside. She remembered baking bellyfill in a pit filled with coals, but this oven was equally magical. A little heat, a little time, and sloppy batter or squishy dough transformed into firm brownies or fluffy bread. Perhaps Earth had more magic than she'd first thought.

As she cleared the table and washed the dishes, Merritt relished the rush of warm water over her skin. She kept humming, feeling the melodic vibration deep in her chest, and realized her sharp longing for the place of trees had faded.

A smile tugged her lips. The smell of baking bread grounded her as effectively as dirt beneath her feet.

Later, she retrieved both loaves from the oven and set them on the counter. As she unwrapped the bellyfill, allowing its spicy aroma to flood the kitchen, the front door opened.

"Merlin's beard!" Tess explained. "It smells *so good* in here!"

Merritt looked up. "Hey! You're home."

"Yeah. My client's conference ended early. It was boring, which is good in the security business. He's less important than he thinks he is." Tess laughed. "Oooh, that bellyfill smells..." She waved her hands. "I'm lost for words. It's too delicious to describe."

"It's spiced." Merritt showed her the colorful, textured loaf. "What do you think?"

"It looks like magic and smells like I need it in my belly right now." Tess tilted her head. "Whoa, look at that! Is that a normal loaf?"

Merritt eyed the golden loaf puffing from its pan beside the bellyfill. "Does it look like it's supposed to?"

"It looks perfect," Tess declared. She dumped her purse on the table. "My feet are so done after standing outside the conference room all day."

"We could have bread for dinner," Merritt suggested.

Tess grinned. "Sounds perfect!"

"There are also brownies," Merritt added.

Tess' jaw dropped. "Merlin's wings! I need to see them."

Merritt placed them on the table for Tess to coo over while she sliced both bread loaves, releasing clouds of fragrant steam into the kitchen. As she set the table, she allowed blobs of butter to melt on each slice. Tess kicked off her shoes and stretched, relaxing as Merritt made two mugs of instant hot chocolate.

"Can't I help with something?" Tess asked.

"Not a thing," Merritt firmly told her. "You look tired." She slid a plate of buttered slices in front of Tess and added the steaming mug. "Dinner!"

Tess groaned with delight. "You can stay."

"Good." Merritt laughed. "It's simple, but…"

"It's perfect," Tess assured her.

She mumbled the grace to Luna, then tried to cram a whole slice of bellyfill into her mouth. Judging by her happy noises, the spices had been a good choice. Merritt nibbled a corner of her slice and plunged into the deep well of memory so intense and vivid that she froze in her chair.

Walls of living branches woven together. Sunlight filtering through green leaves. Ripples of laughter. The smell of wood smoke and baking bellyfill. A long table set with wooden plates, each with a generous helping of fruit, nuts, and buttered bellyfill.

A hand on Merritt's shoulder. "Well done, love."

It was her mother's voice. She turned her head.

It faded before Merritt's memory could reveal any of her people's faces.

"Merritt?" Tess touched her hand. "You okay?"

Merritt blinked. "I...remembered something. A party, maybe, or a big dinner in Lichenvale."

"That's great!" Tess grinned.

Merritt stared at her plate, wrestling with the sudden tightness in her throat.

"Or is it?" Tess tenderly asked.

Merritt swallowed. "I lost so much. The memories remind me of that."

"You did, and it's a tragedy," Tess murmured. "You can regain some things." She smiled. "Like how to bake the most incredible spiced bellyfill."

Merritt raised her head. "You're a great friend, Tess. Anyone ever tell you that?"

"I'm not the one who filled this apartment with the smell of fresh bread," Tess teased. "We're even."

Merritt laughed. "Brownies for dessert."

Uncoordinated footsteps thudded in the hallway. Damian entered the kitchen, hair standing on end, his black trench coat rumpled and the belt flapping loose.

"Hey! How are you feeling?" Tess asked.

"Pissed," Damian growled. He stormed across the kitchen.

"Where are you going?" Merritt queried.

"To work. Where do you think?" Damian grabbed his keys from the hook by the door.

"Shouldn't you be in bed?" Tess frowned. "You don't seem well."

"Yeah, you look sick," Merritt agreed.

"I'm going to catch that son of a bitch," Damian spat.

"Okay, but how about a slice of fresh-baked bread for break-fast?" Tess gestured. "There's plenty!"

"No time," Damian snapped, and slammed the door behind him.

"I don't think he likes me," Merritt observed.

Tess shook her head. "Damian doesn't like anyone. It's not personal."

Merritt found that hard to believe.

Liam's blue car was overloaded. Qenzi sat beside him, and everyone else crammed into the backseat. To Merritt's relief, Tetra sat on one end. Merritt squished between Tess and the door on the other. Antin seemed content to be half in Tetra's lap.

Liam observed as the car rolled down the freeway, "This is illegal."

"It's not a long way," Qenzi reminded him. "We'll reach Manhattan in five minutes."

"Anyone want another muffin?" Tess asked. "Look at me, handing them out like I'm the one who baked them. Sorry, Merritt."

"Go ahead." Merritt grinned. "It's good to see everyone enjoying them. It's my first try at muffins."

"Are there any double chocolate ones left?" Liam asked.

"Two double chocolate, one banana," Tess reported, peering into the container Merritt had brought. Condensation gleamed on the inside from the piping-hot muffins.

"I'll have the banana one," Tetra requested.

Tess passed the container around, and the lucky recipients grunted in appreciation. Merritt shifted her weight, trying to avoid Tess' bony hip digging into hers.

"Where are we going?" she asked for the umpteenth time.

Liam smiled in the rearview mirror. "It's still a surprise, but trust me, you'll love it."

Merritt didn't say it, but she wasn't sure there was anything for her to love in this direction. They'd turned off the freeway and now cautiously rolled between tall buildings that all looked the same to her. A few trees along the sidewalk provided tiny splashes of green as their new leaves trembled in the sunlight. Besides them, Merritt saw only steel, glass, and concrete.

Liam turned his car into an empty parking spot and halted it. "Okay! We're here."

Merritt tumbled from the car and tried to keep her disappointment off her face. She looked at another sheer brick wall, windows barely punctuating the monotony. Rotating, Merritt saw nothing but more city around her. Buildings, sidewalks, streets. Her heart longed for life. She thought she detected green grass, its subtle magic caressing her senses, but she had to be imagining it.

"Here we are." Liam grinned as he locked the car. "Perfect weather for a nice walk."

"It's sunny," Merritt offered. *Walk through this?* The thought of all that concrete and asphalt made her feet hurt.

"Where do we get on, Qenz?" Liam asked.

Qenzi consulted her phone. "Over here. There are the steps."

The troll led them across the street to a series of steel steps that ascended in multiple flights. Merritt winced at the clang of feet on steel.

"Thanks for bringing me on your outing today," she mumbled as she reached the first step. *Even though I would rather be home, baking.*

"Don't thank us yet." Liam chuckled. "You haven't seen what it is."

Tess reached the top first. "Oh, wow! Look at this place!"

Merritt braced herself for yet another building. The stairs led to a concrete pedestrian bridge over the street, and Merritt shuffled after the others, looking for a door.

When she reached the end, she saw rich green foliage.

Merritt gasped. "What is this?"

Her boots crunched on a tangle of plants that flanked the edges of a long platform that ran arrow-straight between the buildings. Rich explosions of vegetation filled the world with color on either side of a concrete path. Bees buzzed among the flowers, which grew in a profuse mass among a diverse array of plants. Nothing was groomed or fancy about these plants. They seemed wild and glorious, like a sliver of Fernwood Deep had fallen from the sky into Manhattan.

Liam beamed at the look on her face. "Welcome to the High Line, Merritt."

"The what?" Merritt whispered.

"It was originally a railway structure, but a few years ago, the city converted it into a unique park," Liam explained. "It's one and a half miles long, and there's plenty to see."

Merritt fell to her knees and pressed her hands into the nearest plant bed, relief coursing through her body when she touched leaves, stems, roots, and damp earth.

"Do you like it?" Tess asked.

Merritt laughed. "I *love* it."

Tetra grabbed a bee. "Ooh, a snack!"

"Tetra, no!" Liam slapped her hand. "They're endangered."

The bee angrily buzzed and swung toward Tetra, then thought better of it and flew away.

"Fine. How about pigeons? Are they endangered?" Tetra eyed a pair on the nearby rail.

"Try to get through the morning without killing anything," Liam implored.

"No promises." Tetra shrugged.

"C'mon, Merritt." Qenzi touched her shoulder. "I've heard there are great art installations. Let's keep walking!"

The farther they strolled through the soaring park between the skyscrapers, the more beauty unfolded before them. Trees shielded them from enclosing walls in places, casting dappled shade on the path. Merritt paused beneath each to touch the bark and feel the kiss of the breeze through the leaves. Later, the park widened into a spacious lawn. The view was breathtaking, with old churches juxtaposed against an ultramodern apartment building.

"Can we sit on the grass?" Merritt asked.

"Sure. I could use a break," Tess admitted. "I got into a fight with a drunk idiot at my security gig last night."

They flopped onto the thick, springy grass. Merritt sprawled on her belly, not worried about grass stains. Contact with the green mattress was worth ruining her jeans.

"A fight?" she asked. "Are you okay?"

"Of course she's okay." Tetra sat cross-legged beside Tess. "She can shoot fire from her fingers."

"I didn't, since my opponent was human." Tess shrugged. "It wasn't a big deal. He was an ordinary asshole trying to hit on my client, a young actress trying to have a nice night out on the town."

"Getting hit on by a gross dude," Qenzi observed. "Sounds normal to me."

"I knocked his lights out." Tess smirked.

"Did the bouncer throw you out?" Liam asked.

"Not this time. They realized what happened." Tess chuckled. "He robbed my client of the pleasure of going out."

"I've been thrown out dozens of times. The key is not to melt the bouncer's face," Tetra announced.

Antin patted her shoulder. "That's not easy for you, my love."

"Face-melting is fun," Tetra whined. "Also, I'm hungry."

"You're always hungry." Qenzi rolled her eyes.

They left the lawn behind and continued down the path, Tetra and Liam bickering all the way. Startling bursts of beauty awaited in every segment. Huge flowering bushes basked in the spring sunshine, and the space opened to another splendid lawn. This one had a magnificent sculpture of a kneeling ballerina with red roses spilling from her plaster hands.

"How do they do that?" Merritt asked, pointing at the ballerina's tutu. It looked delicate, crumpling around the statue's waist, that it was made from tissue paper. When she brushed its edge, it was bronze and plaster.

"I have no idea." Qenzi smiled.

"Magic?" Tetra suggested.

Liam shook his head. "Human-made. It isn't magic. It's art."

Qenzi tucked her arm through his. "I'd argue that's a type of magic. The same type of magic you are."

Liam kissed her cheek. "Thanks, honey."

"Where's the statue of the giant pigeon I saw on the Internet? I wanna lick it," Tetra announced.

They found the pigeon sculpture and narrowly prevented Tetra from licking it by redirecting her attention to a nearby coffee shop. They found a table in the sunshine, with a big window overlooking the lawn that stretched across the city. Merritt sipped a latte and couldn't stop staring at the walk.

"This place is fantastic." She sighed. "Thanks for bringing me here, everyone."

"We all know being in the city makes you antsy." Tess smiled over her coffee. "We'll figure out a way to make you feel more at home."

Qenzi slurped an iced coffee through a straw. Liam gazed at her like she was the most perfect thing he'd ever seen. Tetra surreptitiously munched a napkin, though Antin tried to stop her.

Merritt grinned. "I feel at home. Trust me."

CHAPTER THIRTEEN

Afternoon shadows had faded to evening dusk when Liam steered his car between the shorter buildings and grimier streets in Bay Ridge. Merritt's belly was comfortably full of excellent seafood from La Rose Dansante, a fancy restaurant Tetra had surprisingly suggested. Apart from an awkward moment when Tess had to explain that the lemon water was for dipping her fingers, not for drinking, Merritt had made it through the meal with minimal chaos.

Her full stomach made it hard to keep her eyes open. She leaned her head against the window, her limbs pleasantly tired and her skin sensitive from a mild sunburn. It had been a long time since she'd had a whole day outside, and she loved the feeling.

"You guys are the best," she mumbled. "Thanks."

"We're not done yet." Liam slowed the car as they approached the turn to Little Avalon. "Who wants a nightcap at the Second Fist?"

"Me!" Tetra's hand shot up, almost poking Antin's eyeballs out.

"I'll never say no." Tess grinned. "A glass of Fernwood mead would be the perfect end to this day."

"I agree." Qenzi nodded. "How about you, Merritt?"

"I'd like that." Merritt smiled.

The car turned into Little Avalon, and a blurred figure rushed across the street, clothes flashing in the headlights.

"Shit!" Liam slammed on the brakes.

Merritt grabbed the back of his seat to keep from face-planting into it.

"What in Merlin's name is going on?" Tess growled.

A mass of paranormals filled the street, lining the sidewalks and standing on the asphalt, heedless of traffic. They filled the Second Fist's doorway and clustered around the outside tables, their attention directed to something in the middle of the street, where the crowd was thickest.

"Oh, crap. Something's going down." Tetra opened her door.

Merritt scrambled out to let Tess out. The Lunar Fae's hands glowed with wisps of silver fire. Angry yelling echoed down the street.

"You should get checked for rabies!"

"You should remove that gigantic stick from your ass!"

"How could I have a stick up my ass if I, and I quote, 'shit all over your head?'"

"Oh, boy." Tess sighed. "It's Amber and Aurelio again."

Tetra grinned. "Anyone bring popcorn?"

"We'd better break this up." Tess pushed through the crowd.

"I'm not missing this for the world. C'mon, Merritt." Tetra grabbed her hand. "Best entertainment in Little Avalon, those two."

The faerie shoved through the crowd after Tess, and Merritt had little choice but to go along. They emerged at the edge of the fascinated crowd to see two paras facing each other across the asphalt.

"I don't know, Aurelio. You tell me. You're mean enough to

have two assholes." The werewolf had a wild shock of silver hair and striking yellow eyes. Her torn jeans and white T-shirt hugged a lithe figure, so she looked like she could move gracefully, but she stumbled. Each staggering step drew a jingle from the loose leather straps on her neck and chest.

"That doesn't even make sense!" the orc yelled. "Give me my phone back!" The orc's mustache's edges were almost as straight as the crease in his pants and the lapels of his dinner jacket. His bald scalp gleamed like he'd polished it.

Amber, the werewolf, snickered as she held up the phone. "This old thing? You shouldn't leave your stuff lying around, Aurelio."

"What's she wearing?" Merritt whispered, staring at the leather thing.

"It's a shifting harness. Major fashion for the Weres. They've developed magic that lets it stay on and adapt when you shift shape," Tetra supplied.

"It wasn't lying around. I forgot it on my car's roof," Aurelio snapped. "That is what happens when one has a real job. You get busy and forget things."

"A *real* job?" Amber bared her teeth. "You're telling me that producing priceless works of art isn't a real job?"

Aurelio scoffed. "I'm not sure anything about your art is priceless. I'm not even sure it's art."

Amber threateningly raised the phone over her head. "Take it back!"

"Give me the phone, Amber!" Aurelio yelled.

"*Take back what you said about my art!*" Amber shouted.

"Fine. I take it back, but I'll do you one better. I'll reword what I said." Aurelio folded his arms. "Your paintings are an insult to the word 'art.'"

Amber gasped, then hurled the phone onto the asphalt. The resulting crack made everyone in the crowd wince.

"How dare you!" Aurelio thundered.

"*Hey!*" Tess yelled, clapping her hands.

As they met, a plume of smoke rose from her palms, and Amber and Aurelio hesitated.

Tess marched between them, arms folded. "That's enough. Both of you," she barked.

"Stay out of this, fae. It doesn't concern you." Amber bared her teeth, her canines growing.

"Arrest her!" Aurelio pointed at Amber. "For property destruction!"

"No one's arresting anyone," Tess snapped.

"More's the pity. She should rot in a jail cell!" Aurelio yelled. "Playing that junk she calls music at all hours of the night—"

"Junk? *Junk?* What do you call that wail-y bullshit you listen to at the ungodly hour of eleven in the morning?" Amber demanded. "When any self-respecting werewolf is in bed?"

Aurelio drew himself up to his full height. "I listen to Sylthana opera. I can't expect an uncultured animal like you to understand."

Amber roared and lunged at Aurelio. Tess flung an arm around her chest to hold her back, but she managed to direct a flying kick into Aurelio's knee. The orc bellowed in fury and grabbed Amber's arm.

"Get off her!" Tess barked.

Gray fur sprouted on Amber's arms. The wolf's sudden increase in weight made Tess waver, and Amber dropped to all fours, her shout becoming a snarl. Aurelio scrambled back and raised his fists in a practiced motion as Amber bared her teeth, hackles up on her spine, flattened where her decorative harness crossed her back.

"Merritt?" Tetra nudged her. "You've got something going on."

Merritt looked down. Weeds stretched through the cracks in the concrete, trembling as they grew around her feet. Thorns sprouted from their stems.

"Oops." Merritt fumbled for her amulet and touched the *muffle* rune. The weeds stopped growing.

"*Stop it!*" Tess stepped between Aurelio and Amber. "This isn't necessary."

"*He keeps me awake. I haven't slept a full day in months in* my own home!" Amber roared.

"She howls at night. I haven't slept either!" Aurelio snapped.

Shadow's bark drowned out both voices. The sound slammed into Merritt's chest like it was physical, making her stagger back a step. The crowd gasped and clutched each other to keep from falling. Amber dropped to her belly, and Aurelio fell on one knee with a yelp. Only Tess' wings kept her upright.

The crowd parted. Shadow bounded to the center, hackles high. He towered over Amber, who ducked her head and tucked her tail between her legs.

"*What in Merlin's name is the meaning of this?*" Val thundered.

She strode to Tess, fists clenched, a faint red glow emanating from her skin. Shadow's growl shook the ground.

"Sorry, Val. I was trying to keep them apart." Tess flushed.

"How did this start?" Val demanded.

"She stole my phone!" Aurelio scrambled to his feet.

"He put dog shit in my mailbox!" Amber changed into humanoid form and folded her arms.

"I'm not a canine. Maybe you shit in it yourself." Aurelio sneered.

"I saw you do it, asshole," Amber barked.

"Stop!" Val snapped.

They instantly fell silent.

"You two have been living in Little Avalon for months. You both knew you were moving to a place with different species and cultures before you came here," Val snapped. "Nocturnal and diurnal paras have differences, but neither of you has tried to tolerate the other, and that's the key to living together in peace. You have to show each other a little grace."

Amber and Aurelio glowered at one another.

"In short, get over yourselves, both of you," Val ordered. "This is ridiculous. Try to understand each other."

Aurelio bared his tusks at Amber, who snarled.

"Or you'll find *my* tolerance wearing thin," Val added. "Go home. All of you. There's nothing to see here."

Amber turned on her heel and pushed through the dispersing crowd. Val shook her head, the red light still seeping from her skin. "I need a drink," she muttered.

"Mind if we join you?" Liam asked as the crowd thinned.

Val smiled. "Not at all."

Their little group followed Val and Shadow into the Second Fist, where happy paras filled nearly all the seats. The hubbub hushed as Val entered, then resumed, almost drowning out the dwarven music playing on the speakers.

Dante ran a cloth over the bar and flashed Merritt a smile as the group seated themselves.

"Shoplift anything lately?" he teased.

Merritt smirked. "Three whole days with no accidental crimes committed."

"You go, girl." Dante chuckled.

"Is there something I should know about?" Val asked.

Dante gave Merritt's arm a playful punch. "Yeah. Your girl here bakes excellent thank-you brownies."

Val laughed. "Don't I know it. Beer, Dante."

"Please give me whatever I had the first time I was here," Merritt eagerly requested.

Dante poured beers from the polished wooden barrels and lined them up on the bar for the whole group. Val seized hers and drained it in one long pull, leaving white foam on her upper lip.

"Easy, Val," Liam chided. Merritt noticed that he drank his beer from a bottle. It bore the name *Anvil Brewery* and the words *Non-Alcoholic* in small print.

"Sorry. Another, Dante!" Val called. "If anything drives me to drink, it's those two."

"Did you get the feeling that they're fighting about something much worse than playing music at night or putting dog crap on each other's lawns?" Merritt asked.

Val sighed. "I don't know, Merritt. Speciesist prejudice can run deep. It causes hate that we can't explain or understand when we don't hold those prejudices. Trust me." She inclined her head, blue hair tipping over her shoulder. "I grew up as a five-foot-nine dwarf."

"I agree with Merritt. There's more to their story," Tess chipped in. "It's personal."

"I hope never to find out, and they better quit picking fights with each other so I never have to deal with their bullshit again," Val grumbled. "I have enough on my plate without petty issues."

Merritt didn't think being woken up by wolf howls or wailing music every night was petty, but she said nothing.

"I wish I could tell you Little Avalon isn't always like this, Merritt." Val sighed. "The truth is, this melting pot of species and cultures can sometimes be difficult. Things don't always go smoothly. I'm sorry you had to see that."

"I don't think things always go smoothly in *any* community." Merritt spread her hands. "There were Mavka Elves and one Leshbolg in Wolf Glen, and there was always bickering there, too."

"Thanks." Val grimaced. "Makes me feel like less of a failure to hear that."

Tetra cuffed the back of Val's head. "Don't feel like a failure, asshat."

"That makes me feel better, Tetra." Val rolled her eyes.

"See?" Tetra spread her hands. "Who needs therapy?"

"You, probably," Liam retorted.

"I think Antin's the traumatized one." Tess laughed.

Antin wrapped an arm around Tetra's waist and kissed her

cheek, making bright pink faerie dust trickle from her hands. It smelled like strawberries.

Tension leaked from Merritt's muscles the moment her feet met the rich earth in the place of trees.

Her breath was steamy in the cold air as she strolled across the lawn between the trees. The Brooklyn Bridge was a looming behemoth studded with lights. All the trees had fragile new leaves tonight, and they rustled as a breeze stirred them. The throaty sound caused pleasant goosebumps to rise on Merritt's skin.

She'd come earlier than usual tonight. She hadn't held out long after Tess went to bed. Restaurants and bars on the piers played music and spilled warm light on the lawns. The pathways were quiet enough that Merritt could step behind a tree and take a different form.

Her senses sharpened and her vision blurred, but every movement stood out starkly in the stillness. Scent and hearing took center stage as her massive ears pivoted left and right, capturing laughter from a nearby bar, the hum of traffic on the bridge, and the footsteps of a cautious early caterpillar on a twig.

She flared her nostrils and stepped forward on delicate hooves that splayed when they took her weight. Grace rippled through her as she strolled across the lawn, her damp nose twitching.

Merritt trotted toward the smell in doe form with effortless elegance. Her strength and lightness intoxicated her. She lowered her head, shook her ears, and kicked her heels toward the starless sky. A snort of pleasure escaped her and she leaped, soaring several feet above the ground, then kicked out to the side in a playful twist that stretched her tight lower back.

Freedom!

Merritt landed with barely a sound and accelerated. Her

slender limbs propelled her across the grass in mighty bounds, tail thrown high, ears swept back. The breeze rushed through her whiskers and kissed her skin. She covered half the park in minutes, her limbs stretching and reaching, and trotted to a halt in a thicket.

She panted from exertion, each breath expelling tension from her body, and rubbed her nose on her foreleg. She dropped her muzzle to the ground and sought out the soft blades with dexterous lips. The new grass was delicious her mouth, and she relaxed as she grazed, ears flopping to the sides.

Dinner had not been long ago, so Merritt nibbled only grass for a few minutes before her belly felt full. She folded her delicate legs and lay down, then lifted her nose to gaze beyond the bushes and trees surrounding her. In deer vision, the skyline was a series of blurred spots of light, almost indistinguishable from the stars.

She thought about the High Line's greenery running through the concrete jungle. Humans craved rich earth and blossoming life more than they realized. The thought of the day out with her new friends filled Merritt's chest with warmth, but as she contemplatively chewed her cud, she couldn't suppress the tension in her belly.

Tess had helped her write a document containing her work experience and skills, which she'd called a *résumé*. It wasn't long, but that wasn't why Jackson had handed it back when she asked him to consider giving her a job. It was because of the fiasco with the cocoa and sugar the other day.

Or maybe Lawrence Davies had told everyone how she'd screwed up his geraniums.

She shuddered. What if she never found a job? She'd been in Little Avalon long enough to know that everyone had one and lived independently, paying their own way. Right now, the Eternity Throne paid for Merritt's upkeep. How long would they be content to care for her? What if they stopped?

Tess paid Val to live in the Stonehold House. What if Merritt couldn't?

She shifted her weight uneasily and rose to her hooves. Too late, the scent of humans flooded her nostrils. She tensed, looking around, and realized the two humans she'd smelled hadn't noticed her. They were engrossed in one another. The girl leaned against a tree near the path, her arms wrapped around the boy's neck, and their faces were practically glued to one another. Whimpers of pleasure escaped them both.

Merritt's nose wrinkled. The rampant hormones of adolescence were so thick in the air that she could taste them. She backed away, having no desire to watch as the boy fumbled with the girl's coat. The tiniest sound made her head whip around—the tap of a shoe's sole on the path.

A thin man in a black hoodie edged nearer to the teenagers. Metal gleamed in his hand: the blade of a knife.

Merritt snorted, the alarm call deep and loud, but the man barely spared her a glance. The teenagers didn't hear. They were too wrapped up in each other to notice the mugger approaching them with a weapon.

Merritt dropped to her knees, transforming as she did so behind the cover of the holly bushes. She placed one hand on the dirt, breathing hard, and reached for the amulet with the other. What to do? *Contact?* Val could not get here before the mugger reached those humans.

She touched *muffle*. The suppression of her magic landed on her like a weighted blanket, and she fought the sudden heaviness as she pushed through the bushes and stepped onto the path between the mugger and the teenagers.

"*Hey!*" she yelled. "*Stop!*"

The teenagers jumped and whirled around.

"I wasn't going to—" the boy began.

"Not you," Merritt barked. "*Him!*"

She pointed at the mugger, who looked like he was about to flee.

His gaze traveled up and down her short, slender form, and a sneer lifted his lip. "*Give me your phones!*" he yelled, waving the knife. "*All of you! Now!*"

The girl shrieked and grabbed her boyfriend's arm. He fumbled in his pocket and yanked out a switchblade. It clicked as it snapped open.

"Yeah? You wanna fight?" he yelled, striding forward.

"Don't—" Merritt began.

"I'll take you on, asshole!" The boy swiped at the mugger, a loose, inexperienced blow that cut the air several feet from the guy's face.

The mugger's sneer deepened. He backed up a step and flipped the knife in his hand, holding it more effectively; he had training and experience. The teen and his switchblade didn't stand a chance.

"*Yeah, that's right! Leave us alone! Run away!*" the boy shrieked, swiping the air again.

The mugger hunkered down and focused, and Merritt charged. She bumped into the teenager, knocking him several steps forward, and reached for the mugger with a high-pitched battle cry. He hesitated for an instant, which was all the time Merritt needed. She planted a kick solidly in his groin, feeling the satisfying squish as her boot met his balls.

As the mugger squealed, Merritt grabbed the back of his head and shoved him face-first into the nearest bush. She seized his arm and mashed it against a tree, and the knife clattered from his fingers. He kept screaming and clutching his crotch, and something fell out of his pocket and rattled on the path.

"I had it handled!" the boy protested, raising his knife.

"Run, idiots!" Merritt barked.

"Come on!" The girl grabbed her boyfriend's hand and

sprinted away, shedding high heels as she went. He didn't appear reluctant to go with her.

The groaning mugger rolled to his knees. Merritt turned to flee, but the glint of a streetlight on glass made her pause. The guy's phone lay at her feet, screen cracked after its fall.

Merritt didn't know much about phones, but she knew they contained information.

She bent and scooped it up. The mugger still had his face in the dirt. Merritt tucked the phone into her pocket, spun, and sprinted away. Terrified she'd lose the phone, she remained humanoid as she crossed the park, bolted over the street, and scrambled up a fire escape to the safety of a roof.

CHAPTER FOURTEEN

Merritt's lungs burned as she raced across the last roof to Little Avalon. Her feet scraped and thudded on the school's broad roof, her favorite shortcut to the main street. Deerskin slipped on shingles, and she went down on one knee with a jolt of pain. Had someone heard her? She didn't stick around to find out. Cloak floating behind her, she scrambled over a chimney, raced to the roof's edge, and dropped onto a closed dumpster in the alley behind the school.

Her feet clanged on the dumpster. She stretched out her arms and landed on the alley floor palms-first with barely any impact. Her roll carried her to her feet without losing momentum, and she jogged to the mouth with sweat trickling down her spine.

The phone bumped in her pocket as she slowed to a walk, pulling off her cloak. A glance left and right told her that none of the few nocturnal paras on the street looked twice at her. She exhaled, trying to hide her panting, and draped her cloak over her arm.

With any luck, nobody would notice her.

She hurried upstairs, still breathing hard when she peered around the door into the kitchen. The clock on the wall told her it was ten minutes past two. Merritt listened for several tense seconds but heard no one. Damian would still be at work. Tess was in bed.

She was in the clear.

Merritt glanced at the alarm amulets for Damian's window out of habit. They'd remained dormant for days. Tetra thought she'd scared his would-be assassin off. Merritt wasn't so sure, but she had more urgent problems right now. Nobody could catch her with the mugger's phone in her pocket. If they did, she'd have to admit she'd been sneaking to the park late at night.

Then what? Merritt wondered. Would her new friends even be mad? Hard-learned distrust made her belly tighten at the thought of them finding out. She didn't know how far their tolerance and understanding would go, and she had no desire to find out. Not like she'd done in Wolf Glen.

Merritt hurried into her bedroom and shut the door, then went to the window. She pulled the phone from her pocket and tilted it left and right, catching the streetlight on its cracked surface. Perhaps she could get it to the security guards she'd seen patrolling the park. The ones who'd seen her in her fox form had seemed friendly. They could learn more about the mugging spree using this phone and maybe stop the thieves.

It seemed like a good idea. Merritt could hide it under the mattress in the meantime.

She approached the bed, but before she reached it, it buzzed like a trapped bee in her hands. A yelp escaped her as she jumped back. The phone tumbled from her fingers and thudded on the floor, the sound uncomfortably loud, then buzzed again.

That noise, Merritt recognized. Tess' phone made it when it lay on the kitchen table. She'd never held a vibrating phone before, but Tess always looked at hers when it hummed.

Using her toe, she flipped the phone onto its back. The screen lit up, and a message appeared.

> LUGNUTZ
>
> You in?

"In what?" Merritt whispered.

The screen went dark. Merritt crouched beside the phone and tried to remember how Tess made hers work. She poked the screen, which lit up again and showed the same message.

There had to be more. Merritt frowned and swiped the screen instead. Many more messages appeared between Lugnutz and someone the phone labeled "You," which Merritt assumed was the mugger.

She swiped the screen again, reached the top of the message thread, and read swiftly, her heart thumping.

> LUGNUTZ
>
> Yo. Got an opportunity for you. You available?

> YOU
>
> Yeah. What's up?

> LUGNUTZ
>
> You done good working the muggings in the park. Got plenty of phones, plenty of cash. Boss is impressed with your work. Wants to offer you more.

> YOU
>
> Yeah?

> LUGNUTZ
>
> Muggings are good, but drawing too much attention. Can't keep doing them forever. Gotta move on, but first, one last chance to rake in the dough.

> YOU
>
> I'm listening.

LUGNUTZ

Park's holding an event on March 31st. Outdoor music thing in a tent they're setting up. Minimal security. Marks packed in like sardines. We surround the tent, pull guns, and grab everything they've got. We're in and out in thirty.

YOU

Sounds good. Rich folks?

LUGNUTZ

Tickets are thirty each. I'd say so.

Merritt raised her eyebrows. The details eluded her, but she now knew guns were deadly and could make holes in people. If Lugnutz and his cronies charged into a tent full of humans toting guns, they could cause injuries or worse.

The following few messages confirmed her fears.

LUGNUTZ

There's one more thing.

YOU

What?

LUGNUTZ

Never know when a security guy or some asshole in the crowd is gonna try to be a hero. If that happens, we shoot our way out and clear off. Might be a death or two. You cool with that?

Merritt thought, *How could anyone be cool with that?*

YOU

Killed a guy when I was jumped. Course I'm cool with it.

LUGNUTZ

Just checking.

LUGNUTZ

Hello?

LUGNUTZ

Hello??

LUGNUTZ

You in?

Merritt gulped to wet her dry mouth. The mugger must have been having this text exchange with Lugnutz a few minutes before he approached the unsuspecting teenagers.

They were planning a robbery that could result in casualties. It sounded like it would.

Merritt sagged onto the floor beside the phone, staring at it. What could she do? Give it to Val? Then she would have to explain where she'd been going late at night. Would Val feel betrayed and send her out of Little Avalon, the only place Merritt remembered feeling at home?

What about the human authorities? Merritt wondered, remembering that Isabella had mentioned "cops."

Police, her training supplied. *Law enforcement officers.*

Merritt rubbed her neck, wondering how to contact them. Her training was silent on that front.

She carefully scooped up the phone, which refrained from buzzing again, and wrapped it in a towel before stuffing it under the foot of her mattress where she wouldn't feel the lump. It was March fifteenth. Merritt had two weeks to figure out what to do with the information.

If she didn't, a lot of people could get badly hurt.

The nail salon owner had striking eyes. They had no pupil but looked like twin pits of darkness studded with pinpricks of light that looked like stars. Somehow, they smiled when Merritt shuffled through the doors, feeling like a lost child though Tess was behind her.

"Morning, Trish!" Tess called.

"Tess, good to see you. How are those acrylics holding up?" the salon owner asked.

Her business' layout seemed similar to the hairdresser's, which was no surprise, considering its location in the Stonehold House beside Isabella's. The colors here were equally bold and bright: a black and white carpet, splashy art on the walls, and sophisticated modern furniture in shiny black metal, from the couches against the walls to the coffee table serving them and the two salon tables on the other side of the room. Merritt noticed that those tables had chairs on either side, one for the customer and one for the nail technician.

"They're perfect." Tess fluttered her colorful nails. "As I told Merritt, she'll learn from the best."

"Thank you for offering me a chance," Merritt added, "even though I haven't had any training."

"Hey, not everyone comes from a stable background that allows for a college education, especially not after the war. As a teenager, I worked in a tiny village near the Eyrie as a self-taught nail tech." The Starlight Fae tilted her head, silver hair trickling over her shoulder. Her skin matched her hair. "It was a long time before I saved enough for an official course. I'd love to help you."

"I don't know anything about nails, but I'm willing to learn," Merritt told her.

Tess laid a hand on her shoulder. "Merritt's a fast learner. She taught herself to bake bread, brownies, and muffins in a matter of days."

"I still can't do that after years of trying." The fae winked. "I'm Patricia Storm, but please call me Trish."

"Hi, Trish." Merritt grinned.

"Ready to learn about nails?" Trish asked.

Merritt eagerly nodded. "Ready to do my best."

"That's what I like to hear." Trish beamed.

"Good luck, Merritt." Tess patted her shoulder. "See you tonight."

"See you." Merritt felt a pang of nervousness as Tess strode through the doors and hurried away.

Trish touched her arm. "Scary, right?"

Merritt jumped. "Um, what?"

"This whole thing. Moving from Avalon to Earth. Learning how to function in a world so different from the villages where we grew up." Trish spread her hands. "Trying to get a job."

Merritt exhaled. "Terrifying."

"Sounds like the village where you lived was even more isolated than mine, judging by what Isabella says. Moving to Earth was scary enough for me. I can't imagine how weird it all seems to you." Trish inclined her head at the salon tables. "You'll be fine, though."

Merritt followed her across the salon. "I hope so."

"I know so because this is Little Avalon, the best place in the world." Trish slid into a chair. "The humans and paras here are different. They'll do anything to help a newcomer. You'll do great."

"Thanks for saying that." Merritt sat. "Everyone's been nicer than I could have hoped for."

"You can trust them." Trish held her gaze.

Looking into those startling starlight eyes, Merritt thought about the phone hidden under her mattress and felt an uncomfortable kick in her belly.

"Enough of that!" Trish clapped her hands, and Merritt jumped. "Let's start with the basics. I'll teach you on the job while you keep the place tidy and answer the phone."

Merritt nodded. "I practiced talking on the phone. Tess and Liam helped. Those…" She gestured at the handset on the back counter. "They're much less complicated than the little ones everyone carries around."

"Then you're already halfway there," Trish assured her.

"I know how to clean, too," Merritt added.

Trish chuckled. "I'll teach you your first nail-related skill." She extended her fingers, and Merritt admired the beautiful swirls of colorful polish on each of her nails. "False nails like acrylics are all the rage, and I sometimes wear them, but my forte is painting natural nails with scenes like these."

"Wow." Merritt leaned closer. "These are like tiny paintings. Are they stickers?"

"I use stickers, but these are mine." Trish smiled. "I admit I used magic."

Merritt stared. Trish's nails bore gold and silver comets, twinkling stars, and gleaming nebulae on a navy background. She could not imagine how time-consuming this work must have been.

"I don't think I could do anything like that," Merritt admitted.

"I'm not asking you to." Trish wiggled her nails. "I will teach you how to take the polish off."

Merritt's jaw dropped. "You want me to destroy that?"

"They're chipped, and I'm bored with them. I will paint a spring theme—flowers, bunnies, and sunshine." Trish grinned. "First, we need to get rid of the polish. Soap and water won't do it, or it would come off in the shower."

Merritt nodded. "That makes sense."

"We use this." Trish retrieved a bottle from a nearby cabinet. "Acetone."

She opened the lid, and a nasty sensation crawled over Merritt's skin, like she had stumbled upon deadly nightshade while picking berries. She worked hard to keep her face blank as Trish tipped a few drops on a cotton pad, then applied it to her left pinky finger.

Its intense smell hit the back of Merritt's palate like a punch.

She leaned away as Trish spread the substance over her finger. The beautiful painting vanished.

"See? No effort at all. You don't even have to rub." Trish held up the pad, showing Merritt blue and yellow stains. "It comes right off."

Merritt nodded.

"It's a pretty strong chemical, so don't drink it, but it's safe to put on your skin." Trish pushed the bottle and the roll of cotton pads toward her, then held out her hands. "Your turn. Go right ahead!"

Merritt swallowed her nerves and fumbled a pad from the roll. Her skin crawled when she grasped the bottle, but she ignored the terror in her gut and dripped a little acetone onto the pad. To her relief, nothing happened.

She exhaled. *You're being silly, Merritt.*

"You'll need a bit more," Trish coached.

"Okay." Merritt nodded and tipped the bottle with more confidence.

Acetone splashed over her fingers, its fruity scent filling the air, and the burning sensation was so intense that Merritt couldn't hold back a yelp of pain. She dropped the bottle and pad and scrambled back, clutching her hands to her chest.

"Merritt!" Trish jumped up. "What's wrong?"

Merritt's heart thumped against her fingers. The burn brought tears to her eyes. It felt like she'd plunged her hands into a beehive.

Trish righted the acetone bottle and hurried around the table. "Show me."

Merritt extended her hands toward Trish, and her gut twisted. Scarlet welts rose on her pale skin, matching the splashes of acetone. The thin skin between her fingers was forming blisters.

"Oh, crap. Quick." Trish grabbed Merritt's arm and steered

her toward a sink. She turned on the cold water. "Put your hands under there."

Merritt shivered as she obeyed. The water stung at first, then soothed. Trish rubbed her shoulder as it flowed over her skin and the pain faded.

"Sorry," Merritt croaked.

"You have nothing to apologize for." Trish smiled. "You've probably never come into contact with strong chemicals like this one."

Merritt mutely shook her head. "Except for bleach at Tess' house. It made my hands burn, too."

"Merlin's beard! You poor thing. Seems your skin is more sensitive than most," Trish observed. "Must be a Leshbolg thing."

Merritt shrugged. She had no way of knowing.

"We'd better get you to the clinic," Trish suggested.

"It's okay. You have appointments," Merritt protested.

Trish scoffed. "I can reschedule."

"Seriously, it's fine." Merritt gently withdrew her hands from the water. "Look."

The blisters had faded to the angry red of a bad sunburn. Where the welts had been, only a pink rash remained. Merritt flexed her fingers and felt only vague discomfort.

"Ah." Trish raised her eyebrows. "Fast healing. That's nice to have."

Merritt managed a smile. "I have a few powers." She sighed. "Using acetone doesn't seem to be one of them."

"We could try gloves," Trish suggested, "but that's not the only strong chemical we use around here. It's not even one we consider dangerous." She grimaced. "You haven't met the toxic trio yet—toluene, formaldehyde, and dibutyl phthalate."

The names made Merritt shudder.

"If you're this sensitive to acetone, I don't think it's worth the risk." Trish sighed. "Merritt, I'm sorry. Working here won't be safe for you."

Merritt's shoulders sagged. "I'm sorry for wasting your time."

"Don't say that." Trish grinned. "I got to meet a fascinating new person. Not wasted, trust me."

Merritt appreciated Trish's kindness, but her heart was heavy as she left the salon, keeping her still-sore hands in her coat pockets. She started to go home, but when a snatch of laughter drifted from the door of Isabella's salon, her steps slowed.

An elf and a human sat in the waiting area. Isabella was working on a Woodland Fae's hair, oblivious to the porcupine quills growing from the scalp, which she blow-dried and brushed upright.

I could use a friend. Merritt shuffled into the salon.

"Hey, Merritt!" Isabella called, bending sideways to direct the blow dryer at the fae's roots, making her damp hair stand up.

"Hey." Merritt lingered by the door, feeling stupid.

"You want anything done today? Your hair looks great." Isabella switched off the blow dryer and ran the brush over the fae's hair.

Merritt touched its tips. "Not today. I, uh..."

"Came in to hang out." Isabella beamed. "Awesome. Have a seat over there. I know you like being close to the action." She indicated the chair by the mirror on her left.

"Thanks." Merritt sank into it.

"Girl, what happened to your hands?" Isabella asked.

Merritt told her about her brief trial as a nail technician.

"Aw, man. Acetone did that to you? That's rough. You must be extremely allergic," Isabella sympathized. "I'm sorry to hear it."

"I'll keep looking for work," Merritt mumbled.

"It'll happen. Keep believing. Your big-city dreams will come true." Isabella grinned.

Merritt smiled. "Thanks. What do you call that hairstyle? It looks amazing."

"Doesn't it?" The fae beamed at her reflection. "Nobody does my hair like Isabella."

"Thanks, Macy." Isabella returned her smile. "This is a faux hawk, so named because it's not a mohawk but has similar vibes." She sculpted the front with her brush, not hearing the rattle of porcupine quills. "Macy's hair holds it better than most."

"It's worth the time in the chair," Macy observed.

"You're nearly done," Isabella told her. "Hey, were you there when Aurelio and Amber fought a few nights ago?"

"Boy, was I!" Macy chortled. "What a scene!"

"I can't believe I missed it," Isabella complained. "It was the talk of the town."

"It was crazy. I thought Amber was going to rip his face off!" Macy relished the image.

"It was insane," Merritt agreed. "I can't believe they were so violent about silly things like music playing late at night or during the day."

"Did you really think that was what the fight was about?" Macy raised her eyebrows.

Merritt hesitated. "I told Val afterward that it felt like there was more to it."

"There's *much* more to it." Isabella chortled.

"So much more," Macy assured her.

Merritt leaned back in her chair, forgetting about her painful hands. "Sounds like a good story."

"It's a great story, if a sad one." Isabella spritzed Macy's hair with product and kept sculpting.

"They're far more than disgruntled neighbors." Macy paused for effect. "They're former lovers."

Merritt raised her eyebrows. "No way."

"It's true." Isabella grinned. "This was before my time in Little Avalon, but everyone tells me the same thing."

"They were madly in love. Wildly in love. *Crazy* in love." Macy sighed. "I remember when they moved here. They were among the earliest residents of Little Avalon. They always hung on one another's arms. They were like teenagers, giggling and kissing on street corners. They lived in Stonehold One on the top floor."

Merritt tried to imagine Aurelio and Amber making out like the teens in the park. It seemed impossible. "What happened?"

"The rumors are rampant and delicious." Macy shrugged. "All I can tell you for certain is that things ended badly. They were looking at buying a house together when Val made the small houses by the school available. They wanted to marry and raise a family. Things seemed to be going great."

"Until they weren't," Isabella chipped in. "I've heard different stories about why they broke up. Some say he cheated. Others say *she* cheated. Some believe his family didn't approve of her, or vice versa."

"I heard that Aurelio has a secret lovechild, and Amber found out." Macy grinned.

Isabella raised an eyebrow. "That one seems far-fetched."

"Either way, things ended, and it was messy," Macy went on. "Both were too stubborn to leave Little Avalon, and neither was in financial difficulty. Aurelio is the heir to some lost kingdom, if you believe the stories—"

"Which one shouldn't," Isabella interrupted.

"Not always." Macy smirked. "Either way, they bought both houses they'd been looking at right next to one another."

"Wow." Merritt blinked. "No wonder there's so much trouble between them."

"Wild story, isn't it?" Macy shook her head.

"Hey!" Isabella protested.

"Sorry." Macy stopped moving.

Isabella fixed a few strands of hair going the wrong way.

"I wonder what we can do to make peace between them," Merritt murmured.

Macy snorted. "You're young, dear. You don't know how deep the rifts between jilted lovers can be. I don't think peace is possible."

"I've heard the stories about their drama. Digging up each other's lawns, dumping garbage into each other's backyards... I don't think peace is possible," Isabella admitted. "Things will only improve if one gives up and moves away."

"It's sad to have such friction in Little Avalon." Merritt flexed her fingers, glad to see that only a faint pink mark remained where the burns had been.

"Not only that, but their *neighbors* can't take much more of this. I live down the street from them, and that's bad enough," Macy grumbled. "Amber yells as loud as she can during the night, and Aurelio plays opera at top volume during the day. They're driving the whole street nuts with their efforts to drive one another nuts."

"I'm sure it's unpleasant," Merritt murmured.

Macy shrugged. "I don't mind, but Bob and Anna, the old couple across from me, are talking about moving."

"Really?" Isabella frowned. "That's shitty. If Amber and Aurelio cause people to move, Val will lose business."

"Someone has to do something," Macy agreed. "I don't think either will admit that it's not working and move away. They're both far too stubborn to give up their home."

"Maybe they can reconcile," Merritt suggested.

Isabella chuckled. "Maybe unicorns exist."

Macy and Merritt exchanged looks. Merritt had to drop her gaze to avoid giggling.

Macy changed the subject. "Did you guys hear about the vigilante on the news?"

"What's a vigilante?" Merritt asked.

"Somebody who protects people outside the bounds of the law," Isabella explained. "Like Spiderman."

Merritt nodded, pretending to know who that was.

"What vigilante?" Isabella asked.

"The tabloids are going insane with it!" Macy waved her

hands. "You know there have been all those muggings in Brooklyn Bridge Park?"

"Yeah?" Isabella seized an aerosol can and thoroughly sprayed Macy's hair.

"Some mysterious person is protecting people from the muggers," Macy told her.

Merritt's gut clenched. "Who?"

"That's the mystery." Macy smirked. "A man walking his dog says he saw a giant take on an armed mugger. The mugger fired shots, but they never found any blood."

"A giant?" Merritt squeaked.

"Probably not a *real* giant," Macy acknowledged.

Isabella laughed. "Obviously not."

Macy and Merritt exchanged glances again.

"I bet the guy was high on something," Isabella added. "Especially when you think of what the other victims said."

"The other victims?" Merritt tried to keep her tone normal, but the words came out in a whisper.

"Yeah. Another mugger attacked two teenagers in the park, and the vigilante defended them. Interestingly, they gave different descriptions of the mysterious Good Samaritan." Isabella tapped a few hairs into place. "The boyfriend said it was a ripped six-foot female MMA fighter. The girlfriend said it was an ordinary-looking chick who kicked the mugger in the nuts and ran away."

"Maybe they're not the same person," Merritt suggested. "It could be a coincidence." She cleared her throat. "The first mugger…how did he describe this vigilante?"

"He can't," Isabella told her.

"He's *dead*?" Merritt whimpered.

"No, no. He had a severe concussion. No recollection of the event." Isabella grinned. "Mysterious, right?"

"Maybe it's Val," Macy suggested. "It seems like a her-thing."

Merritt chipped in, "Yeah, it's probably Val."

"You kidding? If Val was involved, she'd have thrown all the local gangsters into jail by now. It wouldn't be the first time." Isabella stepped back. "Okay, Macy. What do you think?"

Macy touched the spiky tips of her hair. "I love it. My daughter is visiting from, um, out of town tomorrow. I'm sure she'll be jealous."

Merritt's shoulders relaxed as the conversation turned to Macy's daughter, but she told herself that she'd have to be careful.

No matter how the place of trees called to her, she had no choice but to stay away.

CHAPTER FIFTEEN

Genevieve purred into her usual space in the shaded carport beneath the queen's tower. Val kept her hands off the steering wheel, allowing the Mustang to park herself. Genevieve did it better.

"Dinner with the queen." Tess wiped her palms on her blue dress. "I can't believe it."

"You didn't have to dress up." Val smiled. "Julie will likely be wearing sweatpants and a T-shirt."

"It's the *queen*," Tess croaked. "Why do you think she invited me? You and Liam go to dinner at the palace all the time, but not me."

"She's always reaching out to Lunar Fae who make a difference in the world." Val unbuckled her seat belt. "Look at the work you've done with the High Magic Division."

"Do you think it caught her attention?" Tess quavered.

"There might be a simpler explanation." Val smiled. "Julie likes you."

"She's amazing, but she's also a regular person," Liam added from the backseat. "Can we get out? Shadow's drooling on me."

Shadow love Liam! Shadow licked his face.

"Shadow! Cut it out." Liam pushed him off.

Val climbed out and folded the front seat to let Liam and Shadow out. The big dog scrambled into the courtyard at the tower's foot, waving tail high.

"A regular person?" Tess hissed as Val opened the trunk. "*A regular person?* This is Queen Julia Artura Pendragon we're talking about. She conquered *Mordred*!"

Val removed a keg of Anvil Brewery's finest IPA from the trunk and balanced it on her shoulder. "You know what I mean."

"I don't," Tess muttered.

"She grew up in the city thinking she was an ordinary human, like you did." Val stumped toward the tower door. "You two have a lot in common. She also recruited you. She clearly sees something in you."

Tess gulped.

"Don't be intimidated. She's cool," Liam told Tess. He raised his tablet, which he carried like a satchel on his hip, and swiped the screen. "Alarm amulets still quiet in Little Avalon."

"For now," Val muttered.

She knocked on the door, and an Aether Elf answered. His willowy body, clad in a midnight blue shirt and black slacks, was topped with a mop of soft dark hair, and his manner exuded kindness.

"Your Majesty." Tess bowed.

"Not tonight." The elf smiled. "You're a guest in my home. Call me Taylor. Need help with that, Val?"

Val eyed him and adjusted the keg on her shoulder. "I'm good."

"That was a stupid question." Taylor laughed. "Come upstairs. Everyone's in the kitchen."

They crossed a living room strewn with toys, blankets, and forgotten snack plates. A solid gold hat stand stood in one corner, and the state-of-the-art TV played an old cop show with the sound off.

"Sorry for the mess," Taylor added. "Toddlers are fun."

A small explosion rattled the windows as they climbed the stairs. Tess jumped, but Taylor did not react.

They followed him into the kitchen. Lilli sat in her high chair, smoke slowly dissipating from her hair. Merlin leaned against the nearest counter with a cup of tea in hand. Julie crashed around in the pantry.

Val placed the keg on the table. "Beer's here."

"Not a moment too soon." Julie emerged from the pantry with a tray of gold goblets.

"Is it necessary to break out the gold tonight, honey?" Taylor inquired.

Julie huffed as she placed the heavy tray on the table. "I forgot to wash the beer glasses. They're still in the dishwasher, covered in dust."

"Tastes just as good from a goblet," Val observed. She tipped the keg onto its side and expertly poured beer into the gleaming receptacles.

"Hey, everyone." Julie waved. "I'll greet you all properly after I get the roast out of the oven."

"May I help with anything?" Liam asked.

Julie straightened, oven mitts in hand, and planted her hands on her hips. "See that, Merlin?"

Merlin was scrolling on his phone. He startled guiltily. "See what?"

"How to be a kind and considerate guest." Julie turned to Liam. "You can fetch plates from the pantry, my precious human friend."

Liam smirked. "Sure."

"Why's my Lilli-billy smoking?" Taylor smoothed her hair.

"I gave her orange juice." Julie pulled a smoking leg of lamb from the oven and placed it on the counter with pride.

"What did she ask for?" Taylor inquired.

"Orange juice." Julie laughed. "How are your side dishes doing, babe?"

Taylor busied himself with the pots on the stove, and Val dispensed the froth-topped gold goblets. She had her back to the door when someone new entered the room, followed by a trilling cry.

"Valeerieeeeeeeee!"

Val turned, grinning. "Rosa! Hey."

Julie's adopted mother spread her arms wide, grinning. Shopping bags hung from her elbows. She pressed Val into a bosomy, perfume-scented hug. The tension melted from Val's shoulders, and she leaned into the embrace.

"Gramma!" Lilli squealed.

"Hey, Mom." Julie pecked Rosa on the cheek.

"Hello, dear. Dinner smells good." Rosa grabbed Val by the chin. "Darling, you're pale. I'm sure you have an iron deficiency."

"Mom, don't start," Julie groaned.

"You must be exhausted half the time. It's all that running around you do, being a duchess and everything." Rosa tutted. "Look at you. I'm sure you're eating nothing but takeout."

"Um..." Val's toes curled.

"You won't be young forever, you know." Rosa gave a throaty laugh. "Not like me, thanks to a lunar explosion."

"A lunar explosion?" Tess gaped.

Rosa turned. "Teresa! It's good to see you. Julia told me you were coming." She grasped the fae's hands. "Do you know the story about how she gave me eternal youth?"

"Um, no," Tess managed. "I thought you simply looked amazing for your age."

Rosa beamed. "I do, thank you. Let me tell you about it."

She wrapped an arm around Tess' shoulders and directed her to a seat at the kitchen table. Val placed a goblet in Rosa's hands as Taylor put the finishing touches on the side dishes. Liam set the table, and Julie carved the roast with ease. Ignoring the toys on her chair's tray, Lilli contentedly played with a teaspoon.

Merlin shuffled over to Val. "A word, Your Grace?"

Val looked up. "Uh, sure." She sipped her beer for fortitude.

"I'd like to hear how Manni…I mean, how Merritt is doing in Little Avalon." Desperation tightened the corners of Merlin's eyes.

Val swirled her beer, thinking. "It's hard to tell."

"Hard to tell?" Merlin raised his eyebrows. "She hasn't caused any minor catastrophes yet?"

"Well, she destroyed the park's lawn, but she did it saving someone's truck from being stolen. I gave her brownie points for that." Val rubbed her neck. "It was less destructive than it could have been."

"That doesn't sound promising," Merlin muttered. "What else?"

"Nothing else. She's fine, except that she relies on Tess for everything." Val sighed. "I don't think Tess minds, but I'm worried that Merritt won't cope on her own in the long term."

Merlin tilted his head. "That's unusual. Merritt was independent quite early in her other placements."

"They were all insular forest communities, Merlin. This is a whole new ball game for her." Val paused. "She's a fast learner, and everyone likes her. I don't blame them. She's smart, fearless, and has no trouble telling right from wrong. I like her, too."

"I sense there's a 'but' coming," Merlin muttered.

Val sighed. "She's had no luck finding a job."

Julie overheard. "The Eternity Throne will pay for Merritt's upkeep. The kid's an orphan because we didn't help her when she needed it." She shot a swift glance at Merlin, who looked away. "We will pay her way for the rest of her life, if that's what it takes."

"It's not the money that worries me, Julie," Val confessed. "It's her well-being. She wants to contribute and fit in. She was distraught after the incident at the park. She feels like she has to earn the right to stay in Little Avalon."

"Does she?" Merlin asked.

Val smiled. "No, but I want her to be happy there. Maybe it's *too* foreign."

Merlin spread his hands. "She'll have to adapt. She has nowhere else to go, Val."

"Then we'll make it work. I only want what's best for her." Val smiled. "Did you know she saved Damian Radu from a professional assassin?"

Julie raised her eyebrows. "She did?"

"How?" Merlin demanded. "Did she use her powers?"

"If they include super senses, then yes. She smelled garlic when nobody else did and alerted Tess, who found an unidentified para kneeling over Damian with a silver stake in his hand," Val explained. "Damian would have died if it wasn't for Merritt."

Merlin beamed, his cheeks flushing with pride. "That's my girl."

"Silver," Julie muttered. "It's very easy to get hold of on Earth, unfortunately. Is Damian safe?"

"As safe as he'll let me make him," Val confessed. "He's not interested in having a guard at his door. He's a stubborn ass, if you ask me."

"It takes one to know one." Julie smirked.

Taylor elbowed her. "Says she."

"Hey!" Julie swatted him with an oven mitt. "Dinner's ready, people. Let's eat!"

"*Food!*" Lilli roared, smacking the spoon on the tray.

They went into the dining room, where tapestries from lunar history decorated the walls. The round oak table's legs sank into a red carpet, and a chandelier hung from the ceiling, shedding the pale light of will-o'-the-wisps enclosed in glass orbs.

"Your dining room is beautiful," Tess murmured.

"You think so? Mom decorated it," Julie told her.

Rosa scoffed. "As if there's anything wrong with that."

"I like it," Tess assured her.

"Glad somebody does," Julie muttered.

"Julia!" Rosa protested.

"Kidding, Mom. Kidding." Julie shot Val a meaningful look.

"It's very pretty, Rosa." Val set her goblet on the table.

"Thank you, Valerie, dear." Rosa beamed. "See, Julia? She has good taste."

Julie muffled a smile. "Sure, Mom."

Silence reigned for several minutes as everyone lost themselves in the meal. The roast was good, but Taylor's side dishes won the day: buttery mounds of mashed potatoes, roasted vegetables with crispy outsides and sweet, fluffy innards, magnificent dinner rolls stuffed with goat cheese, and a crisp, leafy salad. Shadow lay under the table, ecstatically gnawing on the bone.

Liam tore a chunk off a roll. "This is a weird question, Your Majesties—"

"I love weird questions. Everyone asks me boring ones." Julie giggled.

Liam smiled. "Why do you cook your own meals? You have a kitchen full of brownies to serve you anything you like. I bet Queen Esmerelda never saw it."

Julie's shoulders softened at the mention of her late mother. "I don't think Mother could have boiled an egg if she tried. Nor could T a few years ago. He burned water when we started dating."

"Harsh, but true." Taylor inclined his head.

"It was different for me. I went through a rough patch when I left home. Cooking good meals was a privilege I only had for a little while before the war began. I joined the OPMA, and the wheels fell off." Julie's wild gesture indicated chaos. "Those were crazy years. I barely had time to touch the ground, let alone make dinner. I was a recruiter, then a soldier, then a councilor, then the princess, and then the queen. It was a whirlwind."

Taylor squeezed her hand. "A great adventure, but not greater than this one."

Julie tilted her head to look up at him, adoration in her eyes. Moonlight seeped from her wings at his touch. "You're so cute."

"After the war and the Wild Hunt's conquest, we spent a few months mopping up the mess," Taylor added. "That time was nearly as crazy as the war, but we decided to start a family when things settled."

"We sure did." Julie tickled Lilli's tummy, making the toddler squeal. She had a chunk of lamb in one hand and a squashed sweet potato in the other. The rest of her food was smeared over her cheeks.

"I have a Wet Wipe in here somewhere." Rosa rummaged in her purse.

"Then the pregnancy cravings arrived." Taylor shuddered.

Julie snorted. "They were, uh, intense. The brownies were great, but T was better. He understood what I wanted and made it happen."

"I've never Googled so much in my life." Taylor laughed. "Turns out that if you can read and watch a YouTube video, you can cook. Even if your wife wakes up at two in the morning wanting Lobster Thermidor."

"We got into making our own food again." Julie shrugged. "It felt good. It felt...luxurious, to be honest. Turns out time is the biggest luxury of all."

Taylor kissed her hand. "Time with *you*, love."

"Awww." Tess clasped her hands under her chin.

Val thought about Niall and made a mental note to call him when they left the palace.

"You two are so cute together." Rosa pinched Julie's cheek. "Don't you want to make another baby? This one is adorable."

"Mom!" Julie moaned. "Quick, someone start a different

subject. Any subject. She'll tell us what positions to conceive in next!"

"Well, you do know that—" Rosa began.

"I'm having trouble with a couple of neighbors in Little Avalon," Val blurted.

Rosa scowled, but Julie latched onto the topic with relief. "Neighbors? Do they not get along?"

Liam groaned. "You could say that. The latest is that Amber parked her car in front of Aurelio's gate and went to bed wearing noise-canceling headphones. He couldn't get to work, so he pushed it away and ruined the paint."

"He pushed a parked car?" Rosa raised her eyebrows.

"He's an orc," Val added. "She's a werewolf. It's not working. They used to live together in one of the Stonehold Houses, but things ended badly. Now, they're neighbors."

"Both are too stubborn to move away," Liam added.

"I hear that." Taylor muttered.

Julie elbowed his ribs. "Sounds like things are escalating beyond an ordinary neighborly quarrel if they've progressed to property destruction."

Val spread her hands. "They've almost progressed to physical violence. I don't want to take sides or run away from the problem by booting them out of Little Avalon, but I worry that someone will get hurt."

"Orc versus werewolf." Julie nodded. "Could get ugly."

"They stop if I yell at them, but I can't always be around." Val paused. "I don't think that's the solution, anyway. I need a diplomatic way to fix this." She smiled. "A certain king taught me that hitting shit with a hammer doesn't solve everything."

Taylor chuckled.

"Sounds like a wise and benevolent king." Julie stroked his arm. "One his people are lucky to have."

Taylor put his hand over hers.

"I think you should expel them both." Merlin dabbed sauce

from his beard. "They're contributing nothing to Little Avalon. Get rid of them."

Julie interrupted, "You are one of the kindest and most capable rulers in any dimension, Val." She smiled. "You've got this."

Val grinned.

"That's not advice, Julie. It's a pep talk," Rosa complained.

Julie shrugged. "Sometimes that's all you need."

Merritt lined up the four muffins on the table like prisoners awaiting the firing squad. She folded her arms and ran her critical gaze over them, ignoring the delicious scents that filled the kitchen: caramel, banana, cinnamon, butter, sugar, and a crisp hint of blueberries.

The first muffin was crooked. Merritt pushed it back several inches. The second had risen too much. She held up her recipe book to the third and grinned at it. It was perfect.

The click of the front door made her jump. She snapped the book shut, almost squishing the fourth muffin, and a dandelion sprouted from the kitchen table by her elbow.

"Oops!" Merritt picked it and hid it behind her back.

"Hey, Merritt. Sorry to get home so late. We ended up staying at the palace for—" Tess stopped. Her jaw dropped as she gaped at the kitchen.

Muffins covered every surface. They occupied pans on the countertops and bowls on the kitchen table, and lay in rejected heaps on the drainboard. Ingredients covered the table: bags of flour and sugar, cubes of butter, and a massive can of baking powder.

"You've been busy," Tess managed.

"I'll clean up," Merritt promised.

Tess laughed. "Don't worry about that! I love to see you exploring your baking. I assume Damian's gone to work?"

Merritt nodded. "I offered him a banana and cinnamon muffin for breakfast, but he didn't seem to want anything."

"Poor Damian. This assassination thing is getting to him more than he'll admit." Tess flopped into a chair at the table.

"I know you've already eaten..." Merritt began.

Tess extended her hands. "Feed me muffins, woman. All the muffins!"

Merritt giggled. "I was experimenting with different flavors and came up with these four." She pushed them across the table to Tess. "Sorry for the lopsided one and the over-risen one, but I think they'll taste good. Tell me which is the best. I'm trying to choose a batch for Val. I'd like to take her the nicest ones I made."

"I can do that." Tess grinned.

"This one is blueberry and caramel." Merritt indicated the first.

Tess bit into it and closed her eyes. She groaned in pleasure, sagging into her chair. "Merlin's beard, Merritt," she mumbled through masticated muffin. "I feel like I've died and gone to heaven."

Merritt grinned. "It's good?"

"It's incredible." Tess tore off another chunk with her teeth. "I could eat seven of them."

"This next one is apple and cinnamon. I added a pinch of nutmeg. I wanted it spicy." Merritt pointed at the over-risen one.

Tess reluctantly relinquished the first muffin and tasted the second. She had a similar reaction to that one and to the next, which was peanut butter and banana.

"I can't imagine anything being more delicious than these," she declared, gazing at the half-eaten muffin in awe.

Merritt grinned. "Val would like it?"

"Val would love all of them." Tess gestured. "I think the peanut butter one would be her favorite, though."

"One left to try." Merritt pushed it toward her. "This one is dark chocolate chip with salted caramel and a hint of lavender."

"Lavender? So that's why it's slightly purple." Tess inspected it from all angles before biting into it. Her eyes rolled back, and moonlight oozed from her wings in silver tendrils as she emitted a low groan.

"Is it good?" Merritt asked.

"Good?" Tess shook her head. "I don't have the words."

Merritt grimaced. "That bad?"

"What? *No!*" Tess took another bite. "It's fantastic!"

Merritt grinned. "Based on your reaction, I'll send Val a dozen."

Tess finished the muffin in a few more bites and sucked the crumbs from her fingers. "Merritt, I'm not kidding. These are excellent." She studied the others. "I've never had a better one in a coffee shop."

"Thanks, Tess." Merritt gathered the ingredients.

"I'm serious." Tess rose and helped her put them away. "You could make a business out of this. Wait, I have a better idea." She stopped, grinning. "You should apply to become the baker at Hank and Kalyna's restaurant. They need someone to bake breakfast pastries."

Merritt shrugged. "I've only been baking for a week."

"You're doing so well for a beginner. These are pro-level!" Tess gestured with a muffin. "You could become a master baker in months at this rate!"

Merritt laughed. "I don't know about that."

"It's clear that you love baking, and you're great at it. Hank and Kalyna would love to have you. Why don't we take samples to their restaurant tomorrow morning and ask them what they think?"

The idea made Merritt's intestines tie themselves in a knot. She swallowed hard, imagining their critique. It made her toes curl. "I'm not ready," she mumbled.

"They've been talking about hiring a baker for weeks. They could really use you," Tess urged. "You'd have a job you love just down the street."

Merritt bit her lip. "Can I be honest?"

Tess inclined her head.

"I was rejected by a few employers so far." Merritt hesitated. "Not only from jobs, but from homes in my previous placements."

Tess tilted her head. "No one's going to boot you out of Little Avalon, Merritt."

Nervousness thudded in Merritt's gut. *You don't know that I'm the mysterious vigilante of Brooklyn Bridge Park. Would that push you over the edge?*

Tess put an arm around her shoulders. "Hey, I get it. You're not ready to face rejection for your baking right now since it's the one thing you can lose yourself in. I can understand that."

Merritt cleared her throat. "I have another interview lined up tomorrow morning anyway."

Tess grinned. "How did you manage that?"

"I went to the neighbors' houses, trading finished muffins for ingredients—" Merritt began.

"I was about to ask where this stuff came from," Tess interrupted.

Merritt sheepishly grinned. "I saw the recipe for the apple and cinnamon muffins, but we didn't have apples, only chocolate chips. I baked a batch of chocolate chip ones and went down the road to Mrs. Ricci's house. She traded me some apples for the chocolate chip muffins and mentioned that her neighbor across the road loves apples, so I made an apple batch and brought it to her. *She* gave me the lavender."

Tess smiled. "There's no better way to curry favor than bringing delicious treats. How did that lead to an interview?"

"I ended up trading Doctor Oakheart six blueberry caramel

muffins for two jars of peanut butter," Merritt explained. "He said that Trish had mentioned I was looking for work."

"Dr. Oakheart? Doesn't he run the clinic?" Tess asked.

Merritt nodded. "They're looking for a receptionist. It seems like an easy job. I emailed him my résumé, and he asked me to come in tomorrow morning for an interview."

"Sounds like you've had an adventurous and productive day." Tess grinned. "May I have one more chocolate-lavender muffin?"

"As many as you like." Merritt grabbed the container they'd stashed the leftover muffins in and held it out.

Tess took one. "Thanks."

"You're welcome. Um, was Merlin there?" Merritt asked.

Tess hesitated. "He was."

"Did he..." Merritt cleared her throat. "Did he say anything about me?"

The Lunar Fae nibbled the edge of the muffin before responding. "Only that he hopes you're settling in well."

"I'm happy here." Merritt shifted her weight. "I hope someone told him that."

Tess squeezed her shoulder. "Everything's fine. Goodnight."

She headed down the hall, leaving Merritt in a kitchen full of muffins, staring after her.

CHAPTER SIXTEEN

The clinic was uncomfortably cool. Merritt wished she hadn't removed her coat, which now hung on the back of the chair. She felt that getting up to put it on would be awkward, so she forced her attention away from the goosebumps on her arms and concentrated on the Aether Elf across the table from her.

Dr. Oakheart wore his dark hair in a buzz cut, slender ears protruding on either side. His purple scrubs were tight on his powerful shoulders, and stubble highlighted the stern line of his jaw as he scanned Merritt's résumé.

"There's not much to see, sir," Merritt croaked, then wished she hadn't.

Dr. Oakheart looked up with a gentle smile. "That's all right, Miss Vale. My neighbors speak well of you. Richard Branson said to hire for attitude and train for skill."

Merritt didn't know who that was, but she nodded like she did.

"You've made friends quickly in Little Avalon," Dr. Oakheart noted. "I've also noticed that you don't have prejudices against different paranormal species."

Merritt shrugged. "Why should I? We're all valuable."

"That's what I like to hear." Dr. Oakheart pushed her résumé aside and steepled his fingers on the desk. "Despite Queen Julia's efforts toward unity, you'd be surprised how many paras hold onto speciesism. That simply won't do in a healthcare setting, especially in a clinic as complex as this one."

Merritt glanced around the office. "Complex, sir?" The space was mind-numbingly plain. Gray walls met a white ceiling and tiled floor. The only decoration was a calendar on the back wall, turned to January. It was March.

Dr. Oakheart smiled. "Little Avalon Clinic is the first of its kind. We serve both humans and paranormals. It's a complicated balance, especially since we had to hire human doctors to serve the humans. Paranormal medicine relies on magic, which we can't use on human patients since we've never tested it on them. You never know who will walk through the door. It could be an orc with a broken arm, a werewolf with distemper, or a human in labor."

"Wow." Merritt blinked. "That *does* sound complicated."

"Your role won't be technically difficult, but it'll require thinking on your feet," Dr. Oakheart continued. "Your primary task will be to receive and record their issues. Simply put, you'll ask what's wrong and enter the information on a screen. The screen sends it to the triage nurse, who will assign a priority to each patient and a species-specific room and doctor."

Merritt slowly nodded. "Sounds like something I can do, sir."

"I think so, too." Dr. Oakheart smiled. "You'll be helping people, which strikes me as something you'll enjoy."

A job that means something and makes a real difference. Pleasure flushed through her at the thought.

Dr. Oakheart's expression abruptly changed. "Are you doing that on purpose?"

Merritt dropped her gaze to the arms of her wooden chair. Bright green tendrils sprouted from the wood and wrapped around her forearms, their touch so gentle that she hadn't noticed them. As she gaped, a tiny morning glory bloomed on the left one.

"Oh, crap!" Merritt yanked her arms back. The plants shriveled and died. "I'm sorry, sir. I didn't mean—"

"It's all right, Miss Vale." Dr. Oakheart held out a hand. "Does that happen often?"

Merritt ducked her head. "I'm afraid it does, sir."

The silence hung between them like a storm cloud.

"I'm terribly sorry, Miss Vale," Dr. Oakheart murmured, "but in that case, this may not be the right position for you."

"I can control it. Val gave me this amulet, see?" Merritt pulled it from the front of her sweater. "I can muffle my magic."

Dr. Oakheart inclined his head. "I have great respect for Her Grace's magic items, but I don't think that's good enough. I'm terribly sorry. The Veil can't hide plants growing out of the furniture. It's too large a risk to take with a business on the bleeding edge of para-human relations."

Merritt's shoulders sagged. "Sir..."

"I'll recommend you to anyone looking for an entry-level employee," Dr. Oakheart added. His smile was kind, but his tone held flat finality.

It was over. "Thank you, sir."

***

The cold made Merritt wrap her scarf tighter around her neck as she shuffled down the sidewalk, leaving the clinic behind. Little Avalon Academy was on her left. She heard snatches of laughter from the playground. Stonehold Houses lined the rest of the street, and Isabella's salon was up ahead. Merritt pondered stopping in before she headed home. Isabella didn't seem to mind making her feel better after failed interviews.

Potent magic rippled through Merritt's senses. She lifted her head as a joyful bark greeted her from behind.

Merritt! Hi!

Merritt turned and grinned. "Hey, Shadow! Who's a good boy? Who's the smartest boy?"

Shadow bounded up to her and gamboled around her feet, wagging his tail so hard he could barely keep his balance. *Shadow is! Shadow is the good boy! Shadow is the smartest boy!*

"That's right, buddy." Merritt knelt and flung her arms around his neck.

Shadow leaned into her embrace, his fur soft against her cheek. She struggled to hold back a lump in her throat as she hugged him.

Merritt be okay, Shadow gently told her.

"Thanks," Merritt mumbled.

"Is my dog sharing words of wisdom with you again?" Val grumbled.

Merritt released him and stood. Val strolled down the sidewalk, arms bare, impervious to the cold. Her hobnailed boots thudded on the pavement. Today, she sported platinum blonde curls tumbling to her belt.

"I like your hair," Merritt told her.

Val tossed a curl over her shoulder. "Thanks. You good? You seem down."

Merritt hesitated.

Val inclined her head. "Walk with me. I'm letting Shadow stretch his legs. You headed anywhere in particular?"

Merritt shook her head.

"Then let's walk my dog, and you can tell me what's on your mind." Val smiled.

Merritt fell into step beside her as the dwarf strolled along. The gray sky promised rain later, but a fitful breeze tugged at her scarf and coat for now.

"I'm trying to get a job," Merritt blurted. "I really am. It's not that I want to be idle."

Val raised an eyebrow. "Nobody said you did."

"It's important to contribute to the community." Merritt sighed. "But it feels like I don't fit anywhere."

Val smiled. "Hey, you've only had a few interviews and two trials so far. In the New York job market, that's not bad. You might end up going through many more."

Merritt groaned.

"Not what you wanted to hear? Sorry." Val swung her arms. "Are you on your way back from an interview now?"

"Yeah. A failed one." Merritt grimaced. "I applied for a receptionist position at the clinic."

"Isn't that clinic the most amazing thing you've ever seen?" Val beamed. "Both humans and paras can use it. The first of its kind. I'm proud of it."

"You have a right to be." Merritt sighed. "I would have loved to work there, but I can't control my powers well enough yet. The Veil can't hide them all, and I might reveal us to humans."

"Mmm." Val rubbed her chin. "Things would be different in a quieter, more intimate setting like a small business, where you would have other paras to support you. I can see how it would be problematic at the clinic. It gets hectic in there. There's no one to look out for you or cover for you if needed, and emotions run high." She grimaced. "Emotions make it hard to control magic."

Merritt groaned and flexed her fingers, trying not to clench her hands into fists. "Sometimes I wish I didn't have magic."

Val stopped. "Why would you say that?"

Merritt turned to her, surprised by the shock in her tone. "It seems like my powers do more harm than good. They got me thrown out of Wolf Glen. They are making it difficult for me to get a job, if not impossible." She threw her hands up. "What good are they?"

"What *good* are they?" Val echoed. "Merritt, why would Luna make you with these powers if they weren't any good?"

Merritt didn't know how to answer that.

"Powers can make life hard while you learn to understand and control them, but they're never a curse or something to regret." Val met her eyes with fierce intensity. "Your powers are wonderful, Merritt, and they can make the world a better place. *You* can make the world a better place."

Merritt shifted her weight. "I don't know how."

"Neither did I." Val slightly smiled and walked on. "Growing up as a giant dwarf with no hair wasn't easy. I often cursed my differences and wished I could be like the other dwarves. I didn't know then that I was different because I was more powerful than the dwarves, except perhaps my dad. My height, baldness, and the scarlet fog I see when I'm angry all come from being a Warrior of the Red Bear."

"You must have known that growing up," Merritt murmured.

Val shook her head. "I didn't. I thought I was a misfit. I was an outcast, and I thought there was something wrong with me. No one knew the Warriors of the Red Bear had ever existed until I found an ancient dwarven city buried in Mount Adalbern. I learned how to use my powers on my own, much like you are, from my berserker state to my connection to my warhammer and Shadow's shapeshifting ability and destructive roar."

"Destructive roar?" Merritt gaped at the dog as he trotted ahead of them. "I'd like to see that."

"I'm sure you will." Val grinned. "My powers drove me crazy at times. In the end, they're not only a good thing. They saved the world."

Merritt tilted her head. "Merlin said something about Kronos."

"The most dangerous Wild Hunter of all." Val nodded. "He escaped custody, summoned an army of Titans, and attacked my homeland. We'd secured the only weapon that could stand against him—Gaia's Sickle—months before that. Turns out Gaia's Sickle only gets its full power when it's in the hands of a descendant of Gaia."

Merritt's eyes widened. "A Warrior of the Red Bear."

"Nobody could stop Kronos except me," Val murmured. "That's not a boast, by the way. *I* didn't know until I stood before him with the sickle in my hands. Luna's plan made me who I am and placed me where I was at exactly the right time." She smiled. "We don't have our powers to serve ourselves, Merritt. Our powers exist to improve the world."

Merritt gazed at her hands. A few seedlings sprouted from her fingertips.

"Your powers aren't an inconvenience," Val assured her. "They're your gift to the world. Maybe they'll save the world like mine did, or maybe they'll improve it in smaller ways. I don't think the small ways are any less important. Who's to say riding into battle is more heroic and valuable than feeding a hungry family or making a friend laugh?" She grinned. "Who's to say there's no heroism in baking the best lavender chocolate chip muffins the world has ever seen?"

Merritt smiled. "You liked them?"

"I loved them." Val touched her shoulder. "We can all contribute to the world. Your magic is much more than an inconvenience. It makes you who you are. We need to figure out where you can nurture your magic and make it thrive and grow, not suppress it. The clinic job sounded great, but it's not right for you. Something else will be."

"I hope so." Merritt ran a hand over her hair. "I really do."

"I know so." Val grinned. "You'll find your place. I did."

I hope it's here in Little Avalon. I hope you let me stay.

A wet nose butted into her hand, making her jump. Shadow leaned against her, mouth wide as he happily panted, tongue spilling over sharp white teeth. *Merritt powerful! Use power. Be mighty!* He barked. *I turn into bear! Is good!*

Merritt smirked. *I'd like to see that.*

I show you when no humans, Shadow told her.

"Are you two talking without me again?" Val demanded.

Shadow wagged his tail.

"He likes me." Merritt stroked his head.

"More than I'm comfortable with," Val grumbled.

Merritt chuckled. "Are you jealous, Val?"

"A little. He's *my* dog," Val wailed, then laughed at herself.

Merritt joined in her mirth, but a shriek ripped through the merry sound. The terrible sound sailed across Little Avalon like a flaming arrow, leaving shocked silence in its wake. It was a raw, hoarse bellow of pain and fury.

A dagger appeared in Val's hands.

This way! Shadow wheeled and bounded down the street.

Red magic surged beneath Val's skin. She ran after Shadow with shocking speed for a body so muscular. Merritt had to sprint to keep up as they raced to the end of the street. The scream came again as they rounded the corner.

"Shit!" Val hissed. Her glow intensified.

Merritt's limbs lengthened. She slapped the *muffle* rune on her amulet, and her transformation stabilized as they charged up a street Merritt hadn't been on before. Cozy single-family homes with spacious front gardens and big backyards lined the road.

The hoarse scream formed a word this time. *"Amberrrrrrrrr!"*

"Not this again," Val groaned.

Shadow bounded to a house with a white picket fence surrounding it halfway down the street. The big dog hurdled it effortlessly and landed on a paved driveway with his paws splayed and his hackles up, ready for battle. Val ran through the fence without slowing down. Wood splintered when her powerful legs hit it, and she stumbled to a halt a few feet from the orc who stood outside the house, wrapped in a robe.

"Aurelio, what's wrong?" Val barked.

Aurelio wailed, "Look what she's done. *Look what she's done!*"

He spread his arms, indicating the chaos in the front yard. Merritt halted by the ruined fence and surveyed a scene of wanton destruction. A few scraps of manicured lawn remained; the rest was a plowed mass, claw marks ripping through the earth, torn rose petals scattered in the mud, water bubbling from the unrolled hose that lay across it all.

She guessed there had been flowerbeds along the wooden fence separating Aurelio's yard from the next. Now, broken sticks stood up among churned dirt. Their leaves and splintered stems covered the lawn.

"My garden," Aurelio moaned. "My roses! They were Nox roses. They cost me a fortune!" He sagged to his knees, grief written on his face.

Val sheathed her dagger, and the red glow faded from her skin. She frowned at the streaks of mud on the wall of Aurelio's house. They looked like paws had made them.

"Did someone try to break into your home last night, Aurelio?" she asked.

Aurelio shook his head. "Not that I know of, but I sleep with headphones on, listening to my music. It's the only way I *can* sleep, considering my neighbor." He gave a half-hearted sneer, but sorrow still colored his features.

Merritt picked her way across the mud and crouched beside him. "I'm sorry about your roses, Aurelio. I've heard Nox roses are beautiful."

"Beautiful? They're far more than that, young one. They're… they're…" Aurelio lifted a rose petal from the dirt. It was bright red, fading to flame-yellow on the edges. The bush must have looked like it was burning. "They are priceless and perfect," he whispered.

Shadow's nose twitched. *Smell that?*

Yeah, Merritt replied. *Wolf.*

"Do you think Amber—" she began.

"Of course Amber did it!" Aurelio leaped to his feet. "Who else would stoop so low?"

Val paused her lap of the ruined lawn and pursed her lips.

"We should talk to her, Val," Merritt called.

"Maybe." Val nodded at the ground. "These could be hers."

Huge pawprints with deep claw marks meandered across the carnage to the gate.

"My Nox roses," Aurelio moaned. "My wonderful roses!"

"Let's knock on her door." Merritt stood.

"Not yet." Val frowned. "This could easily be an attempt to exploit Amber's and Aurelio's fight for their own gain. They might have made it look like Amber did this."

"You think so?" Merritt asked.

Val grimaced. "It's far-fetched, but innocent until proven guilty, right?"

"Aurelio?"

Everyone looked up when they heard the sheepish voice. A silver wolf with yellow eyes stood at the gate, tail between her legs. Dirt coated her muzzle and stained her front paws.

"Okay, Amber did it," Val acknowledged.

Aurelio lurched to his feet. "*You!*"

Val was beside him before he took three steps. She flung her arms around the powerful orc and effortlessly lifted him off his feet. He kicked and roared, trying to yank his arms free, as Amber shrank back with rising hackles.

"Stop!" Val commanded.

"*You did this!*" Aurelio screamed. "You destroyed my *Nox roses*! You know how much they cost and how much effort they are, but you ruined them! *Ruined!*"

Merritt followed Amber's gaze to the flowerbed. The wolf shifted to human form, pressing both hands to her mouth. Soil still covered her fingers, and horror shone in her eyes.

"Merlin's wings, Aurelio. I'm sorry," Amber ground out.

"Sorry? *Sorry?* Sorry won't make my roses grow back!" Aurelio thundered. "Why would you do this? Why?"

"*You know why!*" Amber roared.

Aurelio's arms flexed against Val's grasp, biceps straining his robe's silky sleeves. "You admit it?"

"I didn't mean to, okay?" Amber threw up her hands. "It's not like I set out to ruin your life, no matter what you tell people. I was drunk. I came back from the Second Fist and found that you'd ruined my yard when you left your hose running into my flowerbed. I thought I'd tear up one or two of your bushes, and then… Then… I was *really* drunk, okay?"

"*You'll pay for this, Amber!*" Aurelio screamed.

"Enough!" Val barked. "That's enough." She gave Aurelio a shake that made his teeth rattle, no mean feat considering he was a full-grown orc. He kept his fists clenched after she released him but didn't attempt to lunge at Amber.

"You both have to stop this," Val snapped. "Whatever went down between you, it's not worth it. This is your final warning. The next time you cause shit for one another, I'll get the OPMA involved. Got it?"

Amber's lip curled, displaying growing canines. "You deserve it, asshole."

"*I'll get you back for this, bitch!*" Aurelio yelled.

"*Hey!*" Val shouted. "*Are you listening to me?*"

Aurelio gave her a murderous look.

"It's not worth it. Cut it out," Val added.

Amber turned on her heel and strode away, arms wrapped around her chest. Aurelio tossed his head and stormed into the house. He slammed the door hard enough that paint flaked from its surface.

"Merlin's long gray nose hairs," Val muttered. "Those two cause so much unnecessary shit for everyone, it's not even funny." She stomped down the path to the street.

"Aurelio seemed upset over more than flowers." Merritt jogged to catch up. "Did you know they used to be lovers?"

"I remember they rented one of the first Stonehold apartments together. I thought they were an adorable couple." Val rolled her eyes. "Turns out I was mistaken. They're a pain in my ass, and each other's." She sighed. "All that fuss over *roses!*"

"Roses are hard to grow." Merritt shrugged. "I get why they're mad. I can imagine how I'd feel if someone threw my brownies on the ground and stomped on them. Even more so if it was someone I used to love."

"I understand that." Val sighed. "I lose my shit if someone moves a tool in my smithy, never mind willingly destroying my work. Trouble is, I have bigger problems than this, Merritt. I have to deal with the duchy's issues on an interdimensional level." She tugged her curls over her shoulders.

"You need someone who can handle conflicts within Little Avalon on your behalf," Merritt suggested.

"Tess and Julie said the same thing. But who?" Val shrugged. "Another problem to solve. Tess was an option, but she's too busy with High Magic Division assignments. You're lucky she showed you the ropes for a few days."

"You seem overburdened," Merritt empathized.

"Not overburdened." Val smiled. "Little Avalon could never be a burden. But overwhelmed? Yeah, a little. There's an easy fix for the Amber and Aurelio thing, though."

"What's that?" Merritt asked.

Val scowled. "Boot their asses out of Little Avalon."

They continued walking in silence. Nerves twisted and coiled in Merritt's belly like she'd swallowed a small snake.

Nobody deserves to lose Little Avalon, she thought. *Not even me.*

CHAPTER SEVENTEEN

It is commonly held in human opinion that croissants derive from the Austrian kipferl. This crescent-shaped bread, made with yeast, is often filled with nuts and has been a beloved staple since the thirteenth century. What the humans do not know is that the fine art of croissant making originated among the brownies—as in the paranormal species, not the confection—of Broceliande during the First Golden Age.

Merritt turned the page, enjoying the soft rustle of paper as she snuggled deeper into her pillows. A gentle rain misted the window, and leftover muffins waited to be snacks on her nightstand. Mrs. Ricci had given her a book about making croissants. "They're not normally for beginners," the orc had told her, "but I think you'll catch on quickly. You might as well start reading it."

Damian had given her a weird look when she'd told Tess she would turn in early and read the cookbook. Then again, Damian scowled most of the time.

Reading the first chapter, *The Noble History of Croissants*, kept Merritt's longing for the place of trees at bay. She forced her thoughts away from the leafy sanctuary and concentrated on the words.

Ancient brownies can describe the time thousands of years ago, before King Arthur trod the hallowed grounds of the British Isles, when brownies nestled amid the warm folds of freshly baked flatbreads left in elven kitchens during the depths of winter.

Merritt bit into an apple muffin. She could picture a cozy elven kitchen in the depths of a Broceliande winter, with snow weighing down the trees and brownies sneaking across the quiet kitchen to roll themselves in fresh-baked bread. She could almost smell the wood smoke from the kitchen fire.

Wait. Merritt raised her head and sniffed. *I do smell like smoke.*

The scent was faint but clear enough to make Merritt spring out of bed. She left the book on the nightstand and slipped into the hall. Another sniff told her the smoke smell was no stronger, but she knocked on Damian's door just in case.

"Damian?" Merritt knocked again.

"What do you want, Merritt?" Damian growled.

Merritt spread her hands. "There's no need to be rude. I'm just checking on you."

"I don't need to be checked on. Leave me alone," Damian snapped.

Clearly, he's fine, Merritt thought. She padded into the kitchen and glanced at the countertops, but no melting rice cooker explained the smoky smell.

It had to come from outside.

Merritt pulled a rain jacket over her shoulders and trotted down the stairs. When she pushed the door open, the smell of smoke assaulted her.

"What *is* that?" a passing werewolf wondered, squinting up at the stars. She pushed a stroller with six sections, one for each slumbering baby.

"I'll check it out," Merritt promised.

The werewolf smiled, displaying long teeth. "Thanks, Merritt. Don't want to bother Val if it's someone having a bonfire."

Merritt thrust her hands into her pockets and strode down the sidewalk, enjoying the excuse to be outside in the rain. It pattered on her hood and splashed on her cheeks, the drops like icy needles on her skin. That didn't bother her. Rain was a gift in a world of plants.

She passed Val's house and Chaplin's Kitchen, which was closed. When she turned the corner, she saw a pillar of smoke, black and thick against the stars, boiling behind the streetlights.

Fear kicked her in the gut. The smoke was near Aurelio's house.

Merritt sprinted down the street and swerved toward the first opening on the right, jumping over flowerbeds and trampling someone's lawn.

Bright orange light flickered ahead. Merritt ducked around the house, scrambled over a low wall, and squeezed down an alley filled with garbage cans. She burst onto the street and froze in her tracks. Her jaw dropped in horror.

Amber's house was a solid block of raging fire.

"No," Merritt whispered. The yellow and orange flames leaped and swirled behind the windows on the first floor, licking through the shattered panes and leaving dark streaks on the paint as they hungrily rose toward the second floor. Smoke poured from the house, writhing like dark tentacles against the sky.

"*Amber!*" Aurelio screamed. "*Amber!*"

He ran around the side of the house, one arm shielding his face, coughing between shouts as he stumbled to the front door. He grabbed the doorknob, flinched, and cried out in pain.

Merritt bolted across the street. "Aurelio, get back!"

The orc slammed his shoulder against the door. It trembled, sparks and soot spilling from the gap above it, but did not budge.

"*Amber!*" he wailed.

Merritt grabbed his arm and yanked him back.

Flames roared over the lintel. A chunk of wood tumbled off it and shattered into sparks and ash where Aurelio had been a second before.

The orc seized her hands, his eyes huge in his brown face. "You have to get her out of there!"

Merritt glanced around. "I don't see her car. She's not home."

"That was what I thought, too," Aurelio sobbed.

A howl rose from the second floor, twining with the heat and smoke spilling from the house. The high-pitched sound produced echoes that made goosebumps prickle on Merritt's arms.

"I didn't know she was in there!" Aurelio cried. "I didn't know, I swear. We have to save her!"

Amber howled again in panic. A window shattered on the second floor. Merritt hauled Aurelio back as glass tumbled to the ground. Amber's silhouette appeared in the window, but yellow flames surged behind her, and black smoke boiled out.

"*Amber!*" Aurelio shrieked.

Merritt shoved him away from the house. "Get back! You'll get yourself killed."

"She'll die in there," Aurelio moaned.

"No, she won't." Merritt shook him. "Aurelio, she won't. Look at me!"

The orc met her gaze, his face a mask of terror.

"She won't," Merritt growled. "I won't let her. *Stay back!*"

Aurelio stumbled away, shaking violently. Merritt faced the house. She slapped the *call* rune on her amulet, but Amber didn't have long. Fire blazed behind all the second-floor windows. Only one spilled smoke from within.

Merritt closed her eyes and thought about silent flight. The tiny lungs of a sparrow could not handle the smoke. When she spread her wings, she had the four-foot wingspan of an eagle owl.

A wild shriek left her beak as she leaped into the air. Barely a rustle accompanied her ascent. The air around the house was rough with thermals and heat-created currents, but Merritt's broad wings outmatched them. She swooped to the broken window, braced herself, and plunged in through the black smoke.

Heat scorched the undersides of her wings, and she banked hard to avoid a blazing bookshelf against the nearest wall.

Her wings carried her to the only perch she spotted that wasn't on fire: a desk. Talons bit into the wood as she turned her head left and right, her vision blurred among the bright flames and dark smoke.

"*Amber!*" she shrieked. "*Amber! Where are you?*"

"Here!" the werewolf whimpered. "Bathroom!"

The doorway that stood between Merritt and the feeble cry was a ring of flame. The scent of singed feathers filled her nose, but Merritt ignored it. She swooped through the blazing doorway, heat searing her wings. Her feathers twitched and curled as they caught fire, but she kept going. The smoke made her air sacs feel charred and tight as she swooped across a bedroom in which flames licked over the sheets and ducked through the opposite door into the cool sanctuary of the bathroom.

The flames touched her skin. With a cry of pain, Merritt snapped back to her usual form. She landed clumsily, knees slamming into the tiles, and had to grab the edge of the tub to keep from smacking her face on it.

"Merritt! It's you!"

Amber was curled up in the bath with a wet towel over her body, holding a damp washcloth to her face. Soot smeared her cheeks, and her eyes were huge.

"The water won't run anymore!" she cried, turning the faucet both ways.

Merritt kicked the door shut, hoping that would keep the fire out for a moment longer. "We have to go."

"*Where?*" Amber cried. "The stairs are on fire. I checked. I can't jump through the window. I'll die!"

Merritt's breath came in painful rasps. Burns stung the undersides of her arms. The thought of growing feathers through the ruined skin made nausea surge in her belly. Frantically, she thought about the forms she could take that might help.

I need to be a dragon, she thought, but she hadn't spent enough time around Alugon. Mimicking his magic seemed impossible.

"I'm stuck here. Now you're stuck here, too," Amber moaned. "You shouldn't have come."

"We'll get through this!" Merritt grabbed Amber's arm. "We'll figure it out." An idea struck her. "Do you wear a harness?"

"*What?*" Amber yelped.

"*A harness*," Merritt shouted. "*A shifting harness for fashion.*"

"*What does that matter?*" Amber yelled. "*Some people frown on them, but—*"

Merritt spotted it hanging behind the bathroom door as the werewolf rambled. She yanked it off its hook, accidentally ripping a hole in the door. Smoke cascaded through it, and embers caught on the splintered edges.

"Here!" Merritt thrust the harness at her. "Put it on!"

"*What?*"

"*Do it!*" Merritt shouted. "I'm getting you out of here."

Amber seized the harness and yanked it over her head. Merritt retreated several steps and spread her arms. The movement tugged at the burns, and the next few seconds were a million times worse as Merritt gritted her teeth and transformed. New feathers burst through her skin, taking root deep in the burned flesh, but they shriveled and failed to grow as they should. When Merritt spread her wings as an eagle owl, she gave a chirp of dismay. Several secondary flight feathers were misshapen or missing from the burned areas on her wings.

"What now?" Amber whimpered.

Merritt stared at her in dismay. Could she summon plants? The stoutest tree would burn in this inferno, but that gave her another idea.

"Wrap yourself in that towel and run to the window," Merritt ordered. "Then change and jump."

"*Jump?*" Amber yelped. "I'll break my neck!"

"Not if you trust me," Merritt snapped.

Amber's gaze strayed to the burns on Merritt's wings. "I trust you."

"Good." Merritt stepped back, claws clicking on the tiles. "Then go!"

Amber yanked the door wide. Heat and smoke poured into the bathroom, burning Merritt's beak, but there were no flames. With a scream of terror and defiance, Amber charged through the door and sprinted across the bedroom.

Merritt opened her wings and followed. Her flight felt unbalanced, and she flapped hard, fighting for each inch of altitude. There was no time to reconsider her plan. Amber was already at the window, flinging the towel aside. She transformed and plunged through as a wolf.

Merritt was inches behind her. The wolf's hind paws had barely left the window when Merritt reached out with her deadly talons. Amber yelped as their tips raked her skin, but the leather strap slid into Merritt's grasp. She flapped with all her strength as her claws took Amber's weight.

She barely slowed the wolf's fall, but Merritt got the few seconds she needed. A mass of plants burst from the lawn beside the house, and their branches tangled into a thick, springy bed that Amber and Merrit slammed into with breathtaking force. Amber's yelp ended in a grunt of pain. Merritt squeezed her eyes shut as she tumbled into the green mass.

The plants thickened as she crashed into them. She braced herself for impact but only felt the branches raking her feathers. Air rushed into her sacs, bringing blessed relief to her burning chest. When the sliding stopped, Merritt lay motionless for several seconds, just breathing.

Smoke stung her beak. Merritt's eyes snapped open as a yelp came from behind her. She struggled to free her wings as Amber writhed, an ember smoldering on her coat. More sparks fluttered toward them from the fire.

"*Amber!*" Aurelio waded through the plants, heedless of the branches ripping his robe and skin. He slapped the ember on the wolf's fur, extinguishing it, and grasped a fistful of the stems to tear them away from Amber. She leaped out and ran into the street, then she dropped onto her side and rolled, crushing the embers to ash.

Merritt exhaled. Her magic wheezed through her cells, almost spent, but she had enough left to transform back. Her human hands allowed her to claw her arms free of the plants, but her shaking muscles wouldn't respond when she tried to stand.

Her vision blurred. She gazed at the flames and smoke roiling from the house and wondered how long it would take for the plants she had grown to ignite.

It got darker above the house. Merritt heard someone grunt as the stars vanished and the weather changed. The drizzle became a deluge, and rain poured onto the blazing house, coming down in sheets, and the leaping flames turned to hissing steam.

No rain fell on Merritt. She squirmed, and gentle hands grasped her under the arms and dragged her from the heap of crushed greenery.

"Shit, Merritt!" Tess crouched beside her on the lawn. "Are you okay?"

Merritt blinked. Her foggy vision improved in the presence of lunar magic. "I'm okay," she croaked, trying to sit up.

Tess helped her. "Oh, ouch. Your arms got burned. What were you thinking?"

"She would have died in there. I had to help her," Merritt mumbled. "I heard Aurelio screaming."

A blood-curdling snarl got their attention. Amber stood in the street, her hackles erect, yellow eyes like smoldering coals. Her tail twitched as she readied to leap. "*You,*" she growled.

Aurelio sat on the sidewalk, head in his hands. He slowly looked up.

"You did this," Amber snarled.

Tess stood. "Take it easy, Amber. I'm sure he had nothing to do with—"

"I didn't mean for it to happen," Aurelio burst out.

Tess froze.

"I'm sorry, Amber. I truly am," Aurelio whimpered. "I didn't think it would get to your house. I wanted to pay you back for my roses. I never meant to hurt you. I would *never* hurt you!"

"You nearly killed me, you psychopath!" Amber barked. "I should rip your throat out!" She stepped nearer.

Shadow's bark froze everyone. The massive dog bounded up the street, teeth bared, red magic crackling like lightning in his coat. Behind him, Val toted her warhammer. Flames roared around its head when she raised it.

"*Tell me what happened here,*" she thundered. "*The truth!*"

"He set my house on fire!" Amber transformed and jabbed a finger at Aurelio. "With me in it. He tried to kill me." Her face crumpled. "He tried to *kill* me!"

Val rounded on Aurelio. "Is that true?"

"I didn't know she was home!" Aurelio wailed.

Val sheathed the hammer after the flames died and marched over to Aurelio, danger glowing in her eyes. He cringed and raised his hands to shield his face, but Val didn't strike. Her fingers closed around his right ear.

"*Owwww!*" Aurelio yelped.

"You're coming with me, asshole," Val barked.

Bent double and whimpering, Aurelio made no attempt to resist.

"Where are you taking him?" Amber rasped.

"To Lillie House. I'll lock him up there until I decide what to do with him. Someone told me not to make decisions regarding justice in my berserker state, but it's *tempting*." She twisted, and Aurelio squealed. "Tess, you have this under control?"

Tess gestured at the rain cloud covering Amber's house. No flames remained, and only wisps of smoke rose from a few places. The house looked sad and gutted, with no lights in the windows and black streaks of soot covering the interior and exterior alike. "I'm good here."

"Get Amber somewhere to stay. I'll deal with this son of a bitch," Val snapped.

She marched off, towing the sobbing Aurelio.

"Are you hurt, Amber?" Tess asked.

Amber stared after Val and Aurelio, arms wrapped around her body. Her harness looked stupid and incongruous against her silky pajamas.

"Amber?" Tess prompted.

The werewolf turned glassy eyes to her. "Sorry, what?"

"Are you okay?" Tess asked. "Did you get burned?"

Amber shook her head.

"We'd better take both of you to the clinic to get checked. I'm sure you inhaled smoke." Tess extended a hand to Merritt. "Can you walk?"

Merritt slowly rose. "I feel better." She brushed dirt from her sweatpants. "I think the earth helped."

"Whoa, it sure did." Tess blinked. "Your blisters are gone."

Merritt craned to see the back of her arm.

"Fast healing? That's useful!" Tess gushed.

"I don't want to go to the clinic." Amber hugged herself tighter. "I just want to go to bed."

"I'll arrange somewhere for you to stay. Give me a second." Tess pulled her phone from her pocket and turned away.

Amber bowed her head, biting her lip. A tear rolled down her cheek.

"Oh, Amber." Merritt approached her. "I'm so sorry this happened. You must've been so scared, hiding in that house when it was on fire."

"It's not that." Amber bit back a sob.

Merritt rested a hand on her arm. "What is it, then?"

"It's… Oh, Merritt, this whole thing is so stupid." Amber raised her head, still weeping. "How could this go so far?"

"Sounds like it's been brewing for a while," Merritt murmured.

"He flooded my yard, and I dug up his roses, but I never thought it would come to *this*." Amber stared at her ruined house. "I never thought he had it in him to hurt anyone. He was always the gentle one. He'd bring me coffee in bed and rub my feet after a long day." Her lower jaw trembled. "How did we go from that to this?"

Merritt just squeezed her arm.

Amber covered her face with her hands. "I still loved him! *I. Still. Loved. Him.*" The words oozed out between choking sobs. "I didn't stop…until now." She dissolved into helpless crying.

Merritt slid an arm around the werewolf's trembling shoulders. She didn't know what to say and hoped silence would be enough.

Tess strode over to them, her brows drawn together. "Okay, Amber. I found you an empty apartment for tonight. You'll be Mrs. Ricci's neighbor. She'll take care of you."

Amber nodded, still sobbing.

"Let's get you home. Both of you." Tess took Amber's other arm.

Between them, they steered the weeping werewolf down the street.

Merritt slept that night, and this time, it did her all the good Tess always promised. She woke long before Damian came home from work. The smells of sugar and cinnamon filled the kitchen when the vampire wandered through the front door. Merritt slid a tray of buttery cinnamon rolls from the oven.

"Morning, Damian!" She beamed.

He blinked. Dark circles lay beneath his eyes, which were red in more ways than one this morning. A scuff mark on his cheek threatened to become a bruise.

"Want a cinnamon roll?" Merritt asked.

Damian huffed and pushed past her to his room.

"Suit yourself," Merritt muttered. She set the rolls on the countertop and gingerly touched the backs of her arms, feeling for burns. The skin was tender, but she hadn't seen any redness in the mirror that morning. Maybe her magic *was* helpful.

Merritt pried the cinnamon rolls out of the pan with some difficulty. They'd insisted on sticking. She made a mental note to check the recipe books for tips on preventing that. Three or four rolls came loose without leaving chunks behind, so she arranged them in a bowl.

She scrawled a brief note for Tess on the magnetic pad stuck to the fridge underneath Tess' neat list: bread, tomatoes, laundry detergent.

Gone to Val's. Back a little later.

Bowl under her arm, she jogged down the steps to the street, munching the ugliest cinnamon roll as she went.

The morning was breathtaking. A flush of unseasonal warmth promised the riches of summer, and the still air was bright with sunshine. Leaves unfurled on the trees that lined the sidewalk, growing when Merritt strode beneath their branches. Several paras smiled at Merritt as they walked by or left for work. She glimpsed Qenzi through the kitchen window and waved. The troll's glasses flashed in the light as she turned her head and waved back.

She found the garage door of Lillie House half-open, Genevieve's athletic lines waiting within. The Mustang amiably honked as Merritt entered the garage.

"Hi, Genevieve." Merritt patted the car's hood.

Genevieve honked again, sparking a flurry of barks from

inside the house. There was a flight of stairs within the garage. The door at the top opened.

Tetra yelled, "*Shadow, shut up!*" The door slammed.

Shadow's barking got louder, and his claws raked the back door as Merritt approached it.

"Shadow, dude! Stop," Val grumbled.

Shadow fell silent, and the door opened. Val stood behind it, sweat shining on her skin. She wore skin-tight pants, no shoes, and a tank top bearing the words *Vanguard MMA*.

"Oh, hey, Merritt. Perfect timing. I was about to get in the shower after an early-morning session." Val blinked at the cinnamon rolls, then looked at Merritt with hope in her eyes.

Merritt grinned. "These are for you."

"Merlin's beard. They look amazing!" Val took the bowl and reverently inhaled the steam rising from the rolls. "Oh, wow. Come on in. These require coffee."

Merritt followed the dwarf into the house, shutting the door behind her. Shadow gamboled around her feet and accepted her gentle touches on his head and muzzle as they went into the kitchen.

"Freshly brewed." Val placed a pot of coffee on the table, where several mugs waited.

"Are you expecting someone?" Merritt asked.

"No, but this is Lillie House. People show up here at random." Val dropped into a chair and poured coffee. "Few bring delicious treats. Want one?"

"I ate way too much of the raw dough to want more, thanks." Merritt smiled.

"Too much of your baking? Impossible. I could eat it to the point of exploding." Val tilted her head. "Hey, Kalyna and Hank are looking for a baker. Have you thought of applying there?"

"I need to improve my skills first. Um, if I might ask, where did you take Aurelio last night?"

"He stayed in my spare room. He's not delighted at being

locked up in there, but I needed to cool down before I decide what to do with him." Val huffed. "*Asshat.* I can't believe he set fire to Amber's house. How are your burns, by the way?"

"Almost gone. I heal fast." Merritt interlaced her fingers. "Are you going to punish him?"

"I have to." Val sighed. "The only question is how to do that. I could turn him over to the OPMA to prosecute under Eternity Law, but since I'm the duchess, I have the authority to mete out justice in Little Avalon for most crimes as I see fit."

"What would happen if you gave him to the OPMA?" Merritt asked.

"A long, drawn-out, likely public court case that would probably end with Aurelio in prison for decades or banished to the prison realm for a time." Val grimaced. "Depends if they find him guilty of attempted murder."

Merritt had heard the stories about the prison realm, where monstrous creatures devoured all magic, leaving its inmates stone pillars—technically alive but stripped of what made them paranormal. She shivered.

"Yeah, I don't like that option either. I have to do something, though." Val shrugged. "I'm leaning toward banishing him, though I doubt he'll try to harm Amber again. I have to give Amber consequences, too. She's caused plenty of property damage." She sighed and shook her head. "It's too much, Merritt. I should have dealt with this shit before it got life-threatening. I thought they could settle their differences like adults."

Merritt scraped together her courage as Val stress-ate a second cinnamon roll. She hesitated. It would be easy to thank Val for her time and leave, but Merritt knew what she had to do.

She squared her shoulders. "Did...um, did Aurelio talk about what happened?"

Val huffed. "Keeps saying he didn't mean to do it. How do you set fire to your neighbor's house without meaning it? I don't have time for his crap."

Merritt gulped, but the pressure in her chest wouldn't let her back down. "I…" She cleared her throat. "I'd like to talk to Aurelio, please."

Val's head snapped up. "You?"

Merritt squirmed under the dwarf's gaze. "I might be able to find out what happened. He might talk to me."

Val studied her. Merritt's ribs felt like they would crush her chest. Finally, the dwarf shrugged. "Can't do any harm. I doubt he'll try to hurt you, and you do have a knack for talking to people, judging by how quickly you got Tetra to like you." She pushed her chair back. "I'll take you to him. If he makes one wrong move, though, I'll slap his head clean off."

Merritt glanced at the dwarf's stout arms and took her words literally.

Val stumped upstairs, Shadow at her heels. Merritt followed them down the upstairs hall. A stout iron bar held the door shut. Its lock was a hefty block of cast iron with blue runes etched around the edges. The magic emanating from the lock and bar made Merritt's skin tingle.

"I don't normally use this as a jail," Val confessed. "It's a precautionary measure against faeries."

Merritt nodded. "The Shajara Elves in Fernwood Deep have faerie shelters too."

Val chuckled. "No wonder Tetra scared the shit out of you when you met. She told me about that."

Merritt grimaced. "She did?"

"Yeah, but I didn't believe the part where you hid in the corner, crying." Val winked.

Merritt groaned.

Val pressed her palm to the iron lock. It flashed red and clicked as it released. Val heaved the sturdy bar aside without effort and knocked on the door.

"Aurelio?" she called. "Merritt wants to talk to you. Shadow's coming in, so don't try anything funny."

A hollow sigh echoed from the room. "I have no intention of pulling any funny business, Your Grace."

"Better not," Val muttered.

She pushed the door open. Merritt was expecting a prison cell, but Aurelio sat on the edge of a comfortable bed with a cheerful floral quilt. A painting of the Eternal Palace hung on the wall. The room featured a baby-blue rug and an en suite bathroom.

Aurelio's cheeks had a nasty gray pallor. He sat with shoulders hunched, hands limp in his lap, eyes on the floor. Shadow padded over to him, splashed his tongue over the orc's hands, and fell to the rug at his feet with a contented sigh.

"Shout if there's trouble." Val shut the door.

CHAPTER EIGHTEEN

Merritt stood with her back to the door, unmoving. Aurelio didn't acknowledge her presence. Several seconds passed.

What am I doing here? Merritt wondered. *I can't find a job in Little Avalon. I'm not even sure I'll get to stay here. Why am I trying to reconcile these assholes?*

That was the trouble, she realized, staring at Aurelio as he huddled in a black sweatsuit. She *didn't* think they were assholes. She saw beauty in both of them and the potential for real justice. Letting Aurelio spend several decades in jail or never get to come home to Little Avalon again seemed unthinkable.

Merritt exhaled. *I know what I have to do.* She crossed the room and sat on the bed a few feet from the orc.

"Please." Aurelio swallowed, his larynx bobbing. "Duchess Eiravel tells me that Amber is unharmed. Please tell me that's true."

"It's true. She's fine. She's staying in an apartment across the street," Merritt explained. "Well, she's physically fine."

Aurelio moaned and covered his face with both hands. "What have I done?"

Merritt tilted her head. "You kept saying you didn't know she was home."

"*I didn't! Her car wasn't there!*" Aurelio cried.

"I saw that. Last night, Amber mentioned it was a good thing she'd taken it in for service, or it would have burned to a crisp, too," Merritt murmured.

"It wouldn't have. I would never have done what I did if I had known she was home. I would never put my Amber in danger," Aurelio muttered.

"You burned her house down," Merritt pointed out.

Aurelio's fingers tightened on his temples. "That's not what was supposed to happen. I was angry about my roses, okay? I spent a fortune on them. They were one of the few things that made me happy after we broke up."

Merritt tilted her head.

"She has a pavilion in her backyard. It caused our first major fight. When Her Grace made those nice little houses available to Little Avalon residents, we tried to decide between two homes, the ones that are mine and hers now." Aurelio wiped his nose on his sleeve. "I liked mine because of its kitchen's layout. She liked hers because of that stupid pavilion. The names we called each other because of it!" Aurelio shook his head, letting his hands fall to his lap.

"What happened between you two?" Merritt asked.

"Nothing. I don't know. It fell apart on its own." Aurelio sighed. "We fought over little things, then bigger things. Then we did more fighting than anything else, so we gave up. That pavilion was the first nail in the coffin for us. I can see it from my bedroom window, and every time I do, it makes me mad."

He clenched his fists. "Mad enough to understand how Amber could rip up my garden and chew my roses to smithereens. I wanted to do the same thing to her. I wanted her to feel the way I felt." He loosened his fists. "I wanted her to see that stupid pavilion burn the way our relationship burned. The house was not supposed to get involved."

"You set the pavilion on fire?" Merritt asked.

Aurelio raised his head. "Idiotic, isn't it? I know that now. I was too angry to realize that. I came home from work and saw that Amber's car wasn't in the garage, so I fetched a gas can and a lighter and sneaked into her backyard. I thought that just the pavilion would burn, but then the wind came, and the flames grew much faster than I thought they could.

"I turned on the hose and sprayed the pavilion down, which helped a little, but I was so focused on it that I didn't see the sparks flying in the wind. They landed on Amber's back patio. When I turned around, her ground floor was on fire. I tried to get in when I heard her scream, but..."

Merritt remembered Aurelio slamming into the front door, trying to break in, as Amber howled in her bedroom.

Aurelio gulped. "I know what I did was wrong. I was so screwed up." He dropped his head into his hands. "*I* am so screwed up. How could I do that to her? How could I let all this get so out of hand?"

"It sounds like you both regret the way your relationship ended," Merritt murmured. "You fight because it's the only connection you have left. You miss each other."

"Merlin's wings, I *do* miss her," Aurelio moaned. "With every breath! Why couldn't I just swallow my pride and apologize?" He shook his head. "There's no going back now."

Merritt patted his shoulder.

The orc raised his head to stare at her as though he'd forgotten she was there. "Why are you listening to me carry on?"

"I'm here to help." Merritt smiled.

"Why?" Aurelio pressed.

Merritt shrugged. "I like doing that."

"You saved Amber." Aurelio bit his lip, the skin stretching

tight over his tusks. "I'll always owe you for that, Merritt, but can I ask for one more favor?"

Merritt nodded.

Aurelio paused. "I'll never get to tell her this in person since I'm facing prison if I'm lucky, but I need her to know. Will you take a message to Amber for me?"

"Sure." Merritt squeezed his shoulder.

Aurelio swallowed hard. "Tell her how sorry I am. That I never meant to harm her, and I've been an idiot all this time. I should never have let her go. I'll always regret it. Tell her—" Aurelio paused, his voice rough with emotion. "Tell her I still love her."

Merritt thought about Amber's words the night before.

"I'll tell her," she promised.

Amber huddled at the table in the bare apartment kitchen. The room had an empty feeling, reminding her that no one lived there. The fridge held no magnets, the sink no dishes, and the countertop no random spices.

The werewolf wore a borrowed sweatsuit several sizes too big. She wrapped her hands around a plain white coffee mug and received Aurelio's message with blank eyes.

"I think he means it, Amber," Merritt added. "He wasn't trying to hurt you."

"Yes, he was." Amber swallowed. "He wanted to burn down my pavilion."

"You *did* tear up his roses," Merritt pointed out.

Amber turned the hollow gaze on Merritt. "He nearly killed me. I don't care what he says now. I never want to talk to him again." She rose.

"Amber..." Merritt began.

"I don't want to hear it." Amber dumped the still-full mug in the sink. "I'm going back to bed."

Merritt left the apartment and wandered down the street. Amber's response weighed on her shoulders like a chain mail blanket. She dragged her feet, boots scuffing on the sidewalk, and trudged toward the back street without realizing where she was going.

So much pain. So many mistakes, Merritt thought. *But there's so much love beneath it all. How can they reconnect with that?*

The smell of smoke still hung over Amber's house. Though its walls and roof still stood, the fire had left it a blackened shell. Its windows looked like eye sockets with only charred emptiness behind them. Aurelio's garden was a mess of churned dirt and ruined flowerbeds.

So much destruction. Merritt sighed.

She wanted to see the pavilion. Amber hadn't seemed to doubt that Aurelio was telling the truth, but Merritt wanted to lay her eyes on the offending structure.

After letting herself in through Aurelio's front gate, Merritt plodded around the side of his house to the cozy backyard. A rose hedge surrounded a rectangle of bright green lawn. Each bush had its own drip head, and he had meticulously trimmed every stem; not a leaf was out of place. The bright yellow and red roses sent their sweetness into the air, contrasting sharply with the harsh tang of soot and smoke.

It wasn't hard to see how Aurelio had gotten into Amber's backyard. Footprints scuffed the white picket fence at a gap between two bushes. Merritt hoisted herself over it with little effort and landed in a similarly beautiful backyard. Well, traces of its beauty remained. There was no tidy lawn here. Ankle-deep grass and wildflowers stretched to the yard's edges.

Before the fire, the pavilion must have been a glorious place to sit on a spring day like this one, but now it was a charred skeleton. A few boards spoke to the domed roof, and the blackened remnants of a bench lay in a charred mass on the floor with the fallen rafters. Vines clung to the bottom, flowers drooping on the dying stems. The support beams smoldered and wisps of white smoke escaped the cracks in the scorched wood.

Merritt's boots crunched on the charred mess. She kicked the ashes away and stood facing Amber's gutted house.

Their voices echoed through her thoughts. *I still loved him. I still love her.* The love she'd seen in them both was painfully honest. She closed her eyes and bowed her head, wondering how things could have gone so wrong. She didn't know anything about love, but in her mind, it conquered and outlasted all things if it was real.

Something stirred against her boot. Merritt felt life around her and hesitated, magic throbbing in her veins. She had to stop...didn't she? She couldn't grow things whenever she wanted.

Could she?

Your powers aren't an inconvenience. They're your gift to the world.

Merritt breathed deeply. This could get her into trouble, but it felt right. She flexed her fingers, allowing the magic to flow through her blood like warm honey. Stems creaked and leaves rustled around her. Flower petals kissed her skin as they grew past.

Merritt didn't try to stop them.

***

"Merritt?" Tess stepped into the street, looking left and right. "Merritt? Hello?"

"She was here a few minutes ago." Amber peered over Tess' shoulder. "I don't think she went far."

Tess rubbed her neck. "Where would she go? She's not home."

"She's a grown woman. Well, she's a grown whatever-she-is," Amber pointed out. "I'm sure she's fine."

Tess gritted her teeth. "Why did she talk to Aurelio? She might get in trouble."

"Aurelio wouldn't hurt her," Amber blurted.

Tess stared at her. "He set your house on fire."

"It was an accident..." Amber's voice trailed off. "I understand that now. Look, maybe she went to my house to investigate if she's poking around and asking what happened."

"Good thinking." Tess set off.

"I'll come with you." Amber trotted after her.

Tess' long limbs made short work of the trip. As they turned the corner at Chaplin's Kitchen, Amber's nose twitched.

"Do you smell that?" the werewolf asked.

Tess frowned. "What?"

Amber's eyes widened. "Flowers. *Loads* of flowers."

Tess' skin prickled: potent magic. She gasped as they approached Amber's house.

"*Merlin's glowing splendor!*" Amber yelped.

Tess' jaw dropped.

The blackened husk was no longer visible. Plants engulfed the ruined home, the green of life replacing the blacks and grays the fire had left behind. Creepers spilled from the windows, blanketing the walls with fragrant flowers. Grass stretched over the floors, punctuated with wildflowers, and lilac and hydrangea bushes filled the space between the two homes. Tess mused that it was difficult to see that there *were* two homes. They appeared to be one.

"Wow," Amber whispered. "Do you think—"

"Let's go see," Tess murmured.

Amber led the way to the front door, their feet sinking into the thick grass. The rich carpet extended across the house, scattered with bluebells and nasturtiums, and jasmine engulfed the back door. Tess had to clear tendrils away to turn the knob, and leaves and petals fluttered down like confetti when she pushed the door open.

If the houses looked wonderful, the backyards were a symphony of botanical splendor. Here, short grass made the space seem larger. Meadow-like lawns were interspersed with rosebushes whose flowers ranged from classic red to a pale blue Tess had never seen outside Avalon.

"Oh," Amber whispered. "Look at the pavilion."

"Was it always like that?" Tess asked.

"No!" Amber laughed. "It was ordinary. Wood painted white. Not...*that*."

"*That*" was four flowering trees, their branches interwoven to form a tall dome. Creepers wrapped around their trunks, and thick gray-green moss covered the floor. Only a few splinters of charred wood offered a glimpse of what the pavilion had looked like a short time ago.

At its center, Merritt sat cross-legged on the moss, her splayed hands pressed against the earth. Her head hung, red curls obscuring her face. Pale green magic oozed from her skin.

"Did you know she could do this?" Amber murmured.

Tess shook her head. "I don't think *she* knew she could do this."

Amber brushed a fingertip across a scarlet rose by the back door. "Aurelio would love this."

Tess stared at her. Tears shimmered in the werewolf's eyes as she gazed at their interlaced gardens.

"I'll be right back," Tess muttered.

She jogged into the house, pulled out her phone, and hit Val's contact on the home screen.

The duchess answered on the second ring. "Tess, what's up?"

"Can you come over to Amber's house real quick?" Tess asked.

"Sure. Everything okay?" Val asked.

A plant sprouted at Tess' feet as Val spoke. In seconds, it budded and opened a bright yellow buttercup.

"I think so." Tess grinned. "Oh, one more thing."

"What?"

Tess inhaled. "Would you bring Aurelio?"

"*What?*"

The tickle of a leaf on Merritt's cheek made her open her eyes.

Greenery surrounded her. The sunlight dappling the moss was green-tinted and cool. Color inundated her, from the wildflowers in the lawns and the gorgeous rosebushes between them, and the air was heady with the smells of fresh earth and flowers.

She slowly rose and wandered across the lawn, unsure of what to do next. Should she tell someone? Her gut thumped at the thought. Would Amber or Aurelio be angry? What about Tess and Val?

Merritt froze halfway to Amber's back door, uncertain.

Tess' head popped around the door. "Merritt! Psst! Come over here!"

She didn't sound mad, to Merritt's relief. The Leshbolg jogged to the back door, and Tess grabbed her by the arm and towed her inside.

"Merlin's tooth abscess, girl! You didn't tell me that your powers could do this," Val rumbled. She stood on the grassy carpet in what used to be the living room. Shadow ecstatically rolled in the grass, paws in the air, making happy doggy noises.

"Uh..." Merritt began.

"Shhh!" Tess gestured her nearer. "It's working!"

Merritt and Val joined her by the half-closed door and peered outside.

Amber and Aurelio wandered between the rosebushes, following the gently curving grass paths Merritt had created. Amber had her arms wrapped around her chest. Aurelio interlaced his hands behind his back. They said nothing, but their eyes were wide as they stared at the beauty around them.

"This is a ridiculous idea," Val grumbled.

"Shhh!" Tess chided.

"He committed arson," Val hissed.

"She attempted assault. Give it a minute," Tess murmured. "I think things are about to change."

Amber's borrowed sweater was too long. She had to shake the sleeves away from her hands before she could touch one of the ice-blue roses.

"Have you ever seen one this color?" she asked.

Aurelio's head swiveled to her; her tender tone surprised him. "Not on Earth. They don't occur naturally." He gazed at the rose. "Only magic could do this."

"You've told me that before." Amber tilted her head. "I remember teasing you about your lockscreen being a blue rose when we met."

Aurelio smiled. "I remember."

Their eyes met. Aurelio's hands tightened behind his back. Amber looked away, but her hands fell to her sides. She hooked a few wild strands of silver hair behind her ear as she strolled toward the pavilion.

"How pretty is this?" Aurelio murmured.

"It's better than it used to be, and you know how much I loved it the way it was." Amber brushed her fingertips over a trunk.

"You did." Aurelio sighed and leaned against another tree, hands in his pockets. "I should never have fought you on which house you wanted, Ambs. I could've remodeled that kitchen."

Amber turned to him, flower petals landing on her hair. "I could have built a pavilion in your backyard. We could've had one exactly like this if we'd hired some Shajara Elves."

They gazed at one another, the silence lengthening. Merritt held her breath.

"This was so stupid," Aurelio murmured.

"It was." Amber shook her head. "Why did we let anything get between us, Aurelio?"

"I don't know. It was like we stopped paying attention.

Stopped trying. I wish we hadn't." Aurelio lowered his head. "I know it's too late, but I need you to know how sorry I am for what I did. All of it. Spitefully playing my music, flooding your flowerbeds, and especially *this*." He gestured at the house.

Tess, Merritt, and Val cringed back so that he wouldn't spot them listening.

"I hurt you, but I never meant for the fire to harm you." Aurelio bit his upper lip with his tusks. "I tried to burn this pavilion down. I have no excuses, Ambs, nor do I ask anything of you. I just want you to know I'm sorry."

Amber brushed petals from her hair. "I'm sorry, too."

Aurelio looked up. "You have nothing to be sorry for."

"Of course I do. I tore up your garden. I was drunk, but I knew what I was doing. I wanted to hurt you." Amber grimaced. "I would have bitten you the other night if Tess hadn't stopped me. I'm truly sorry."

Aurelio's shoulders softened.

"Can you forgive me?" Amber asked.

The orc's eyebrows rose. "Forgive *you*? Amber, I should be asking for *your* forgiveness."

Amber stepped nearer and rested her hand on his arm. "I should've given it to you long ago. You have it now."

Tears shimmered in Aurelio's eyes. He placed his hand over hers, and their fingers interlaced.

"Awwww!" Tess sighed. "Merritt, it worked!"

"All I see is two idiots continuing to be idiots," Val grumbled.

"Don't be so grumpy, Val. Look at them." Tess beamed. "Can you see them continuing to cause problems for Little Avalon?"

Val's expression softened. "I guess not."

The orc and werewolf left the pavilion and walked to the back door hand in hand.

"Delightful," Val muttered.

Tess flung the door wide. Neither half of the couple seemed surprised to see that they had an audience.

"Merritt, did you do this?" Aurelio asked, gesturing at the garden.

Merritt swallowed. "Yes."

"It's beautiful." The orc beamed. "Look at it. Roses and wildflowers growing side by side. Why did that never occur to me?"

"We're sorry about all the trouble we caused in Little Avalon." Amber grimaced.

Aurelio rubbed his neck. "I'm still your prisoner, Your Grace."

Merritt held her breath.

"You sure are, asshole," Val muttered. "Holding hands in a flower garden is cute, but it doesn't change the fact that you both caused property damage and threatened each other's lives in *my* duchy. I don't take that lightly."

Aurelio hung his head and released Amber's hand. "I'll accept whatever penalty you decide on, Your Grace. I'm aware of what I've done."

"There'll be no more trouble from us," Amber added. "We've made peace, real peace, perhaps for the first time."

Val cracked a smile. "You'll be on thin ice with me for the rest of your lives, both of you."

Amber's eyes widened. "Does that mean you won't send Aurelio away?"

"It means I've decided on his punishment." Val folded her arms, muscles tightening her jacket's leather. "Aurelio, you will rebuild Amber's house at your expense. I expect this place to be spotless when it's done, understand? Better than it was."

Aurelio blinked. "You...you're letting me stay?"

"This might be a good opportunity for remodeling." Merritt smirked. "I thought the kitchen could use a better layout."

Amber beamed and gripped Aurelio's hand. "Yeah. Me too."

"What's more, both your asses are going to the NYHQ," Val added. "You're in dire need of anger management training. Qenzi arranges sessions with the training orb to help you with your issues."

Aurelio eagerly nodded. "That sounds good, Your Grace."

"It's a punishment. It shouldn't," Val snapped.

Aurelio struggled to hide his smile. "Yes, Your Grace."

"We dread it." Amber giggled.

"One last thing." Val's eyes narrowed. "I was lenient this time. Do not expect me to be lenient again." Her tone dropped an octave, and red light flashed behind her eyes. Shadow gave a rumbling snarl.

Amber and Aurelio leaned back.

"Yes, Your Grace," Amber squeaked.

"Good." Val blinked, returning to her usual self. "Get started on this house and never cause shit again. Clear?"

The couple eagerly nodded.

"Let's get out of here." Val exhaled. "I need a drink."

"It's eleven in the morning," Tess pointed out.

"I need two drinks, then," Val muttered. "Let's go to the Second Fist. I'm buying."

"Is it open?" Merritt asked, jogging to keep up as Val strode from the house.

"I don't give a shit. It's never closed for *me*," Val announced.

Merritt didn't doubt it. She followed Val into the street, dropping a hand on Shadow's head to pet him as they walked.

"Merlin's mustache boogers! I'm glad that's over." Val rolled her neck, grimacing at stiffness. "That was one drama I didn't have the energy for. I was ready to throw Aurelio in the locker. Amber, too."

"Turns out that wasn't necessary." Tess smirked. "All they needed was a beautiful flower garden."

"I don't think it was that simple," Merritt volunteered.

Val tilted her head. "It wasn't, but you did a great thing, Merritt." She laid a hand on the Leshbolg's shoulder, engulfing it in her iron-hard palm. "You did something I've never been good at. You really understood the problem. In this case, you saw the perfect solution. You did more than grow a garden." She paused.

"You did the most important thing anyone in Little Avalon can do."

"What's that?" Merritt asked.

Val grinned. "You brought people together. That's what makes Little Avalon special. That's what it's here for…unity in diversity."

"Unity in diversity," Merritt murmured. She liked the sound of that.

CHAPTER NINETEEN

"Well?" Merritt asked. "What do you think?"

Tess sat at the kitchen table, still wearing her Stonehold Security Services shirt and body armor vest. Her purse lay on the corner as she surveyed Merritt's first-ever cookie.

"It came out a funny shape," Merritt mumbled, biting her lip.

"I think it's cute." Tess smiled at the cookie, which had a weird blob on one side. "It's unique! But what counts is how it tastes."

Merritt nodded. "Right."

"What flavor is it?" Tess asked.

Merritt hooked a strand of hair behind her ear, smearing her face with flour. "It's a sugar cookie. I thought I'd start with something simple."

"Simple, yet delicious." Tess raised the cookie. "Here goes."

Merritt held her breath as the Lunar Fae bit into the cookie. The small scar on her left cheek indicated that it hadn't been an easy day at work, but the tension melted from her shoulders as her eyes closed and she slumped over the table.

"Wow, Merritt." Tess took another bite and talked around a mouthful of crumbs. "This is amazing."

"You like it?" Merritt grinned. "I used magic to enhance the flavor."

"It's the best," Tess moaned.

"I made plenty." Merritt indicated the tray on the counter. "Let's take them to the Second Fist when we meet friends for drinks tonight." She'd never met friends for drinks before Little Avalon, or not that she could remember, but it was a regular occurrence these days.

Tess finished the cookie. "We can't do that. The Second Fist sells its food. I'd say I was sorry, but honestly, I want them all. Is Damian around?"

"He's gone off. I'd say he's at work, but it's Saturday night, so I doubt it." Merritt shrugged. "Maybe he's working extra to catch whoever tried to kill him."

Tess cleared her throat. "Maybe." She rose. "I'll shower and change. Then we'll go."

"I'll clean up the kitchen." Merritt grinned. "This'll be fun."

Tess met her eyes and smiled. "Yeah. It sure will be."

She hurried off, and Merritt hastily tossed things in the dishwasher and wiped off the table, then changed into her favorite knee-length dress with long sleeves and a turtleneck. It was the same jade green as her eyes, and given the fire in the hearth at the Second Fist, it would be more than warm enough.

Tess met her at the front door in a bold red skirt and a black blouse that made her skin look milk-pale, plus black tights. They strolled down the street, smiling at neighbors out for runs or walking their dogs, wyverns, or miniature pegasi.

"Tetra keeps encouraging me to try a shot of faerie wine," Merritt mentioned. "Is that a good idea?"

"*No!*" Tess yelled.

Merritt jumped.

"Sorry." Tess cleared her throat. "No, it's not. If three cocktails put you on your ass, a shot of faerie wine could kill you."

Merritt laughed.

Tess grabbed her shoulders. "Look into my eyes. I am serious. They dip their arrows in faerie wine to poison small animals like baby moose when they hunt them."

Merritt blinked. "I thought you said *small* animals."

"Have I taken a faerie wine shot in my life?" Tess paused. "Yes. Did it end with me dancing on the table singing *I Work Hard for the Money* while trying to flash Dante? Also yes. Val carried me home over her shoulder. It was not a good night."

"Wait." Merritt grinned. *"Dante?"*

"Do *not* try the faerie wine," Tess ordered.

Merritt cleared her throat. "Okay."

Tess released her. "Good. Glad we're clear on that."

She opened the Second Fist's door and stepped inside.

Merritt followed. "I was thinking of tasting…oh!"

A cascade of balloons tumbled from the ceiling and bounced off Merritt's head and shoulders before drifting to the floor. In her surprise, a few plants sprouted from the floorboards, and several balloons popped with loud bangs that couldn't drown out the yell from the crowd in the bar.

"Surprise!"

Merritt blinked. "Wh-what is this?"

Every face in the Second Fist was familiar to her, and everyone grinned. A huge banner hung behind the bar. It read, Welcome, Merritt!

Dante strode up to her with an overly toothy grin and placed a tankard of dwarven ale in her hand. "I know it's late, but this is your welcoming party."

"A welcoming party?" Merritt whispered. Tears clogged her throat, making it hard to talk.

"We're all glad you're here." Dante slapped her shoulder. "C'mon! I've reserved the best seat at the bar."

Merritt drifted across the room, gaping at everyone as they waved and smiled. How had she made so many friends in such a short time?

She slid onto a stool beside Val. Shadow lay at Val's feet and wagged his tail when he spotted Merritt.

Merritt hi! Shadow tired. He yawned and closed his eyes.

"Hey, there's our favorite gardener." Val slapped Merritt on the back, almost causing her nose to slam into the bar. "Oops, sorry." She offered her tankard for a toast.

Merritt tapped hers against it. "Thanks for coming, Val."

"It's good to see you settling in so well." Val smiled.

Merritt inclined her head. "I still don't have a job."

"We're not worrying about jobs tonight," Tess interrupted. "We're celebrating you." She perched beside Merritt.

"I like the sound of that." Val grinned.

"Love the new tankards, Val. They feel more para—" Tess glanced around, spotting Hank and Isabella in the crowd. "They feel more authentic," she corrected.

"Thanks, but they were Dante's idea." Val nodded at the new owner. "He's the brain behind the Second Fist these days, remember?"

Dante smiled as he poured beer into another tankard. "Thanks to you."

"To think you were wasting your brain at college." Val chuckled.

"Hey!" Qenzi protested. "I heard that."

Merritt turned to Tess. "This is really amazing." She paused. "Thanks for doing this."

Tess laughed. "I'm flattered, Merritt, but this wasn't me." She nodded at a table near the back. "It was all them."

Merritt stared. Amber and Aurelio sat at the table, facing each other. They held hands under the table, their postures relaxed as they talked and laughed. Aurelio wore a suit and tie and sipped expensive Southern Avalonian wine from a stemmed glass. Amber slurped ale from a tankard and chewed up chicken wings, bones and all. Aurelio politely declined a sticky wing when she offered him the basket.

"They arranged this?" Merritt asked.

"Sure did." Dante slid the tankard across the bar to Qenzi. "They wanted to show their appreciation for your help. Aurelio especially mentioned his blue roses. Amber punched him for it, and they play-wrestled for a few seconds after that."

"They look happy," Merritt murmured. "Different, but happy. I should go over and thank them."

"Maybe later." Tess smiled. "I don't think we should interrupt them. Look how much fun they're having together."

"They haven't set fire to one another's shit for several days, which is all I'm asking," Val grumbled. She checked her phone and smiled. "Ah, there we are. Merritt, there's someone I'd like you to meet."

Val rose as the Fist's door opened, and a tall stranger entered. Though Merritt had never seen a picture of Val's boyfriend, she instantly recognized him. "Smoking hot were-deer" summed it up nicely. The tall Were had short, sand-colored hair and the most limpid eyes she'd ever seen. There were dark rings beneath them, and he vaguely smelled of disinfectant.

"Hey, honey." Val wrapped her arms around him.

The weredeer melted into her as he placed a kiss on her head. "Mmm. Sorry I'm so late. Bartholomew's wyvern thought swallowing the squeaker from his favorite toy would be a great idea. Had to remove it before his bowels started to rot."

"You know rotting bowels are my favorite topic for party conversation," Val teased.

His arms tightened around her. "My bad."

"It's cool." Val turned, her smile holding a softness Merritt hadn't seen in her before. "I'd like you to meet my favorite person in the universe, Doctor Niall Wynthorn." She added the title with pride.

"It's just Niall." The weredeer extended a hand. "You must be Merritt. Val's told me so much about you."

Merritt's toes curled, but Niall's smile was friendly as she shook his hand.

"Your magic feels familiar," she blurted and immediately regretted it.

"Excuse me?" Val's eyebrows rose.

"I get it." Niall winked. "Us woodland folk have to stick together."

Merritt longed for the floor to swallow her, but Val laughed. "C'mon, Niall. I'm sure you need a drink after those stinky bowels."

Merritt didn't return to her stool. She gazed at the paras gathered around the tables, laughing over their drinks, and warmth budded and bloomed in her chest. "It seems impossible," she murmured.

"What does?" Dante asked, pausing with a tray of drinks in hand.

"Sorry. I didn't mean to interrupt you." Merritt followed him as he strode to a table near the back.

"No worries." Dante smirked. "Care to share the thought you were voicing aloud?"

"It seems impossible that everyone is here to celebrate me," Merritt mumbled.

"Why?" Dante raised an eyebrow. "Haven't you ever had a birthday party?"

Merritt shrugged. "I don't know when my birthday is. Or if birthdays are part of Leshbolg culture, for that matter."

"I'm sorry." Dante winced. "That's crappy."

Merritt smiled. "Don't be sorry." Her tone softened. "Little Avalon is a new world for me. I think things will be different from now on."

"Trust me, they will." Dante stopped. "Four Iron IPAs." He slid the drinks onto the table.

Three elderly human males occupied the table, playing cards, but they made Merritt's skin crawl. When she looked at the cards, she couldn't quite make out the numbers and figures on them.

"Thank ye, Dante," one muttered, his accent vaguely similar to Val's but so broad it rendered him almost incoherent.

The fourth figure at the table wore a deep blue robe with swirls of silver embroidery. His hood cloaked his face in shadow, but when he reached for his tankard, silver light seeped from beneath his skin.

Merritt gasped. "Merlin?"

"Shhh!" Merlin hissed, tipping his hood back. "Keep your voice down. I don't need the whole universe to know I'm here."

Merritt glanced around. "Wh-why not?"

"My fame and incredible handsomeness attract more attention than necessary," Merlin grumbled. "This is your night, not mine, stupid little waif."

Merritt blinked. "Oh. What are you doing here?"

"What's anyone doing here? Trying to drink my beer in peace," Merlin muttered.

"Sorry." Merritt backed away.

The nearest old man clicked his tongue. "Sit yer wee arse doon, lass. The old bampot dinnae mean it."

Merritt stared, trying to decipher the sentence, and got it when the old man pushed a chair out near her.

"Who's to say what I mean?" Merlin growled into his beer.

Merritt slid into a chair, looking at the cards. They remained a mystery to her.

"Val told me about what you did." Merlin sipped, foam smearing his mustache.

Merritt looked horrified. "They were happy about it."

"I know," Merlin grunted. "I was congratulating you."

"Oh." Merritt cleared her throat. "Thanks."

"Things are different here, Merritt." Merlin lowered his tankard and studied her over the rim, his blue eyes stabbing through her. "You'll find your place. I'm told you haven't found somewhere to work yet."

"Not yet," Merritt confessed, "but everyone's been kind. I'll keep trying, sir, I promise. I'll find something."

Merlin's mustache twitched as if to hide a smile. "I know." He waved his tankard. "That's all I wanted. You can go away now."

"Gae on, lass." The nearest old man patted her hand. "Away wi' ye. Get blootered wi' yer muckers."

Mystified, Merritt slid from her chair and retreated in haste, almost colliding with Damian as she hurried away.

"Hey!" Damian snapped, shielding his drink with one hand.

"Oops!" Merritt stopped. "Sorry."

"Watch where you're going," Damian growled.

"I made cookies," Merritt squawked.

Damian stared at her. "What?"

"I mean, how are you?" Merritt asked.

"Peachy," Damian spat.

He shoved past her and marched to an unoccupied table in a back corner, where he flopped into his chair and stared into his tankard without drinking the contents.

Val had saved Merritt's seat by placing the warhammer on it. She removed the massive weapon as Merritt approached.

"Merlin's here!" Merritt hissed, wide-eyed.

"I know." Val sipped her drink. "I invited him."

"Damian, too," Merritt added.

"I invited *him*." Tess raised her eyebrows. "Good to see that he came."

"He doesn't like me." Merritt sighed.

"Not necessarily. I heard that he's received death threats at work." Tess grimaced.

Val's head snapped up. "What? Death threats?"

"Scary letters, boxes full of venomous spiders, that sort of thing. He was telling his mom about it on the phone, and I overheard," Tess admitted.

Val huffed. "He still won't let me post someone at his window to keep an eye on him."

"I know death threats are part of his line of work, but this seems different." Tess shook her head. "I wish he'd let us help him."

"Poor guy," Merritt murmured.

"We can only help him as much as he'll let us," Val pointed out. "Besides, tonight is about something different." She nudged Merritt. "It's about *you*."

Merritt grinned.

"Bottoms up, girlfriend." Val waved her tankard. "I'm told you are a hilarious drunk. I wouldn't mind seeing that."

"I don't think—" Tess began.

Merritt grinned. "We have Fernwood dew at home, Tess?"

Tess groaned. "Yes, but—"

Merritt raised her tankard to her lips and chugged. She slammed the empty tankard on the table, breathless and a little nauseated, and the Second Fist rang with cheers.

Tess shuffled into the kitchen, yawning, barefoot in her pajamas. She held her laptop under her arm and ran her hand through the tangles in her long hair.

"Oh, hey." Merritt looked up from the dough she was rolling out. "Is it morning already?"

"It's six AM." Tess slid into a chair. "I'm not complaining about waking up to the amazing smells of your baking, but how long have you been up?"

Merritt shrugged. "I got bored."

"Who could ever get bored with sleeping?" Tess yawned. "I feel like I don't do enough of it these days."

"You got in late last night," Merritt observed.

"Yeah. We tracked a changeling through Istanbul most of

yesterday. The time difference screwed us, but we found him in the end." Tess placed her laptop on the table. "Was the job application keeping you awake?"

Merritt weighed her answer. "Sort of."

"Let's see if they've responded yet." Tess smiled. "Sorry I couldn't check for you yesterday evening."

"Don't apologize." Merritt scattered chocolate chips on the smooth dough. "I'm grateful that you use your computer to send my job applications."

"Anytime. Tech can be overwhelming on top of your first introduction to Western society," Tess acknowledged. "You seem much less overwhelmed these days, though."

"I'm ready to learn more." Merritt nodded.

"Then I'll talk to Liam. He's been waiting in the wings for the big moment of getting you a phone." Tess grinned. "Okay, let's see... Here it is. They responded."

Merritt's heart thumped. She'd sent her résumé to the school for an entry-level teaching assistant position in its Were class.

Tess turned the laptop around. "Here."

Merritt leaned closer to the screen, and her heart sank as she read the response aloud. "Dear Ms. Vale, we regret to inform you that the position was filled." She sighed. "Aw, crap."

Tess grimaced. "I'm sorry."

"I'll have to keep trying." Merritt slid the laptop toward her. "Thanks for the help."

"You could always talk to Hank and Kalyna," Tess suggested.

Merritt curled the edge of the dough and slowly rolled it up before responding. "Maybe." She bit her lip.

"Thinking of keeping your baking as a hobby?" Tess asked.

Merritt shook her head. "I'd love to do this all day, every day." She patted the roll and smoothed the edges. "And beggars can't be choosers, but it means a lot to me, Tess. I want to get it right."

"I understand." Tess yawned. "Okay, I'd better take a shower and prepare for a day of babysitting a rich European guy's daughter while she explores the Big Apple."

"These will be ready before you leave," Merritt told her.

"I have no idea what 'these' are, but I'm here for them." Tess grinned.

She trudged off to her room, and Merritt selected a sharp knife to cut the chocolate roll into chunky segments. This time, the dough's consistency seemed right. It bounced back when she cut it, leaving her with perfectly round rolls.

She glanced through the kitchen window, which overlooked the street, as she arranged them on a sheet pan lined with parchment paper. If Damian came home at the time he usually did, maybe the smell of the baking rolls would have been enough to entice him to try one.

The street was still dark, barely lightened with the beginning of dawn. A Were bundled in a coat and a scarf against the chill hurried down the sidewalk, looking small and endearing from Merritt's vantage point.

She replaced the freshly baked bellyfill in the oven with the chocolate rolls. The bellyfill loaf steamed through its magically altered cabbage leaves, making Merritt's mouth water. She'd found that leaving it to cool slightly before removing the leaves enhanced the flavor. It trailed fragrant steam across the kitchen as she strode to the counter by the window, where a sourdough loaf was on the rise.

A familiar figure caught Merritt's eye through the window. She stood on tiptoe to peer at the sidewalk below, where Damian strode toward their building, coat collar flipped up against the first rays of the sun, his stylish hat pulled down over his ears.

"I'll get you to try my baking one way or another," Merritt whispered.

A shadow darted from the alley across the street from Damian. Merritt froze. Had she imagined it?

She leaned closer to the window, keeping her hands off the

hot sheet pan, and squinted at the alley. Something stirred in the gap between two Stonehold Houses. The outline was vague enough that Merritt thought she was seeing things until she spotted a shadow on the concrete. Whatever concealment spell was in use didn't hide that. When Merritt squinted harder, she spotted the outline of something clutched in the shadow's fist.

Something that had a sharp point.

"Crap!" Merritt yelped. *"Tess!"*

She got no response. The shower had to be drowning out her words, but there was no time to waste. The shadow slipped across the sidewalk and sheltered beneath a tree directly across the street from Damian.

Merritt pushed away from the window and scrambled across the kitchen. She flung the door open and leaped down the stairs three at a time, clinging to the rail for support.

"Damian!" she bellowed, having no idea if he could hear her. It seemed to take an eternity to reach the ground floor. Merritt crashed through the door and stumbled into the street, half expecting to see the vampire unconscious on the sidewalk.

Damian trudged toward her, head low, hands in his pockets. His slouched shoulders suggested he hadn't seen the shadow that darted across the street, the arm with the stake lifted high.

"Damian, look out!" Merritt screamed.

The vampire's head snapped up, his scowl revealing his fangs. "What do you want, Merritt?"

The shadow was mere feet away. No time to consider the implications of anything but saving Damian's life. Merritt clenched her fists and yelled with effort. Tree roots burst from the street beside Damian, sending pieces of asphalt flying. The vampire leaped back with a yelp as the roots writhed like snakes and formed a solid wall.

In mid-leap, the shadow crashed into the root wall, sending splinters in all directions, and the concealment rippled. Damian whipped around as the shadowy figure stumbled back. The spell snared on the roots and tore away from the attacker like a cloak.

The vampire's face twisted. "Who in Merlin's name are *you?*"

His attacker stood in the street, breathing hard, a silver stake gleaming in her hand. The female orc had black tattoos like slashes across both cheekbones. She'd filed her tusks to needle points and wore all black, her clothes tight-fitting.

"The last face you'll ever see," she hissed and lunged.

Merritt's options flashed through her mind as the assassin darted around the root wall and slashed at Damian with the stake. The vampire leaped back and raised his hands, his nails lengthening into claws.

She knew what would happen if she touched the *amplify* rune. She could feel the potential sizzling in her blood, her magic straining against her fingertips, longing to lengthen them into wooden clubs, but she'd just won over the residents of Little Avalon. What would they think if she turned into a seven-foot male Leshbolg?

Damian hissed, fangs lengthening. The assassin flung the stake, but he slipped aside, and it missed by several inches, slamming into the root wall instead. Its proximity made Damian stagger, fangs growing shorter as he fell to one knee.

Merritt would help him in a different way. She clenched her fists and emitted a growl of defiance. The assassin seized the silver stake, but the roots grew feet in seconds. With a yelp of alarm, the assassin clung to the stake, bracing her feet against the roots as she tried to pull it free.

The stake slipped out with a crunch, and the assassin fell several feet, landing almost soundlessly. She whipped around to face Damian, who'd retreated a short distance and held his curved claws aloft.

"You can't fight me. Not while I hold silver in my hands!" the assassin hissed.

"Maybe not." Damian nodded at Merritt. "But *she* can."

Merritt knew what he meant. The roots shook in response to her magic. Every cell cried out for her next command. Her fists clenched, and the leaves rustled.

The assassin threw back her head and laughed. "Her?"

"That's right." Merritt grinned. "Me."

She raised a hand in a motion like an uppercut. A root cracked through the sidewalk, shot to the assassin's arm, and wrapped around the stake with snake-like speed. The assassin roared and swung her other hand in a wild punch that met the root with a painful crack. She screamed and released the stake.

The root retreated into the earth, dragging the stake with it. Damian exhaled relief and raised his hands, pale claws as sharp and curved as a cat's, then lunged.

The assassin dodged. Fabric ripped when his claws caught her hoodie, but she danced back on nimble feet and ripped a switchblade from her pocket. Merritt held her breath, but the blade was steel, not silver.

Assassin and vampire danced back and forth across the sidewalk. Merritt could do little except hold her breath as knife and claws traded slashes. The assassin jabbed at Damian's belly. He spun away and swiped toward her face. She twirled to avoid his blow, which was a mistake. Damian's other hand closed around her left arm, and his claws dug into her flesh.

The assassin shrieked and raised her right hand, switchblade at the ready, but Damian met it with a sharp blow to the wrist that knocked the knife out of her grasp. He twisted her arm, and she squealed and doubled over. She tried to writhe out of his grasp as her blood coursed over his hands, but Damian planted a kick in the back of one knee that sent her to the ground.

"You're under arrest!" he barked, knocking her onto her face. The orc tried but failed to resist as he yanked her hands behind her back. "You'll answer to the Eternity Throne for your crimes."

"Shit!" the orc hissed.

Damian ripped off his belt and wrapped it around her wrists, securing them behind her back.

"*Damian!*" Val thundered. "*Merritt!*"

She charged toward them, bare feet slapping the sidewalk, wearing checkered sweatpants and a tee shirt that read *tell your dog i said hi*. Her warhammer blazed with red fire.

What happen? Shadow raced beside her, hackles bristling.

"It's under control, Your Grace." Damian rose, wiping his bloody hands on his pants. "We caught the assassin who tried to kill me."

"We?" Val demanded.

Merritt tucked her hands behind her back. The root wall unraveled and plunged below ground, leaving massive holes in the street and the sidewalk.

Merritt squeaked.

"Merritt saved my life." Damian met her eyes. "I would be dead if it wasn't for her."

A burst of applause startled Merritt. She jumped and looked around. Several dozen paras had gathered in doorways and windows nearby, a few venturing as far as the sidewalk to watch. They clapped their hands. Tetra wolf-whistled.

Val raised her eyebrows. "Good job, kid." She slapped Merritt's back, almost knocking her to the ground. "That only leaves one question. Get her up, Damian."

Damian seized the orc by her uninjured arm and dragged her to her feet. Val slung the warhammer onto her shoulder, flames still hissing. She swaggered up to the assassin, who raised her chin and met Val's eyes, only the slight tremor of a lower lip betraying her terror.

"Okay, bitch. Here's how this shakes out." Val planted her free hand on her hip and cocked it. "You tell me who sent you, or I will shove this burning hammer so far up your ass, you'll puke flames."

The assassin's jaw clenched. "You can't do that to me. It's against your precious Eternity Law!"

"I'm the duchess here, stupid." Val smirked. "I do what I want." She clasped the warhammer with both hands. "Last chance. Tell me who sent you."

"I never betray my clients!" the assassin barked.

"Suit yourself. Damian, bend her over." Val readied the hammer.

"Stop! Stop! All right, all right." The assassin shivered. "It was Norton Barbados."

"*Him?*" Damian frowned. "I should've known."

"Who is he?" Merritt asked.

"One of the many assholes my intelligence put in jail." Damian's eyes narrowed. "I'd like to know how he hired you from prison."

The assassin glanced at the hammer. "I'll tell you anything if you agree to have me tried under Eternity Law."

Val grinned. "Fine by me. I'll call the OPMA." She pulled out her phone. "Hey, Bianca. What's up? We're good, thanks. I'm calling because I've got a present for you."

CHAPTER TWENTY

Isabella's fingers massaged Merritt's scalp, caressing the tension away. Merritt kept her eyes shut, enjoying the steady pressure and the warm water as Isabella rinsed the shampoo from her hair.

"I'd like to try a new conditioner." Isabella held up a bright purple bottle. "It's supposed to be great for shaping curls. Mind if I use you as my guinea pig?"

"A small rodent often kept as a pet?" Merritt asked, frowning.

"A test subject." Isabella chuckled. "I forgot you're not from around here."

"Oh. Sure." Merritt grinned. "I don't mind."

Isabella rubbed the conditioner into her locks. "Hang tight. It needs to stay on for a few minutes, which gives me time to start on my next customer."

The row of chairs by the door contained several other paras, including Tess. She hopped up when Isabella called her and dropped into the chair beside Merritt's. She sighed with contentment as she lowered her head to the basin's rim.

"This is seriously the best part of my week, Bella." She shifted her weight, getting comfortable.

Isabella directed a stream of hot water over Tess' abundant hair. "Sweet of you. Hey, do you guys know what happened to the street in front of your apartment building?"

Merritt and Tess exchanged sidelong glances.

"Gas leak," Tess mumbled.

"Wow. Must've been bad." Isabella worked shampoo into Tess' hair.

"Yeah," Merritt muttered.

"Did you hear the end of the saga with Amber and Aurelio?" Isabella added.

Merritt shifted in her chair. "What happened?"

"They're living together again." Isabella giggled. "Can you believe it? After Amber's house fire, they apparently decided to mend their fences. Amber's living in Aurelio's house with him. My real estate friend told me they approached her about selling Aurelio's house in a few months. They're thinking of moving into Amber's after they finished rebuilding it."

Merritt beamed. "That's awesome."

"I know! Who would've thought it could end that way? I'm happy for them." Isabella chuckled. "Though I might miss the drama. Little Avalon's gossip is now a tiny bit less juicy."

"I'm sure something new will come up." Tess laughed. "Never a dull moment in this place."

"Your turn with the conditioner, Tess." Isabella twisted the Lunar Fae's hair into a knot. "You want it cut, Merritt?"

Merritt enjoyed the warm water as Isabella rinsed her hair. "Not today. I like it the way it is, but you make the curls look so much nicer."

"Let's see if this new product works like I think it will." Isabella squeezed water from Merritt's hair and wrapped a towel around it. "Move over to the chair so I can dry it."

Merritt rose. The salon door opened, and a few quiet giggles emanated from the ladies waiting in the chairs by the door.

"Hey, Damian," Isabella called. "Are those for me?"

"No." Damian cleared his throat. "They're…they're for Merritt."

Merritt raised her head. Damian stood in the doorway, pale cheeks flushed. He wore the usual rumpled suit with a broad-brimmed hat and clutched a bunch of flowers in his left hand and a cake box in his right. The price tag still clung to the top.

"Oooh, they *are?*" Isabella cooed.

"Yeah." Damian shifted his weight. "I- I owe her an apology, but I feel like this is, uh, bad timing." His gaze dipped to the cape around Merritt's neck.

"It's *perfect* timing!" Isabella clapped her hands.

Damian squared his shoulders and marched across the salon like a prisoner to the gallows, then stiffly held out the cake and flowers.

"I know you like baking and gardening," he got out. "I thought these would be good."

Merritt stuck her arms out from under the cape to take them. "You didn't have to."

"I did." Damian mopped his brow. "I've been a real ass to you. You were new and could've used my help and support as your housemate the way Tess has helped and supported you. Instead, I was an asswipe."

"It's okay." Merritt smiled. "Really."

"It isn't." Damian squared his shoulders. "Listen, I know a little something about feeling rejected. It can't have been easy to leave your home so often before you came here. I bet you arrived hoping things would be different, only to have your new housemate give you the cold shoulder."

Merritt didn't know what to say since he was right.

"I'm shit at this," Damian muttered. "I'm trying to say you're welcome in Little Avalon, and you make this place better. There." He shoved his hands in his pockets. "I fixed it."

"That's not how it works," Tess protested.

Merritt dumped the cake and flowers on the nearest table, flung her arms open, and charged Damian.

"Aw, crap," the vampire whimpered.

She wrapped her arms around him and squeezed. Damian grunted and half-heartedly squirmed.

Merritt released him. "Thank you for saying that."

"Yeah, yeah." Damian smoothed his jacket. "Whatever."

"Are you joining us for drinks tonight?" Tess asked, still leaning back over the basin. "Bella and I are going to the Second Fist. You're obviously also invited, Merritt."

"I could do that." Damian almost smiled. "It's late. Bye."

He stomped out of the salon.

Isabella laughed. "*Now* may I dry your hair?"

"Thanks." Merritt flopped into the chair. "Wow, this cake looks...um..." She leaned over it and grimaced at the gooey blobs of greasy buttercream clinging to crumpled vanilla cake.

"Awful?" Isabella suggested.

"I was going to say 'unappetizing,'" Merritt confessed.

Isabella shrugged. "It's the thought that counts."

"I'm glad Damian's coming with us tonight," Tess observed. "It'll be good to have all three housemates out together."

Merritt glanced at the calendar on the back wall, which was visible in the mirror as Isabella fussed over her hair. Isabella marked off the days in bright pink highlighter. Only one day was blank: March 31st.

She had never done anything with the phone under her mattress. Her fists clenched as she made a decision. "I can't make it tonight. Would tomorrow night be okay?"

"Tomorrow night is fine with me." Isabella held a sheaf of Merritt's hair back with a crocodile clip.

Tess asked, "Why not?"

Merritt smiled at her reflection. "I have somewhere to be."

Tess raised an eyebrow. "Where are you—"

"Don't interrogate her, Tess." Isabella cut her off. "Merritt's a grown woman who's settled in Little Avalon nicely." She squeezed the Leshbolg's shoulder. "She can do as she pleases."

Tess smiled. "That she can."

A knot unraveled in Merritt's chest when Tess didn't press for details.

She didn't want anyone in Little Avalon to know her plans for that night.

Merritt couldn't make herself invisible, but to the mass of humans gathered on the section of the place of trees known as Pier Three, she might as well have been wearing the invisibility garment the assassin used when she attacked Damian.

Her twitching nose, adorned with whiskers, helped her make her way along the borders of the flowerbeds surrounding the vast lawn. She paused to wipe her nose with tiny paws and sat on her haunches, ears turning, protruding eyes taking in the wide view of the world.

She sat in plain sight of the humans, but none noticed the tiny shrew huddled by the flowerbeds. Merritt cleaned her whiskers again and sniffed the air. She missed details, though she saw movement clearly. She made out the stage on the lawn near the waterfront, staccato bursts of music emerging as the band checked their instruments. A mass of humans on folding chairs or blankets were ensconced on the lawn. Far beyond the stage, Manhattan's skyline was a blur of lights to Merritt's rodent vision.

Her nose and whiskers knew everything. When a human couple strolled past, she smelled aftershave, perfume, sweat, and laundry detergent. The air they displaced stirred her whiskers. She tilted her head left and right as her tiny ears picked up the odd thump of music.

Then she smelled what she'd come here looking for: gunpowder. Her orb training told her gunpowder propelled bullets out of guns. The metallic and acrid scent made it easy to pick out the armed people in the crowd.

Merritt focused. A tall, lanky human shambled past, pants riding low on his hips and his ball cap pulled down over his eyes. She couldn't see the gun from down here, but she smelled it.

There's one. I have to find the others.

Merritt scampered across the lawn, dodging and weaving to avoid the massive feet that thudded like the boots of giants around her. Her delicate paws felt the vibrations, telling her when to swerve or stop. The odd squeal from a frightened human told her when they'd spotted her, but she sprinted away before anyone could give chase. The humans seemed happy to let her escape.

She wondered how they'd become the dominant species in this dimension if they couldn't even catch a harmless shrew.

She paused, tail twitching, when she located another armed human, then another, and another.

Dismay knotted her gut as she completed the lap of the lawn and darted into a tiny gap between the wooden posts bordering the trees and shrubs at the lawn's edges. Her diminutive heart fluttered in her ears seventeen times each second.

Twelve. She counted twelve armed gangsters.

How many bullets can each gun shoot? she wondered.

A Glock fires fifteen to seventeen rounds, her orb training supplied.

Wow, look at you being helpful for once, Merritt silently muttered. She scanned the crowd as the sun sank low and spotlights switched on to illuminate the crowd and stage. How many were there? A hundred?

Fifteen rounds for each of the twelve gangsters would outnumber these victims almost two to one. Merritt didn't like those odds.

She slunk over to the lanky human she'd scented first. He

hung around near the back of the crowd, his right hand continually twitching toward his waistband. She guessed that was where he'd concealed his weapon.

Merritt perched on the grass a few inches behind the human and debated her options. Call Val? She shook her head and bared her needle-like teeth. *No.* Little Avalon had accepted her. She couldn't tell anyone about this.

Besides, she knew she could take these guys if she could lure them away from the humans.

She stepped back, bowed her head, and transformed. The human scratched his ass, oblivious to her presence. Merritt blinked as her human vision showed her the ugly black butt of a gun sticking out of his waistband.

The buzz of a phone made her tense, but she had the presence of mind not to jump. The human yanked his phone from his pocket. "Yeah?"

"Ready?" someone growled.

That has to be the one Lugnutz calls "Boss." Merritt seized the opportunity.

"Yeah, I'm—" the human began.

Merritt grabbed the butt of his gun and yanked it out of his waistband.

"What're you doing with this?" she asked playfully.

The human whirled. "Oh, shit!"

The person on the phone screeched, *"What? What?"*

"Some bitch got my gun!" the human hissed.

"Were you planning to cause trouble with this thing?" Merritt waved it.

The human ducked. "Crap! Boss, we got a problem." He lowered the phone. "Give me that!"

"Why should I?" Merritt held up, making him cringe. "You're planning to use it to hurt people."

"Give it *back*!" the human spat. "Boss, what do I do?"

"Stay where you are!" Boss ordered. "We can still pull this off.

Don't make any noise. Boys, get that weapon back before she draws attention to us!"

A thrilling chord rang across the park. The deep, soulful sound came from the wooden instrument near the front of the stage, which the orb said was a *cello*. A drum joined the cello's powerful notes. It sounded like the music from one of the weird movies Tess liked, the speciesist human-made ones with desperately inaccurate orcs in them.

The human made a wild grab for the gun. Merritt danced aside and aimed the barrel at him. He leaped back.

The audience didn't move. Their eyes were nailed to the stage, wrapped up in the music. A few people slipped out of their chairs and hurried around the crowd's edge, heading for Merritt and her opponent.

"You'll kill somebody with that thing!" the thug hissed.

"Like that's not what you planned to do with it?" Merritt retorted.

She had their attention. Now, to lure them away from the humans.

Merritt waved the gun. "You want this, boys?"

"Keep that bitch quiet!" Boss hissed through the phone.

"Come and get it!" Merritt giggled, then sprinted into the trees.

They'd come after her. They'd want to shut her up before she told anyone about the armed men at the performance. She didn't look back as she sprang over the low fence and bolted into the park.

Leaves touched Merritt's face and bushes were thick against her knees, but no roots tripped her, nor did any branches whip across her skin. The plants bowed and rustled as they moved out of her way. Magic flowed through her from their presence, and she felt like she could run forever.

She had to hold herself back from full speed to allow the

humans to remain in sight. After they left the concert behind, they raised their voices.

"Get in front of her, Longlegs! Cut her off!"

"How'd she get your gun, idiot?"

"Stop! Yo, bitch, stop!"

Merritt laughed and kept running. Her boots met concrete with a jarring impact. She skidded, uncertain, seeing lights to her left and darkness to her right. Merritt swerved to the right and raced down the path. Trees rose on one side, shielding her from the sight of any humans using the park. On the other were the docks and dark water stretching to Manhattan's shoreline.

Merritt slowed to a jog, then stopped. Magic burned in her veins as she turned to face her pursuers, dark silhouettes pounding down the path toward her. They were the only humans she could see. Their guns glinted as they raised them.

"Shoot her! Shoot her ass!" the unarmed human squealed, jumping up and down. She guessed from his build that he was the one they called Longlegs.

"No, fool. We need her to stay quiet," a burly man with Boss' voice snapped. "Look, girl, I don't know what you're on, but you've got nearly a dozen guns pointed at you. Put that piece down, and you don't need to die tonight."

"Not right away, anyway," a toothless man whispered, creeping up behind Merritt. She let him go, though his words made several others give throaty laughs.

"Put it down," Boss ordered. Gold glinted on the chain around his neck. He held the gun steady with both hands, aimed at Merritt's heart.

If she took all of them down fast, no one else would get involved. No innocents would get hurt.

She vaguely aimed the gun at the men as she raised her free hand and traced the rune for *amplify* on her emerald-encrusted amulet. Then she pressed it. Magic struck her like a thunderbolt. This time, she was ready for the transformation.

When his eyes opened, he towered over the gangsters. Roots curled into the shape of feet were braced on the concrete. His fingers creaked like branches as he curled them into fists.

"What...what the...what..." Longlegs stammered, stumbling back.

A gun clattered to the ground. The man without teeth staggered back, mouth wide, eyes huge as he stared at Merritt.

"*Pick up your gun!*" Boss thundered.

No Teeth turned. "We gotta get out of here!"

"No, we gotta fight that thing." Boss switched his aim to No Teeth. "Pick it up, or I'll shoot your head off!"

No Teeth snatched up his weapon. Merritt rounded on him as he emitted a high-pitched porcine squeal and fired. Bullets punched into the impenetrable bark over Merritt's abdomen as he strode toward No Teeth, raising his fists. No Teeth stumbled off the path and tripped on the incline, landing on his back.

Merritt counted rounds as he stood over the screaming gunman. "You wanted to do *what* to me?" he demanded in a roar like a gale through a thick canopy.

No Teeth pointed the barrel between Merritt's eyes. Merritt slammed both fists into the human's torso, which produced a nasty cracking sound. No Teeth was squishier than he'd expected.

"Ewwww," Merritt spat, retreating as he shook blood from his fists.

A bullet struck Merritt's hip, but he felt no pain. Splinters flew from him as he whirled to face three men advancing on him, firing their guns at his upper thigh. Merritt roared and swung his arm, sending all three men flying with one blow. They hit the concrete path with crunches and thuds.

Longlegs lunged to grab one of their guns and raised it to aim between Merritt's eyes. Before he could fire, a knife plunged into Merritt's knee.

The blade found nerves and flesh beneath the bark.

Merritt threw his head back and bellowed in pain. Boss yanked his double-edged knife out of Merritt's knee, face twisted with fury, and slammed it into his thigh. The blade cut through the bark, but it didn't hurt.

Merritt gripped the handle, which was as slender as a toothpick in his large fingers. Boss yelped as Merritt yanked the knife out of his leg in a shower of bark crumbs. He flung the blade away, hearing the distant splash as it fell in the water, and seized Boss by the neck.

Boss' squeal ended in a splutter. He clawed at Merritt's fingers, trying to pry them off his neck, which felt as soft as jelly in Merritt's grip.

"*Over here, you son of a bitch!*" Longlegs shrieked.

"*Now, boys!*" another man shouted.

Seven guns fired at once, their report deafening. Pain blossomed through Merritt's other knee. He dropped Boss and whirled to face the men. Sound and flashes of light beat against his senses as more impacts evoked pain in his knee, their bullets repeatedly striking the same spot. A trickle of dark green sap trailed like blood over his shin.

Merritt stumbled back.

"*Kill it, boys!*" Boss shrieked. "*Kill the monster!*"

Merritt's foot met the grass on the park side of the path, and magic surged through him, erasing the pain. Merritt raised both hands, clenched his fingers, and roared as his hands changed. His fingers sank into his palms and disappeared. Wood creaked and bark grew as his fists became heavy clubs that ended in bark with knots that stood out like spikes.

"*Kill it! Kill it!*" Boss screamed.

Merritt swung his new arms, then clobbered Boss with enough force to launch him across the path. His scream ended in a crack as he landed beside the water.

Terror screwed with the men's aim, so bullets ripped into

Merritt's thighs, feet, and belly, but he barely felt the impacts. He charged the remaining men with wild swings. Longlegs dodged the first blow, which then mowed down four men like Merritt was cutting grass. Two more collapsed when Merritt swung his other fist.

Only Longlegs remained. He aimed and squeezed the trigger as Merritt straightened. The bullet clipped Merritt's cheek, leaving a streak of burning pain. His clubbed hand crunched into Longlegs' chest and flung him back. He hit the water and sank.

"Oh, crap," Merritt rumbled. He hadn't meant to kill the stupid asshole. He stomped down the bank, roots growing like tendrils from the soles of his feet to get purchase in the mud. The clubs receded, leaving fingers behind, and Merritt grabbed the rapidly sinking Longlegs by the ankles. He dragged the unconscious human out of the water and dumped him on the bank.

Breathing hard, Merritt looked around, hands hanging by his sides. His moss hair trailed over his shoulders. Several humans groaned and writhed on the dirt, but none were in any shape to hurt innocent people. Not tonight. The music still played in the distance, a rousing melody rising against the backdrops of the city lights and stars. Merritt closed his eyes and took a moment to enjoy it.

***

When she opened her eyes, she was humanoid. Her wet jeans clung to her boots as she plodded up the riverbank to the path. The thought that the humans might see her face made her fret, so she looked at them. They were all unconscious.

Jimmy Barton didn't remember her. She'd clearly hit *him* hard enough the first time. She had hit these guys a lot harder.

There was blood on the grass on the bank near the path. Merritt's stomach lurched.

A *lot* harder.

She edged closer to No Teeth and grimaced when she saw his torso. It was mincemeat, with exposed bones where his ribs had shattered. No Teeth was *extremely* dead. Merritt hadn't set out to kill him, but looking at his glassy eyes and remembering the expression in them minutes ago, she couldn't muster any remorse.

Humans were more fragile than she'd expected. If these idiots didn't get help soon, more might die.

A car door slammed nearby. Merritt scampered into the trees and peered around a trunk at the blue and white police car. Two cops stepped out, guns drawn. One spoke into the radio on her shoulder. "On scene at a possible ten-thirty-four S."

Merritt had no idea what that meant, but her orb training told her that the police helped people. She pushed through the brushes and stumbled onto the path near the car. Both cops jumped and swung their weapons around to her.

"Um, hi," Merritt managed, holding her hands up.

The cops lowered their guns. "What's going on here?" the female officer asked.

Merritt dodged the question. "There's a bunch of people lying over there. It looks like someone beat them up bad."

"Beat them up? Do you know about a shooting that happened here, ma'am?" the male cop demanded.

Merritt cleared her throat. "There was shooting, but none of them have guns right now. They need help."

"The 911 call reported gunshots," the female muttered. "The caller also said—" She stopped. "Did you see anything...odd?"

"Odd?" Merritt asked, pulse thudding. She'd thought no one could see her.

The cops exchanged glances.

"Odd, like what?" Merritt pressed.

"It's probably nothing," the man conceded, "but the caller reported a giant tree-man attacking the gunmen."

"A giant tree-man?" Merritt raised her eyebrows. "I didn't see anything like that, sir. I was at the concert and came across these injured people, that's all."

The cop nodded. "All right. Please wait over there so we can take your statement."

"Yes, sir." Merritt strode toward the concert instead.

As the cops rounded the corner, the female cop grumbled, "Full moon in New York City, amIright?"

The male cop laughed.

Merritt broke into a dead run toward home.

CHAPTER TWENTY-ONE

The abrasion on Merritt's cheek had stopped burning when she hurried up the street toward home. Drunken singing echoed from the Second Fist, combined with overly loud music. It covered her footsteps as she slipped into the building and climbed the stairs with all the energy she could muster, but she plodded when she reached the third floor. Her limbs felt as frail and useless as dry branches.

She pushed the door open and stumbled into the kitchen, almost colliding with Damian.

"Ooh!" Merritt jumped. "S-sorry. I thought you were, um, at the Second Fist with the others."

"It's one in the morning. Tess didn't last that long." Damian looked up from his sandwich. "I brought her home before lunch."

"Um, okay." Merritt edged toward her bedroom.

Damian's gaze pinned her to the wall like thrown daggers. "You're keeping secrets, aren't you?"

Merritt froze.

"Got blood on your cheek." Damian touched his.

Merritt resisted the urge to brush it off. No words came to her lips.

Damian inclined his head. "Not asking." He raised his sandwich.

"You're not?" Merritt croaked.

Damian bit into it and chewed before speaking. "Nope. Not my business. You saved my life, so I know I can trust you. Good enough for me."

Merritt grinned. "Damian—"

"Go away. Don't ruin a good sandwich," Damian interrupted.

Merritt gratefully darted down the hall to her room.

A long shower did little for the aches in her muscles and joints. Sleep clogged the corners of her eyes as she changed into her little-used pajamas and fell onto the bed, sinking her head deep into the pillows. She stifled a yawn as she gazed at the blank TV screen. Maybe the reporter would have a story about what had happened in the place of trees.

She reached for the remote, but the screen turned a brilliant silver before she touched it. Merritt yelped and shielded her eyes with one hand as a tinny voice came through the speakers.

"Hello? Hello? Oh, wow, I love the wallpaper in here. It's got Liam Miller written all over it."

Merritt lowered her hand and gaped at the screen. She wasn't sure how the TV had turned itself on and didn't recognize this show. The character on the screen stared directly at Merritt with striking eyes whose color shifted through a range of blues and greens as the light met them. Her pale silver skin was luminescent, contrasting with black hair in a pixie cut.

"There you are. Sorry. Did I scare you?" the Lunar Fae asked.

Merritt hadn't seen many paras on TV. She leaned forward, gazing at the beautiful fae in awe.

"Hello?" The fae waved a hand. "Merritt? Can you hear me?"

Merritt jumped.

"There we are." The fae grinned. "How are you?"

"Are...are you talking to me?" Merritt croaked.

"Do you see any other Leshbolgs in the room?" the fae impatiently demanded. "Yes, I'm talking to you."

A quiet voice rumbled offscreen. Merritt couldn't make out the words.

"Oh, yeah. You're right, honey." The fae's expression softened. "Sorry. I forgot that scrying screens aren't part of the cultures where we've placed you. Think of it like FaceTime."

"Like what?" Merritt squeaked.

"Yeah, that doesn't work either." The fae waved dismissively. "I can see and hear you, and you can see and hear me, even though we're dimensions apart. Get it?"

Merritt nodded. "Who...wait. You seem familiar." She gasped when the penny dropped. "Merlin's wings! You're *her*."

The fae grinned. "Hey."

"Your Majesty, my Queen." Merritt scrambled off the bed and bowed.

Queen Julia Pendragon sounded sad when she spoke. "That's a funny way to greet someone who failed your entire species."

Merritt raised her head.

"I'm sorry for your loss, Merritt." The queen's eyes darkened to midnight blue. "I should have been there to save them."

"You were fighting in the Deep, Your Majesty. Killing Mordred." Merritt paused. "Saving the world. My people died, but Mordred's cult killed them, not you. They would have killed many others if you hadn't stopped him."

The queen tilted her head, studying her. "Merlin's right. You *are* wiser than you look."

Merritt couldn't work out if that was a compliment.

"Merlin tells me you're finding your place in Little Avalon." The queen smiled.

"I love it here," Merritt confessed.

The queen raised her eyebrows. "Not enough that you don't need to visit Brooklyn Bridge Park occasionally."

Merritt gulped. "Your Majesty?"

"Don't look so shocked, Merritt. I *am* the queen of all dimensions. My secret agents are everywhere." The queen grinned. "I know you turn into a guy when you're mad. I also know that you took out twelve violent gang members in about sixty seconds tonight."

"They were going to hurt people," Merritt whispered.

The queen held up a hand. "I know. Don't worry, I'm not going to tell Val. This is between you and me, though I encourage you to trust her. There's nobody more trustworthy than Val."

Merritt swallowed hard.

"I didn't call because you're in trouble, Merritt." The queen lowered her hand. "I called to congratulate you on kicking ass."

"You did?" Merritt managed.

"Yeah. Okay, the OPMA might take a dim view of your extracurricular activities, but I don't." The queen smirked. "You saved a lot of people tonight, Merritt. You kept the peace." She smiled. "Don't stop."

Merritt gaped.

"One thing, though." The queen raised a finger. "Please avoid revealing magic to humans. Mind wipes are expensive and a pain in my ass."

Merritt ducked her head. "Yes, Your Majesty."

"Thanks. Keep kicking ass in the name of peace and unity, got it?" the queen added.

Merritt couldn't smother a grin. "Yes, Your Majesty."

"If anyone asks, *especially* Merlin, we never had this conversation." The queen winked. "Bye, girl."

The screen turned black. Her reflection was the only face she now saw.

She fell back onto bed and squashed the pillows against her face. The tension left her body, and sleep wrapped around her like a plush blanket.

The kitchen at Hank and Kalyna's restaurant was the opposite of Mrs. Ricci's. No adornments dared come near its sterile surfaces. The stainless steel on every appliance and surface gleamed, polished to a spotless shine. Range hoods loomed over the many burners, towering stacks of trays on wheels waited in rows against the wall, and ample space between the countertops and central island allowed several chefs to work at once.

Right now, the kitchen was orderly and still. Hank and Kalyna sat at the island as Merritt came in with two more covered trays she'd retrieved from the back seat of Liam's car.

"Those the last ones?" Liam asked, popping his head around the door.

Tess glanced at Merritt, who nodded.

"That's it. Thanks for the help, Lee." Tess beamed.

"Stay for breakfast, Liam," Kalyna offered.

"I have to run." Liam grinned. "Qenzi and I are scoping out wedding venues." He waved and left.

"Finally," Hank grumbled. "I thought he'd *never* plan his wedding to that nice girl. When I met my Mary, there was no messing around and wasting time." He scoffed. "We got married a few weeks after I proposed."

"Don't be a grouch, Hank," Kalyna chided.

"I'm not a grouch," Hank grouched.

Merritt stood awkwardly opposite them, watching.

"If you're not a grouch, I'm Elvis Presley," Kalyna teased.

Hank rolled his eyes. "This generation has no respect for the elderly."

"Elderly, sure. Geriatric? Probably not." Kalyna elbowed his ribs.

Hank wagged a bony finger at her. "I'm warning you, young lady!"

Kalyna laughed. "We're forgetting that we're here for a job interview. The best kind—one with samples to taste." She turned a warm smile on Merritt. "I see you brought plenty."

Was that a good thing? A bad thing? Merritt tried not to panic. "Um, I wanted to showcase my…versatility."

From the corner of the room, Tess gave her an encouraging smile.

"I'm not complaining." Hank chortled. "More for me."

"These smell too good not to taste." Kalyna gestured at the covered tray on the left. "What are they?"

Merritt unclipped the cover and slid the tray nearer. "A few of my favorite muffins. This one is lavender and dark chocolate chip." She pointed at another muffin. "This is blueberry caramel."

"Lavender? In baking?" Hank demanded. "Are you out of your mind, girl?"

Merritt's mouth turned dry, but she forced a smile. "Try it."

Hank suspiciously sniffed the muffin before tearing off a piece. He popped it into his mouth and grimaced, waiting for a bad taste. As he chewed, his eyes widened. "Wow," he mumbled.

"The flavor balance is outstanding, Merritt." Kalyna raised her eyebrows. "You've made it herbal and rich but not too sweet. How's the texture for you, Hank?"

"The fluffiest muffin I've ever had." Hank took the rest of the muffin from Kalyna's hand. "Give me that."

Kalyna laughed. "We have other things to taste." She reached for the blueberry caramel muffin. "Tell us more about your job experience, Merritt. You're a recent immigrant from…Europe?"

Merritt licked her lips to wet her sandpaper-dry mouth. "I have no job experience, to be honest."

"How long have you been out of college, girl?" Hank demanded, raising a shaggy eyebrow.

"I didn't go to college. Things were different where I grew up. Everyone worked together to sustain the village. We didn't have jobs," Merritt confessed.

Hank grunted. "No job experience, but plenty of *work* experience. Does that sound right?"

Merritt's shoulders relaxed. "Yes."

"Wow, this is heavenly." Kalyna raised the half-eaten muffin to the light and admired it.

"I have sugar cookies and brownies, too. They're more basic," Merritt confessed, "but I tweaked the recipes to make the brownies moister and the sugar cookies crisper."

She uncovered the second tray. Hank and Kalyna eagerly reached for the samples within.

"You have any family in New York City, kid?" Hank asked, snapping a sugar cookie in half with a delightful crunch.

Merritt shook her head.

"What made you come here, then?" Hank shoved half the cookie into his mouth.

"I didn't know where else to go," Merritt confessed. "I had trouble finding my place in the world." She smiled. "I think this is it, though."

"Sure seems that way," Tess chipped in.

"Little Avalon has a way of being that for people. Somewhere to belong," Kalyna agreed. "I've never had such a wonderfully sticky chocolate brownie, Merritt. It's excellent."

"Great cookie, too." Hank waved the other half. "Wants icing, though."

Kalyna tasted the other half. "It'll be perfect with icing. How are you with art?"

"I don't know," Merritt confessed. "I've never tried it."

Kalyna pondered her, chewing. "I have a feeling you'll be good at it. These cookies are popular when they're decorated, especially around the holidays. Would you be willing to try?"

Merritt eagerly nodded. "I'll try anything."

Hank grinned. "That's the spirit. What do you have in there?"

"This is different." Merritt opened the last tray. "On the left, I have buttered slices of an ordinary sourdough loaf."

"What's *that*?" Hank asked, eyes widening as he gazed at the soft, pale loaf beside it.

"That's a traditional dish from my hometown." Merritt bit her lip. "It's different, but I thought you might like it. It's called bellyfill."

As Hank reached for the bellyfill, Kalyna's and Merritt's eyes met over his head.

"Magic?" Kalyna mouthed.

Merritt nodded, and Kalyna raised her eyebrows. Merritt couldn't tell if she was annoyed or impressed.

Hank bit into a piece of bellyfill, and his jaw dropped.

"Wow, kid." Hank gulped. "I've never tasted anything like this before."

"Let me try." Kalyna tore off a chunk and ate it. Her eyes widened. "Mmm, that's unique."

Unique? Merritt clutched the tray's cover with white knuckles.

"I love it!" Kalyna beamed.

"It's great. Try the sourdough, Kalyna. It doesn't have that mushy texture you get sometimes." Hank handed her a slice.

Kalyna tasted it. "Incredible. How long have you been baking, Merritt?"

Merritt's toes curled. She'd been dreading this question. "I made a lot of bellyfill in, uh, Europe." She guessed it was true. "I've only been baking other things for a few weeks. I'm not an experienced baker. I'm excited to learn more, though."

"I'm sure of one thing." Hank folded his arms, deadpan.

"What now, Hank?" Kalyna asked.

Hank's grin spread over his face. "It means you're a wildly talented baker! You're pulling this off with only weeks of experience?" He jumped up and extended a hand. "Kid, you're hired!"

"Hank!" Kalyna laughed. "You do remember you have a partner, right?"

Merritt froze.

"C'mon, Kalyna. We both know we won't find another baker like this one in a hurry," Hank grumbled.

Kalyna snorted. "I'm pulling your leg." She rose. "Hank's right, Merritt. Congratulations. You're hired."

The words were music to Merritt's ears. She couldn't stop grinning as she shook their hands.

"I'll give you a list of the recipes we plan to start with on our breakfast menu," Kalyna added. "You can work on those for a few days before we launch our breakfasts. I'd also like you to bake pitas for our lunches and dinners. That'll save us time in the kitchen later. We'll keep you busy."

"I can't wait," Merritt gushed. "Thank you so much. I've been dreaming of this job."

"You're welcome, kid." Hank beamed.

"Thank *you*, Merritt." Kalyna inclined her head. "I see a lot of potential in you."

"You'll do this restaurant good," Hank added.

Kalyna agreed and promised to email Merritt's employment contract and other details to Tess.

They left Chaplin's Kitchen together, Merritt carrying the empty trays in a stack. She felt as though her feet didn't touch the ground. The sunshine seemed brighter and the morning more beautiful.

"You're floating," Tess observed.

"I can't believe I got the job." Merritt laughed. "This is amazing, Tess!"

"It really is. I think it's time you and I went to Gold, Manns, and Sax and opened a bank account that's all yours. You need a phone, too. Liam will be overjoyed to help you with that. He's been waiting for his big moment to introduce you to tech." Tess nudged Merritt's shoulder. "Things are coming together for you."

"I feel like I can contribute to Little Avalon now." Merritt's cheeks hurt from smiling.

"You do that simply by being here." Tess touched her shoulder. "We all like you."

"Even Damian, these days." Merritt giggled. "I don't remember ever being excited about the future, Tess, but I am now. It could hold so many good things."

"It *will* hold so many good things," Tess corrected.

Merritt believed that.

Dinner arrived in square cardboard boxes. Tess carried them into the kitchen with a triumphant air, like a berserker returning with the head of their enemy. Steam trickled from the cracks in the boxes' lids and smelled like cheese and something freshly baked.

"Pizza's here!" Tess called, sliding the boxes onto the table.

"Be there in a minute," Damian yelled from the hall.

"Quick question." Merritt frowned. "What *is* pizza?"

"What is pizza?" Damian stomped into the kitchen. "Have you been living under a rock, girl?"

"Damian!" Tess protested.

"Pizza is life," Damian proclaimed.

Tess snorted. "You're not wrong."

Damian flipped the nearest box open to reveal a round flatbread covered with tomato sauce, cheese, and toppings. "Merlin's dimples, *that's* a perfect pizza."

"No, it's not." Tess pulled a face. "It's got pineapple on it, weirdo."

"Full of shit, as usual," Damian grumbled, pulling up a chair. "Pizza is the ultimate superfood."

"Pizza clogs your arteries, but that doesn't mean I won't destroy this one." Tess opened the second box. "Merritt, *this* is a real pizza. Feta cheese, basil, cherry tomatoes, and a drizzle of olive oil."

"No meat?" Damian shook his head. "That's not a pizza. That's cardboard covered in string cheese."

Merritt giggled. "I'll try both."

"Fair's fair." Tess tore a slice off each pizza and slid them onto a plate. "Here you are. Oh, hold on, I'll open a bottle of wine."

"Not for me." Damian raised a hand. "Pizza for breakfast is one thing, but I'm on duty."

Merritt chose the chair opposite Damian's as Tess produced a bottle from the cabinet and uncorked it.

"Thanks for eating with us." Merritt smiled.

Damian's pallid cheeks turned pink. "Tess and I used to have my breakfast and her dinner together all the time. I'm hoping that can be the case again."

"I think it can. I'm sure I can come up with a recipe that works as both." Merritt grinned. "Maybe I can make batches of two muffins, one sweet and one savory, at the same time."

"Muffins for dinner? Only a Lunar Fae would be absurd enough to consider the idea," Damian growled.

"Stop fussing." Tess slopped wine into three glasses, giving Damian's only a splash. "Damian, you have to join in with one sip for the toast."

"I can do that." Damian grasped the stem of his wineglass.

Tess held hers aloft. "To Merritt's new job."

"Hear, hear." Damian clinked his glass with Tess'.

Merritt held hers out, and Damian and Tess tapped their glasses against it. She sipped the rich, spicy flavor of Fernwood wine and smiled. "You guys are the best. Thank you. Tess, I'll always owe you for helping me get settled in Little Avalon."

"Don't mention it." Tess inclined her head. "I'm paying it forward, that's all. Val helped me find my place in the world. I can help you find yours."

"Damian, thanks for not being an asshole to me anymore," Merritt added.

Damian rolled his eyes. "Try the pizza."

Merritt bit into each slice in turn and, despite relentless pressure from Tess and Damian, declared that she couldn't pick a favorite because both were perfect. She devoured three more slices before Damian excused himself to go to work.

"Three slices left over," Tess observed. "Let's put them all in the same box and stash them in the fridge. The only thing better than fresh pizza is leftover pizza."

"I'll do the dishes," Merritt offered. "You had a long day."

"Thanks, Merritt." Tess refilled her wineglass. "I wouldn't mind an extra few minutes to relax in the tub before bed."

The fae padded from the kitchen, and Merritt made short work of tidying up and preparing a fresh batch of dough to rise overnight. She left everything in order, with the surfaces polished, the loaf pan on the counter, and the sourdough starter fed and happily bubbling. Come Monday, she'd be baking in a different kitchen. The thought of all the equipment at Chaplin's Kitchen made her hands itch in anticipation.

That was Monday, though. For tonight, Merritt had other plans.

She scampered into her room and turned on the TV. A few presses of the remote took her to the news channel. Brooklyn Bridge Park was calling. Merritt wanted to see where the latest mugging hotspots were.

Keep going out there and kicking ass in the name of peace and unity.

A few boring stories played on the screen about the scandalous mess of human politics. Merritt watched without interest. She was about to turn off the TV and head to the park to inspect it herself when the screen finally cut to the usual reporter standing in the park. Its vivid greens spoke of spring. She stood before a lawn, looking out of place in a well-cut suit as a group of kids played ball.

"The unusual incident that took place in Brooklyn Bridge Park on March 31st remains a mystery." The reporter stared fiercely into the camera. "After a 911 call reported shots fired near an open-air concert in the park, police discovered several members of a local gang dead or badly injured on the riverfront. A single witness described a fantastical scene that beggars belief: a seven-foot-tall, disfigured giant beat the gangsters to death.

The police investigation failed to reveal any further details about this strange event."

Merritt exhaled. The gangsters weren't talking. For now, her cover was safe.

"However, the attack has had a significant effect on the mugging problem that has plagued the park for several months. Since this incident, no muggings have been reported in Brooklyn Bridge Park or the surrounding neighborhood." The reporter stiffly gestured at the playing children. "Gang violence is at an all-time low in this part of Brooklyn. Residents once again feel safe visiting the park, knowing gang activity no longer poses a threat."

Merritt turned off the TV and stared at the blank screen, unsure of how to feel. The happy kids pleased her, but the emotion knotting behind her sternum wasn't pure joy.

It was dismay.

What am I going to do at night now?

Merritt left the couch and wandered to the window. She pulled the curtains wide and threw the window open, allowing the city sounds to drift in: barking dogs, blaring sirens, and bursts of laughter from the Second Fist. Beyond Little Avalon's quiet rooftops, the city was an endless expanse of lights: rectangular windows, headlights, and a boat's lights on the dark river.

Merritt smiled. Brooklyn Bridge Park was safe for now, but there was a whole city out there, teeming with trouble. Ripe with possibility.

RENÉE'S NOTES

FEBRUARY 15. 2025

Thank you for reading the first book in this new series and here on the back! I love these characters, and I am excited to continue the story with all our old favorites, and some new ones. Plus I get to bake in these! What's not to love?

Kelly and Nat and Izzie are coming to visit!

(Edit: Yay! Can't wait to see you all - Kelly)

It's the spring reunion. We get together at my house in spring because everyone loves my garden. The people that owned it before me had great taste in plants, and we all enjoy seeing the lilac and forsythia and wisteria and new roses bloom between mid-March and the first week in April, so it's a pajama party again! Fortunately, I have a well, so I do not have to beggar myself keeping it all watered, and there is plenty of room for my girls.

Don't worry, Jo will supervise, so we won't get too wild. I do have some special adventures planned for them this time. Massages and capybaras! More on those in the next author notes, since I know you are all wild to learn about the large South American rodents.

I do wonder how the garden will evolve this year since it was a very dry winter. We have only had about an inch of rain so far, and normal is four to five inches by now, most in January and early February. We won't have a stunning wildflower show in this state this time. When we have a rainy winter here in Arizona, and for that matter, in New Mexico and Nevada as well, we have lupines, something yellow I don't know the name of, orange mallow, and tiny white flowers all over, plus California poppies where passing motorist have flung seeds out the window. It's a real thing. I have now done that myself in my favorite canyon, and I was hoping to see them bloom this year, but I can't go through it until construction is finished next autumn. Oh, well. They'll bloom without me. I shall see them the next year, since poppies reseed.

Don't smell the saguaro flowers. They use a urea-like scent to attract bats to pollinate them. Not pleasant.

In honor of their visit, or maybe because it was a very quiet winter, I got inspired and changed my whole kitchen around. I moved the stove and put live-edge shelves over it. The woman who crafted them out of a raw plank of black acacia inlaid tiny bits of turquoise in the edges, so they are amazing and very special. I also had a pantry and spice shelves built. It's been tiresome living in dust, but it's all rewarding now. I can find the gochujang and the chipotle pepper powder now! I am lucky to live in a town with very fine craftpeople. My carpenter is amazing, and he hand-built the pantry doors as well as custom-building the spice shelves over the mess of a wall behind where the stove was formerly. I am in awe of his talent!

Of course, the minute I painted the walls, I started planning the new decorations (because you can't have blank walls) and went on Etsy. It seems I am on a rabbit kick, since I bought several handcrafted tiles with rabbits on them. Most of the potters are in the UK, but that's fine because Nat and Izzie will bring them over for me.

As always...

As always, big thanks to everyone at LMBPN. I sincerely appreciate my editor, the JIT team, and you, the readers! We authors couldn't do it without you. Kelly and the ops team work their butts off to get our books into your hands.

Until we speak again, I hope your skies are sunny and your days are filled with happiness and good books.

Renée

BOOKS FROM RENÉE

Para-Military Recruiter
(with Michael Anderle)
Drafted (Book 1)
Recruiter (Book 2)
Accepted (Book 3)
Lead (Book 4)
Recruited (Book 5)
Soldier (Book 6)
Tactical (Book 7)
Officer (Book 8)
Leader (Book 9)
Victor (Book 10)
Appointed (Book 11)
Councilor (Book 12)
Royal (Book 13)
Princess (Book 14)
Peacemaker (Book 15)
Queen (Book 16)

Valerie Stonehold

(with Michael Anderle)
Security For Hire (Book 1)
Shieldmaiden of the Modern Realm (Book 2)
Arbiter of Shadows (Book 3)
Jewel of the Night's Mantle (Book 4)
Echoes of the Anvil (Book 5)
The Iron Bear (Book 6)
Guardian of Little Avalon (Book 7)
Protector of the Sleepless City (Book 8)
A Hunt No More (Book 9)

Merlin's Waif
(with Michael Anderle)
A Little Waif Justice (Book 1)
Bet on the Waif (Book 2)

Piercing the Veil
Dangerous Opportunities (Book 1)
Dangerous Responsibilities (Book 2)
Decisions To Make (Book 3)

Reincarnation of the Morrigan
Birth of a Goddess (Book One)
The Way of Wisdom (Book Two)
Angelic Death (Book Three)
A Cold War (Book Four)
A Battle Tune (Book Five)
Broken Ice (Book Six)
A Torn Veil (Book Seven)
Sins of the Past (Book Eight)
The Wild Hunt Comes (*Book Nine*)

The WereWitch Series
Bad Attitude (Book One)

A Bit Aggressive (Book Two)
Too Much Magic (Book Three)
Were War (Book Four)
Were Rages (Book Five)
God Ender (Book Six)
God Trials (Book Seven)
The Troll Solution (Book Eight)
Winner Takes All (Book Nine)

Callie Hart Series
Thin Ice (Book One)
Cold Blood (Book Two)
Feelings Run Deep (Book Three)

CONNECT WITH THE AUTHORS

Connect with Renée

Facebook: https://www.facebook.com/reneejaggerauthor

Website: https://reneejagger.com/

Connect with Michael Anderle

Website: http://lmbpn.com

Email List: https://michael.beehiiv.com/

https://www.facebook.com/LMBPNPublishing

https://twitter.com/MichaelAnderle

https://www.instagram.com/lmbpn_publishing/

https://www.bookbub.com/authors/michael-anderle